The Coincidence of Hope

A NOVEL

J. Willis Sanders

ISBN: 978-1-954763-29-6 (paperback)
ISBN: 978-1-954763-31-9 (hardcover)

BUGGS ISLAND BOOKS

Printed in the United States of America
Cover design by MiblArt

The version of the lyrics for Poor Wayfaring Stranger used in this book is in the Public Domain, from William T. Dale, 1893, www.cpdl.org.

Author's Note

This is my first novel. Having undergone numerous rewrites over the years, it also has become a three-book series. Although each is complete in itself, they read much better if they are read in order.

For those who care to know the list and the order, it starts with this novel, *The Coincidence of Hope,* followed by *The Yearning of Hope* and *The Gift of Hope.* Naturally, I call them my Hope Series.

The Yearning of Hope is about two characters from *The Coincidence of Hope* (not Joe and Elaine), because I wanted to further explore them. I'm pretty sure readers will want that too. To see if they do, they can read the first chapter in the back of this book.

The Gift of Hope continues about ten years after the end of *The Coincidence of Hope.* Of course, you'd rather read it than have me tell you about it. I'll include its first chapter at the end of the second book when it comes out. I plan to release all three before the end of 2022.

As most authors might say, to write well, we must share the perspective of our characters, shirking our own perspective while we write. As a fan of perspective in all its forms, I hope these novels are a reflection of perspective, for what finer way to understand a person than to place ourselves within their situation?

Please enjoy,
J.W.S.

Also by J. Willis Sanders

The Eliza Gray Series
The Colors of Eliza Gray
The Colors of Denver Andrews
The Colors of Tess Gray

The Outer Banks of North Carolina Series
The Diary of Carlo Cipriani
If the Sunrise Forgets Tomorrow
Love, Jake

The Hope Series
The Coincidence of Hope
Coming in 2022: *The Yearning of Hope* and *The Gift of Hope*

Writing as J. D. James for the Reid Stone Series
Reid Stone: Hard as Stone

Readers: In the back of this book, you'll find the first chapter of *The Yearning of Hope,* coming later in 2022.

Amazon Reviews of *The Diary of Carlo Cipriani*

"This is the story of a shipwreck. No, a survival story. Actually, it's a history lesson worked in to the tale of Carlo's life after a shipwreck told as entries in a diary to Carlo's daughter. Wait, it's also a love story from earlier in his life, and again now. An impressive work of fiction."

"Many twists and turns, lots of tragedy but always hope. At several points you are not sure what is real and what is the narrator's madness due to his loneliness. A very satisfying resolution answers all our questions."

"This is fascinating tale of survival, both of shipwrecked sailors and of how wild horses came to live on the Outer Banks. I enjoyed the characters and the character development, as well."

Amazon reviews of *If the Sunrise Forgets Tomorrow*

"What a captivating book. I read it in 2 sittings because we just couldn't put it down. Brought tears to my eyes!"

"To be honest, I wasn't certain I would enjoy this book. I've read other books at in the Outer Banks and a lot of them seem to be sloppily written and just capitalizing on the setting to prey on die-hard OBX readers. I was pleasantly surprised to find it very well written and descriptive. It was easy to visualize the island, the characters, and the story as it all unfolded."

"This book was captivating and it was difficult for me to put it down. If you like a touch of history and have a love for Ocracoke, this is a great book to read. It was very descriptive and made me feel like I was there. Virginia and Ruby are typical sisters who are loving each other one minute and the next they are disagreeing. I enjoyed the strength they displayed as they overcame many obstacles. A Great Read!"

The Coincidence of Hope

Visitors

The Ardennes American Cemetery
Neuville-en-Condroz, Belgium
December 6, 2011

Surrounding Joe Matthan, hundreds of white crosses fill the vast cemetery. Beyond them, in front of a backdrop of leafless trees, each bone-gray in the dawn, an American flag hangs from its pole. The sun rises. Through the trees its light slashes the crosses with crimson, followed by orange, followed by yellow. Each cross is a reminder to humanity of the offerings beneath them, many forgotten. The sun climbs. The shimmering globe bursts above the trees. Frost sparkles on the brown grass. Here and there, patches of snow glitter with rainbow hues. Another day is born. Another day to live. Another day to die. The stone crosses now reflect the light, white and crisp, and Joe is on the way to find his own grave.

For decades it's the same thing: wake up inside a body not his, muscles not his, bones not his. Even the brain isn't his, nor the touch, nor the vision or hearing, nor the taste or smell. Although he shares them all with each body's owner, he is unable to control a single muscle. He is a ghost, a spirit, an essence clinging to this strange existence. He has no idea why, yet it is so. Each host either eats breakfast or doesn't, dresses or doesn't, or puts on a robe and stares in a mirror or out a window. Sometimes they don't get up. Sometimes they cry.

Sometimes they smile. Sometimes they marry. Sometimes they divorce. Of all the things they might do, most vary. Some go to work and some don't. Some kiss a significant other and some don't. Some wake their kids for school and some don't. Joe prefers the hosts in a happy marriage. Kids are a plus.

He hates how it doesn't always happen that way.

A few days ago, when his last host, a fifty-eight-year-old plumber—he loved running a model train around the Christmas tree for his grandkids—died from colon cancer, he found himself within the body of a young man dressing in a United States Army uniform. This morning the young man is miraculously looking for Joe's headstone in the Ardennes American Cemetery in Belgium. The memorial center's chaplain said some people are coming to see Private Matthan's grave for the first time, and it's the young man's job to attend them during the visit. Although Joe is excited to see who's coming, he's afraid to see his own grave. Death isn't fun, but living this way isn't fun either. He's gotten tired of it over the years, although bored is a better word.

Within the multitude of white crosses—5,329 to be exact, 792 of them unnamed— the young man searches. His breath plumes. Sunlight melts the frost, and the droplets dapple his black shoes. The air is fresh and clean. The crisp smell reminds Joe of a mid-winter snowstorm blanketing his parent's farm; the young man's musky antiperspirant does not.

He turns, takes a few more steps, and stops at a cross to lean closer.

Joseph S. Matthan
PFC, 106th Infantry Div., Nebraska
Dec. 17, 1944

Joe nods his phantom head. *That's me all right. I wonder why my body wasn't shipped back home. It isn't like my injuries were bad enough to keep anyone from seeing it.*

Nodding as if acknowledging either the location of the grave or the sacrifice, the young man stands.

It's then that Joe sees a freshly dug hole, small and rectangular, in his grave. The young man scratches his head as if he doesn't know anything about it. The chaplain didn't mention it, so it must be a mystery. He and Joe see something in their peripheral vision, and the young man turns.

In the distance, leaving the huge memorial building constructed of gleaming marble, three figures enter the morning sun. One, an elderly woman, walks slow and a bit stooped over. The second, a middle-aged man with blond hair, carries what resembles a small chest made of dark wood, wrapped in clear plastic. The last is the uniformed Army chaplain.

The three people come closer. The elderly woman's face grows clearer, along with the face of the blond man.

Then, like the exploding grenade that ended Joe's dreams of life and love so long ago, the ghostly remains of his heart bursts with astonishment as he recognizes who these two people are.

Chapter 1

Artillery

December 17, 1944
The Ardennes Forest, Belgium

In a huge field bordered with evergreen trees, snowflakes drift down in hesitant spirals, slowed and scattered by gusts of winter wind. A formation of airplanes roars in the dawn, on their way to bomb or strafe men and equipment. Beneath the snow-covered trees, three 105-millimeter Howitzers aim black mouths at a gray sky. Soldiers in drab-green coats, pants, and filthy boots—more brown than black from the frozen mud caking the worn leather—wait. Some raise cigarettes past shivering chins to cold lips. Some attempt to warm hands with clouded breaths. Burning embers of tobacco flare red. A gust of wind steals the smoke.

At a radio, another soldier clamps a hand to a pair of headphones over his ears. His eyes dart. The coordinates come in.

One after the other, the waiting men shove explosive shells into place. They think of baseball, hot dogs, warm beds. They think of wives and sweethearts, perfume and kisses, movie theaters on Saturday nights.

A single hand, white in the dawn, drops. Barrels recoil. Flames gout. Tires bounce. Snow shudders from the limbs. Shock waves thud into the men, deafening them despite hands over ears. They silently pray each shell finds its target. Silently pray the war ends soon.

Acrid smoke burns nostrils. Freezing air stings throats. Hands grip cold brass. Fingers go numb. Boots scatter clods of frozen earth. Breaths cloud faces. The dance of loading and firing continues.

As does the praying.

Chapter 2

Targets

They wear uniforms with swastikas. They hear the distant concussions of artillery. They hear the rounds whistling in and run and duck and clamber beneath downed evergreens and dive into smoking craters filled with mud and snow and the bitter smell of burned gunpowder and the iron aroma of bloody corpses. They pray for misses. Pray for an end to the war. Pray regardless of knowing most of them will be dead in the next few minutes.

Explosions shatter trees. Men scream. Men cry. They call for their mothers. They call for their fathers. Shrapnel rips arms and legs. Fragrant evergreen splinters pierce abdomens, chests, heads, eyes. Falling tree trunks compress bodies both dead and alive. On trees still standing, snow shudders from needled limbs in wet blankets.

The volley slows. Flames lick. Fires crackle. The terribly wounded pray for death. Lying inside a smoking crater, a man rises to look. He doesn't hear the whistle of the round that transforms his head into pink mist.

Huddled in a ball several downed trees away, a soldier cries and vomits. He wipes his mouth, checks his rifle. The Americans will be coming, and like everyone else, he's out of ammunition.

The concussions return. The shells whistle. He has one grenade and dare not search the bodies for more. Like a badger filled with desperation, he burrows deeper into the frigid earth beneath the tree. The scent of fresh-turned ground reminds him of Mother's flower garden.

Just close your eyes and play dead, my son. Let them walk by if they come. Live for another day. Live for a chance to return home.

The explosions stop. Smoke burns his nostrils. No one screams. No one moans. No one calls for their mother or father.

No one prays for death.

He closes his eyes. Hope instead of death. Life instead of death. Sleep instead of death. Let them pass.

Please let them pass.

He wakes to the sound of brush cracking. Through a narrow slit between the ground and the tree trunk, he sees two Americans. Rifles at the ready, they take short, hesitant steps toward him. Their eyes scan left, right, then return forward. They stop, nod at each other, and continue.

One American is blond, like him. The other is black, likely from one of the artillery units that reports said were overrun near Wereth. Some of the men said the captured black Americans were tortured. War is torture enough, why torture captured men?

Beyond the Americans, from behind one of the trees left standing, the profile of a German helmet juts forward. The blond German recognizes his corporal's stringy black hair. One of the cruelest men he's ever met, he enjoys wounding men and finishing them off with his bayonet. He hasn't fired a single bullet or thrown a grenade, so he must be out of both. The man's also a coward, attacking from the rear every chance he gets.

The Americans near the area. Trees still burn. Smoke still rises. The blond soldier stops, takes a yellow ribbon from his pocket, and ties it around his wrist. The black soldier says something. Although his tone is derogatory, he smiles. The blond soldier replies. They continue their start and stop patrol.

A few steps later, the blond soldier pauses for water from his canteen. Done drinking, he raises the ribbon to his nose. What memories exist within those yellow strands? Likely those of the young woman at home who gave it to him. He starts forward again, and snow from a branch falls to cover him in white crystals. The black soldier laughs. The snow-covered soldier brushes it from his collar and digs it from his coat pocket. Then they start forward yet again.

Hating how he must take the life of these Americans—one in love and one who understands the warmth of humor—the German unclips the grenade from his belt. Why can't they pass to the left or right? He's sick of killing. Sick of war. The Americans spread ranks, so his throw must be accurate to get both. If not, he'll be forced to use his bayonet.

I know you hate killing, my son, but you have a right to life as well as anyone. A right to love and to be loved. A right to return home to your family.

Do what you must to survive.

Chapter 3

Transformation

To Joe Matthan, home is as far away as far away is.

He runs a gloved finger beneath his nose. Either do that or let the moisture clinging to his nostrils freeze. This place, this country, this frigid air surrounding him, is nothing like home.

He closes his eyes.

Closes his eyes and draws Nebraska near.

Summer mornings with Mom's Sunday breakfasts. Summer afternoons with his girl fishing. Summer nights beneath starlit skies, moonlight lapping waves and swirls upon the river bank. Elaine's kisses and caresses. Sweet-breath whispers. Promises and hope and—

The truck that carries the remainder of Joe's platoon along a snow-covered road lurches to the side. His fellow soldiers, plus three members of a black artillery battalion who joined them a few days earlier, sit beside and facing him. They wear standard-issue drab-green winter uniforms: Heavy coats. Gloves. A scarf if you're lucky. Winter-weight pants and leather boots. All useless in the hellish cold of the Ardennes Forest. The freezing air burns his sinuses. Judging by the bursts of white haze from each man's flaring nostrils, it burns theirs too. Most wear stony stares while cigarettes tremble between shivering lips. The sour stench of unwashed bodies cuts through the cold, not dissimilar to corpses—both German and American—that thaw on the side of the road in morning sun.

Yes, home *is* as far away as far away is.

And so is Elaine.

The truck slides again. The C-ration breakfast churns in Joe's gut. His throat thickens with pork and beans.

Inhale. Exhale. Again.

The truck stops and his sergeant jumps out. "Joe, James, you're up." Joe follows. His boots slip in the slush as if he were on a frozen pond back home.

James joins them. The sergeant flips a lighter open, touches the yellow flame to a cigarette. Smoke leaves his nostrils in twin jets. He returns the lighter to his pocket.

"Artillery blasted this area to hell. I'm dropping you guys here and two more about a hundred yards down the road. Orders are to check for enemy survivors we can question. Get in, get out, be here in thirty minutes when we come back. Got it?"

"We'll be here," Joe says.

The engine roars. Bitter diesel exhaust hangs in the air. Joe returns the sergeant's quick wave, then faces the dense growth of evergreens lining the road. "More dead Germans. Screw 'em."

"Damn right," James says. His throat muscles tighten with a hard swallow. "Especially after what they did to my unit."

This is the first time James says anything about how he joined Joe's platoon. Joe wants to ask and doesn't want to ask. It's an obvious sore spot with the man he's gotten to know over the past few days. "What artillery battalion were you with?"

"The 333rd. Well, it *was* the 333rd. We got separated at some spot in the road called Wereth. Germans showed up out of nowhere."

"You're lucky you got away. I keep hearing how the Nazi's are killing Jews. No telling what they'll do to black guys."

"You do know the only reason what's left of us are mixed with you white boys is 'cause there ain't enough of us to make up an artillery battalion."

"Hey, I don't make the rules. All I care about is you covering my back while I cover yours."

"I don't mind doin' that. My grandma would skin me alive if I treated you different 'cause you're white." James steps toward the evergreens. "Let's see if we can find a wounded German and blow his brains out."

Snow crunches underfoot. The trees, tall and scaly-barked, filled with fragrant needles, enclose them. Up ahead, where artillery struck, trees flame at their bases, adding the bitter note of burning sapwood to the breeze.

Joe stops to take a yellow ribbon from his pocket, and James shakes his head. "C'mon, man, that ribbon ain't gonna bring you no luck."

"I told you my girl gave it to me." Joe ties the ribbon around his left wrist. "That's all the luck I need."

"Hope you don't get blowed up. Hate to say I told you so."

"I wouldn't be too fond of it myself." Joe raises his rifle. Time to get his mind on the job so he can make it back home to Elaine. "You know the deal—ten steps, stop, look, listen, do it again."

"Gotcha. Just like deer huntin' back home."

James steps about a dozen paces to the right. Joe starts forward slowly, stops after ten paces, and so does James. They scan the area, acknowledge each other's nod, and move forward again. Three more start and stop patterns later, they enter an all too familiar nightmare: Trees lie scattered, blasted by direct hits from artillery. Bits of clothing, arms, legs, helmets with swastikas, and rifles with bayonets litter the mud and snow. Joe eases around a huge crater, where the dark earth explodes with loamy aroma like on the farm back home. Smoke rises from the blasted ground in a twisted, ashen spiral. The slight breeze curls the gray haze into what the old folks in Alma call a ghost grin.

Joe steps around another crater and stops. A legless corpse wearing a German helmet lies in the smoldering hole. The shade leaves the frozen body odorless. Sightless eyes stare. A single lock of brown hair curls from beneath the helmet and wavers in the breeze. The mouth gapes like one of these craters, black with glistening quartz stones for teeth.

Good day, my American friend. It is a fine morning for a stroll in the woods, is it not? How would you like to trade places with me? How would you like to trade places with me? How would you like—

Joe clamps his eyes shut. What an imagination—great for daydreaming about Elaine but not for this mess. He clears his throat. "I see why Sarge said to make it quick. No way anyone's alive in here."

"Keep an eye out." James nods toward a German at his feet, the chest a mass of blood and gore. "Don't wanna end up like that."

Ten paces later, Joe stops beside a tall evergreen. A breeze rustles the branches and snowflakes drift down, dusting his arms with white crystals. He tips his helmet back. The thickly needled boughs are still covered. How can that be when everything else in here is blown to hell?

He swallows icy water, returns the canteen to his belt, raises the stained and frayed yellow ribbon to his nose. It doesn't matter that the scent of Elaine's hair is as faded as the ribbon. He closes his eyes; she kneels before him on the patchwork quilt and gathers her hair. *Tie it where I'm holding it, okay? Tie it like you would your shoelaces.* Joe leans close, slides the yellow ribbon under her hands. Her hair smells like summertime, sweet as morning dew on ripe strawberries. The fine curls on the back of her neck flutter with his breath. Was he even breathing then?

He opens his eyes. Time to get back to—

Woomph!

—reality?

A cloud of glistening snow envelopes Joe, and James's rich baritone laugh echoes in the forest. "Man, that tree sure dumped a load on you. Maybe that'll get your mind off that gal until we get back to the road."

Joe leans over to brush the snow from his neck. "It's gonna take more than snow down my collar to make me stop thinking about Elaine." He digs one last bit from his coat pocket. "Let's finish and get out of here. I'm ready for a cup of that powdered crap the Army calls coffee."

"Can't argue that." James takes a step. "Tastes like Sarge filters it through his stinkin' drawers."

Joe moves forward again, the ends of the yellow ribbon dangling from his wrist. What he wouldn't give to be at home with Elaine, holding her in the moonlight beneath millions of stars. Maybe soon … maybe—

BOOM!

Pressure blasts him upward. Light and heat sears his eyes. He falls, and snow soft but cold presses into his cheek and one eye. Blood fills his mouth, salty and thick. He tries to cough. Tries again. Nothing but a choked gurgle bubbles in his throat.

Elaine's brown eyes plead, but he can't raise his head to look for her. Despite the searing pain in his chest, like molten maggots burrowing into his heart and lungs, he manages to shove his hand with the yellow ribbon through the snow. It shakes and shudders: a dead leaf on the oak at the river back home. If he can just touch her, just reach out and touch her ...

I have to believe you'll come back to me, Joe, I have to believe you'll come back to me, Joe, I have to believe—

On a huge tree lying in the mud and snow, its trunk splintered and twisted, Joe's hands rest. Did he black out? If he did, how did he get here? The explosion sounded like a grenade. If it was, maybe the concussion stunned him and he stumbled to this tree. Why's he so tired? It's like he's been fighting someone. What's wrong with his hands, anyway? Spread against the tree, they sting from several bloody cuts. Shrapnel from the grenade? Why are they black? Did he get burned? What happened to the blood in his mouth? Why isn't Elaine's ribbon on his wrist?

He tries to stand. Hands firmly against the tree, chest heaving, he remains there, arms and legs locked into position as if he were that German's frozen body.

Am I paralyzed? Why can't I—

His thigh and calf muscles tighten. He eases around. His hands scrape the tree and pain flares. *What the hell? I wasn't trying to move and I moved. Why can't I talk? I'm trying to but my mouth won't move.*

On the ground several steps away, beside another tree in the snow and mud, a German soldier is dead. He lies on his stomach with one side of his face visible beneath his helmet.

His breath doesn't plume from his open mouth like it does Joe's mouth. Steaming blood covers the side of his face and stains the snow beneath his head. One eye is visible. Open and unseeing, it's partially filled with either bloodstained snow or white gore from the fatal head wound. He must be the guy who threw the grenade and James got his wish to blow a German's brains out. Where *is* James anyway?

Again, without making the attempt, one of Joe's black and bloody hands moves. It touches a sore spot on his face and pulls away to reveal blood on a fingertip. Then it rises to his pocket, takes out a metal mirror, and holds it in front of his face.

James's reflection looks back.

This is crazy! Joe tries to throw the mirror down, but the black hand returns it to the pocket. He tries to look around but his head—like a scarecrow's head on a post back home—refuses to move.

I can't—I can't—

Joe's vision swims in a river of confusion, the same as when he received his notice to report for duty and knew he had to leave Elaine and his family and everything he loved. Blackness tugs him into a well of unconsciousness: deep, cold, without focus or form.

Joe awakes. He's lying face down with his hands—no, James's hands—digging in the snow. The tree isn't in sight, so he—they—aren't where they were before, near the dead German. Joe has no idea what has happened to his friend, but blood bubbles in his throat like when the grenade exploded, sending shrapnel burning into his chest. Almost like wine, the taste of sour grapes mingles with the iron flavor of blood.

What the hell happened after the grenade exploded? He must be dead, but the minister back home never said anything about a person's soul going into another person when they died.

James coughs blood. A blast of cold, like the snow that fell down Joe's collar from the evergreen tree, grips his neck with an icy hand. A tremendous wave of pressure, like the pressure wave from the grenade, clutches his entire body, followed by a flash of bright light, again, like from the grenade.

James's chest heaves and collapses, and cold enfolds Joe's consciousness. It's as if he's flying through a night sky: no moon, no stars, frigid air swirling about him. An incomprehensible amount of time passes. The disorienting cold falls away in a sudden rush. Warmth surrounds him, as if he were standing beside the wood stove in the hardware store back in Alma. How will he ever make it home to Elaine by existing in the bodies of the living?

A woman, almost a human skeleton dressed in rags of clothing, holds the small body Joe is within. On a wooden bunk, beneath another one overhead, she rocks back and forth, humming some kind of song. Hesitant and high-pitched with despair, the notes vibrate in her throat and against the small body's cheek, pressed against her chest.

Dim light tumbles through dirty windows. The odor of human excrement, mixed with the sickly, sweet scent of decaying flesh, fills the building.

The body coughs. The woman strokes the forehead. "Shh, Johan, shh."

Johan coughs again, and Joe tastes blood. The boy's lips separate. "Ima." His voice is a weak, dried husk of a whisper.

The woman pulls Johan to her, pressing his cheek against her ribs even harder. "Shh, my son, shh. We'll be free soon." Her heart flutters within her chest like the wings of a bird longing to escape this cage of a concentration camp. She rocks the boy harder, until her back strikes the wall behind her with an empty, muffled thud. The low, monotone notes of her humming—a mix of song and anguish—grow louder.

The icy hand grips Joe's neck.

The woman's warm tears spill onto the boy's face.

The wave of pressure grips Joe.

The boy's eyes lock open. A rasping exhale empties his lungs.

The flash of light almost blinds Joe.

The woman pulls the boy's face into her heaving chest, and her pitiful wail fades as Joe leaves her dead son.

A yellowed ceiling appears above Joe. The person he's in is lying on a hard surface of some kind. To his left, two men roll a sheet-covered body away. To his right, wearing a surgeon's mask, a doctor pulls a sheet over the ashen face of a man. While he trades bloody gloves for clean ones, a woman dressed in a white nurse's cap, a gray blouse, and a white apron, leans over Joe. "Don't worry, love, you'll be fine in no time." Her accent is British. "You'll take a short nap and be good as new."

"Where's— Where's me mum?" The girl's voice, also with a British accent, is weak and edged with tears.

The doctor leans over the girl. "Your mum's right outside waiting. Now be a good girl and lie still."

The girl's face twists into a grimace. "My leg, it—it hurts."

The nurse holds the girl's hand. "Now, now, sweetheart, the doctor's taking a look. What's your name? You're such a pretty little thing, I'm sure you have a pretty name?"

"Eliz—" The girl swallows. "Elizabeth."

"There now, see? A proper British name for a proper British lady."

The doctor lifts the sheet over the girl's legs. "Nazi bastards. I need to take—"

"Doctor, please," the nurse says, her voice firm.

"Damn!"

Elizabeth strains to raise her head. Joe strains to see why the doctor cursed again. A stream of blood spurts across his mask, matching the dripping streak across his chest.

"Hold her," the doctor says. "I've got to do it now or we'll lose her."

The nurse takes Elizabeth's hands in hers and presses her chest down on the girl's. "Look at me, love, just look at me. It's going to be all right I swear it is, just look at me." The nurse's breath smells of fish and cigarette smoke.

Something metallic clatters near the doctor. Elizabeth's eyes widen as he picks up a scalpel. He lies across the uninjured leg and her shrill, keening cry echoes throughout the room as the cold blade slices through skin, muscle, and tendon. Her head falls to the side. The weakened heart thrums. The diaphragm expels short, ragged breaths.

The doctor exchanges the scalpel for a saw. "Hold her now, just a bit more."

Elizabeth screams again, a long, anguished shriek that empties her lungs as the rasping cuts of the saw's teeth send vibrations up her leg.

"Got it." The doctor picks up a suture. "Let's stop this bleeding."

Elizabeth's vision dims. Joe can barely make out the nurse's blue eyes.

Then ... not at all.

The cold hand grips Joe's neck. The wave of pressure squeezes. The flash of light momentarily blinds him.

The nurse turns. "I'm afraid she's gone. I should—" She wipes a tear from her cheek. "I should tell her mum."

The doctor grinds his teeth. Joe tastes sugar and milk from the man's last cup of tea. The doctor snaps off the rubber gloves and jerks the bloody mask from his face. "Didn't she say her name was Elizabeth? She's the last person to die from that building collapse. Damned Nazi bastards."

"But you said …?"

"I had to give her some kind of hope, didn't I? Let me be." The nurse leaves the room. The doctor goes to Elizabeth's side. "I'm sorry, sweetheart," he says, wiping a smudge from her forehead. "So sorry." He closes the lifeless green eyes, pulls the sheet up over the blonde hair filled with dirt. A hot tear trickles down his cheek and falls to the sheet. It expands like a gray thunderhead in a sky filled with white clouds. Two men come and roll Elizabeth away.

The doctor leaves to shuffle along a darkened hall, head down, mumbling unintelligibly.

He enters a room, turns on a lamp. Yellow light spreads a circle on a desk and a chair. From a drawer, he takes out a bottle, a small glass, a revolver, and sits. He spins the cylinder, removes all the bullets but one, snaps the cylinder shut. Glass filled, he downs the bitter alcohol, slams the glass to the table, and drives the cold barrel of the gun into his temple. His hand shakes. Another hot tear rolls down his cheek. A loud click shatters the silence.

And another.

And another.

Gun on the table, remaining drops drained from the glass, once more he curls his finger around the trigger and drives the barrel into his temple.

Again, the cold hand falls upon Joe's neck. Again, the wave of pressure squeezes him. Again, he waits for the flash of light to nearly blind him. All three, no doubt, are the warnings of death.

And life within another person.

Insane.

Insanity.

What kind of living is this?

The doctor slowly pulls the trigger. "What kind of living is this? Humanity destroying itself? Children dying at the whim of a madman?"

The hammer tightens its rearward arch against the spring. He holds it there. Holds it there.

He and Joe close their eyes.

Chapter 4

Not a Merry Christmas

December 17, 1999

In his car seat, Sam places the tip of his finger on the window and purses his lips, sticky from a recent candy cane.

"Mmm."

His lips separate, pucker, and warm breath flows through his vocal cords, vibrating just so.

"Ooo."

His tongue lightly touches the roof of his mouth.

"Nnn."

He grins. He remembered the word for the big white thing in the sky without anyone telling him.

Joe tastes the candy canes' peppermint sweetness as if he had just licked and crunched one himself. Sam's two-year-old eyes continue watching the moon, and Joe enjoys the view. He did the same thing as a kid in Nebraska, but here in Kansas, the moon looks exactly the same. If only he could see it from home one more time.

Sam's breath fogs the glass. He touches the haze with tentative fingertips and snatches them away.

It's cold, isn't it, Sam? Don't worry, we'll get warm at home when

Hope has all of us working on the decorations. Listen to her, I never heard an eight-year-old get so excited about Christmas.

"… and Daddy, this year you can hold up Sam so he can put the angel on the tree. I think he's big enough this time." She faces Sam. "Whatcha think, Sam? Can you do it?"

Sam whirls around, claps his hands, and raises them over his head. "Cwismuss twee, Hope!"

All right then. My little buddy gets to put the angel on the tree this year. I can't think of a better way to end the day.

Hope describes stringing lights on the tree to Sam, fingers fluttering and weaving, dipping and diving. Sam watches intently, chin moving in time with her hands.

Butterflies. That day Elaine and me were lying on the quilt in the shade of the old oak, two yellow butterflies, like tiny pieces of stained glass, flitted around us. Elaine said they were looking for the perfect flower. I laughed and said I'd found mine. Hope's hands remind me of those butterflies. I'd sure love to visit the river again. Maybe one day I'll—

A cold draft chills the back of Sam's neck.

Is that on Sam's neck or my neck? Did someone open a window? Sam, look at your dad. Come on, buddy, he's right in front of you.

Joe waits. Sam doesn't turn.

Maybe I'm overreacting. I don't think I ever left someone after only a year.

Concentrating again, Joe tries to make Sam turn away from Hope to look at Adam for the source of the cold air. Like with all the other people Joe has been with over the years, all he does is make Sam scratch the skin below his ear.

"What's wrong, Sam?" Hope asks. "Got an itch?"

"Itch, Hope."

Her grin reveals a space where two front teeth fell out

recently, now exchanged for two quarters from the Tooth Fairy. "Then scratch it," she says.

Sam's nails scrape his neck. The car slows. Adam turns off the main highway. The headlights illuminate a railroad crossing sign

Two more miles to home. Maybe I'm wrong about—

The familiar wave of pressure squeezes Joe.

It can't be happening now, dammit. How could that—?

"Let's sing, Mommy," Hope says. "Jingle bells, jingle bells ..."

In the front seat, Rachel turns around to face Hope. "Jingle all the way."

"Oh, what fun ..." they both sing.

"Fun!" Sam squeals with laughter, claps his hands again, and Adam's eyes appear in the rear-view mirror, crinkled with a smile.

Please don't do this—why do I have to—

"It is to ride ..."

This makes no sense, how can Sam—

Adam's eyes are still visible in the rear-view mirror. He doesn't slow the car for the railroad crossing. Sam raises a finger and points. "Light, Hope."

Hope whirls around. Her ringlets of golden hair mix with a blinding whiteness coming in through the window behind her. "Daddy! Mommy! It's the—"

It's the train? No! Take me and leave Sam alone! Leave them all alo—

The train's shrill horn blasts into the night, startling Sam into a scream.

Rachel spins toward the metallic squeal of the train's brakes. "Adam, go!"

Adam hits the accelerator, jerking them all backward. The train plows into and through the car. Tearing metal screeches. The straps securing Sam into the car seat break, releasing him into the freezing night air.

The train continues down the tracks, brakes locked and screaming, sparks flying. What's left of the car cartwheels along the gravel fill beneath the tracks, spewing its contents along the ditches lining the woods.

The rear seat, with Sam's empty car seat, lands upside down near the woods.

Sam lands near Hope. As he reaches for her still hand, an intense bolt of white light ejects Joe from the little boy, and the family he loves so well.

Chapter 5

Becoming Kurt Bauer

An unfamiliar heartbeat thumps, hesitant and slightly off-time. Blood whooshes through veins and arteries but slower, like molasses dripping in long, brown strings from a Mason jar. The chest rises and falls with steady breaths.

Sam and Hope, Adam and Rachel—the Lewis family, all gone in an instant. To be Joe again and cry it all out—it hasn't been that way in so long, he can hardly remember. Experience tells him he won't learn anything about his new body until he calms down from the Lewis's deaths.

"The name Matthan has a special meaning," Dad once said, patting Joe on the back when he was a kid. "The hope of God."

Dad's statement sounded fine back then, kind of like Joe's name is a gift. Instead of a gift, his life is a curse. In the Ardennes all those years ago, death had caught him like a wolf catches a newborn calf in the spring. The calf bawls for only a second. In the woods its throat is slashed. It gurgles and kicks in an attempt to free itself from the savage incisors until blood pools beneath its head. Another life transformed, to exist within the wolf that wears Death's black cloak and carries the long-handled scythe that slashes whenever and wherever Death pleases.

The Bible says Lazarus was raised from the dead. Joe can't

count the times he's been raised, so he might as well take Lazarus's name instead of Joe. *No, forget that stuff and find out where you are and who you're with. That's what's important now.*

Joe imagines deep breaths, cleansing and calming, and he gradually sinks into the man's muscles and bones. He's nothing like Sam. Sam's two-year-old body felt clean and new, and being with him reminded Joe of standing on the porch the last year he had been alive, a crisp spring breeze blowing through his blond hair. The man also feels stiff and scratchy, like an old woolen overcoat Joe's grandpa used to wear. Like his grandpa, the man radiates maleness and age.

Okay, old man, you're an old man. That means I might not stay with you very long. Hell, I'd rather be with an old coot like you instead of another kid like Sam. At least it won't be a surprise when you keel over from a stroke or a heart attack.

The old man moans. Joe senses drowsy confusion. The man rolls over, roots in his pillow like a nursing piglet, and relaxes into sleep. *Go ahead and rest, I'll be right here waiting. Huh, like I have a choice. Well, I guess I can use the time to see if I can figure out what happened to Sam and Hope and Adam and Rachel.*

Joe concentrates on his last moments with Sam: When Hope mentioned Sam and the angel. When her fingers fluttered in the air. When she sang and Rachel joined in. When Sam said "light" and when the train's headlight blinded him and the horn blared, scaring them all out of their minds.

How the devil did Adam forget the train tracks? Hell, he forgot them just like I forgot them, because we were paying attention to Hope and Rachel singing and to Sam laughing.

This would have been Joe's second Christmas with this family. He wanted to see red and green and gold wrapping paper, with matching bows and ribbons, flying when they opened their presents. Rachel had mentioned Christmas dinner, and he wanted to taste mashed potatoes and gravy and turkey and stuffing in Sam-sized bites. Rachel and Adam would've gone to the living room afterward, while Hope and Sam played with their new toys.

And since these parents loved books and often read to the children, Joe had hoped for the simple pleasure of a bedtime reading of *The Night Before Christmas*. After all, he had seen a copy on Hope's nightstand last night when Adam carried Sam to his big sister's room for a hug and a kiss, and to say in his pure little boy's voice, "'Night, Hope."

The man moans again.

Joe once dreamed of having his own family with Elaine, even one like Sam's. Realistically, those dreams aren't possible anymore. Still, the insanity of his own situation proves the impossible is sometimes possible. *Like grandpa used to say, cain't give on yer hopes, boy. Dream big or don't dream at all.*

The years roll back: pages of lives lived and gone after the doctor shot himself in Britain. No memory compares to the story the Lewis's sometimes told friends and relatives concerning Hope and Sam meeting for the first time.

It happened in the hospital, on the day after Sam had been born. Adam had given Hope a boost to see Sam for the first time, as he was having his breakfast in Rachel's arms.

Hopes eyes had opened wide. "Hold me still, Daddy," she had said, leaning toward Sam's head. "I want to see what special smells like."

Joe's life consisted of more pages of lives lived, ripped from the novel of his life at eighteen, leaving him hoping beyond hope for another chance at life, another chance with Elaine. Hope had kept his dreams alive all the long years of his so-called life, and it's all he has left to cling to.

I'll miss Sam and Hope, and Adam and Rachel. There're so many things I'll remember about them, but I hope they're not living a life like mine. I wouldn't wish this on anyone, not even my worst enemy.

As difficult as it is, Joe shoves the sadness from his mind. *It's time to pay attention to this old guy and see who he is and where I am. I just hope I'm not stuck in a version of some old Scrooge who hates Christmas.*

A scratch and a moan later, the man rolls onto his back, rubs crusty sleep from his eyes, and stretches. Two gnarled hands extend into Joe's view. "All right, Kurt, time to rise and shine." The man's gravelly voice vibrates in his throat.

'Kurt' is it? Well, Kurt, it's about time, you slow old fart. Don't break your neck getting out of bed. I don't want to set a record for the shortest visit I've ever had with anyone.

Kurt slides his legs from under the covers; his warm feet plop onto the cold floor. *Durn, old man, where are your slippers?* Kurt shifts on the bed as if he's about to stand, his old joints a bit sore, and Joe readies himself for the effort.

Instead of rising, Kurt faces a nightstand. A glass bowl filled with curlicued seashells sits on the far side, a yellowed paperback beside it. On the side nearest the bed, a framed photograph sits under a reading lamp. Images of dogwood leaves artfully incise the lampshade's cream-colored paper surface. On the lower edge, a name is written in blue ink. Although Joe can't make out the signature, he admires the fine work, likely handmade.

Kurt brings the photograph near his squinting eyes, smiles for a moment, and returns it to the nightstand. He continues to stare at the picture and so does Joe. The picture is of a woman, maybe in her mid-sixties. She wears a large straw hat with a yellow ribbon around the base. The ends dangle as her head tilts back. Graying hair frames smooth cheeks, except for a few faint wrinkles around eyes a shade or two lighter than black coffee. A smudge of dirt—closely matching the deep brown of her eyes—marks one cheek. She also wears a red-checked apron and holds the corners up with gloved hands. The apron contains four ears of corn, each still in green husks, each adorned with yellow tassels, along with two tomatoes. Behind her in a garden, corn stalks stand at attention. Tomato vines, supported by trellises, rest at ease.

Joe's mental mouth waters at what must've been served for supper that night. When did he last taste ripe tomatoes off the vine and fresh buttered corn on the cob?

He looks at the woman again, paying more attention to the best part of the photograph, even better than corn and tomatoes. Her radiant smile transforms an average face into a glowing face, as if she's daring the camera to take a less than acceptable picture of her.

I've always been a sucker for a pretty smile, and she's cute too. Joe attempts to roll his eyes. *Doggone, have I lost what little sense I've got left, by thinking a woman who's got to be in her sixties is cute?*

Huh, with everything I've been through, I wouldn't doubt it for a country minute.

Chapter 6

Memories

Kurt picks up the picture again, touches his wife's cheek, and returns the picture to the nightstand.

What memory should he relive this morning? The day he took her picture at the garden or—he picks up the bowl of seashells—their trip to the Outer Banks of North Carolina? He raises the bowl to his nose. If he sniffs hard enough, he can smell the salt air, feel the warm breeze on his face, and imagine her fingers slipping into his as they stroll the beach.

She had driven her retirement present to herself, a new SUV with four-wheel-drive, half way across the country. Seeing the wild descendants of the Spanish Mustangs that lived on the slender barrier island north of Corolla was one of her reasons for buying the four-wheel-drive, the other being that Kurt had told her of his interest in driving down to the tip of Cape Hatteras to try his luck at surf fishing.

During the long drive south on Highway 12, when the rising black and white spiral of the Cape Hatteras Lighthouse towered ahead of them, they added two more visits to their agenda. She wanted to see it at night, while the light shined across the Atlantic. He wanted to see it in the daytime, to challenge his legs by climbing the 257 steps to the top.

Whenever he looks through their picture album, Kurt tries

to recall other parts of their lengthy adventure. There's a picture of them at the red brick Currituck Beach Lighthouse, but he can't remember if they climbed it or not. There's one of the Bodie Island Lighthouse, which they drove by because it was raining. Then there's one of the Ocracoke Island Lighthouse, short, stubby, and painted white. He remembers its squat form, but can't quite recall the narrow, winding roads leading to it. But of all the things they had seen and of all the places they had been, what his heart chooses as special keepsakes from the trip are their two visits to the Cape Hatteras Lighthouse.

On their nighttime visit, the lighthouse was closed, so they parked at the old site where it had been located before being moved inland to protect it from the encroaching ocean. Stopping at the ring of old stones marking the original location, they ran their fingers over the cool, chiseled surfaces, then strolled by the glow of the full moon to where the Atlantic surf met the Outer Banks of North Carolina.

The waves were abnormally calm, swishing to their final resting place on the sand. Endless stars twinkled like millions of shimmering eyes watching them from the cloudless sky. They made a perfect backdrop, yet, when Kurt glanced up from his seat on the sand, he barely noticed the tiny specks of light. His wife's head moved slightly, timed with the beam reaching across the Atlantic, the warm salt breeze blowing her graying hair about her face. She turned his way, and the moonlight reflecting off the water illuminated tears on her cheeks. He started to ask why but waited. If anything was wrong, she would tell him in her own time. She sat beside him and looped her arm under his.

"You know what amazes me, sweetheart? Here I am, a

retired English teacher, and I can't find the words to describe how I feel about this place. How many people have seen that light? How many couples have stood right here and talked about it? It's been here for almost 150 years, so there's no telling who has seen it. I just wish we visited before it was moved away from the beach."

The next morning, after breakfast at a local diner, they arrived as the gate to the lighthouse visitor's center was opening. On this day, Kurt stores two more memories into the recesses of his mind. One, not so special, is how he only climbs about two-thirds of the way up those 257 steps. He didn't care, because his other memory—more special than he ever imagines—chisels itself into the stone of his recollections. This is his wife at her best, all smiles, no tears, full of joy.

Kurt waited by one of the tall, narrow windows, attempting to cool off in the breeze, and her white tennis shoes appeared above him on the black-painted metal stairs. She smiled at him over the railing, and his vision blurred into the scene he would always remember: the day she walked down the church aisle thirty-five years ago in her wedding dress, smiling in exactly the same way as she did now.

She joined him by the window, to lay her head on his chest and give him a hug. "Thank you for letting us come all the way out here."

"Thank me?" Kurt asked, chuckling. "You did all the driving."

"And I'd do it all over again, in a heartbeat."

"I would too, sweetheart, I would too." He looked toward the top of the lighthouse. The light beaming its way across the Atlantic had been bright last night, brighter than the full moon could ever be, but it couldn't hold a candle to his sweetheart's beautiful smile.

* * *

Joe assumes the lady in the picture is Kurt's wife. He also assumes she's dead since she isn't here, and Kurt's remembering something about her, or either he's *trying* to remember something about her. *Unless Kurt's having some kind of dementia, maybe I'll stick around long enough to find out more about her. I hope he's okay though, my positive karma's pretty well used up. Maybe he has a grand-kid or two we could visit and perk him up.*

Because of Kurt's aching joints, Joe expects him to ease up from the bed slowly. Instead, he rises with one smooth movement. *Maybe I misjudged you, old Kurt. That lady might have kept you young. How many more surprises have you got for me?*

As Kurt ambles around the bed, Joe tries to see as much of the room as possible. A few pictures of a boy at various ages and another glass bowl of seashells sits on a dresser. Kurt nears a bathroom, and a small, round object that resembles a medal, which hangs on the corner of some kind of framed document near the door, catches Joe's curiosity.

That looks like a German war medal. It even has a World War II German soldier's helmet and a swastika on it. I can't get a break. Here I am, losing the perfect American family at Christmas to a train, and I'm stuck with some old German guy. What the hell is next?

Kurt continues to the bathroom, slips his feet into slippers, and opens his pajama fly at a toilet.

Takes a while, huh? Joe mentally smiles. *Maybe that's because you don't have much to work with.* The man goes to a sink. *Look, don't forget to leave your slippers by the bed in the morning. It must be winter wherever we are, and that durn floor was cold.*

Kurt washes his hands and fills the sink with hot water, wets his face and spreads shaving cream on his gray stubble.

Joe attempts a mental frown concerning the German medal. *Given my situation, I should've learned by now not to think the worst when I join a new person. All right, Kurt, let's see what you look like while you whack your whiskers off.*

Hazy blue eyes stare back from a face at least in its seventies. Kurt's nose has a peculiar bend to one side, and sun spots dot his weathered, wrinkled cheeks. A white bandage covers the upper half of his left ear.

What happened to your ear, old man? Did you get too much sun out in the garden?

Turning his head like an owl, Kurt scrapes more whiskers. On the craggy forehead, a faded, pink scar starts just over one eyebrow and ends at his hairline above his other eyebrow.

You get that in the war? I know, your wife took a frying pan to your head one night after you got home late. I guess I'll find all that out if you don't keel over anytime soon.

Who am I kidding? You'll probably live to be a hundred. Look at you, you made it through the war and married a woman with a sweet smile and had a son while I get to be a traveling ghost of some sort. On top of that, I get to look at you every day until you kick off and be reminded of what I missed because one of your buddies threw a grenade my way.

Joe stops his rant. How would James handle this situation? During the few days he knew him, they talked about how people sometimes mistreated each other. When it came to understanding things that made no sense, James's grandma, who he lived with in Grandy, North Carolina, had shared some advice after being in a fight or two when he was a boy, which was some of the best advice Joe had ever heard. "Give folks a chance," she would say. "Who a person is, James, is on the inside. People are afraid to get to know you because they're blinded by your outside. *And* 'cause, deep down, they're scared of what they don't know."

Yep, I used her advice a lot over the years, so I should use it now, while I get acquainted with my new old German friend, Kurt.

Chapter 7

Perspective

Okay, old man. I admit I was blinded by your outside and not knowing you, not to mention that doggone German medal. Get your day going and I'll do like James's grandmother said and give you a chance.

Kurt wipes leftover shaving cream from his face with a warm washcloth, brushes his teeth, combs his hair, and applies a few swipes of deodorant. In the bedroom again, he dresses in socks, faded jeans, and an olive-drab long-sleeved shirt, similar to what Joe wore as part of his cold-weather uniform. On a chest at the foot of the bed, he sits to trade his slippers for a pair of broken-in work boots, goes to the dresser to stuff his pockets with a pocket knife, wallet, keys, and follows the aroma of coffee down a hallway that leads to a kitchen.

Boy, does that smell good. Sam wasn't old enough for coffee and I missed it. Tell you what, old man, I'll let you alone and see what this day brings. Unless you shock me any more than you already have—and I don't see that happening—I'll shut up so I can figure out exactly where in Germany I am.

* * *

Kurt fills his mug. There's nothing like waking up to the smell of a fresh pot of coffee, and the new programmable coffee maker does a great job. His wife used to get up first on the weekends to make coffee while he slept. She never had to call him either. Without fail, as the last drops fell into the decanter, the aroma drifting into their room teased him out of bed. Cancer took her two years ago, and this is just one of a thousand different ways he misses her.

Under a Cape Hatteras Lighthouse magnet on the refrigerator, a note reminds him to go by the hardware store after selling his last box of spinach at the local Farmer's Market. He touches the top of the tiny lighthouse, where a drop of white paint shines, added by his wife after they returned from their trip.

"Has it really been two years?" He lowers his hand to his side. "Might as well be two-thousand, much as I miss her."

* * *

Sad and a bit slow, Kurt's actions concerning the lighthouse are familiar to Joe. He understands missing a loved one, especially when that someone had been the love of his life like Elaine had been his.

A cardboard box of fresh greens, spinach maybe, sits on a nearby counter. *I hope that stuff isn't Kurt's breakfast.* Kurt takes two pieces of what appear to be homemade bread from a plastic bag and drops them in a toaster, easing Joe's concerns about the greens. There's no way Kurt will eat toast with spinach on it. Nostrils flaring at the aroma of toasting bread, Kurt fetches a jar of apple butter and a package of cream cheese from the refrigerator, confirming Joe's guess about spinach on toast. The bread pops from the toaster, and Kurt sits at the table with his meal: one slice of buttery toast with cream cheese, one with the cinnamon sweetness of apple butter, every bite washed down with hot coffee. Joe's phantom mouth waters with every bite.

Breakfast done, Kurt dons a faded jean jacket, a red-plaid cap with ear flaps folded up, and steps outside. A Labrador retriever, tail wagging, and a matching yellow cat rubs his legs. "Darn it, you guys, I forgot to feed you." He fills their bowls and goes back out. The dog prances and the cat meows. "All right, all right, here you go."

Hey, old man, your dog reminds me of mine when I was a kid. It's nice you have pets like I did in Nebraska. Joe raises a phantom eyebrow. *Wait a minute, he's speaking English with a slight German accent. How'd I miss that?*

Kurt retrieves the box of spinach, closes the door, and gives his pets another rub. "Okay, you two, time to hit the road." On the way to an old SUV, his breath clouds in the cold air.

Joe tries to read the dusty license plate. *That doesn't look like a foreign plate, I've seen a few of those. N, E, B, R—is that? It says Nebraska! I can't believe it, I made it back home! Well, I should've known that because of that lighthouse on his refrigerator. Wow, this old man sure threw a welcome wrench into my assumptions. Now, how the heck did a German soldier—if that's what he is—get to Nebraska?*

* * *

Kurt sets the box of spinach in the passenger seat and climbs in to fasten his seat belt. He cranks the SUV and circles the driveway. Gravel crunches under the tires of his wife's old retirement gift. A miniature Cape Hatteras Lighthouse swings from the rear-view mirror.

The path that led him to Nebraska from World War II Germany never fails to amaze him. He didn't even mind getting captured and sent here to help farmers in the fields. Most, like George and Betty Edwards, were fine people. If they hadn't offered him a home before he returned to Germany, on the premise that he had no family to return to, who knows what might've happened to him. Sure, some townspeople had treated him like the enemy for a while after the war, but people like the Edwards, people whose kindness he truly appreciated, had made him feel like family.

"And the rest is history," he says, giving the gently swinging Cape Hatteras Lighthouse a nudge.

Chapter 8

Home

You sure got a thing for lighthouses, Kurt. Where are we going anyway?

The SUV passes a field of brown corn stalks, waiting for a farmer to harvest the golden ears peeking from the dried shucks. Minutes later they pass a field of wheat stubble, where another farmer has already completed his work. A few miles later, Kurt's head turns toward a sign that marks the town limits of Alma, Nebraska, population 1,134.

Alma? My Alma? You've got to be kidding me. All this time I've been hoping to find my way back home and here I am!

The old man scratches his neck, waves at someone, and continues through town, to park beside a sign that reads "Alma Farmer's Market." He climbs from the SUV, turns for the spinach, and someone slides their hands around his waist and squeezes. He and Joe look at the small hands. "I know who that is," Kurt says. "Are you trying to hijack me and steal my spinach, old gal?"

"No, old man," a feminine voice says. "I'm just stealing a squeeze from your broken-down body is all. You can keep your spinach." The arms hug once more, let go, and Kurt turns around. The woman, with permed gray hair and quick blue eyes, wears snug jeans and a pink sweater.

"Hey there, Ruthie, who're you calling old? Your egg-laying days are far behind you yourself, old hen, but this old rooster can still crow when he needs to." Kurt attempts a weak imitation of a rooster crowing, pauses, and fakes a coughing spell.

This guy's a mess, but I think this funny lady might help bring it out of him.

Ruth takes a cell phone from her pocketbook. "Should I call 911 before you toss a tonsil, old rooster?"

"No 911 for me, old hen, not yet anyway. You're right though, about all I'm good for these days is growing spinach and keeping Ex-lax in business."

Ruth burst out laughing, Kurt joins in, and Joe shares the old man's wheezing chuckle. *What a pair. If these two aren't married they ought to be. I bet there'd never be a dull moment if they were together twenty-four seven.*

Kurt takes the box from the SUV. "Let's go sell my last box of spinach. We'll have a bite of lunch after."

Ruth winks. "You got yourself a deal."

They stroll alongside various vendor booths while Joe attempts to recall Alma. Some of it's familiar, but not a lot. For one thing, there's never been a Farmer's Market or the new Christmas decorations hanging from the lamp posts lining Main Street. *Didn't I see a new post office? I wonder—*

Elaine! I haven't even thought about her since we get to town. Could she still be here? Could she still be alive?

At a booth, Kurt places his spinach on a table alongside Ruth's bread. "I hope I get a good price for this last box. That'll be it for a while."

"Don't you need to pick up your order from the hardware store?" Rush asks. "I'll work on selling my bread and your spinach while you're gone. That'll save you from making the trip later."

"You know what, Ruthie? You're one smart and considerate lady. Now I know why my wife thought so much of you."

"Aw, go on," Ruth says, waving the comment away. "Stop being nice before you throw me off my game. Besides, how long did it take you to figure out I'm smart and considerate? Your wife—and my best friend I might add—knew it the minute I warned her about old roosters like you."

"If you don't know my opinion of you by now, maybe this will help." Kurt kisses her cheek. "Besides, we both know you're full of fertilizer."

"All spice here, old rooster. Wouldn't life without spice be a mediocre meal?"

"Got that right, Ruthie. Mediocre meals—or conversation—never happen around you. I'll be back quick as I can. Then we can head over to the diner and see if you can spice up that stuff Bill calls meatloaf."

The hardware store? Kurt can't be going to the same hardware store that was here before I left. One of the big chains has probably put it out of business by now.

A few blocks later, when Kurt parks, the store front amazes Joe. *Look at that, the same old door. I wonder …* Kurt opens the heavy wooden door with a plate glass center, which rings a bell at the top. *Yep, that sounds exactly like the same old brass bell that rang every time I walked in all those years ago.* The old man strides the center aisle, glancing about at the interior of the store, and Joe marvels at what he sees. *It's the same old store, exactly like I remember. It even has the old wood stove in the aisle on the way to the counter.*

* * *

Kurt brushes his hand along the cool metal of the wood stove, smiles a slight smile, and stops at the counter. "Morning, Jimmy."

"Hi, Mr. Bauer. I know why you're here." Jimmy faces the back of the store. "Hey, Dad, it's Mr. Bauer!"

John Hansen, an older version of Jimmy, only heavier, with graying hair and eyebrows, rounds a corner with a box and brings it to the counter. "There you go, Kurt. Hope it does the job."

"Morning, John, I'm sure it will. Don't total my bill yet. I might get some seeds."

"Sure, but the next shipment is two months away. Don't you want 'em fresh?"

"Well, I like to look around. No matter how many times I've been in this old store, I never know what I might find. Besides, I like your store's ambiance. You know what that means, right?"

"Uh-huh. It means it smells like my son's feet."

Jimmy frowns at his father; both older men laugh.

At the seed racks, Kurt gives them a glance and leaves to stroll around the store, waiting for one of the most significant memories of his life to appear like a ghost from his past. Nearing the seed racks again, he stops to place his palm on the edge of the dented and scarred wooden counter that runs the length of the store, stacked with all manner of hand tools.

During these visits, Kurt knows he's been watched on occasion. He knows he's being watched now, due to John and Jimmy's murmuring voices. Regardless, nothing can distract him, possibly not even a tornado. He closes his eyes, opens them, and smiles. His memory is primed once again, to be run through his mind on the drive home like an old movie, flickering and dim, but still able to tell its story.

Kurt pays his bill and turns with his purchase. Glancing around the old hardware store again, filled with dusty shelves, musty smells, and the voices and faces from his past, he goes to one of the wooden benches by the dinosaur of a wood stove and sits, placing the box beside him. Hands resting on the edges of the bench, he rubs the smooth wood, polished by generations of sitting Alma patrons, and closes his eyes like he did at the counter earlier.

Wood smoke. The clank of the door closing whenever someone took a notion to add another piece of seasoned oak or hickory. Ashes in the floor, glowing bits of wood mixed in. A brass spittoon, missed to the point of dark tobacco juice stains on the heart-pine flooring, amber with age.

Those days are long gone now. At least the old wood stove is still here: a comforter and a reminder and a cast-iron, pot-bellied ghost from the past.

John installed a new gas furnace over twenty years ago, likely in need of replacement now. When he took the stove pipe down in preparation for removing the old wood stove, some of his older clientele protested so much—Kurt included—John left it. After being a centerpiece for old men to gather around for so long, no one cared if it was never used for heat. John admitted to Kurt how he thoroughly understood. He also told Kurt he had worn his own share of wood from those benches, spending many an afternoon listening to the Alma elders tell stories, spin yarns, and talk politics over the years.

* * *

Kurt's standing at the counter with his eyes closed puzzles Joe. Either he was remembering something like he did with the picture on his nightstand, or dementia was setting in. When

Kurt completes his purchase and sits on the old bench in front of the stove, Joe's concern comes to an amazing end. Finally, after all these years, he gets to see something he never thought he'd see again: the old wood stove, blackened with age. Even through it radiates no heat, it burns with a cherished memory.

Would you look at that, it's really here, the old wood stove.

As Kurt's stiffened fingers squeeze the edge of the bench as if it were a baseball bat Joe had as a kid, Joe retrieves pieces of his own hardware store history. Like an angler hoping for the catch of a lifetime, he concentrates, slowly reeling in memories from ages ago, careful not to rush, afraid they'll break the fragile line of his past that connects him to Elaine.

Kurt opens his eyes, slowly raises his head, and Joe can almost see Elaine's beautiful brown eyes looking down at him.

Chapter 9

More Memories

All I wanted was to earn money for college. Then Dad suggested I ask Mr. Hansen—I guess he's a relative of this John Hansen—about using the store to give music lessons. As simple a thing as that was, it's a day I'll always remember.

* * *

Joe stands at the counter with his guitar case. "I know it's a lot to ask, Mr. Hansen, but I'd sure appreciate it."

Mr. Hansen, in his storekeeper's white apron, rubs his dark beard. "Well now, this is an interesting proposition, young Mr. Matthan. How much do you propose I charge for the use of my fine establishment?"

"I didn't think about that. Could I teach you instead and start paying after I get a few customers? If you like music, that is."

"How about an audition to help me make up my mind?"

Joe sits on one of the benches by the wood stove and uncases the guitar. "Did my father talk to you about this?"

"Sure did, said you could sing too. I was joking about getting paid. I wouldn't dream of taking money from a young man trying to better his education. Maybe I'll take lessons so I can play that new music on the radio. What they're calling bluegrass."

"I like that music too." Joe strums the guitar. "This thing needs tuning."

He turns the keys until each string matches another at certain locations on the fretboard. Not knowing where to start, he plays a simple chord progression, adds a few lead-in notes, and stops to see what Mr. Hansen says.

Hansen nods. "How about singing one?"

Not wanting to make a mistake, Joe watches his fingers while changing chords. An old song comes to mind, so he attempts to calm his nerves by playing the progression until the rhythm flows smooth and solid.

"I am a poor, wayfaring stranger, while traveling through, this world of woe."

A pair of girl's white and black leather shoes, complete with white socks and shapely legs, steps into view. He stops playing. About his age, she holds three or four schoolbooks in her arms. She wears a below-the-knee-length blue dress, a white sweater, and her long, light-brown ponytail hangs behind her, tied with a yellow ribbon.

"Please don't stop," she says. "I love that old song."

Joe places his fingers on the neck of the guitar. The girl steps closer and reaches out to rest her fingertips on the strings near the soundhole. Then, while he still holds the chord, she strums the guitar. She does this again, slowly takes her hand away, and Joe follows it back to its owner.

Is she the same girl?

Unlike anyone he's ever known, she transforms into a beauty he's never seen, and all because of her stunning smile.

Mr. Hansen clears his throat. "Do like the young lady says, Joe, finish that tune."

"I'm Elaine Johnson," the girl says. "Someone at school said you were giving lessons here at the store."

"Today's my first day. I was asking Mr. Hansen about it, and he wanted to hear a song." Joe faces Mr. Hansen. "What do you think?"

"Fine with me," Hansen says, taking a pencil from behind his ear. "We'll see about my lessons later. I'm going back to work so you can talk business."

Joe faces Elaine. "I'm Joe Matthan. I don't think I've seen you at school. What grade are you in?"

"Tenth."

"I'm in the eleventh. Maybe that's why."

Elaine sits beside him. "Could be, not that it matters." She places her books on the bench and slides closer. "Can you show me the chords in that song? Please?"

Adrenaline tingles along Joe's spine. He wants to run, or at least to slide over enough to not feel the warmth of her leg touching his. His breath hitches in his throat and he doesn't know why. His legs tense, ready to stand. Maybe if he closes his eyes, she'll slide back over. Instead, she slides so close their shoulders touch, then takes his left hand and places her hand within it. Her hands, smooth and warm, feel great. The smell of fresh air in her hair is crisp and clean. Joe has no experience with girls, especially this close and personal. A few years back, Alma experienced a small earthquake, and he could swear his insides were experiencing one now.

Elaine places their hands on the guitar neck. "Joe-o-o-o, I'm ready-y-y-y."

Her breath tickles his ear. She grins and he blinks. "I'm sorry, I was … I was trying to remember those chords."

"Didn't you just play them?"

"I did, but— Elaine, why are you sitting so close to me?"

"I'm this close so you can help me make a chord, silly."
"Oh, okay. If you say so."

Chapter 10

Lunch

Kurt eases up from the bench and rubs the old stove's black surface, and the cold metal comforts Joe. *What a day that was. Making a guitar chord was the last thing on our minds. Where could Elaine—*

Slam!

Doggone, old man, can you close that SUV door a bit easier? You'll scare a person half to death with all that racket. One thing's for sure, you'll bring him back to reality.

Where was I? Oh, yeah, the day Elaine and I met. Where could she be? What a dumb question. It's not like I can tell her I'm back if I saw her. I just hope she had a happy life, even if it meant finding someone else.

Joe calms his thoughts while Kurt returns to the Farmer's Market. He'll observe the couple and take the day as it comes. If he sees Elaine, great. Either way, he's stuck inside Kurt, and no amount of complaining will change that.

At the Farmer's Market, Kurt joins Ruth as she makes the last fold in her tablecloth. "Well, Ruthie, I see you sold everything. Did you think about running off to the south of France with the proceeds?"

"I almost had enough money to do just that after Bill Jenkins bought all your moldy spinach. Would you believe he offered to buy all my bread too? Only if I gave him a discount, of course. There's no telling what he makes selling my bread. That's one of the reasons so many people eat at his diner and he knows it."

Kurt's grizzled eyebrows twist into a knot. "He bought all my spinach? Which, by the way, was *not* moldy."

"His wife has them on a dark-green-diet, whatever that is."

Kurt snorts laughter. "Huh, something's gonna be dark green if they eat all that spinach."

"You've got that right." Wiping the table to a shine, Ruth eyes Kurt. "You're in a good mood. Did you enjoy your visit to the hardware store?"

"Old things enjoy other old things. I bet you'd enjoy visiting the Pyramids."

"Pyramids?" Ruth waves the paper towel in Kurt's face. "Why you old geezer, are you trying to say I'm as old as the Pyramids? Better watch out before my spice gets too hot for you to handle."

"*Me* try to say you're that old? Would you expect anything else?"

"You're right. I'd think you were ill if you got all sincere on me. Let's go to the diner and pay for the privilege of eating my own bread. While we're at it, let's stop talking about being old. If we do, maybe we'll remember what it feels like to be young again."

"That's a fine idea," Kurt says, offering his arm. "Take my strong and masculine arm and we'll be young until I head back home and my Ex-lax kicks in."

I hope the Ex-lax kicks in after you get home instead of before, old man. We'd be a sight with our collective behinds shining on the side of the road. Joe shakes his phantom head. *Being here makes me miss Elaine all over again, especially after going into the old hardware store. I think I need a break.*

Joe mentally closes his eyes, which closes out Kurt and Ruth's words to an ignorable murmur.

* * *

At the diner, Kurt hurries around the SUV and opens Ruth's door. Climbing out, she takes his arm. "Aren't you the gentleman, opening my door for me."

"You've got me mixed up with somebody else, old hen. I came around here to tell you it's your turn to buy lunch."

"Old rooster, I really should know better by now than to give you any claim to being a gentleman. After all, you corrupted my best friend."

"You know darn well Lainey corrupted me. Then you came along and corrupted her even more." Kurt winks. "But it was a good kind of corrupting."

He climbs the steps and holds the door for Ruth, who enters. "She was something, wasn't she? I miss her more than I can say. Now there's a lady with spice."

Bill Jenkins, balding and wearing a white mustache and a stained white apron, leads the couple to a booth. "Kurt, Ruth sure drives a hard bargain. Wouldn't drop a penny on her bread." They sit, and he leans close to Kurt's ear. "I'm glad that's the last of your spinach. I told my wife if she kept feeding me that darned stuff, the doctor would think I was a Martian the next time he took a stool sample."

All three chuckle. Bill hands them menus, and Kurt motions him to lean closer. "Speaking of stool samples, Bill, I think I'll have the meatloaf special." Ruth looks up at the diner owner, lips compressed, eyes crinkling at the corners, and they all burst out laughing.

Bill takes a pad and pencil from an apron pocket. "Ruth, what can I get you today?"

"I'll have the chef salad with plenty of spinach. I won't be seeing my doctor for a good while yet." They all chuckle again, and Bill leaves, saying he'll be right back.

"Ruth," Kurt says, "the line was good but your timing was off. The most important part of a good joke is the delivery. I learned that from Lainey."

"I know that you knot-head. I learned more from her than you realize. I'm just holding back some of the more amusing ways she taught me of torturing you. Remember though, the more you talk, the more likely I am to use them sooner than later."

"'Knot-head?' That's a new one." Kurt reaches over the table to shake Ruth's hand. "I better shut up. Being tortured takes away my appetite."

"Too bad, I'm about to torture you again. When were you planning to tell me what the doctor said about your ear?"

"My dermatologist sent off a sample. Whatever it is, she's sure she got it all. I'll worry about it when I go back next week and get the stitches out." He gingerly touches the bandage. "Can we talk about something more uplifting than my ear? It's not my best feature anyway."

Ruth sips lemonade. "You've got a better one?"

Kurt laughs and clinks his glass to hers. "There you go, Ruthie, that's what I call timing."

"Thank you, sir. I thought it was pretty good myself."

She taps her newly polished nails, a glossy pink, on the glass, and Kurt waits. Those tapping nails are always a warning she's got something on her mind.

The nails stop tapping. "Have you heard from Joseph

lately? Is any of the family coming home for Christmas?"

Bill brings their plates. Kurt waits until he leaves. "He called the other day. They're too busy to make the trip. You know how it is."

Ruth's bright eyes dim a notch. "Today's families have so much going on, don't they? We did too when we were young, but it's nothing like now. Personally, I enjoy the simple life."

Kurt clinks her glass again. "Me too, Ruthie, me too. Most of the things people let take up their time are rarely as important as they think they are. Some folks are on the go all the time. Rats running on a wheel getting nowhere."

"I suppose you're right."

"Maybe, maybe not. I might be doing the same thing if I were in their shoes."

"That's true." Ruth tilts her head to the left. "What about priorities? There, on the other side of the room, is an example. A whole family out on a beautiful Saturday—having lunch together—and the children have their cell phones glued to their ears, probably talking to somebody else instead of each other. If you ask me, those things need to be re-named."

Kurt chews meatloaf, nods and swallows. "They're having lunch together, that's something. As far as their toys, I don't fault them for that, but I do fault them if they let their toys cause them to ignore each other. You can't be a family if you don't take the time to communicate." He pauses for a swallow of lemonade. "Listen to us, sounding like old folks when we said we'd try to be young the rest of the day. Tell me what name you have in mind for a cell phone, and we'll let that subject alone."

Ruth pauses, rolls her eyes, and cups her ringed fingers around her lips. "How about dumb-ass phones?" Kurt coughs, almost spraying Ruth with meatloaf. She gives him a napkin. "Laugh all you want. Am I right or what?"

Wiping his lips, he nods toward the family. "When I see something like that, Ruthie, I guess you've got a point."

* * *

On the way back to the market. Kurt glances at Ruth, who, quite uncharacteristically, has nothing to say. He parks, unclicks his seatbelt, and so does she. "What are you doing the rest of the afternoon, old rooster, relaxing?"

"When do I get to relax? Wait a minute, I take that back. Since there's nothing to tend in the greenhouse, I could install that heater. You?"

"Would you be up for a picnic at Lainey's Grove tomorrow?"

"I haven't been there in a couple of weeks." Kurt climbs out and opens Ruth's door. "Want to come around one?"

"It's a date, old buzzard."

"There you go with that old stuff again. What happened to feeling young?"

"You know us women-folk, we love bending the rules." Eyes crinkling, Ruth touches the tip of his nose. "Any rules dealing with you men that is. See you tomorrow."

"Wait a minute, old hen. What kind of rules do us men-folk get to bend?"

"Only the ones we let you." She opens her car door. "But the trick is knowing which ones they are, and we don't give away that information easily."

As Kurt drives down Main Street, the lighthouse figurine swings from the rear-view mirror. Visiting the old hardware store has set his blood to warming, like when he met his wife there. Talk about love at first sight. He grins. Or love at first fight. What a day that was, a day he'll relive on the way home. He flips the radio on, finds a big band station, and taps his fingers on the steering wheel in time with the jazzy rhythm.

* * *

Joe wakes from his half-nap. *What the heck are you so happy about, old man, tapping your fingers like that? Yeah, I heard you and Ruth talking. It sounds like she was best friends with your wife when she was alive. It also sounds like you and Ruth might be more than friends. What would your wife say if she saw you carrying on like that?*

Oh well, I guess I should perk up and try to get a better look at Alma in case I missed something on the drive to the market. There's the post office again, nothing like the old one. Got a new water tower, I see. There's the hardware store again, hardly changed. Kurt must not have looked at it the first time we drove by, and I missed it. I had no idea I'd make it back, but even after over fifty years, I'm glad I did. I just wish I could find out what happened to Elaine.

Joe tries to smile at his hardware store memories. How many more can he remember? Bits and pieces? Every minute? Especially the minutes he spent with Elaine? Even the painful ones? Why put himself through all that? He tries to smile again. The answer is as simple as a summer afternoon at the river with Elaine, because the majority of all those minutes he spent with her are the ones he wants to relive over and over again, and right now, since remembering is all he has, remembering is all he can do.

Chapter 11

First Date

Three Fridays after Joe met Elaine, he leaves school with his guitar case and strolls along main street in Alma. At the Army recruiting office, he can't ignore how he'll be eighteen next year, or what that means with World War II raging. Sure, he understands how young men should do their duty to defend the country, but he doesn't want to die doing it.

Farther along, he passes the post office on one side of the street and the new movie house on the other, where *Sahara* with Humphrey Bogart played last weekend and *Lassie Come Home* with Roddy McDowall is playing this weekend. He's dying to ask Elaine out. Regardless, he doesn't make enough money at the part-time job Mr. Hansen offered him, stocking shelves in the hardware store. Then again, no one besides Elaine ever asked to take guitar lessons, not even Mr. Hansen, and even if Joe could spare the money, he's too shy to ask her out.

After her lesson, they sit on the bench by the wood stove with a cold bottle of pop apiece. As usual, Joe's quiet and, rather uncharacteristically, Elaine's quiet too. She empties the bottle and places it on the bench. "What do you do for fun besides play the guitar?"

"I like the outdoors." Joe stares at the half-full bottle in his hands. "Most of my time outside is spent working on the farm. That doesn't count, I guess. When I get a chance, I like to fish in one of the ponds on our place."

Watching him, Elaine taps her chin with a fingertip. "Hmm, since you like to fish, have you tried the Republican River?" She lowers her hand. "My brother caught a huge catfish out of it at a place on the Edwards' farm. I've never seen a catfish. Thomas cleaned that one before he brought it home. He said they have whiskers. I'd like to see a fish that has whiskers. I know where the Edwards' farm is. Thomas said it's a nice place to have a picnic."

Being subtle isn't one of Elaine's strong points. Joe holds in a grin. "Oh, that's true all right, catfish do have whiskers. They meow like a cat too."

Elaine's normally smooth brow furrows as if a tractor is plowing it full of rows. "Really? They do that?"

Joe laughs. She punches his arm and slides so close their legs touch. "Don't you make fun of me, Joe Matthan. The only way I'll believe it is to see it, and the only way that'll happen is if you take me fishing."

"I might have to work that day."

"I didn't say what day, you bozo." She faces the wood stove but stays by his side. "You like to eat, don't you? What kind of sandwiches do you like? Do you like potato salad? How about chocolate pie?"

"What's that got to do with fishing?"

"Just answer the question. You can do that, can't you?"

"I can answer it, but I still don't see—"

"Hush and answer already."

"Sure, I like to eat. I like sandwiches. I like turkey, ham, whatever, I'm not hard to please. Will you tell me—"

"Good, because that's what we're having for lunch tomorrow when you take me fishing." She offers her hand. "Deal?"

Joe opens his mouth but nothing comes out. He takes her hand and shakes it firmly. As exasperating as she is, he looks forward to tomorrow. If nothing else, even if they don't catch a single fish, it'll be an interesting day.

That night during supper, he mentions his plans to his parents, leaving out the part about taking Elaine. He still doesn't know what to make of their amusing relationship, but he enjoys being around her more than anyone, including his small circle of friends.

* * *

During dinner with her parents and her brother, Thomas, Elaine sips lemonade.

She wants to learn more about Joe. She also hopes to discover if their relationship can grow beyond guitar lessons. It's obvious how a spark of some kind is flaring between them, and though he's frustratingly shy at times, his artistic side with his music arouses her curiosity. She also enjoys teasing him and making him laugh, and she loves laughing with him, and since his timid personality is changing for the better, she can't wait to if she can get him to shed it entirely.

Taking a chance to stir the quiet at the dinner table, she tells her parents about the fishing trip. "That sounds nice," her mother says, "but I don't think I've ever known you to be interested in fishing. Have you, Albert?"

Her father's fork pauses on the way to his lips. "Not that I know of."

A slight grin plays around the corners of her mother's mouth. "Well, Miss First-time-fisher-girl, are you planning to use our leftovers for bait?"

"I didn't think catfish ate—"

"I'm talking about Joe."

"No, Mom, I'm not trying to catch Joe. I've always wanted to see what a catfish looks like. Isn't that right, Dad?"

"Sure, honey, whatever you say." He smiles at her mother, who winks. Elaine returns to her food. Her parents know her well, sometimes *too* well.

Thomas ate quietly during the interaction, likely exhausted from working on the farm after school. After dinner, Elaine asks him what kind of bait he uses for catfish, and he says he uses worms dug from the rich soil near one of the animal stalls. She wraps the leftovers, takes an empty tin can from the trash, and finds a shovel in the barn. In no time at all she's filled the can with soil and lively, wiggling worms and covers it with tin foil. Joe should be surprised at her digging their bait. Most boys think girls avoid worms and bugs like they avoid going into the hardware store with their dads.

***

Saturday afternoon, Joe parks the truck at Elaine's house. Go to the door or wait? He starts to get out when the screen door slams open and Elaine runs out to meet him. She wears faded jeans, a red-checked flannel shirt, a slight smile, and her long hair streams down her back, minus the yellow ribbon she normally wears. "Hey, Joe," she says, opening his door. "I need help with lunch."

"Why?" he asks, following her to the white painted farmhouse. "Do I look like I eat that much?"

Elaine opens the door. "You're still growing, so I packed a side of beef." Joe rolls his eyes and follows her into a kitchen, where Elaine's mother is folding clothes at a table.

"This is Joe Matthan, Mom, the so-so guitar player and singer I was telling you about. I'm giving him a fishing lesson today. Joe, this is my mother. If you're nice to me, she might let you call her Mary."

Ignoring the comment, Joe faces Mrs. Johnson. With light brown hair, the same height and features minus the faint smattering of freckles across Elaine's cheeks and nose, she resembles her daughter, but a bit worn from farm life, like his own mother. He offers his hand. "It's nice to meet you, Mrs. Johnson."

She takes his hand. "It's nice to meet you, Joe. Elaine's been talking about you ever since you two met."

"She has? That's—"

"I told her she can use my old wedding dress when she needs it."

Joe half-smiles. Maybe Elaine gets her teasing from her mother.

"Albert—that's her father—plans to build an addition onto the house too."

"Is Elaine getting a bigger room?"

"We need room for you and Elaine and the babies. When's the wedding? I think a June wedding would be grand. We need to make plans, okay? We're halfway into May already."

Married?

Grandchildren?

June wedding?

Hurry because it's May?

Joe's knees buckle. He drops into a chair at the table. Elaine comes over to rub his back. "Mom, you scared him to death! Tell him you're joking."

"I hope so." Joe stands. "Because if she isn't, I'm gone."

"Don't run off, Joe. I'm teasing Elaine because I know how she can be. Let's start over." Mrs. Johnson takes his hand. "It's nice to meet you, Joe. Elaine is looking forward to your fishing trip. I hope you two have a wonderful day."

"Thanks." Joe releases her hand. "It's good to see where Elaine gets her teasing from." He grins at Elaine. "It's even better to hear her squawk like a hen laying an egg."

"Thanks a lot, Mom. I'll never hear the end of that." Elaine takes three paper bags from the counter, gives Joe two, and takes a cloth bag from the refrigerator. "Mom let me use an old laundry bag for our drinks. We can tie it to a tree limb and hang it in the river to keep them cold. Good idea, huh?"

"It's hard to beat a cold drink on a hot summer afternoon, fishing or not."

Elaine goes to the door. "See you later, Mom."

"Okay, honey, good luck with the fishing. And Joe" —she nods toward Elaine— "good luck with this one too, in case she teases you into next week. Please have her back before supper time."

Joe puts their lunches and the drinks in a wooden crate in the truck's bed. In the cab he reaches for the key. "I understand you a lot better now. Your mother is as crazy as you are."

As he turns the key, Elaine punches his arm. "Now just you wait a minute, Joe Matthan."

"Gotcha." The old truck rumbles life, and he laughs.

Elaine shoves his shoulder. "What's so funny now?"

"What's funny now is your mother. I think I like her. A lot."

"I thought you seemed more relaxed."

"You call what she did relaxing?"

"I should have gotten you a mirror."

"A mirror? Why would I need a mir—"

"So you could've seen the look on your face, like a *rooster* laying an egg."

Joe makes a growling sound in his throat. She's right—he must've been a sight. She's right about being relaxed too. Seeing Elaine's mother get the best of her was worth it.

At the end of the driveway, he stops to check both sides of the deserted country road, turns right, and eases the pickup into second gear. Dust rises from the tires. The transmission's steady whine echoes back from every fence row they pass. He glances at Elaine. "What's the biggest fish you ever caught?"

"I've never been fishing in my entire life. I hope you can teach that better than you can teach guitar."

"Like the student had nothing to do with it?"

"Maybe, but if you can't teach me to fish, we sure won't have any for supper after we get married."

Gripping the steering wheel with both hands, Joe laughs hysterically like Elaine. If they keep this up, he might have to pull over to stop from driving into the ditch.

Chapter 12

Catfish Kisses

Joe checks his watch. Twenty minutes of conversation about school and how he taught himself the guitar have passed. "Shouldn't we be there by now?"

"I think it's—" Elaine points. "There it is. See that road by the no trespassing sign?"

He pulls into the road and stops. "Do we have permission to fish here?"

"Fish? Is that why we're here?"

"What other reason would we—"

"I'm teasing. You take things too seriously."

"Too seriously? What do you mean by—"

"Yes, Joe. Dad called Mr. Edwards last night. He said we could come anytime as long as we clean up after ourselves. Satisfied?"

Joe lets out the clutch. "Just making sure." A tire rolls into a rut. The truck bounces. Its springs squeak. A moment later, despite his best efforts, it happens again. "Too bad this road isn't a little smoother. I could hide a cow in some of those ruts."

"Oh, please. Want me to drive?"

"I got it. Just let me know when the tires on your side start to slide off into those miniature Grand Canyons."

About a mile later, he parks near a huge oak tree. Elaine

jumps out and runs to the river, sun-streaked hair billowing behind her. Joe catches up, and they stop on the river bank beneath the oak.

"It's beautiful here," Elaine says.

"I'm sure your brother was talking about fishing instead of how it looks."

As her chest rises and falls from her run, her eyes reflect the sun on the water. Joe takes a deep breath. "Still, beautiful is a good word." Did he just say that? Did he *really* just say that? If the sight of her looking across a river makes him say things without thinking, what does it mean?

She turns his way. "What?"

"I said, uh … yeah, the river looks nice. Let's get our stuff."

On the way to the truck, he stops. "Doggone it. I was gonna dig some worms and forgot. I guess we could catch some grasshoppers or crickets."

Elaine covers her mouth, but she can't hide the mischievous glint in her eyes.

Joe continues to the truck. "You're always laughing at something. What's so funny now?"

She lowers her hand. "I thought it might be fun to watch you running around trying to catch grasshoppers."

With two bags of food and his fishing gear in hand, Joe walks toward the river. After a few steps, Elaine stops. "Is there anything in the truck we can sit on?"

Joe searches the cab but doesn't see anything. Tilting the seat forward, he finds a folded quilt and takes it out. "This might work, but it's kind of dusty."

In the shade of the tree, he and Elaine shake the quilt. Dust billows while her grinning face appears with each shake. They spread the faded patchwork out in the soft carpet of lush grass.

"You know," Joe says, smoothing out a corner, "if we wanted, we could fish while we eat."

Elaine stands. "We don't have any bait, remember? Let's eat first." She sits cross-legged on the quilt, takes a foil covered can from one of the bags, and gives it to Joe. "I made this just for you. I hope you like it."

He removes the cover. "You're kidding. You want me to eat dirt?"

It's not dirt, silly. It's a new kind of chocolate cake you eat with your fingers. Taste it and see what you think."

Joe sticks a finger in the gritty, somewhat slimy contents and pulls his finger out with a fat, wriggling earthworm dangling from it. Elaine bursts out laughing and he flips the worm, which lands on her lap. She hands him the worm. "I'm trying to impress you with my cooking skills and you won't even try it? I bet a catfish will like it."

He drops the worm in the can. "I bet Thomas dug them. You wouldn't dare get your dainty little hands dirty."

Elaine crosses her arms. "I may be a girl, but I'm not girly."

"Let me see your fingernails." She holds out her hands, and Joe inspects each nail. "Uh-huh, clean as a whistle."

She jerks her hands back. "I know how to use a brush to wash the dirt from under my nails, Joe Matthan."

"Okay, okay, I believe you. Let's eat, or do you want to traumatize any more worms?"

"We want them to wiggle when we use them for bait, don't we?"

"That's true. So where are the turkey and ham sandwiches, potato salad and chocolate pie?"

Elaine gives him a sandwich. "This one's ham but there's another with turkey. We had both for dinner last night. Mom said I could take the leftovers."

Joe removes the crinkly wax paper. "Between you and your mother, there can't be a dull minute at your house. When do I meet your father?"

Elaine's chin drops. "I don't believe it. I had to practically drag you to the house, and now you want to meet my dad."

"You know what I mean. What kind of a person is he?"

"He's pretty quiet. Knowing me you wouldn't think so. Mom can make him laugh, but I think he works too hard. He's like you, he needs to take it easy more often."

"Having a good dad means a lot. My parents are like that. I think you'd like them."

"Maybe I can meet them soon." Elaine unwraps her sandwich.

Joe takes a bite of potato salad. Except for the gentle whisper of the river rolling by, and the occasional flutter of oak leaves overhead, they eat in silence.

Swallowing the last of his sandwich, Joe tosses the wad of wax paper at Elaine. She glances at him, tears on her cheeks, and turns away.

"I'm sorry, Elaine, did I hit your eye?"

"I … I need a minute." She wipes her eyes with a napkin.

He steals glances at her between bites of a second sandwich. She puts her leftovers away and kneels in front of him on the quilt. "You told me you're seventeen. Are you worried about the war? You never say anything about it."

Joe almost says how that should be a clue but doesn't want to be rude. "Well, you never say anything about it either."

"I go to my room when Dad listens to the war news. Then you hear about local people, like Charles Edwards, and you can't get away from news like that. Did you know he was killed when his submarine sank? He was an only child too. I hope the damn war ends, and soon!"

"I hope it ends too," Joe says. "I mean, I get why we're fighting, but who wants to die?" He lowers his head. "I want to live … I want to live and do all sorts of things."

"I want you to live too, Joe." Elaine's voice is a whisper, almost pleading. She places her hands on his cheeks and lifts his face. "Maybe you've noticed and maybe not, but I like being with you." She kisses his forehead, sending a tingle up his back. He leans forward, hoping for their first kiss.

"But," she says, tousling his hair, "if you ever accuse me of not digging worms again, we might have a problem." She smiles, completely spontaneous and beautiful, and Joe smiles too. How does she do it, lightening his mood and making him feel like everything will turn out all right, even about the war?

"Elaine Johnson, you're too much. Do me a favor and don't ever change."

"Never gonna happen. Let's clean up so Mr. Edwards will let us come back. Then we'll see who catches the first catfish."

Trash put away, Joe cuts two forked sticks with his pocket knife and pushes them into the ground at the river's edge. Elaine brings the quilt over and holds two corners out to him. "Help me spread this again."

"You want to fish sitting on a quilt? I thought you weren't a girly-girl."

"You said we could fish while we eat. Besides, isn't fishing supposed to be relaxing?"

"Not if one pulls a rod into the river."

Although Elaine surprised Joe by digging the worms, she doesn't care for sticking a hook through one. He baits one hook and casts it into the river, rests the rod on one of the forked sticks and does the same with the other rod. She sits on the quilt. He waits by the forked sticks.

A warm breeze brings the sweet scent of honeysuckles from a thicket upriver. Overhead, a flock of crows wing by, cawing as if they're looking for a cornfield to attack. On the opposite bank, a white-tailed deer with her spotted fawn creeps toward the water. They take hesitant drinks, ears flicking, and blend into the woods again.

Joe lets his attention go from the rod tips to Elaine. She looks his way as if she's studying a side of beef at the butcher shop, eyes tracking him up and down. He doesn't mind, in fact he likes it. It's the first time a girl looked at him like that.

She faces the river again, and her profile resembles some of the paintings in his history textbook: steady eyes, strong profile. Her confident ways—not being afraid to dig worms or drive the truck in the rutty road—attract him. Still, her other characteristics, the teasing and humor, attract him too. Maybe he should sit beside her. If he does, he might get another chance at a kiss.

She looks his way again. "Thomas and Dad said fishing reels have something called a clicker that makes a noise if a fish takes the bait. You could make those reels do that and get us a drink and sit on the quilt."

Holding in a smile at her *taking the bait* comment, because that's exactly what he's doing, Joe sets the reel clickers and opens two bottles wet from the river, gives one to Elaine and sits beside her with his own bottle. They tip the bottles up and take several cold, fizzy swallows. A few more swallows later, they put the empty bottles with their lunch trash.

Elaine takes a yellow ribbon from her pocket and tries to tie her hair in a ponytail, but every time she tightens the knot, it comes loose in her fingers. "Could you help me with my hair? I'll hold it while you tie it." She hands him the ribbon. "Please?"

Joe stares at the yellow ribbon. "I never tied hair. Is there a special knot?"

She faces the river, kneels in front of him, and gathers her hair. "Tie it where I'm holding it. Tie it like you would your shoe laces."

The silky strands of hair at the base of her tanned neck flutter with his breath. He leans close to sniff the scent: sweet like summertime and— What the heck is he doing? He slips the ribbon under her hair and their hands touch. Hers are soft and smooth, warm as the blood rushing to his face. He snugs the knot. "I guess that'll work."

She whirls around and stares, cheeks flushed. He stares back. What will she do if he kisses her? Just leans forward and—

Whir-r-r-r-r!

They spin around. A catfish is taking the bait on one of the rods. Elaine jumps up to grab it. "I got it, I got it!"

"I'm glad to see that," Joe says, getting up from the quilt. "Do you know what to do?"

"Stop being a know-it-all man and tell me."

He touches a lever on the reel. "This stops the line from going out. I'll flip that, but you need to hang on tight and pull back hard to set the hook."

"That sounds simple," Elaine says, spreading her feet apart and adjusting her grip on the rod. "I don't know why I got so excited."

"Ready?" he asks. She nods and he flips the lever. She jerks the rod and the tip bends toward the river, pulling her down the bank.

"Joe-o-o-o! He-e-e-lp!"

Joe grabs her around the waist and pulls her back to the quilt, steadying her while the fish takes line and the rod tip plunges. "Want me to take it?"

"And let you catch the first fish? You've lost your guitar-picking mind."

"Just trying to help. You know, if you can't handle it."

"Oh, please, I can handle this and anything else I have to handle, including whatever this stupid war does to Alma."

The fish makes another massive surge, pulling her down the bank again. Without screaming for help this time, she manages to stop short of the water.

Joe admires her tenacity, but it's hard not to laugh. "If you get tired, I can help hold the rod while you reel."

She struggles back up the bank, slipping in the mud. Beside the quilt, she re-grips the rod and squares her feet. "Are you sure this is a fish? Maybe it's a log, or maybe the hook is hung on a rock. Can the current make the line jump around like that?"

"No way, Elaine. I bet that catfish is meowing at you right now, about to laugh its whiskers off."

"I'll meow you when I—" The fish makes another huge lunge. Elaine slides in the mud down the bank. "Joe-o-o-o, he-e-e-lp!"

Joe grabs the doubled-over fishing rod, pulls back hard to take some of the strain, and they return to the edge of the quilt. "Even if you don't land that fish, I'm enjoying this. I sure would like to see how big it is."

Sweat beads on Elaine's forehead. "I would too, but—"

Pop!

They fall to the quilt in a tangle. Elaine sits up. "You broke the line on purpose, Joe Matthan!"

Lying on the quilt, Joe laughs so hard his stomach aches. Elaine falls back beside him, laughing just as hard. As their laughter slows, Joe rolls over to face her. "Now tell the truth, what else would you rather do on a Saturday afternoon? Oh, I know, you'd rather do your hair and your nails and put on a dress, right?"

"What? I told you—"

"How about perfume? I bet you'd love some Essence of Earthworm."

Elaine grabs the can of worms. She digs a gob of dirt out and jumps on top of Joe, straddling him. "I might like Essence of Earthworm. Let's put some on you and see."

"I don't think so," he says, catching her hand on its way to his face. "Don't blame me for teasing you. You and your mom are good teachers."

"We sure are." Elaine jerks her hand away, grabs his arms, and pushes them beside his head to the quilt. "Gotcha."

"Oh, really? You think I couldn't get up if I didn't want to?"

The pressure on Joe's arms lessens. Gorgeous brown eyes with flecks of green in the centers come closer. A feeling similar to when he tied her hair comes over him, but more intense, like his breath hanging in his throat. This is nothing like when they met in the hardware store, when he didn't even like her sitting close to him.

The pressure lessens even more. "Joe?"

"Yeah?"

Elaine leans close to kiss his forehead and his nose. Her lips pause above his, warm breath teasing. They kiss, kiss again, and Joe swears he's died and gone to Heaven.

Smiling, she pulls away. He rises with her, slips his fingers into the soft hairs at the base of her neck, and brings her back down for another kiss.

Yep, he's died and gone to Heaven, and that's just fine with him.

Chapter 13

First Love

Elaine lets Joe pull her down for another kiss, then lies beside him to rest her head on his chest. The aroma of fresh air clings to his shirt. His stomach muscles—firm beneath her fingertips—rises and falls. She listens to his heart beat a counter-rhythm to his breathing, similar to the timing of the first song he sang for her. Why isn't he saying anything after all their amazing kisses?

"You're mighty quiet, Mr. Matthan."

"Just lying here, but …"

"Do I have to tickle it out of you?" She digs her fingers into his side.

"Sorry, not ticklish."

"That's no fun. Any boyfriend of mine has to be ticklish."

"I was just thinking how I never thought I'd be kissing my guitar student. Well, my *only* guitar student."

"Or your fishing student either." She hugs him tight as he laughs.

Elaine can hardly believe what's happening. She had no idea she'd fall in love, and only a few weeks after meeting Joe in the hardware store, with his curly blond hair and his guitar.

"Okay," he says.

"Okay what?" she says.

"You're the one who's quiet now. Quiet's not an Elaine Johnson thing."

"Can't I be quiet?"

"It depends on why."

Elaine says nothing. Admit her feelings or not? Take a chance on him breaking her heart or not? After all, he'll probably get drafted when he turns eighteen and go off and get himself killed. Then again, the war could be over before he turns eighteen. And he is sweet. And he is nice. And he is good looking.

"What do you think of us kissing?" she says.

"I could ask you the same thing," he says.

"I kiss every boy I go out with. You're nothing special."

"Then why were you looking at me while ago like a farmer getting ready to bid on a prize beef steer at auction?"

"I—"

"I'm not done yet. What about when you sat in my lap at the hardware store the day we met? What about batting your eyelashes? What about asking me to ple-e-e-ase show you those guitar chords? All that, plus jumping on top of me and holding me down so you could suck my tonsils out, and you don't think I'm special?"

Elaine pinches his stomach. "I didn't sit in your lap *or* suck your tonsils out. Besides, you pulled me down for that last kiss."

"How was it compared to all those other guys you've kissed?" Joe snorts laughter. "How many are walking around Alma without tonsils? How many are—"

Elaine jumps on top of him like she did earlier, pinning his arms down. "Will you shut up? I'm trying to tell you I love you."

"Oh, really?" Joe's eyes focus down. The collar on her shirt hangs open, so he must be looking at her cleavage.

"I thought you were shy. Stop looking down my shirt."

"Stop advertising."

"Do you love me or not?"

Joe's lips—a wrinkled tight line that can't decide whether to purse or smile—sputter. He laughs long and hard, raising Elaine up and down like when she rode a goat as a girl of about eight in pigtails. She rolls off him and waits, arms crossed. He stops laughing and shoves her knee. "You have a funny way of telling someone you love them."

"Do you or not? I don't have all day."

"I'm not sure." Joe touches his throat. "I'm worried about my tonsils. If I marry you, I won't have them five seconds into the honeymoon."

Elaine sniffles and turns away. "That's what I get for caring about a jerk."

Joe touches her arm. "Hey, I'm just teasing, okay? Don't cry."

Jerking her arm away, Elaine gets up. "Take me home, I'm done with you." She walks toward the truck.

Footsteps swish in the grass behind her. "Sheesh," Joe says, "I'm just messing with you."

"Kiss my—"

"After all, I wouldn't kiss just any girl, or take just any girl fishing."

She turns around. "And?"

"You aren't crying." Joe leans down to look her in the eye. "Your eyes aren't even red."

"I don't cry when I'm mad, my nose runs."

"Oh."

"Is that all you've got to say."

"Well, no, not really."

"And?"

"You sure are making this hard on me." Joe's lips sputter like they did earlier. He laughs again.

"Heaven help me," Elaine says, "I've gone and fallen in love with a guitar-playing goofball."

"That's okay. I'm in love with a girl who can't fake crying with a hoot."

"You really mean that?"

"Which part? You were faking and you know it."

"You know what I mean. You said you're in love with me."

"No more jokes. I wouldn't say I love you if I didn't mean it. All my teasing comes from being around you."

"That's good, because you're about the shiest boy I ever met. You need to loosen up if we're gonna get married and live in that room Dad's gonna add to the house." Elaine takes him by the hand and leads him back to the quilt. "Lie down, Mr. Jokey Matthan, and tell me what you love about me."

"C'mon now," Joe says, pulling his hand free. "Don't tell me you're one of those girls who needs their boyfriend to hang all over them and tell them they love them all the time."

Elaine points at the quilt. "Down. Now." He lies down and she lies beside him, head on his shoulder, hand on his chest. "Spill it," she demands. "What do you love about me?"

"It's your mom I like, unless …"

"Uh-huh, unless I can cook like her."

"Gotta keep my priorities straight. Man cannot live on kisses alone."

"Don't you worry about that. I'll keep you loving other

things when I hitch my wagon to yours."

"Things like this?" Joe asks, grabbing her bottom.

"Grab all you want." Elaine pats his hand. "That's *all* you'll grab."

* * *

Joe lets go of Elaine's bottom. He wouldn't have done that if she weren't so jokie all the time. Still, it was wrong, and still, he does love her. "All right, Miss Essence of Earthworm, I love you for lots of reasons. A girl digging worms is a start. Another reason is how I'm nowhere near as shy as I used to be. Another reason is your butt fits my hand great and your bra is stuffed, and not with tissues."

"I'll take those as compliments," Elaine says. "It's not like I wasn't looking at you like you were a prize steer on the auction block while ago."

Joe points up. "I like how the light shines down through the oak leaves. I forget what it was about, but some kid teased me in the fourth grade so bad, I kept to myself from then on. It was on my mind all the time, and figured I couldn't trust anyone except Mom and Dad and my grandma and grandpa and my other kin. When we met at the hardware store and started getting along like we do, I didn't think about that kid anymore."

Elaine raises her head off his shoulder to look him in the eye. "You thought about him all that time?"

"I sure did," Joe says. "When something bothers you like that kid did me, you don't have to think about it to make you not trust anyone."

Elaine lowers her head to his shoulder again. "What's that got to do with the light in the leaves?"

"It might sound silly, but you sort of brought me out of my

own shell … sort of out of the dark of the leaves, know what I mean?"

"Goodness gracious, aren't you the deep thinker, Mr. Expert Catfisherman?"

"You're the one who kept bugging me about why I love you. Now it's your turn to tell me why you love me, other than my beefsteak-behind you've been ogling."

"That's the only reason," Elaine says, patting his chest. "That and your huge tonsils that drive me wild."

"Uh-huh," Joe says, his voice sarcastic. "I knew it all the time."

"Shut up. I loved the challenge of getting you to not be so shy. I love your artistic side of playing the guitar and singing too. Your beefsteak-behind is a just a plus."

"What about my fishing ability?"

"I'll let you know when we catch enough catfish to take home for supper. That'll be a good way to break the ice with Dad."

"Do you have a phone so I can call my folks? We got one right after the war started."

"We got ours last year. Mom loves it so much that Dad has to run her off it to do farm business for the war."

Joe reels in the unbroken line to check the bait. Not a nibble. He casts it back out and ties another hook on the line the big catfish broke, baits it and casts it into the river. Sharing a drink and a piece of chocolate pie, he and Elaine wait to see if a hungry catfish will consider one of their earthworms for lunch.

Chapter 14

Meeting Parents

Joe finishes the bumpy drive from the river and steers the truck onto the main road. "All right then, you finally got to see what a catfish looks like, whiskers and all."

"Those fish filets will surprise Dad. Thanks for taking me fishing."

"It was your idea, you know."

"I didn't have to twist your arm." Elaine pokes his side. "Just tempt you with Mom's cooking." She slides close and holds his hand, surprising Joe. She must *really* love him if she doesn't mind him smelling like fish.

At her driveway, he turns into the narrow path to the house and slows behind a plow hitched to a red tractor. Dark sod clings to the plow's shiny blades. As the truck's brakes squeak to a stop, Mr. Johnson, washing his hands at the well house, raises his head. Dressed in the standard farmer's wide-brimmed straw hat, coveralls, and work boots, he's about Joe's height.

Joe rubs his chin. If he were Elaine's father, how would he react if he saw some boy he's never met pulling up to his house with his daughter sitting close beside him?

"Your dad looks busy. Go ahead with the fish. I'll come back some other time."

"I thought you were ready to meet him? The fish *should* help."

"We won't tell him about the one that got away, right?"

"He'll like that story. Mom will too."

Elaine pulls him to where Mr. Johnson is drying his hands. "Dad, this is Joe Matthan. You remember me telling you and mom about him taking me fishing, and you know he was teaching me guitar at the hardware store. I never learned the guitar, but I caught a catfish today. We brought some home for supper too." She opens the paper bag to show him the catfish fillets. "You and Thomas were right about their whiskers."

Elaine's father offers his hand. "Albert Johnson, Joe. It's nice to meet a guitar-playing fisherman." He grins. "Or is that a fishing guitar player? Can you do both at the same time?"

Joe recognizes the farmer's grip: rough but strong, able to perform any task, but gentle enough to help deliver a farm animal into the world when the need arises.

Joe releases his hand. "Mrs. Johnson and Elaine are a lot alike with their joking." He winks at Elaine. "I bet you could tell me some interesting stories about your daughter."

"That's a true statement if I ever heard one. What I want to hear is how she caught a catfish."

Tempted to shove Elaine to tease her, Joe doesn't. "The funniest story is about the one that got away, Mr. Johnson."

"Isn't that the way it always is? I'm looking forward to hearing it."

Elaine nudges Joe toward the well house. "Wash your fishy hands before you call your parents. Dad, I invited Joe for supper. Can you check with Mom?"

"I'm going in, honey. I'll ask her."

Joe rinses and dries his hands. Mrs. Johnson meets them at

the door. "I see you made it back with supper." She takes the bag to the sink, dumps the fish out, and runs water over them. "Was the river pretty? No snakes, I hope."

"Only one." Elaine eases up behind her mother. "It was huge." She brushes her fingertips along her mother's bare calf, and her mother whirls around.

"Oh, you, don't *do* that!" She flips a dishtowel at Elaine. "You know how I am about snakes." She tosses the dishtowel by the sink. "Joe, Albert said you're staying for supper. Do you need to check with your folks? Elaine, show Joe where the phone is. Joe, if you want to clean up before we eat, Elaine can show you the bathroom."

Elaine wrinkles her nose. "He is sort of stinky."

Joe sticks his tongue out at her. "You're not as fresh as a flower either. You smell more like a stink-weed than a rose."

"Will wonders never cease?" Mrs. Johnson says. "I do believe you've taken the shyness right out of him, Miss Fisher-girl. Let Joe call his folks before they worry."

Elaine shows him a telephone in the hall. When he starts to dial, she pokes his side. "I don't think there's anything to your stink-weed comment, Mr. Matthan." She sniffs her fingers. "I'll wash in case there is." She leaves for a door at the end of the hall.

Joe finishes dialing, and Dad answers. Joe tells him about catching the fish and staying at Elaine's for supper.

"You didn't say you were taking Elaine," Dad says. "How many fish did you catch?"

"Four, but we lost a huge one. I'll tell you that story when I get home. It was hilarious."

"Ask Elaine if she'd like to join us for Sunday lunch. I'd love to hear that story from both of you."

"I'll ask her." Dad's invitation amuses Joe. Elaine gets to be nervous about meeting his parents like he was nervous about meeting hers. "See you and Mom later."

"I'll tell your mother about supper. Get home at a decent time."

As Joe cradles the phone, Elaine's hands encircle his waist. "Can you stay?"

Trying to control his grin, he turns around. "Mom told Dad she's heard rumors about you. They said I should get home right away."

"What rumors? Who said—"

Joe laughs, and she smacks his chest. "Oh, you, I've created a tease monster. I deserve it, huh?"

"That's okay. I love you anyway."

Elaine glances left, right, kisses him, and points at the door at the end of the hall. "See that door, Mr. Stinky-man? Go wash up."

Joe salutes and turns sharply, marches down the hall and stops after a few steps. "You know we wouldn't be having fish for supper if we relied on your fishing skills."

"Look, Joe Matthan, you were the one who broke my line on purpose because you knew my fish was gonna be bigger than any you've ever caught. Go wash up, I'm hungry."

* * *

Joe swallows his last bite of fish and faces Elaine. "I didn't think to ask, where's Thomas?"

Mr. Johnson lowers his fork. "Some of his friends took him on an overnight fishing trip."

"Yeah? Maybe I should've gone."

Elaine smacks Joe's hand. "I don't think so."

Mrs. Johnson stands with her plate. "I'll handle the dishes.

Elaine. Take Joe to the living room."

Mr. Johnson follows and sits by a radio. Elaine sits on a sofa and pats the cushion beside her. Not wanting to press his luck with her parents, Joe sits another cushion away.

Mr. Johnson turns the radio on. Static pops and crackles, until the Bing Crosby song *People Will Say We're in Love* plays clearly. Elaine rubs Joe's hand, and Mr. Johnson clears his throat. "I normally listen to the news broadcast about the war after dinner, Joe. I wish it would end soon. Boys like you should stay home instead of going to fight in Europe and the Pacific if they can. Do you plan to stay in Alma and farm after school?"

Joe's glad to have the conversation steered away from the war. "I'd like to study hybridizing and disease resistant farming. When disease or pests destroy crops, I see how hard it is for my dad. I'd like to help farmers everywhere, especially here. I think it would be interesting work."

"I didn't know that," Elaine says, batting her eyelashes at him. "It sounds so-o-o-o fascinating."

"There's a lot you don't know about me. I bet there's a lot I don't know about you either. Why don't you fill me in?"

"I like to read, so I'm thinking about getting an English degree." Elaine's tone is serious, so she must mean what she's saying. "English includes grammar, so it includes the study of books and their authors. That's literature to farm boys like you."

"Oh, so you want to be an English teacher. I can see you wearing glasses and carrying an armload of books. You'll make a great old maid."

"You'll make a great hog farmer, Mr. Pigheaded joker."

"As far as studying ways to help farmers," Mr. Johnson says,

"I'd appreciate anything that can help us be more productive." He lowers the radio volume. "Are you good with a hammer and a saw? Mary and me think it's time to start on that room addition she told you about."

Elaine scoots forward on the sofa. "Mom told you about that? She's so bad."

"You're just as bad and you know it, Elaine. I've been sitting right here watching it."

"I don't mind," Joe says. "I'd rather be around a person who's fun instead of a stick-in-the-mud."

"Me too," Mr. Johnson says. "Between Elaine and Mary, there's rarely a dull minute around here."

Mrs. Johnson comes in to sit in a chair across from Mr. Johnson. "Let's hear this big fish story you two mentioned during supper." Before Joe can speak, the radio news comes on with the announcer broadcasting the day's war reports. "Albert," she says, "please turn that off. The last thing we need to hear is news about more of our boys dying in this war."

* * *

Joe checks his watch, almost nine, and stands. "I better get home. Thanks for supper."

"You're welcome." Mrs. Johnson says. "Thank you for taking Elaine fishing too. I'll laugh about that story for a long time to come." She stands.

"Come back soon," Mr. Johnson says, rising from his chair. "Catfish or not, I'm looking forward to hearing more about those farming classes you want to take."

Mrs. Johnson opens the screened door. "Elaine, why don't you walk Joe out?"

"Good idea, Mom. He might get lost on the way to his truck." Goodbyes finished, Joe and Elaine stroll through the cooling night air, which carries the earthy aroma of the sod on the plow.

At the truck, Joe snaps his fingers. "I almost forgot. My dad invited you to lunch tomorrow. Can you make it?"

"What time? I can ask now."

"About one. We might have leftovers from Saturday. Mom sometimes fries a chicken when we get home from church."

"It should be fine. I'll get there a little before one."

"I'll pick you up."

"You don't have to. I've been driving tractors and trucks around this farm ever since I could see over the steering wheel."

Elaine's farm experience impresses Joe. He's never heard of a girl driving tractors and farm trucks, let along digging worms. He sticks his hand out. "See you tomorrow."

"If you think you're leaving without giving me a goodnight kiss, you're crazy." Elaine stands on tiptoe and pecks his cheek. "And since all you offered is a handshake, that's all you get."

"C'mon, you're teasing, right?"

On tiptoe again, she wraps her arms around his neck. "That's another thing I love about you. I can keep you guessing."

Chapter 15

Parents Plus Responsibility

A little before one on Sunday, Elaine parks behind Joe's truck. She starts to raise her hand to chew a fingernail but stares at the house instead. Now she knows how Joe felt when he met her parents. He walks out the front door, taking long, loose strides, running his fingers through his blond hair, and opens the truck door. "Do I need to drag you inside like you did me yesterday?" She opens the door, and he takes her hand to twirl her around. "Look at you, all prettied up."

"You really think so?" She wears her best Sunday dress, bought last year, a bit snug in the bust and tied with a matching belt at the waist. Her mother said the gray material, which falls just below the knee, sets off Elaine's brunette ponytail, tied with another yellow ribbon.

Joe lets her hand go. "Nah, you look decent is all. You're just fishing for compliments and I'm giving you a worm."

"I'll give you a smack if you keep messing with me."

"Are you nervous like I was yesterday?"

"Maybe a little." Elaine takes a jar filled with daffodils from a circle of dishtowels on the truck seat. "I brought these for your mom."

"Too bad, she hates daffodils."

"Someone doesn't want a goodbye kiss later."

"Like I'd let you leave without one." Joe slips his hand into hers. "Let's go"

His parents step onto the porch, smiling and talking. His mom, with shoulder-length dark hair and delicate features, except for her full lips, wears a blue knee-length skirt and a white blouse. His father, dressed in dark slacks and a tan shirt, resembles his son, except for his shorter hair, wider shoulders, and an inch or two difference in height, him being taller than Joe, who's close to six feet.

Elaine and Joe climb the steps. His mom opens the door. "I remember, Will. How could I forget?"

Joe goes inside and holds the door for Elaine. "What are y'all remembering, Mom?"

Will comes inside. "We were talking about how you two remind us of ourselves about a month after we met."

Joe introduces Elaine to his mom, whose name is Sarah. Will shakes Elaine's hand. "Joe told us about your fishing trip at the river. I'd like to go myself, but I don't get much of a chance to fish."

"I've been looking forward to meeting you," Sarah says. "I've never heard Joe talk so much about anyone."

Elaine gives her the daffodils. "I picked these from around our house this morning."

"These will look nice on the table. I like your idea of the Mason jar too."

Joe faces Elaine. "Mom stayed home from church and made roast beef with all the trimmings. I don't know what she does to it, but it melts in your mouth."

"It sure does," Will says. "I bet she could make an old shoe taste good."

"Not when we have cows, Dad."

They all laugh. Sarah leads them through a doorway, "Come along, everything's ready."

"It smells great," Elaine says, sitting beside Joe. "You didn't tell me your mother was such a good cook."

Will unfolds his napkin. "Like your own mother, I'm sure."

"She is," Joe says. "I told you about the fried catfish we had last night. We had leftovers from Elaine's Friday night dinner for our lunch yesterday. Mrs. Johnson's chocolate pie was great."

Sarah brings a platter of sliced roast beef with carrots, potatoes, and onions to the table. The delicious aroma rises with the steam. "Will, would you say grace, please?"

They all hold hands, and Elaine closes her eyes. Joe rubs his thumb back and forth along her fingers, and a surprising warmth gathers deep inside her. She licks her lips. The warmth intensifies. She bites her lower lip. What's she doing having such feelings—sexual feelings—during the blessing? Joe releases her hand.

During the meal they discuss various subjects, including Elaine's plans for studying English and Joe's plans for studying crop science.

Sarah refills Elaine's glass with lemonade. "How are the guitar lessons going?"

"I don't have the knack for it like Joe. I love music, but when it comes to a guitar, my fingers won't do what my brain tells them. I think Joe is a genuine artist. I like to hear him play, and sing too. He did teach me how to fish yesterday, so I finally saw a live catfish. I learned they actually have whiskers too." She elbows Joe. "Tell your parents about the big one you made me lose on purpose."

"Go ahead. I'll tell them when you exaggerate something,

but I'll make sure they hear my version of you sliding down the riverbank in the mud."

Elaine tells the story. When the line breaks and they fall to the quilt, Sarah and Will laugh so hard they take napkins from the holder and wipe their eyes. Elaine grabs a napkin too. "I was so mad when I lost that fish. All my so-called fishing teacher did was laugh like a maniac, saying he never had that much fun fishing."

"I wish I had been there," Sarah says. "The way you describe the river, it sounds like a nice place for a picnic."

"It is," Elaine says. "There's a grassy area under a big oak tree. The river is right there beside it."

Sarah faces Will. "You need a break. Call Mr. Edwards and see if we can have a picnic there. Do you think your folks would like that, Elaine?"

"I can ask."

Sarah takes her and Will's plates to the sink, and Elaine stands. "It was delicious, Mrs. Matthan. Can I help clean up?"

"Let's clear the table, I'll wash the dishes later. Who feels like a walk?"

"Let Joe and Elaine go," Will says as he stands. "I'll help with the dishes."

In the back yard, Elaine and Joe stroll toward a huge, red barn. The aroma of hay, pungent like an herb garden, flows on the breeze blowing from the direction of the loft. They near a pasture. Cows graze on new grass while several more water at a pond in the distance. Beneath the fence, a yellow blanket of daffodils sways in the breeze.

Elaine points. "Did your mom plant those?"

"She planted ten bulbs there a few years ago. Before she knew it, she had all these."

"Would she mind if I picked one?"

"Pick all you want."

Elaine goes to the riot of yellow and picks one of the largest daffodils she's ever seen. She returns to Joe and looks into his blue eyes, hints of gold near the centers. "Mom says there are legends about daffodils. One is they're a sign of a new beginning. So, Mr. Joe Matthan, what do you think about our new beginning?"

She taps his nose with the yellow bloom and runs away, laughing. Behind her, Joe's feet pound the grass. He pulls the ribbon and her hair falls free. She runs faster, tall grass brushing her legs. Nearing another daffodil patch, he grabs her by the arm. She stops and laughs, hardly able to breathe.

"I won't accuse you of" —Joe pauses for a breath— "being a girly-girl anymore. You sure can run." He holds out the ribbon. "This is all I could catch. Want me to tie your hair?"

"I'll leave it down." She slides the daffodil stem behind her ear, then puts the ribbon in his pants' pocket. "Maybe I'll tie it later."

Joe's throat muscles work with a hard swallow. He obviously didn't expect her to put her whole hand in his pocket, near a certain *very* private place.

And neither had she.

Driving over, she had considered some of the feelings she had experienced since their first kiss, feelings she hadn't experienced before, feelings like when he held her hand during the blessing earlier.

"Something's been on my mind. I think we should talk about it."

"What? When we're going fishing again so I can laugh my butt off at you?"

"This is something that scares me."

"I know, you're scared you're gonna actually fall in the river next time."

"Since you're *obviously* trying to make up for being shy since the fourth grade by cracking a joke every chance you get, I'll show you instead of telling you."

Elaine runs her fingertips along his brow, down his nose, and pauses at his lips. She stands on tiptoe and kisses him, a lingering, warmth-sharing, lips-parting kiss that sends tingles of unfamiliar anticipation up and down her spine. She wants to continue, wants to kiss his chest, wants to taste the salt on his skin, wants to— She drops to her heels. "Was any of that about fishing, smart aleck?"

"Not unless you want to kiss a catfish like that."

"Shut up and tell me you know what I'm talking about."

"All jokes aside, I've thought about *that* too."

Elaine smirks and he smirks back. "Don't look at me like that," he says, "you know what I mean."

"And?"

"I guess it's not something we want to happen."

"Tell another lie, Joe Matthan."

"Didn't I just say I know what you mean?"

"You better. I want to be married when that happens. We're not gonna stop kissing, so how do we keep things from going too far?"

"After what you just did to me, that might be tough."

"Tough?" Placing her hands on her hips, Elaine moves closer to Joe and stares him in the eye. "Are you saying the big, strong, he-man can't handle it?"

"You're the one who said you were scared. You don't have a problem—as you say—handling it?"

"I didn't say that, but— Well, when it comes to girls, boys are weak. That's just the way you are."

Joe crosses his arms. "You think you're stronger than me when it comes to that because you're a girl?"

"Like I said, that's just the way you are."

"What's that by the fence?"

"Where?

He points. "Over there."

"A cow, what about it?"

"Look again."

"It's a bull, so what?"

"That's right," Joe says, tapping her nose. "Bull."

Elaine slaps his hand away. "You're the one full of bull. I see I need to prove you wrong by letting you do the same thing to me that I did to you."

"Not the same, coward. You're so much stronger than me, remember?"

"As long as you're a gentleman."

"Close your eyes."

"What happened to being a gentleman? What happened to please?"

"Please then, with sugar" —he grins— "and chocolate pie on top."

Remembering their chocolate pie kisses at the river, Elaine almost changes her mind. Instead, she closes her eyes. Whatever he has in mind, she can handle it. He pulls the daffodil from her hair and moves behind her, the swish of grass betraying his steps. "You better behave back there," she says.

He brushes her hair aside. "Hush, you had your turn." He blows on her neck.

"Is that all you've got, tickling my neck by blowing on it? It better be, since you say you've never had a girlfriend."

"I'll put it this way—for future reference, I'll do to you what I think I'd like done to me. Got it?"

"You might as well give up. I can handle whatever you do better than you can."

Joe pulls the dress's collar aside and runs his fingertips along the sensitive skin where her neck joins her shoulder. It tickles like when he blew on her neck, but this tickle is more of a tingle that traces a line of anticipation to her shoulder blades. He lightly kisses her neck, tongue swirling small circles on skin even more sensitive. She shivers and he stops. Then something else touches her neck. Something soft and supple. Something enticing and sensual and as warm as droplets of summer rain falling from an almost cloudless sky.

The daffodil.

Sensations Elaine has never known course through her rapidly warming body. Her breaths come in tiny, ragged gasps; she moves her head aside for him to kiss her neck again. She wants more, as much as he can offer. His hands on her breasts, anywhere and everywhere and—

She spins around. "Okay, okay, you were right!" Pausing to catch her breath, she watches him smile—slight and satisfied— but his chest rises and falls exactly like hers does.

"You see what I mean, Mr. Matthan. How do we keep our kisses from going beyond kisses?"

He clears his throat. "Yeah, that was intense. What if we promise to not let our kisses go too far? I guess that sounds simple, but it might work."

"What you're saying, I guess, is if we're getting to the point where ... well, you know, one of us should just say—hey, hold on, wait a minute, we promised, remember?"

"Not all that, but you know what I mean. A promise means you're trusting another person to honor their word. If we make a promise—especially about that—we better keep it."

"I can do that," Elaine says, nodding. "But there's something else we need to do."

"What's that?" Joe asks.

"Do what your mom said and have our families meet at the river for a picnic. They might as well get to know each other, right?"

"Good idea." Joe takes her hand and they walk toward the house. "We'll figure out a day when they can take a break from farm work and do exactly that."

Chapter 16

A Mother's Fear

Careful not to spill the glass of lemonade, Sarah Matthan rises from a sharp pain beneath her behind and takes a stick from beneath the quilt. Thank goodness for lemonade in this heat, even in the shade of the huge oak at the river.

She glances over her shoulder. Will and Albert lean on the hood of Will's truck, likely discussing farming and their work loads because of the war. Down by the river, sitting on a huge log, Joe and Elaine talk quietly, sometimes laughing.

Across from Sarah, Mary Johnson raises her glass. "Here's to ice. What would we do without it?"

"You and your sense of humor. I'm sure Elaine gets hers from you."

Mary points toward the log. "Aren't they a pair. I've never seen her laugh so much."

"Joe certainly has taken to her." Sarah sips lemonade. "They might act like kids but they're almost adults. Sometimes it's hard to think of them that way."

"They have mature ideals too, since they're considering college." Mary glances toward Joe and Elaine. "I don't know if this is a good thing or not. Along with her sense of humor, Elaine reminds me of myself at her age."

"How do you mean?" Sarah shifts on the quilt to move off

another stick. She'd rather be comfortable while hearing what Mary will say, which sounds like she's about to admit to something interesting.

Mary circles a fingertip around the edge of the glass. "I was—and still am—headstrong. I sometimes wonder if she might try to talk Joe into sneaking off and getting married." She looks Sarah in the eye. "I'd love grandchildren, but at the right time."

"I doubt they'd run off and get married," Sarah says. "They're some of the most level-headed young people I know."

"Joe might get that from you, but Elaine doesn't get it from me." Mary sips lemonade. "At least not from my younger self. What were you like when you and Will met? I hope you don't mind me saying so, but he's an attractive man."

The question surprises Sarah, but for only a second. Farm wives don't normally tell each other how handsome their husbands are. "It's a good thing I got to know you before you said that, Mary, or I might drown you in the river. When Will and I met, I'm sure it was the same with you and Albert." Sarah sips lemonade. Elaine laughs as Joe tickles her. Sarah lowers her head and turns away.

"What wrong?" Mary asks, touching Sarah's arm.

"Joe will be eighteen next May and I can't stand the thought of his birthday and how he might get drafted. I'm afraid of how that would affect Elaine too."

"Thomas is sixteen, so I understand. Yes, when I met Joe— and later, when Elaine told me he was seventeen—I thought the same thing. I'm sure you heard about the Edwards losing their son a couple of months ago. He was in the Navy on a submarine. Can you imagine living in a metal tube under the ocean?"

Sarah slings the leftover lemonade in the grass, almost losing her grip on the cool, damp glass. "I don't care to imagine any of it. All I want is for the war to end and for my boy to stay here and have a life with your daughter. Elaine is an extraordinary young woman. Joe used to be shy and fairly quiet. She seems to have brought him out of his shell, or woke up part of his spirit. I'd feel blessed to have her as my daughter-in-law."

Elaine tousles Joe's blond curls.

"I feel the same about Joe," Mary says. "Elaine's always been outgoing, but now she seems more focused. I guess it's because she's thinking about a future with him. Maybe we shouldn't let our fears get the best of us."

"That's easy for you to say." Warmth rises in Sarah's cheeks. It's not like her to speak without thinking, although it's true how Mary's son might avoid the war altogether, unlike Joe.

Mary touches Sarah's arm again. "I only meant how positive thoughts are better than fearing the worst."

"I realize that. I'm sorry, I shouldn't have …"

"Don't think anything of it. I'd feel the same if Thomas were seventeen."

Elaine rests her head on Joe's shoulder.

Regardless of Mary's words, Sarah can't shove her fears away. Every time their children laugh, she can't ignore the reality that might shatter their lives with Joe's next birthday.

Will and Albert stroll down from the trucks. "Sarah," Will says, "it's about time we get home."

"Us too," Albert says.

"I suppose you're right." Sarah stands. "I'll tell Joe and Elaine." Nearing the laughing couple, she forces a smile. "Okay, you two, your fathers say it's time to go."

Elaine glances at Joe. "Mrs. Matthan, will it be okay if Joe and I stay and build a fire and watch the stars come out?"

The talk with Mary about their younger years gives Sarah pause. Considering what might happen next May however, she understands Elaine's request. "It's all right with me, but I can't speak for your parents." Sarah faces Joe. "Or your father."

"Can you ask him?"

"We'll see."

Sarah returns to Will, Mary, and Albert. "Guess who wants to stay and build a fire and watch the stars?"

"I have an idea," Will says, slipping his arm around Sarah's waist. "You and me, right?"

"Well, darn," Mary says. "I was about to tell Albert the same thing."

"I don't know if that's a good idea," Albert says.

Mary kisses his cheek. "We can always go home and misbehave."

"As you well know, my forever joking wife, I meant Joe and Elaine."

"Phooey on you, Albert Johnson. If we can't trust our children, who can we trust?"

* * *

Elaine waves to her parents as they leave. Mom did a great job of talking Dad into letting her and Joe stay. Joe waves too. "I'm glad I drove so we can stay, but if I had a daughter ..."

"You wouldn't raise her so you could trust her?"

"It's not her I'd worry about. You heard how your mom had to talk your dad into it."

"He knows I can handle you." Elaine shoves Joe's arm. "Like our moms have been handling our dads all their lives. Besides, Mom knows I'm a good girl."

"Yeah, right," Joe says, returning the shove. "Like you were a 'good girl' when we talked about our promise."

"You were the one teasing me with a daffodil, Mr. Pervert Matthan. Every time I see one now, that's all I think about."

"Good, that's exactly what I wanted." Joe gets up from the log. "I'll get the quilt from the truck. I'll make the fire out from under the tree for a clear view. We can spread the quilt and be ready for the stars."

Joe returns with the quilt. Elaine drops an armload of dead branches she gathered from beneath the oak. Joe uses the smaller branches to form an inverted V. She spreads the quilt while he adds larger branches.

Elaine drops to the quilt cross-legged. A strange feeling, as if a butterfly is fluttering inside her chest, makes her take several deep breaths. Ever since their first date she fantasized about being alone with him here at night, even to the point of guilt. He strikes a match and holds it to the small sticks. The flames flicker into the thicker branches, setting those alight. Heat rises within her, flowing in waves that reach her innermost places, intense and inviting yet frightening at the same time.

* * *

Watching Elaine watching him, Joe adds more limbs to the fire. She unfastens the top button of her dress. She's either warm or teasing. Teasing isn't a good idea. More buttons undone would be a *great* idea, but only if he were some guy who doesn't love her. Still, being here with her alone magnifies his feelings of wanting to see the lace of her bra, the curve of her breasts.

The flames rise between them; dancing apparitions of orange and yellow reflect in her eyes. She shares a slight, angelic smile, one that touches him deeper than any kiss or caress. Temptation flares, warm and sultry as a hot August night. Biting his lower lip in an attempt to replace temptation with pain proves useless.

He joins Elaine on the quilt. "I think that'll keep the chill away."

She slides her arm under his. "You're awfully hot." She touches his other arm, his chest, and lingers there, fingering a button. Firelight flickers on her face and neck. Her chest rises and falls sharply. She faces the river, licks her lips, and Joe swallows. Does she remember their promise? She better, because he isn't sure he can keep it by himself.

Elaine faces the fire again. The flames reflect on her lips as well as in her eyes, both golden. She faces the river again, and her profile becomes an artist's rendition: a portrait to hold and never let go. Joe's heart stutters like a tractor engine starting on a cold morning. He collapses to the quilt. Elaine kisses his cheek and settles into the crook of his arm.

"Thank you."

"For?"

"For being you. For loving me. For helping me figure out how to handle our scary feelings that have been threatening to burn me like the fire is burning the wood."

"I'm glad it isn't just me. I can't begin to put into words what I felt when I saw you sitting here. I wish I had a camera. I'd have taken your picture and have some great artist use it to paint your portrait. After that they might as well throw the Mona Lisa in the trash."

Elaine pats his chest. "Now Joe Matthan, that's your heart talking, not your head." She points to the sky. "I think it's time to watch the stars."

In the dimming twilight, the faraway pinpoints of light wink into view. The constellation Hercules, named after the Greek warrior, appears, reminding Joe of the soldiers fighting around the world. Then Lyra, named after the lyre, a stringed instrument also common in Greek lore, comes into view, reminding him of his guitar. This thought calms him, allowing him to think back to the day when he met the young woman he now holds in his arms.

Bathed in the dying firelight, they talk quietly, serenaded by the crackle of glowing embers. A breeze rustles the leaves overhead; the aroma of wood smoke drifts their way. Crickets chirp in the grass nearby. Some unknown animal scurries in the woods behind them: maybe a white-tailed deer, a racoon, or a cottontail rabbit.

Joe turns to kiss Elaine's forehead. She snuggles deeper into his shoulder, hair soft against his cheek.

An owl's *who-who-o-o* echoes from across the river, almost as if it's asking Joe who's next to leave Alma for war. Not him. Not now. But what if the war isn't over by his birthday? If not he'll have to register. Will the war be over before he's drafted and has to go fight? If not, how will he handle it? More importantly, how will Elaine handle it?

He closes his eyes. Too many questions—none he wants to think about. May—and his birthday—will get here soon enough.

Chapter 17

A Father's Love

May, 1944

Waiting on the porch swing, Will expects Joe back from Alma anytime now. He's gone to register for the draft, and Sarah's in the bedroom crying. She said she'd have it under control before he gets back.

The spring morning blooms with promise: Cows graze in the pasture; calves butt their udders for milk. In the yard, not far from the watchful eyes of several clucking hens, chicks scratch and peck in the yard, *peep-peeping* and running back to the hens when the rooster struts near. In the maple tree shading the porch, new leaves, green with life, flutter in the breeze.

Will takes a pocket knife to his dirty fingernails. Considering where Joe is and what he's doing, the season holds little hope for his family, as well as other families across the country.

About a half mile up the road, dust rises from behind a tree-lined hedgerow. The dust comes closer, followed by the hesitant whine of a downshifted vehicle. Joe turns in, pulls up to the house, and climbs from the truck. Will puts the pocket knife away and stands. "How'd it go, Son?"

Joe climbs the steps. "I feel like I'm a traitor to Elaine, that's how it went."

Will returns to the porch swing. "Let's sit here a bit." He nudges the worn oak planks. At the bottom of the swing's arc, their shoes scrape the floor. The chains creak. At the top, the hooks squeak in near-silent, high-pitched sighs.

Hints of Will's baby boy remains in Joe's face, more-so in his blue eyes. On his first day home as a newborn, wrapped and warm, Will and Sarah gave him his first ride on the porch swing.

"I'm proud of you, Son."

"Why's that?"

"You're doing your duty. America doesn't have a chance at staying free if we don't stand up to Germany or Japan."

"Well, I wouldn't be me if it weren't for you and Mom." Joe pauses. "I can add Elaine to that list too. Do you think she changed me? I thought she might, but not as much as Mom thinks. Now that I look at it, I think she's right."

"Your mother and I always knew you were quiet. That's better than being a blabbermouth."

"I guess."

"We were hoping you'd open up as you matured, but we didn't know how to make that happen. Now Elaine—amazing young lady that she is—has figured that out."

Will allows the conversation to falter. A breeze blows from across the road, bringing the earthy aroma of several fields they recently plowed. He's never shared the next bit of information with Joe and doesn't want his voice to betray his emotions.

"The first time your mother and I brought you outside, we sat right here and took turns holding you. This swing holds memories I can't remember, but that's the one I love the most. My fondest hope is for you and Elaine to build memories here in Alma. I'd love nothing more than for you to swing your children here one day. You two are as right for each other as any two people I've ever met."

Joe smiles; his eyes don't. "We're glad you and Mom and Elaine's parents think we're a good match. We're glad you trust us too."

"How do you mean?" Will asks, curious because it's a different subject.

"I mean like when y'all let us stay at the river alone that night to watch the stars. Remember the day you and Mom met Elaine? We promised each other we wouldn't make any mistakes we might regret."

Joe's revelation surprises Will. Knowing his son like he does—his son who just turned eighteen, his son who's mature to the point of being responsible about making love—fills him with even more pride.

The moment is serious—he tries not to smile—but he once thought the same thing about his parents as he's about to tell Joe. "You probably don't like thinking about your mom and me having the same feelings as you and Elaine have now, but we do. That means we had them at your age too. It's natural to have those feelings—it's unnatural to fight them—so any person who does has an exceptional character. That's you two in a nutshell. Your mother thinks so too." Will pauses. Will Joe understand the underlying meaning behind what he's about to say? "We hope that strength will get you both through anything."

"You're not very subtle, Dad. If you're talking about the war, I'm not worried about me as much as I'm worried about Elaine.

I don't know what she'd do if something happened. She's strong, but something like that ..."

"Have you talked to her about it?"

"I don't—" Joe's lips tighten. "I don't know how."

"I need to ask you something." Will stops the swing. "You know me, I'm a realist. I think the best way to handle a problem is to face it head on, not hide from it."

"Hiding from something makes it worse. What do you want to ask?"

"If you have to go fight" —Will's throat tightens— "and you don't make it back, wouldn't you want Elaine to have a happy life without you?"

"Well," Joe says, pausing like he's considering the question, "I think she'd want that for me if it were the other way around."

"Since you haven't told her that, you need to." Will hesitates to let that statement sink in. "Then, no matter what, she'll know you want what's best for her." He's pleased with how Joe understands his last point, but another point is more important. "Even if that means she meets someone else."

Joe's eyes narrow. "You could've left that part out, Dad."

"Life goes on, Son. Would you want her to be alone the rest of her life?"

"I, uh ... I don't like to think about her with another man. You know, kissing her and stuff, or her kissing him back and liking it."

"That's part of life," Will says. "She wouldn't like you to kiss another woman either, but I doubt she would want you to be alone if something happened to her."

Joe rubs his forehead. "Well, that *would* be pretty doggoned selfish. What if I don't say anything until I know I have to report for duty?"

"That's why I mentioned it. Now you'll have time to figure out what to say. It won't be easy, you know."

"She won't like it, but it makes sense how I'd want her to be happy because I love her."

Will pats his son's shoulder. "I think she'll understand even if she says she doesn't. Besides, like we just said, she wouldn't want you to be alone the rest of your life if your roles were reversed. If you think it'll help, you could ask her that."

"I will if I need to. I just hope I don't have to bring it up."

Chapter 18

A Family's Decision

July, 1944

At the kitchen table, peeling potatoes for supper, Sarah wipes sweat from her brow. Another blistering hot afternoon, no clouds and no rain in sight.

The front screened door opens with a squeak and shuts with a bang. The clock over the stove says it's time for the mail. What once had been an enjoyable stroll to the mailbox with Will made her cringe with each step after Joe registered, so she stopped going. Minutes later the barn door slams. She starts to yell out the back door, but at the recognizable strike of an ax biting into a piece of wood, she doesn't. If Will needs to chop wood on such a hot day, he might like a cold glass of lemonade.

She stops at the barn door. The strikes of the ax aren't their usual rhythmic thudding when either Will or Joe splits wood. The sound resembles lightning strikes during those violent thunderstorms that often blow in on days like this. Afraid of startling Will in the middle of a swing, Sarah peeks in the barn door. Her husband is shirtless; perspiration pours off his chest. The seasoned lengths of oak firewood don't stand a chance as he swings the ax in a high arc and abruptly downward, sending each piece flying to the side. Sarah starts to go in but doesn't. Part of the moisture dripping from Will's face isn't sweat—some of the droplets streaming down his cheeks are tears. He groans with each savage blow, places another stick of wood on the chopping block, and repeats the torturous cycle.

Still afraid she'll startle Will, Sarah slowly opens the door. Sunlight illuminates him. He spins around; the ax slips from his fingers and thumps to the dirt floor.

Sarah sets the glass on the chopping block. "It came, didn't it?" Will wraps his arms around her and heaves with heavy sobs that eventually fade to sniffles. She wipes his sodden hair from his forehead. "I wish I had known this was so hard for you."

"I thought I was doing the right thing by keeping how much it bothered me to myself. I guess I thought it would help you and Joe." Will shakes his head. "I'm not sure if that was the right thing to do, but I do know I don't want to lose my son to some war because of the delusions of a maniac." He nudges the ax at his feet. "If Hitler were here right now, what I did to that oak would be nothing compared to what I'd do to him."

Sarah gives Will the lemonade, picks up his shirt, and takes his hand. "Let's go inside." She leads him to the house, intending to leave his anger with the pile of shattered oak.

He sits at the kitchen table, and she gives him a dishtowel. Wiping his face and chest, he stares at his glass. She pours herself lemonade and sits across from him. What can she do to make him feel better? She doesn't want to lose Joe either, but she doesn't know how to deal with it any better than Will does.

The real issue—one she hasn't realized—surfaces in her thoughts. All this time she's been worrying about her own feelings instead of Joe's. How could she have not seen that?

"Will, I think I've finally realized that all I've been doing over the past few months is grieving over what could happen to Joe instead of believing he can come home. I should've supported him by being strong like you."

Will raises his head. "If Joe caught me acting like I did, he'd think I had no faith in him making it though the war."

"I hope he hasn't thought that about me," Mary says, failing to keep the worry from her voice.

"I hope he hasn't thought that about either of us." Will rubs her hand. "I'm sorry I didn't tell you how I felt about it. If I had been more honest—more open—I might've handled that letter instead of getting upset. You're absolutely right about Joe needing our strength and support." Will takes an envelope from his pants pocket. "And that's what we'll give him when he reads this."

Sarah nods. "Let's wait until tomorrow. I'd hate to ruin his Saturday night with Elaine."

* * *

Sunday, Joe trades church clothes for everyday clothes and finds Mom and Dad at the kitchen table. He starts to ask about lunch but doesn't. Their somber expressions—no smiles and downturned eyes—are similar to when they attended the last family funeral.

Dad pulls out a chair. "Son, how about having a seat with your mother and me?"

The burn of adrenaline creeps up the back of Joe's neck. They were unusually quiet last night and this morning, so his draft notice must have come in yesterday's mail. "I guess I don't need—" He clears his throat. "I guess I don't need to ask what this is about."

"Please," Mom says, "this is hard enough as it is."

Joe sits. Dad gives him an envelope from his pants pocket.

"Remember how we talked about facing problems head on?"

Joe opens the envelope and reads, unsure how to feel about the reality that has just smacked him in the face.

"I have to report to the train station in Holdrege this coming Saturday. From there I go with other inductees to Fort Leavenworth in Kansas for basic training. Now I need to tell Elaine, and I just don't know how to do that."

"Invite her for supper," Dad says. "I'm not sure if it'll help, but we'll be glad to sit with you when you tell her."

"Please consider it," Mom says. "I want to tell her she's more than welcome to come by and visit, day or night. I can teach her your favorite recipes, and she can tell me more about her plans for college when you come home."

"*When* I come home?" Joe lowers his head. "You mean *if* I come home."

"You know better than to say that." Dad's decisive tone surprises Joe. "Raise your head and look at your mother and me, this is important."

Joe raises his head.

"We've decided that kind of talk does no one any good around here, especially not you. I wish we had realized it before. We're sorry, okay?"

Joe agrees with his parents. Not only is believing he'll come home good for him, it's good for Elaine. He doesn't want to give her false hope, but hope exists. To act as if it doesn't is wrong. He grins at Mom and Dad. "You two must be the smartest parents in Nebraska."

"Just Nebraska?" they ask together. Everyone laughs.

Joe stands. "I'll call Elaine."

"Let me call her," Mom says. "You menfolk find something to do so we can have some time to ourselves."

* * *

Sarah meets Elaine at the front door and takes her to the kitchen. "Joe and Will are checking a fence on the other side of the farm. They'll be back soon."

Elaine sniffs. "Is that roast beef like we had before?"

"It sure is," Sarah says, sitting at the table. "Let's have a chat."

Elaine sits. "When Mom or Dad use that tone, it makes me worry."

"Good. That means you'll do better than I just did when you talk to your own children about a concern one day." Sarah tells Elaine about Will's rage the day before, including how she hadn't realized the sadness she'd been exhibiting concerning Joe was affecting everyone. "Will and I sat right here and decided the gloom had to stop. We need to be more positive around Joe."

"I understand what you mean." Elaine hesitates. "But when I think of what could happen …"

"Don't think about it like that," Sarah says, keeping her voice firm. "Think about Joe coming home without a scratch. That needs to be—has to be—our attitude from now on."

"It won't be easy, Mrs. Matthan, but I'll try."

"Good. Now, don't you think it's time you called me Sarah? You might as well, right?"

"I can do that, Sarah, but like I said, the other's going to be hard. Still, Joe needs to believe he'll come back. That is, if he has to leave."

Footsteps clomp on the back porch. Joe and Will come inside.

"Just in time," Sarah says.

"For what?" Joe asks Elaine. "Is Mom teaching you how to

make roast beef?"

"For this." Elaine hops from the chair. "Mr. Matthan, Joe's mom asked me to call her Sarah. Would you allow me the honor of calling you Will?"

Will offers his hand. "How do you do, Miss Johnson? I'm Will Matthan, Joe's father. I'd be pleased if you'd call me Will."

Elaine shakes Will's hand. "How do you do, Will? I've heard some fine things about you. Your son, on the other hand …"

Sarah smiles at Elaine's addition. She couldn't ask for better young woman to be Joe's wife one day.

"That reminds me of the day we shook hands and agreed to go fishing," Joe says. "Remember?"

"Better than you I bet," Elaine says. "You always forget making me lose that huge catfish."

"Is this story about shaking hands something else you haven't told us?" Sarah asks.

"It's almost as funny as the fishing trip," Joe says. "I'll tell you while we eat."

"*I'll* tell them while we eat," Elaine says. "That way they'll get the *whole* story."

* * *

After supper, Elaine follows everyone to the living room. Sarah goes to the screen door leading to the front porch. "It's a shame to look at four walls when we can watch the sunset." Sarah and Will take two chairs. Elaine sits with Joe in the swing.

She has a feeling—and not a good one. If she's right, Sarah's conversation and today's invitation are hints. During supper she had also considered Sarah's advice about supporting Joe, and the more she thought about it, the more it made sense. Still, she can't stand the thought of losing him.

Joe eases them back and forth on the porch swing. The movement Elaine usually loves nauseates her until she's forced to swallow the feeling in her throat, thick and prodding her to vomit. Tears come, blurring her vision. She turns away.

Songbirds flit in the maple shading the porch. Crickets chirp in the shrubbery. The sun sinks toward the horizon. The last of the evening breeze settles, bringing the sweet fragrance of a rose arbor at the opposite end of the porch. The sun seems to hesitate, its light a fading curtain of red satin that announces the end of nature's evening show.

Elaine turns away from it all. Silence consumes the porch. Just get it over with already. Time to cry and be done with it. The man she loves is going to war and she might never see him again.

Joe reaches into his shirt pocket. Elaine squeezes the swing's armrest, forcing white paint under her nails. Nausea rises in her throat again. He takes out a folded envelope. "This came in yesterday's mail." His voice is low, ominous. "I have to be at the Holdrege train station Saturday morning at ten. I guess a lot of other guys will be there too. From there we'll go the Fort Leavenworth in Kansas. I don't know what happens after that."

Elaine's heart jackhammers in her chest. She turns to lay her head on Joe's shoulder and wrap her arm around his waist. How can this happen now, after loving him for only a year?

Joe takes her in his arms. She tucks her face into his shirt. No, she needs to be strong like Sarah said. Clenching her teeth, she sits up and palms tears from her cheeks. The bones are hard, but she needs to be harder for Joe. "I hope you don't think you'll keep me from seeing you off. Besides, I need to know where the train station is so I can pick you up when you come back home."

Joe fingers moisture from the corners of his eyes. "Leave it to you to make me smile at a time like this."

"Maybe I should go with you." Elaine faces Sarah. "What do you think, Sarah? If all the women who are as upset as we are go to fight, I bet the war would end in no time."

Elaine," Sarah says, after they all finish laughing, "I couldn't agree more."

Chapter 19

One Last Night

At breakfast Friday morning, Joe doesn't say much. He and Elaine want to go to the river tonight alone, and he's afraid his and her parents will want to go too.

Dad looks at him over the top of the newspaper. "Do you and Elaine have plans later?"

"We, uh … you could say that."

Mom pulls the paper down to reveal Dad's grin. "He's teasing you. We overheard you talking to Elaine on the phone last night about going to the river alone."

"You don't mind?"

"Not as long as we have supper together before you go. Does fried chicken and mashed potatoes and green beans tempt you?"

"Does it ever. Throw in a chocolate pie and you've got a deal."

* * *

The day lingers, muggy and warm. After supper, Joe washes his sour armpits and dons a fresh shirt. It hasn't rained in over two weeks. During the drive to Elaine's and to the river, every vehicle traveling the dirt roads leaves a curtain of dust. Across the endless fields of growing corn and wheat, heat waves shimmer above them.

Joe parks near the oak. Is this the last time he'll see this place? No, he can't think like that. Elaine has been positive all week, constantly talking about their future. Ruining their night is the last thing he wants to do.

He takes the quilt from behind the seat and they stroll hand-in-hand, grass crunching beneath their feet. Grasshoppers whir and scatter; two land on wisps of broom straw that droop with their weight. The straws rise again with the sultry breeze; the grasshoppers take flight, wings clattering.

Elaine stops at the river's edge. "It's hard to believe, isn't it?"

"What is?" Joe says, nudging her arm. "That the river's so low?"

"No, silly, that we had our first date here over a year ago."

"I'm teasing but you're right. I've heard Dad talk about how time sometimes seems to move quicker than others."

"The last year's definitely been like that." Elaine takes the quilt and gives him two corners. They spread it like they did on their first date fishing. Joe can hardly believe this is their last night together, unless he makes it back from the war.

Lying on the faded patchwork, he concentrates on the river's whisper to calm his fears. Elaine caresses his cheek with fingertips feather-soft and cool, and her lips form that perfect half-smile he loves so much. "I love you, Joe. More than I ever thought possible."

"I love you too." He wants to say more, but the words hang in his throat. Instead, he kisses her fingertips in turn while searing her brown eyes and the splash of freckles across her nose into his memory.

She pulls her hand free to trace a sensitive path from his forehead, to his brow, then along his nose to pause at his lips.

He closes his eyes. If he can sear her touch into his memory, like with her eyes and her freckles, he can keep her in his heart until he's able to hold her in his arms again.

She fingers the top button of his shirt, unfastens it, and continues down his chest. At the final button, Joe places his hand on hers. "That might not be a good idea."

"Trust me, okay? I'm not going to do anything we'll regret."

She finishes the button. "I'm getting up for a minute, close your eyes."

Joe blanks his mind. This is their last night together. Whatever Elaine is going to do is all right with him. Well, unless it's stripping naked and lying on top of him. That *really* might not be a good idea.

* * *

Elaine rises from the quilt. The promise she and Joe have kept for more than a year screams for her to stop. She banishes it with a shake of her head, unbuttons her dress to the waist, and pulls her arms from the sleeves. The damp cloth falls from her shoulders. She takes her bra off. The breeze kisses her bare skin with a mixture of heat and cool. Is Joe feeling the same anticipation as she does? His chest rises and falls in rapid, shallow breaths. At his sides, his hands clench the quilt. Yes, he feels it exactly like she does.

Their promise hangs in the balance. Still, she wants this one simple thing. No, she needs it, has to have it. It's just one touch. What will one touch hurt?

She sits astride him. Taking his hands from the quilt, she presses them to her breasts and closes her eyes. This simple caress tempts her. Causes deeper stirrings within her. Stirrings that take her breath away. Joe's fingers gently squeeze. His hips move; hers respond as if they have a will of their own. She pulls his hands away. Such a simple touch leading to so much temptation. She hadn't known, how could she have known?

"I'm sorry," Joe says. "I shouldn't have done that."

"I shouldn't have done that either." She lies on his bare chest and their bodies sear together, like two embers, red and glowing in the first fire they shared here. She concentrates on the beating of his heart, the intimate touch of bare skin on bare skin. Her love for Joe gradually banishes desire to a secondary corner of her mind, saved for when he returns.

"Do you have any idea how much I want you?" she whispers. "I've even thought about getting pregnant, but I don't know if that will keep you at home."

He wraps his arms around her. "When the time comes, I want it to be right in every way possible. Using you like that would be wrong."

"I wasn't planning on letting you touch me just now." She rises enough to kiss his nose. "I guess I'm one of those weak girls."

"You're one of the strongest people I know. What did you have in mind when you—you know?"

"What I'm doing now. I can't think of any more words to say that will let you know how much I love you, so I wanted to lie here, our hearts as close as possible. Maybe they can say more to each other than we can with words alone."

Joe traces circles on her back with his fingertips. His warmth radiates from him, spreads to intimate places of her body, tempting her to writhe against him again. "Close your eyes while I get dressed. You should too."

The evening passes with talk of college, marriage, children. Before the sun sets, Elaine places Mom's camera on the driftwood log, still there from last August. She sets the timer, runs to Joe's side at the river, and the shutter clicks, recording the end of a perfect afternoon.

In the truck, she grabs Joe's arm as he turns the key. "You realize I'm driving you to Holdrege tomorrow, don't you?"

"Why not? Maybe we can find a diner where you can buy me breakfast."

"I'll tell Mom and Dad and you can tell your folks. They can meet us at the train station after."

Joe turns the key. "You sure are smart" —he grins— "for a farm girl."

Elaine pokes his side. "Just for that, *you* get to buy breakfast."

* * *

Late from breakfast, Joe hurries through the train station and enters the morning sun shining on the boarding platform. He stops to look over the heads of several other families with young men ready to board the train too. Down toward the huge, black locomotive, clouds of steam hissing from somewhere near its wheels, his and Elaine's parents wave. Thomas waves also, a camera hanging from his neck.

Elaine waves back. "I see my brother got Mom's camera off the kitchen table like I told him."

The train's horn blares; Joe flinches at the blast to his eardrums. "I hope I have time to tell everybody bye."

Everyone takes turns giving him quick hugs. Mom kisses his cheek. "You stay safe, Joe. You need to come back to us."

Thomas laughs. "You've been talking to my mom, huh, Mrs. Matthan? She's ready for some grandchildren."

"Good idea," Albert says, patting Joe's shoulder. "I'll have that extra room built by the time you get back."

The horn blares again; Thomas aims the camera. "Come on,

Elaine. Give your sweetie some sugar before he leaves."

Elaine takes the yellow ribbon from her hair. "This is the ribbon you tied my hair with on our first date. I want you to tie it around your wrist for good luck."

Joe puts the ribbon in his pocket. "Hey, great. I *know* I'll come back now."

"All aboard!"

Joe glances at the conductor standing in a car's doorway. Elaine wraps her arms around him for a kiss. "You come back to me, Joe Matthan. I love you more than I can say."

The train's horn blares again. Joe grabs Dad's hand; Dad pulls him into a bear hug. "I love you, Joe. Take care."

The cars shudder and bang.

Joe hugs Mrs. Johnson. "How about some fried catfish for my welcome back supper?"

She pats his cheek. "That's a deal, Joe."

Stuffing the ribbon in his pocket, Joe grabs his suitcase and runs to jump into a doorway of one of the shuddering cars. He turns for one last look at Elaine, who waves wildly. He waves back and she screams, "I love you!"

* * *

As the train clatters along the tracks away from Elaine, she covers her face and cries. Arms surround her. Voices tell her Joe will be back before she knows it. She can't stop crying. Mom says she needs to stop before she makes herself sick. Dad squeezes her shoulders. Silence is his comfort, either that or he's about to cry also.

Other families cry all around her. Each, she knows, is like her, missing their loved ones already, unsure if they'll ever see them again.

121

Chapter 20

Final Song

The barracks door opens. "Mail call, you lonely boys, mail call."

Joe closes his foot locker and sits on his bunk. Elaine or his mother or father usually writes him over the weekend, and the letters come mid-week instead of Friday. He'll let his platoon have their excitement and stow his laundry after.

The mail clerk finishes, turns to leave, and spins around, envelope in hand. "Almost forget you, Matthan." He tosses Joe the envelope.

Joe rips the letter from Elaine open.

Dear Joe,
Your mother's not well. She told me not to write because you'd worry. You know her, if you call, she'll only say not to come, but I really think you should. Call me before you leave and I'll pick you up at Holdrege. I'd say more but I think she should tell you herself.
Love, Elaine

Joe runs out the door to find his commanding officer.

* * *

Elaine smiles hugely when Joe steps off the train. He comes running, drops his duffel bag, and wraps his arms around her for a kiss. As much as she loves this moment, he's sure to ask about his mother after the kiss.

"I can't believe how much I missed you," he says. "Well, after that kiss you do. Is Mom better?"

"She was never sick. Joe, I—."

"But your letter said—" Joe's mouth falls open. "You lied to me?"

Elaine wipes tears. "Joe, please, I—"

"I never thought you'd lie to me about my own mother."

"I had to see you, Joe. I—" Her voice breaks; tears run down her cheeks. "I've been trying to be strong, to not worry you. You'll be leaving soon to go to Europe and … and …"

She covers her face. Why can't he understand? Why can't he take her in his arms and tell her everything will be all right? Why can't he—

The train's horn shatters the silence.

Joe slips his arms around her; she buries her face into his shoulder. She shouldn't have doubted him. He'll never stop loving her—never!

Wiping her eyes, she pulls away. "I hope you're not too mad. I never thought I'd lie to you either."

"I *was* mad. This whole thing, it's— I guess what I'm trying to say is we never know how we'll handle things until they happen. I don't care who says they know, they don't know." He lifts her face and she smiles. "That's what I wanted to see," he says. "Now, is there any way I can get one of your everything-is-okay-now kisses?"

"Just one?" Elaine asks, standing on tiptoe to wrap her arms around Joe's neck. "How about two or three, or maybe a dozen?"

"I'll take three right now and a dozen after we eat." Joe pats his stomach. "I'm starving."

With the required number of kisses complete, Elaine drives them to the same diner where they ate breakfast the day he left. Families fill the seats, most with somber looking young men having their final meals before they leave like Joe left in July.

The waiter takes their orders. Elaine reaches across the table for Joe's hand. "Joe." His brow wrinkles. "Yes," she continues, "you know that tone, so stop looking at me like that. I think you'll want this too."

"You think I'll want what?"

"I want to get married."

"Uh-huh. To me, right?"

"I've already talked to the Justice of the Peace here in Holdrege. I lied about my age and told him I didn't have a birth certificate. You won't need one since you're in the Army. He said he'd perform the service. He might not believe I'm old enough, but I think he and his wife have a soft spot in their hearts for soldiers and their girls who want to get married before— Well, before the soldier has to leave home."

Eyes blinking, Joe leans back. "Really? You've done all that?"

"I want us to get married," Elaine says as seriously as possible, "and I won't take no for an answer. I told Mom and Dad I'm staying with a friend tonight and I'll go to school from there tomorrow. We can spend the night at the river and I can have you back tomorrow in time for the train."

Joe stares. Elaine doubts he's ever seen her this determined. Still, as he well knows, her stubborn streak has shown itself on more than one occasion. "Okay," he says, lacing his fingers together on the table, "let me think about this."

The food comes; they eat without talking. He has to be

considering everything, has to be admitting all the bases are covered. Even though the timing is off concerning their future, the timing is off about everything. He better realize that, or they'll both be under arrest for the biggest fight this diner has ever seen.

He plucks a napkin from the holder. "What time does he get back from lunch?"

"Who?" Elaine asks.

"That Justice of the Peace you've got wrapped around your little finger. We want to be first in line, don't we?"

Elaine jumps from her seat and kisses him—looks at her future husband's sweet, embarrassed, red-cheeked expression and kisses him again.

Meal done and cash on the table, they hurry to the office around the corner and wait, either leaning against the building, arms crossed, or shifting their weight from foot to foot. Joe glances at his watch. "I guess Justices take long lunches."

Eventually, the short, round official arrives. "Hello again, young lady. I take it this young man in uniform is the husband-to-be?"

"He sure is. If you're ready, we are."

Elaine wears the same dress she wore when she met Joe's parents. Joe already looks handsome in his uniform. The vows are simple, and both say them with every sincerity. They kiss. The justice's wife cries and congratulates them. Elaine asks her to take a picture of them with Mom's camera.

At the general store, they buy food for the evening, then drive straight to the river from Holdrege. Driving through Alma and risk someone seeing them is out of the question.

Rain has satisfied the parched landscape several times over the last two months, making the long drive on the dustless country roads bearable. Elaine glances at Joe several times during the drive. She actually, finally, almost unbelievably, is Mrs. Joe Matthan.

At the river, when they park, she holds her hand out toward Joe. "Let me see the marriage certificate. I haven't had a chance to read it."

He takes the paper from his pocket and unfolds it. "Would you believe I miss-spelled my last name? I guess this honeymoon is over before it starts."

She jerks the paper from his hand. "Uh-huh, I watched you sign it, remember?" She takes a quick glance and puts the paper in her purse. "I don't know. Maybe I should make you wait for a honeymoon until you get back from Europe."

"Yeah, right," Joe says, his tone sarcastic. "We're not going anywhere until we do what we came here to do, and you know it."

They take everything to the oak, and Joe picks up his duffel. "I'm getting out of this uniform before I make a fire." He goes behind the huge oak.

Elaine spreads the quilt and adds a few more blankets and a couple of pillows she'd snuck from home. Dressed in farm clothes, Joe gathers wood and assembles the sticks and branches. She waits on the quilt barefoot, growing acutely aware that she'll treasure this night the rest of their lives, exactly like the evening their parents let them stay to watch the stars.

Joe glances up from time to time while lighting the fire. Does he remember that night? This night will be altogether different. Why is he taking so long with that fire?

Elaine unbuttons the dress and pulls the bra through a sleeve. Holding the dress to keep it from falling, she allows one bare shoulder to shine in the brightening firelight.

Joe glances her way again. He rises from the fire, joins her on the quilt, and slips his hands around her waist. "Did I ever tell you how Mom taught me a few dance steps? Too bad you didn't sneak my guitar out of my house, we could have some music for our wedding dance."

"You're good," Elaine says, patting his hands, "but you're not good enough to keep your arms around me and dance and play the guitar at the same time. Sing the song you were singing at the hardware store the day we met. We can dance to that."

Joe hums the tune. They sway to its rhythm.

> *I am a poor, wayfaring stranger*
> *While traveling through, this world of woe*
> *Yet there's no sickness, toil nor danger*
> *In that bright world, to which I go*
> *I'm going there, to see my father*
> *I'm going there, no more to roam*
> *I'm only going, over Jordan*
> *I'm only going, over home*
> *I know dark clouds, will gather 'round me*
> *I know my way, is rough and steep*
> *Yet beauteous fields, lie just before me*
> *Where God's redeemed, their vigils sleep*
> *I'm going there, to see my mother*
> *She said she'd meet, me when I come*
> *I'm only going, over Jordan*
> *I'm only going, over home*

On the last line, Elaine joins in with a high and haunting

harmony. She's never sung for him, being somewhat shy about it, but her voice seems an acceptable counter to his.

"Wow," Joe says. "We've known each other over a year and you're just now singing for me? That was incredible. If I had known—"

She covers his mouth. "If you *had known* what? I'd be too embarrassed to sing in public."

"You? Elaine Johnson? My Elaine? Embarrassed?"

"You're forgetting something, Mr. Matthan. If you need a hint, it has something to do with my last name."

"What's wrong with— Oh … oh, yeah."

"I'll 'oh, yeah' you. Never mind, I know it's a lot to get used to. Thank you for singing. That song is sad but it's full of hope too. It's strange no one knows who wrote it. There's no telling how old it is."

Across the river, the full moon's curve rises above the tree-lined horizon. It casts a magical glow around them while it reflects on the water's glassy surface.

"The moon's nice." Elaine turns Joe toward the rutted path that descends down the hill from the main road. "But I like the stars too."

In the sky over the tree-lined rise, stars twinkle like lightning bugs scattered over the fields surrounding her house on many a summer's night. A meteor streaks by; the brilliant line of white dies almost immediately. She closes her eyes to etch this moment into her memory, then raises her palm to Joe's cheek. "Remember the promise we made? The only promise we need tonight is to love each other always."

He pulls her close. "I've felt that way for a long time. No matter what happens—even if I don't make it back—I'll always be with you. Like with that song, I don't know what waits for us after we die, but as long as hope lives, I think anything's possible."

The thought of being without him—and what that means—fills Elaine's eyes with tears. "Nothing is promised us, but I promise I'll always love you. Remember that talk you and your father had? If our roles were reversed, I'd want you to find someone else. I can't promise I'll do that—I don't know how I could. What I do know is right here, right now, I don't want to think about any of that. I have to believe you'll come back to me, Joe—I *have* to. Can't we hold onto that hope?"

"That's all I want, too, Elaine." Joe takes her face in his hands, kisses her, and the full realization that she has nothing more to fear—unlike their last evening here—rushes in. She responds completely, burying her face into his neck after their lips part. "I love you so much," she whispers. "I've wanted you for so long."

"I can't tell you how many times I've thought about this night." He smiles, kisses her nose, and says in an official sounding voice, "*Mrs.* Matthan."

He turns her around, traces tingling lines along her neck and shoulders with his lips, then pulls the yellow ribbon. Her hair falls in soft waves against her skin. The dress and panties drop at her feet. The chill night air prickles her arms and legs with goosebumps. His clothes join hers.

With Joe's warmth in her arms, Elaine re-lives that August evening under the stars, this time with no stopping, no starting, no ending, no beginning. Stories from school friends say making love hurts the first time. Instead, she only feels a single sharp pain, soon replaced with the most intense need she's ever felt in her life, which turns into the most intense pleasure she's ever felt in her life. She drifts along on the magic of their special place, the moonlight and firelight joining about them as their bodies entwine again and again. Exhausted, they snuggle against each other, warm in their blankets. She sleeps, waking occasionally to gaze into the fire and at Joe. No, she isn't dreaming. She sleeps again, never wanting to wake, never wanting to leave this place, never wanting anything—

But hope.

Chapter 21

Goodbyes

"Joe-o-o-o … Joe-o-o-o."

Someone calls Joe in sweet, perfect, sing-song-up-and-down syllables. He rolls onto his back and groans. Is he dreaming?

"Joe-o-o-o … Joe-o-o-o." Is he dead and an angel is singing to him? *"Time to wake u-u-u-up."*

Something soft and warm touches his cheek, and he opens his eyes. Elaine is beside him, caressing his face with her fingertips. "Good morning, sleepy head. You looked as peaceful as this place makes me feel."

"Good morning to you, darlin.'" Joe kisses her." I hope you slept well."

"'Darlin'?'" Elaine asks, crinkling her nose. "Where'd that come from? Never mind, I kind of like it. As far as sleeping well, I don't remember the last time I slept *that* well." She tousles his hair. "Maybe it's because we couldn't get enough of each other."

"We never ate either." Joe grins." We really went at it, didn't we? What if we had eaten first?"

"Oh, please. If we did it any more than we did, *you* might have ended up at the doctor's office."

"I'd prove you wrong if we had time." Joe glances at his watch. "Nope, I've got to catch that train."

"The food's probably spoiled," Elaine says, propping herself up on her elbow.

Joe yawns and stretches. "It's a long train ride back to Kansas. I hope we have time for breakfast in Holdrege."

Instead of commenting, Elaine rolls over onto him. Her body is warm; her silky hair is soft. Her eyes, liquid brown and sensual, speak volumes. So does her lingering kiss.

And Joe can't help responding.

Sitting up, she moves with an elegant and exquisite rhythm, and the morning sun rises to bathe her in gold. Joe can't believe what he's seeing. Or feeling. She closes her eyes, continues her motion, and collapses to his chest.

"See," she whispers in his ear, "we still had time."

* * *

Joe turns onto the main road and floors the accelerator. Gravel clatters beneath the truck. Mile after mile the noise continues. Elaine alternates between giggling, kissing his cheek and neck, and running her hand over his chest. They arrive at the diner with fifteen minutes to spare. She promises to send him a copy of their wedding picture, plus copies of the one they had taken of themselves on the log at the river and the one Thomas had taken at the train station, right after she gave Joe the yellow ribbon. At the train station, they hug and kiss and say their goodbyes.

Joe boards the train and slides the window aside to wave. Elaine waves crazily with both hands. The breeze from the cars stirs a dust devil around her, scattering her hair about her face. The train curves away to the south.

And she's gone.

The distance grows between them, but the vision of Elaine smiling and waving has etched itself into his mind.

Rolling along with a gentle, rhythmic shudder, the steel wheels squeak when they bump over the occasional crossing. A couple of miles out of town, the shrill whistle shrieks its warning as the train slows for a herd of cattle on the tracks. The pungent aroma of fresh manure hints at their presence.

Joe settles back against the seat and closes his eyes to relive his and Elaine's wedding day, including their dream-like honeymoon night at the river. The memory gives him the confidence to believe he'll return. Their love will see them through. This is just the beginning. All their dreams of their future together will be inscribed in stone at some special and immortal place.

And even the insanity of a world at war won't dare ruin one single hope.

Chapter 22

The Unexpected

December, 1944

Elaine raises her hand to be excused from class. In the bathroom, she vomits for a third time, rinses the bitter mess from her mouth with water from the sink, and burps as she shuffles to the office to ask if she can leave to visit the local doctor. The flu is going around. If she has it, she wants to warn Mom and Dad and Thomas so they can stay away from her.

She drives the truck through a gray day, with low, rolling clouds spitting sleet. In the examination room, Dr. Roberts asks about her and Joe's families and about Joe, commenting that he hopes her young man will return soon. She explains her symptoms, the vomiting and queasy stomach. He examines her, checks his notes, and removes his glasses.

"Elaine, you don't have a temperature, so I don't think it's the flu. Are your monthly cycles on time?"

"With the war and all, and with Joe leaving, I haven't thought about it, why?"

"Well, because I think you might be—"

"No … you don't mean …"

The doctor nods. "If you've missed your cycles, and if you

and Joe have been together, I'm pretty sure you're going to have a ba—"

"I'm … I'm going to be a mother?"

The doctor nods. "That's right, that's what I think."

Elaine jumps off the examining table and dances a circle around the room. "I'm going to have a baby!" She stops. "AND I'M GOING TO HAVE JOE'S BABY!" Thought after thought runs through her mind, Joe being the first. She can't wait to tell him.

Dr. Robert's caterpillar eyebrows twist into an intense knot. He probably thinks she got pregnant out of wedlock.

"Please don't worry, Dr. Roberts. Joe came for a visit in late September and we got married."

The caterpillars relax, and Elaine hugs him. "I can't wait to tell Joe. He'll love being a dad."

* * *

Intent on telling Mom and Dad how she and Joe got married, including how they're going to be grandparents, Elaine drives home. Thoughts fill her head, both happy and hopeful. As soon as she tells them, she'll write Joe.

She pulls into the yard, mud splattering beneath the truck, and runs to the house, splashing through puddles. At the top of the steps, one end of her loosened yellow hair ribbon falls across her shoulder. She brushes it away, opens the screen door, and stops. On the sofa, Mom and Dad cut their eyes toward each other and then toward her. She goes inside; the screened door slams behind her. "What's going on?"

"Your teacher called and said you were sick, so we expected you." Dad pats the sofa. "Sit down, honey, we need to talk."

Mom stands and takes a step toward her. Her deep brown eyes are filled with concern. "I need to ask you something, and you need to be honest."

Elaine glances at Dad, who holds an opened envelope. An open envelope? What could—

"Look at me and listen," Mom says. "Are you and Joe married?"

The tension building in Elaine's shoulders releases. If that's what this is about, however they know, she'll be glad to tell them, which she should've done when she came home after her and Joe's last night at the river.

"Joe managed to get a short leave the last week of September and we got married. How do you know? I was coming home to tell you now."

Mom returns to the sofa. "Come here and sit with your dad and me." Although apprehension tightens Elaine's chest, she sits. Dad hands Mom the envelope, and she faces Elaine. "This letter is addressed to a 'Mrs. Joe Matthan.' I opened it when I saw that name. I hope you'll forgive me."

"There's nothing to forgive, Mom. I hope you both can forgive us. I wanted to get married before Joe left for Europe. We're sorry for not being honest."

Dad leaves the sofa, slides a chair over, and sits to face Elaine. He takes one hand and Mom takes another. The adrenalin burn of fear tingles along Elaine's back and into her throat. "Is this about Joe?"

Mom's head drops. Her tears wet Elaine's hand.

"Mom, why are you crying?" Dad lowers his head too. "Dad, look at me, what is it? Talk to me!"

"Elaine, I'm sorry, but we—" He raises his head. "But we don't know how to tell you this. The letter says Joe is missing in action."

"That doesn't mean he's— He said he'd be careful. He said

he'd do everything he could to come back to me." Elaine jumps from the sofa. "Joe can't die, I don't know if I can live without him!"

Mom raises her head. "We know it doesn't mean the worst, but we have to be prepared for—"

"Don't you dare say it, Mom. Don't even think it."

"Let me talk, you need to understand this. I want Joe to come home as much as you do, but you have to realize—"

"I don't have to realize *anything*." Elaine backs away from them. If they keep saying Joe is dead, she'll run outside and drive away and never come back.

"Elaine, please, we—"

"I won't hear it! Joe's coming home! They'll find him and he'll write. He'll be perfectly fine and I can tell him everything. You can't ask me to give up on him!"

Mom's chin trembles. A single teardrop rolls down Dad's cheek, which Elaine has never seen. "Dad, I—"

Someone knocks on the door and Elaine whips around. Her yellow hair ribbon twists and turns to the floor between her and the man she's seen delivering telegrams in town— telegrams that can only mean one thing.

Cold recognition slaps her face. Anger and heart-wrenching anguish smash against her throat. It hangs there building, tightening. She can't breathe, can't think.

"*No-o-o-o-o!*"

She collapses to the floor, throat raw from her scream. Gray clouds her vision. Barely visible, the yellow ribbon lies near the door. If she can just touch it, even with one reaching fingertip, Joe will come back to her like he said he would.

But the slender strand of yellow—along with her hopes and dreams for a lifetime of love—fades to black.

Chapter 23

Desperate Parents

Albert drops to his knees beside Elaine and rolls her from her stomach to her back. His desperate daughter's fingertips were almost touching the yellow hair ribbon before she fainted and her forehead thumped to the floor. She told Joe to wear it for good luck, and Albert had prayed as hard as he knew how that it would work. Now it hadn't, and she had lost the love of her young life, evidenced by the man with the telegram. Still, he had never dreamed his and Joe's family would be facing such a tragedy.

Mary comes from the kitchen with a wet dishtowel. She brushes Elaine's hair from her forehead and places the dishtowel there. "As much as I hate it, I think we know what that telegram is about."

"I think Elaine knows too, or she wouldn't have screamed and fainted." Albert goes to the porch and motions the man away from the door. "I suppose that telegram is for my daughter."

"I'm sorry about what happened, sir. This isn't the first time I've had a young lady faint like that." He gives Albert the telegram. "Elaine Matthan, correct?"

"I wish it wasn't."

"I'm sorry for your loss."

Albert watches the man walk back to his car, parked a good way behind Elaine's truck, which must be why they didn't hear him drive up. He opens the telegram. *We regret to inform you* confirms how his daughter's husband—the son-in-law he didn't know he had—is dead because of this damned war.

Inside, Mary is placing a pillow under Elaine's head. "I heard most of that."

Albert squeezes the back of his neck, the muscles knotting with tension. "I can't imagine what Will and Sarah are going through."

"Heaven help us, Albert. They don't know Joe and Elaine are married."

"We'll tell them when we can." Albert takes Elaine's yellow hair ribbon from the floor and kneels beside her and Mary. "That's not something I look forward to."

"I'm worried about Elaine. She should have woken by now. Carry her to her room while I call Dr. Roberts."

Albert takes Elaine in his arms. It's been years since he's carried her like this, and he'd give anything if he didn't have to do it now. He settles her in bed, takes off her muddy shoes, and pulls a quilt over her. It's also been years since he tucked her in like this. He puts the ribbon on her dresser and goes back to the bed.

Mary joins him. "I caught Dr. Roberts before he left the office. He's on his way."

Albert fingers a lock of hair out of Elaine's eyes. "How in the world do we handle this?"

"All we can do is our best and hope that's enough."

"If only it were that simple. I'll make coffee to help with this raw day. I can hear the doctor when he comes too."

When the percolator steams on the stove, Albert takes a cup

from the cabinet. Three sharp knocks announce the doctor. In the living room, Albert opens the screen door. "I'm sorry to keep you from going home, Dr. Roberts. Did Mary tell you why Elaine fainted?"

"Is she still unconscious?"

"I'm afraid so. She screamed and fainted when she saw the telegram delivery man. You know Joe Matthan, the boy she was seeing? He was killed in Europe."

* * *

Dr. Roberts notes Albert's choice of words: *the boy she was seeing.* That likely means Elaine hasn't told her parents about marrying Joe. If that's the case, they also don't know she's pregnant.

"I'm sure she's all right, Albert. Yes, Mary told me about Joe. News like this can be hard for a loved one to accept." He drapes his coat across a chair and adds his hat. "Elaine isn't the only young lady I've had to visit when the word came. A few fathers and mothers have needed something to calm their nerves as well."

He questions his next words. It's best to break the news with as much tact as possible.

"Let me take a look at Elaine. It had to be a shock to find out her husband has been killed."

In the middle of turning toward a hall, Albert faces the doctor. "How do you know they got married? We just found out ourselves. We don't think the Matthans know either."

The doctor pats the concerned father's shoulder. "Let me take a look at Elaine. Then we'll have a talk."

Albert leads him to a bedroom, where a quilt covers Elaine. Mary sits at the bedside, gently wiping her daughter's brow with a towel. She turns in the chair. "She still hasn't come

140

around, Dr. Roberts."

"She's had a severe mental shock, Mary. It's a shame about Joe." He takes a blood pressure cuff from his bag. "Let me see how she's doing." He checks Elaine's blood pressure, listens to her heart, touches his palm to her forehead. How to tell her parents about the pregnancy? It doesn't matter how, because his dilemma isn't as important as the safety of his two patients.

"Her vital signs are good. As I was telling Albert, news like this can be hard on a young woman." To give weight to his next sentence, he pauses. "Especially a young woman in her condition." Albert and Mary look at each other with puzzled expressions, then at him. It's time to spell it out. "Make sure she gets plenty of rest and healthy food. She needs her strength and nutrition, and so does the baby."

"Baby?" Mary says, her voice rising. "Elaine's going to have a *baby?*"

Albert shuffles to a chair and sits, his face pale. The doctor silently prays he won't have another patient on his hands. He closes his bag. "She stopped by today, saying she's been sick to her stomach. When I told her why, happy wasn't the word for it. She actually jumped off the examining table and twirled around, saying how she couldn't wait to tell Joe. I can't imagine getting such happy news, then getting such heartbreaking news right after it. I'm sure that's why the shock was so great."

Mary faces Albert. "Call Will and Sarah, they need to know about this." Albert, his pallor almost normal, rises from the chair and leaves. Mary stands too, although a bit unsteady on her feet. "Dr. Roberts, I'm— Well, I'm afraid of how Elaine will react when she wakes up. Do you have any suggestions?"

The doctor pauses; the struggle is obvious. Mary wants to do the absolute best for her daughter and grandchild. Other than that, he can't imagine what she's going through. If it weren't for this damn war. …

"Just be the parents I know you and Albert are. Love her … hold her when she cries … and give her time. It's going to take that and more before she feels like living again."

"That sounds like the best advice I could hope for."

"She *must* take care of herself too, for her and the baby's sake. It should help if she remembers she has a very important and precious part of Joe still with her."

"I hope so. Regardless, this is going to be difficult for everyone concerned. For the life of me I can't put myself in Will and Sarah's shoes, but I know they'll help too."

The doctor stands. "Of course they will, Mary, of course they will."

Mary heaves a deep sigh. "I think it might be a lot harder without a baby in the picture. Perhaps this little one will be a blessing we can all rally around. If I have anything to say about it—and I do—he or she will be the most loved baby in Nebraska."

In the living room, Doctor Roberts finds Albert on the sofa with a cup of coffee. "You have an exceptional daughter and wife, Albert. I'm sure you'll have an exceptional grandchild as well. Let me know if you need anything." He dons his coat and hat. "Remind Mary I'll need to start seeing Elaine regularly, beginning next month. If she doesn't wake in the next hour or so, give me a call. Take care now."

The doctor leaves the sad home. He's tired—*damn* tired. Tired of war. Tired of seeing happy wives turned into desperate widows. Tired of fatherless children. Tired of seeing mothers and fathers grieving as only mothers and fathers can when they lose a child. Tired of nurses losing their lives overseas as well and its effect on their loved ones.

A few miles outside of town, he passes the Matthans in their truck. Sarah holds a tissue to her eyes. Both of Will's hands grip the steering wheel. Any other time the doctor would wave. Instead, he says another silent prayer, this one for the two families to be able to gather around daughter and daughter-in-law and help her through such an impossible situation. How many families across the country are going through the same thing? Too many, no doubt. Perhaps, during their time of grief and pain, they'll have the same love and support Elaine will have.

The doctor sets his hat on the passenger seat and passes a hand through his thinning hair.

The sun is almost set behind the clearing western horizon. The first star twinkles into view in the east.

"Hope. Where would we be without it?"

Chapter 24

Facing Reality

Albert waits at the screen door while the Matthans walk from their truck. How to break the news of Elaine's pregnancy? Not without Mary's help, that's for sure. He holds the door open. Sarah, with red eyes, and Will, his lips a tight line, come in.

Albert closes the door. "I can't tell you how sorry we are about Joe. Mary and me loved that boy as if he were our own." Albert rubs the tightening muscles in the back of his neck. "I hate all this, and … and I don't know how we're going to handle it."

Tears flowing, Sarah hugs him. Will blinks, swallows, and places his arms around both of them. They separate, and Albert wipes his eyes.

"As sad as this is," Will says, "Elaine made Joe's last year on earth special. I'm going to miss him—I probably don't know how much yet—but I'm going to miss seeing them together. It was" —Will wipes his eyes— "it was like all the holidays wrapped in one."

"That's exactly how I feel," Sarah says

"I can't tell you how much I enjoyed having Joe around," Albert says. "He and Elaine … well …" Before his trickling tears become a river, he turns away.

"How's Elaine?" Will asks. "You said she fainted when she saw the man with the telegram?"

Albert faces them again. "Dr. Roberts said she'll be fine."

"That's good. I'm sure she was shocked when—" Will tilts his head to one side. "Why did Elaine get a telegram? I thought they were for the next of kin?"

"That's why I called. Let me see if Mary can step away."

Albert returns with Mary. Sarah hugs her and they both cry. Will fingers moisture from his own eyes and so does Albert. He goes to the kitchen for tissues, hands them out, and suggests they sit.

Sarah wipes her cheeks. "Elaine isn't awake yet?"

"Dr. Roberts said she should wake soon." Mary balls the tissue in her hand. "I'm sorry we asked you over."

"Don't be sorry for calling," Will says. "If there's anything we can do to help Elaine, anything at all …"

Albert glances at Mary. "We asked you over because we found out a couple of things you should— Well, you *need* to know." Albert takes a breath. He might as well start with the letter. "The mail came while Elaine was in town. One envelope was addressed to a 'Mrs. Joe Matthan.'"

Will slides forward in the chair. "Why would it be addressed like that?"

"Because— Well, you'll see. Mary regrets it but she opened it. It was from the Army, it said Joe was missing in action. I suppose you got the same letter addressed to you."

"We did," Sarah says. "Right before we got the telegram."

"I wish I hadn't opened that letter," Mary says. "The only thing we could think is Elaine and Joe had gotten married without telling anyone."

"We asked her when she got home," Albert says. "They got

married in late September, and she said they were sorry for keeping it secret. I don't blame them one bit. Those two wanted to get married and I'm glad they did."

"If that's the case," Will says, "I'm happy they spent time together as husband and wife before … before Joe …" Will's throat muscles tighten as he swallows.

Albert hopes the final news will be more welcome—perhaps so welcome it will help everyone get over the immediate grief overwhelming them.

"We need to tell you one more thing. I'll be honest, at first it was such a shock, I didn't know how to feel. Now that I've had a little time to think about it …"

"This is more news about Joe and Elaine," Mary says. "I happen to believe it's a miracle."

"I'm as ready for a miracle as I've ever—" Sarah stops midsentence. "No … Elaine's pregnant?"

"That she is," Mary says. "Dr. Roberts told us Elaine stopped by today because she was sick to her stomach. I think she was about to tell us before she fainted, since she admitted to her and Joe being married. Dr. Roberts had to tell us because Elaine will need her rest. We'll have to make sure she takes care of herself too."

"That means Joe—" Sarah wipes her eyes with the tattered remains of the tissue. "Joe didn't know he was going to be a father."

"We're all going to be grandparents?" Will asks. "Good Lord above, all this sadness and a ray of hope shines through. Unbelievable."

"We need to do all we can to help Elaine," Sarah says. "That's what's important now, her and the baby."

"Mom? Daddy?"

Albert runs to Elaine's room. When's the last time she called for her daddy? She's sitting up in bed. He holds her but she doesn't cry. It's like there's a dam inside her, blocking off her pain. He eases away, not sure what to think.

* * *

Elaine jerks upright in bed. The vision of the man holding the telegram—including the reason he was on her doorstep—bursts upon her. Emptiness engulfs her; it bites at her heart, numb from so much pain. Why isn't she crying? Joe's dead. She should be hysterical, grieving, almost dying herself. Her room is empty. "Mom? Daddy?"

Heavy footsteps echo in the hall. Dad runs in and holds her, only to pull away. His eyes ask questions she can't answer.

"I can't cry, Daddy. Why ... why can't I cry?"

The Matthans come in. Sarah rushes over and holds her. The grief Elaine just questioned engulfs her. Struck by another realization, one that adds another layer of heartache, she cries even harder. Not only has she lost Joe, Sarah has lost her son. Their crying gradually slows to sniffles. Sarah holds her at arm's length.

"Elaine, I couldn't love you more if you were my own daughter. That goes for Will too. Day or night, you're welcome in our home, okay?" Tears threaten again. Elaine can only nod.

Mom comes over. "Sweetheart, we called Dr. Roberts when you fainted. He told us about you having a baby. You realize we're all here for you, I know, but I want to make *sure* you know."

Sarah goes to Will. Dad kneels by the bed. "Honey, we'll do whatever it takes to get you through this. That means helping with the baby too."

Mom glances back at the Matthans. "We all consider this

baby a blessing. I've already decided our grandchild is going to be the most loved baby in Nebraska."

"Knowing your mother like I do," Dad says, "I think she means it."

"Darn right," Will says. "Sarah and I understand why you and Joe got married."

"We need to say goodbye," Sarah says. "Elaine needs her rest." She comes over again. "I realize we have a lot to deal with. We'll get through it because Joe would insist. I know that as sure as we're all standing here. I'll stop by tomorrow."

"Thank you for coming," Elaine says. "I know you're hurting too." A fresh wave of tears threatens, but a ray of hope stops them. "Now that you and Will know about Joe and me getting married, I can think of you as family. Yes, I know I can count on you." She pauses, amazed that the faintest of smiles hints at the corners of her mouth. "But I knew that before, didn't I?"

Sarah hugs her. "I'm sure you did. See you tomorrow, I love you."

"I love you too, both of you."

"Try to rest and do what the doctor says," Will says. "Like Sarah said, we have a lot to deal with, but sure as I'm standing here, I know Joe is somewhere looking forward to the birth of his son or daughter as much as we all are put together."

"That includes Thomas," Dad says to Elaine. "He's probably wondering why you left him at school."

"Let him wonder," Elaine says. "Just remember to tell him he's going to have another fishing partner when you pick him up."

Chapter 25

A Realization, a Picnic and a Photograph, and an Enemy

Having just finished one of several nightly crying episodes, Elaine rolls over in bed. Warm tears track down her temples and pool in her ears. Except for last week, when Mom insisted she venture into the kitchen at meal times, she's stayed in her room since Joe died.

Often, her heart aches as if it's lost its will to continue beating, as if it's drying up, about to be blown away in a bone-numbing Nebraska snowstorm. If she allows it, the pain is overwhelming, but after a few nights of hysterical tears, Joe's wishes for her happiness tease themselves into her thoughts. It's then that she recalls their wedding and honeymoon by the river. It's then that she thinks of the result of that night. It's then that she can feel his love warming her, existing within the tiny body inside her. As the grief from Joe's death gradually dulls, she holds onto these positive thoughts more often. After all, she has them because of Joe.

On her bedside table, a small hourglass sparkles in the lamplight, and she spends countless hours watching, turning, watching. One night, after turning the hourglass over and over endlessly, an epiphany of sorts reveals itself. Time can do many things, and it might even heal her heart. She turns the hourglass one last time. But the sands of time will never scour away her love for Joe. Yes, eventually she has to move on, both for her and her child, but she'll never stop—no matter what—loving Joe.

* * *

Elaine wakes. A spring shower, one of several this April, whispers a waterfall of sound against the tin roof. Illuminated by the orange light of the rising sun, water streams down the window pain. The top sash is open a bit, and the smell is fresh and clean, foretelling the changing season.

She turns the lamp on beside her bed. Under the dim light, glowing like a jar of weary fireflies she caught on many a summer evening as a child, she studies each of the three photographs of her and Joe, which includes the picture of them when they were married. She's never shown this particular photograph to anyone and finally understands why: she couldn't share—didn't dare to—or he might be lost forever, because the photograph is all she has left of him. This can't be further from the truth.

The rain gradually stops, leaving a smattering of shimmering droplets on the window. Someone knocks on her door. Instead of tucking the pictures away, Elaine keeps them in her hand.

"Elaine," Mom says, "can I come in?"

"I'm awake."

The open door allows the aroma of coffee and bacon in. Mom pulls a chair to the bed. "Do you feel like breakfast yet?" Her eyes lower. "What do you have there?"

"Something I should have shown you and Dad before now. Will and Sarah too."

"You mean the pictures of you and Joe?"

Elaine offers the pictures. Mom studies them one by one, glancing from each to Elaine. At the last picture, her eyes open wide. "Is this when you and Joe got married?" Tears trickle down Elaine's cheeks. Mom takes an always-available handkerchief from her pocket.

Wiping her cheeks, Elaine nods. "I'm sorry I didn't show it to you before now. I just figured out why, I think. Can we get copies made? I want to have two framed—one for my room and one for Sarah and Will. They really should have one."

Mom returns the pictures. "We can check the next time we're in town." She takes the handkerchief from Elaine. "But I need a favor."

"What's that?"

"I expect to get a picture too."

Elaine shoves Mom's arm. "You *better* want one."

The wrinkles lining Mom's forehead, nearly constant since Joe died, smooth away to a suggestion. "Your father and I have been talking. If you'd still like to go to college later, we'll be happy to take care of the baby. It'll be a while before you can go, but you still can."

"I can't think about that now, Mom."

"The option's there, when the time comes." At the door, Mom starts to close it.

"Mom?"

She peeks around the door. "Yes, honey?"

"When the time comes."

* * *

Elaine leaves the doctor's office. Behind her, Mom laughs. "You remind me of our ducks waddling at the pond."

"I bet you did your share of waddling with me and Thomas, smarty."

"I sure did. Waddle yourself to the truck so we can get home and show your father those pictures."

Driving along main street, Mom slows for a young man crossing in front of them. Because of his blond hair and similar height, Elaine can almost swear he's Joe. "Do you know who that is?"

"He's the German prisoner helping the Edwards," Mom says, turning her head toward him. "There's Mr. Edwards behind him."

The two men stop at the hardware store. Mr. Edwards points at something in a display.

Elaine whirls the window down. "Go back to Germany and leave us alone!" she yells. The men enter the store, apparently not hearing her above the noise of the busy street.

At home, Dad meets them at the door. "They just announced the end of the war in Europe, can you believe it?"

Elaine runs to her room and cries. If the war had ended a few short months ago, Joe would be home soon.

Having gotten her cry out, she walks down the hall for supper. The phone rings as she passes it; she takes the call. "Johnsons."

"This is Sarah, Elaine. I imagine you've heard the news. If you're like me, I have mixed feelings about it."

"I know. If the fighting in Europe had ended a few months ago, Joe would be coming home."

"I guess we should be thankful."

"It's hard, but Joe would want that."

"I was calling to suggest we all meet at the river for his birthday next month."

Elaine doesn't reply. She hasn't visited her and Joe's special place since their wedding night, and she's afraid it will bring back too many agonizing memories. Still, she'll have time to frame her and Joe's wedding picture for the Matthans and give it to them then.

** * **

On the day of the picnic, Elaine arrives at the river early to have some time to herself. The morning air chills her, but she welcomes the sun's rays as she watches the rolling water. The old oak stands majestically, making its seasonal attempt at acquiring a new suit of green foliage. The driftwood log she and Joe used as a seat is gone, washed away during one of many spring storms.

At the oak, to relive her and Joe's last night together, she leans against the coarse bark. Just as he starts to sing *Poor Wayfaring Stranger*, the slow rumble of an engine and the intermittent squeak of suspension springs comes from the direction of dirt path. Did Mom and Dad come early? Or maybe Joe's mom and dad?

The truck—one of the two she passed at the Edwards' house—tops the last rise, bounces down the path, and stops on the other side of the oak upriver. The same German prisoner she saw in Alma hops out. Elaine leaves the oak and strides toward him, fists clenched. "My family's having a picnic here and you need to leave—right now!"

Retrieving his fishing gear from the back of the truck, the man throws it back in and slams the door behind him. A gray gout of gaseous exhaust blasts from the tailpipe. The truck backs up, spins around, and bounces up the rutted path. Tires spin. Fenders rattle. Dust swirls.

Satisfied, Elaine returns to the oak. Still, she feels a twinge of shame at her reaction, which may have been overreaction. Regardless, some strange person shouldn't intrude on her time here, especially when that strange person is a former German soldier.

At the oak again, she sits, leans against it, and closes her eyes, ready to hear Joe finish the song. The squeak of springs and a metallic rattle comes from the path again. She jumps up and grabs a fallen branch. That German will wish he never came to Alma when *she* gets through with him. The truck, with the Matthans inside, comes into view. Elaine throws the branch away. Thank goodness she doesn't have to look at the German who bears such an eerie resemblance to Joe again.

She helps the Matthans carry food to the oak. At her truck, she gets the bag with the framed wedding picture, pauses, and goes to the Matthan's truck for the old quilt behind the seat. At the oak, Sarah eyes her but says nothing. She probably realizes how many memories are stored in its old stitches.

They spread the quilt and sit. Elaine opens the bag with the picture. "I'm sorry I didn't show you this before, but it took me a while to realize you might need it as much as I have." She gives the framed photo to Sarah.

* * *

Will slides closer to Sarah. She holds a picture of Joe and Elaine. "Is this when you two got married?" she says.

"It sure is. Do you like it?"

Sarah clutches the picture to her breast, and tears stream down her cheeks. Will imagines it feels like Joe has come home, even if in this fleeting manner. Elaine hugs Sarah and cries too, and Will wraps his arms around both of his most special ladies. Will Elaine's scars from Joe's death ever heal? Or Sarah's? Or his own?

Sarah gives him the picture. Seeing his son on his wedding day, Will cherishes the fact that Elaine gave Joe so much happiness in so short a time. Wiping his own eyes, he faces her. "Have we ever told you how much it means to us that you and Joe found each other?"

"Oh!" Elaine places her hand to her stomach.

"What's wrong?" Sarah asks.

"Yes, Will," Elaine says. "I know how much it means to you that Joe and I found each other." She places Sarah's hand on her rounded tummy. "And this little monkey knows it too."

Sarah's hand rises and Will grins. Sarah glances at him, then returns to Elaine. "Do you mind if Will …?"

"Not at all."

"Are you sure?" Will asks, his cheeks warming. "If it's too personal …"

"Phooey on that. You need to say hello too."

Sarah places his hand where hers was. As he concentrates, a tentative push raises his hand, followed by another. He takes his hand away. "He feels like a strong young fellow to me."

"How do you know he's a he?" Sarah asks.

"Why not? I *do* have a fifty percent chance of being right, you know."

Elaine crosses her hands on her stomach. "Joseph Albert Matthan. I haven't thought about a girl's name. I'll find out if I need one in a month."

Up the path, a transmission whines as it's downshifted into low. Albert and Mary pull up. Everyone helps carry food to the quilt.

Thomas joins them minutes later. He'll be eighteen in a few months. With the war in Europe over, he should be able to stay home. Will is glad for the young man. Still, for a fleeting moment, the anguish of Joe not being there tightens his throat.

***

Done with lunch, Elaine joins Thomas on the riverbank while he fishes. To Will, they could be her and Joe standing there on their first date. He looks away. If the vision follows him home, he might not be able to hold his tears in until he can get to the barn.

"Albert, Mary, I'm happy Thomas will avoid the war. As we all know, it's taken too many of our boys."

"We appreciate the thought," Albert says. "You doing okay these days?"

"Well, sometimes Joe's death gets to me. You and Mary won't have to go through what Sarah and I have, and I'm glad."

Albert gently claps Will's back. "I understand. There's nothing I'd like more than to have Joe standing right there with Thomas and Elaine." Albert leans close and gives Will's shoulders a squeeze.

The warm embrace comforts Will. He and Albert have grown close since Joe's death, and he cherishes his friend's gentle ways and understanding demeanor.

"You're just like Elaine, Al. Joe told me how she could always turn a serious moment into a light one." He grins. "He also told me how Mary teased him about rushing them to get married on the day she met him. That tells me where Elaine gets her humor from."

The sun begins its downward slide toward the horizon, all golden with the promise of a new beginning.

Will marvels at how well the day has gone.

Joe would be pleased.

* * *

When everyone rises from the quilt to leave, Elaine keeps her seat. "I'd like to stay a while. Do you mind leaving the quilt,

Sarah?"

"Please keep it. Since you and Joe used it here, I'm sure it means a lot to you."

The three trucks rattle and squeak up the path. In the last one, Thomas waves.

Elaine lies on the quilt, still warm from the presence of her two families. The tree's branches sigh with the slight breeze, bringing back her conversation with Joe concerning how they were falling in love.

The baby moves. An arm or a foot traces a raised line across the surface of her tummy. She places her hand there, reassured by the gentle nudge.

"Don't worry, sweetheart, Mommy's here."

The leaves above her rustle as if they're Joe whispering, *I love you.* She doesn't know whether to cry or smile.

"And Daddy's here too, sweetheart. Deep inside our hearts."

Chapter 26

Birth

Lightning brightens Elaine's room. Thunder rattles the window. Hail pounds the tin roof. Wind howls around the corners of the farmhouse. Sweat beads her forehead. Contraction after contraction wracks her body as Mom lets her squeeze her hand.

"Just a bit more," Dr. Roberts says. "We're almost there."

Through the haze of pain compressing Elaine's middle, Joe's face appears. Instead of allowing the agony to consume her, she imagines his arms around her, imagines his strength helping her, imagines his love for both her and his child. As the edge of a scream tightens her throat, she clenches her teeth and pushes.

"Here he comes," Dr. Roberts says. "He's— Mary, I need you."

Elaine jerks up from the pillow. "What's wrong?"

"Lie down." Mom's voice is stern. "Let the doctor do his work."

"Elaine," the doctor says, "he's coming out behind first, and I think the umbilical cord is wrapped around his neck."

Elaine drops to the sweaty pillow. Hasn't she lost enough already? Joe and now Joseph?

"Push hard, Elaine. One more time so I can get him out."

Teeth clenched again, Elaine holds another scream and pushes."

"Unwrap the cord while I hold him, Mary. I'll pop his behind to get him breathing." Three sharp pops come from behind the sheet over Elaine's raised legs. "I don't understand," the doctor says. "He should be crying by now. Scrub him with one of those towels, Mary. Gotta get him pink instead of blue."

"Oh my God, he won't move," Mom says. "Why won't he move? Come on, Joseph, Elaine needs you."

"I'm sorry, Mary, I don't think he's going—"

"*Waaaaaahhhhhhhhhh!*"

"You rascal," Mom says. "You're teasing us exactly like Elaine would tease us."

"He's a loud young fellow," the doctor says, chuckling. "I do believe he's saying, 'Look out Nebraska, here I come.'"

"I'll clean him up while you finish with Elaine," Mom says.

Elaine holds the pillow over her face and cries. She might as well have died if she lost Joseph too. Thank God he's all right.

Mom coos while she cleans him. "Okay, Elaine, it's time to hold this handsome young man. He looks exactly like a miniature Joe."

Elaine tucks Joseph in the crook of her arm. "Hey there, Joseph. Did you finally decide to see what the world looks like after you scared me half to death?" She studies his pink face. "Look at those blue eyes, you *do* look like your daddy." She chokes back a sob. "I'm so sorry he couldn't be here. I promise I'll tell you all about him one day. I'll take you to our special place too—you'll love it as much as we did."

Mom takes Joseph. "We need to let Dr. Roberts put in a stitch or two."

The doctor finishes his work. Mom returns Joseph to Elaine. "I better scoot and tell everyone you two are okay."

Minutes later, footsteps clomp in the hall. Dad sticks his head in the doorway. "Hi, honey, care for some company?"

"Why not? The more the merrier."

Joseph's four grandparents pile into the room.

"Will," Mom says, "Elaine told me what you said about the baby being a boy. She's holding our new grandson, Joseph Albert Matthan."

Everyone circles the bed to take turns holding the squirming bundle. They marvel at the never-ending wonder of new life, commenting on the perfection of every tiny finger, of every tiny toe. Elaine's cheeks ache from smiling. The previous Sunday at church, the minister preached the Bible story concerning the origin of the rainbow. Joseph, the timely reminder of hope, along with her ability to smile again, means the same thing: a rainbow of promise after the storm.

Dr. Roberts comes in. "Elaine, Joseph is as healthy a little man as I have ever helped bring into the world." He picks up his black satchel. "Mary, Albert, call if you need me. I'll phone in the morning to see how these two are doing." He steps to the bedside. "Congratulations, Elaine. I think Joseph is ready to take on the world." He glances back at the four grandparents. "And with a group of loving people like this to help him along, he's already got a head start."

Thomas sticks his head in the door. "Hey, Sis. If my new fishing buddy is big enough to fish in six months, maybe Santa will bring him a new rod and reel for Christmas."

* * *

Holding Joseph's plump self in her arms, Elaine points at the Christmas tree. "Can you see your blond hair and blue eyes in the ornament, Joseph?"

Mom hangs another glass bulb on a cedar branch. "I bought these so he can. Do you think he can?"

"If he can," Dad says, draping strands of tinsel on the tree "you won't know it until he's old enough to tell you. I'm glad I saved a cedar when I cut back those fencerows. I love the smell."

Mary eyes him. "As much as you love the smell of that ham in the oven?"

"It depends on what Sarah's turkey smells like." He glances at his watch. "She and Will should be here any—"

Knock-knock.

"That must be them." Elaine holds the door open. Will brings in a foil-wrapped turkey. Sarah brings in a still-steaming pan of dressing.

"Merry Christmas," they say together. Will takes the turkey to the kitchen and returns to tickle Joseph's chin. "How's my chunky grandson? Are you ready to eat up the world?"

Dad hangs the last strands of tinsel on the tree. "Good idea, Will. I'm ready myself."

* * *

Stuffed with turkey, ham, dressing, green beans, mashed potatoes, and pumpkin pie, Elaine sits beside Thomas in the floor to hand out presents. On the sofa, Mom and Sarah take turns holding Joseph. Dad and Albert are in chairs at the end of the sofa. Everyone lets Joseph pull ribbons and bows and tear wrapping paper to help open their presents.

Presents done, Will gives Elaine an envelope from his pocket. "This is from Sarah and me, and Joe too."

She takes a letter from the envelope, along with a check. She reads the letter.

Dear Elaine,
I'm sorry if you're reading this because we both know what it means.
I won't say more because I know you'll cry, and I don't like to think
of you being unhappy. I told Mom and Dad to give you my college
money. When you can, I want you to go to school so you can be a
teacher. I know you'll be great at it. Please do this for me. More
importantly, do it for yourself.
Love always,
Joe
P.S. I want you to have my guitar. Don't forget to sing and be happy.
I want that for you more than anything.
Love, Joe.

Elaine clutches the letter to her chest. Regardless of Joe's wish, she can't help crying. Joseph lets out a cry himself, and Mom hands him over. Grinning, he pats Elaine's cheeks, giving her no choice but to grin along with him.

Will goes outside and comes back to place Joe's guitar case under the tree.

"You know," Elaine says, "I never could get the hang of playing that thing. Maybe Joseph will try it one day."

Thomas shoves Elaine's shoulder. "Maybe I should give it a try and show you how it's done."

Elaine shoves him back. "You'd give it up as soon as spring gets here. You know how you like to fish."

Will laughs. "Thomas, since I don't have time to use Joe's rod and reels, you can have them. Just make sure you drop off a catfish fillet once in a while."

Thomas gives Will a thumbs-up. "Thanks, Mr. Matthan, it's

a deal."

"As far as the guitar," Will says, "you're right, Elaine. Maybe Joseph will like to play it one day. Or if not him, maybe his grandson or great-grandson. Anyway, I'd like to see Joe's guitar stay in the family."

"I'll make sure it does. Thank you both for everything." Elaine glances at the check. "Did Joe have another job I didn't know about? There's no way he made this much working at the hardware store."

"It includes what we saved," Sarah says. "We want you to have it, so no arguing."

Elaine sits Joseph in Mom's lap and goes to the Matthans. "I don't know what to say."

Sarah stands. "Thank you is fine but hugs are better." Elaine hugs her.

"Don't forget your father-in-law," Will says. Elaine hugs him too.

"Also," Sarah says, "you can thank us by doing what Joe said. Be happy—have a happy life. If that money can help, we're glad for you to have it. The only thing I ask is when you go to college, please let us help take care of Joseph. We've gotten Joe's old baby bed out and cleaned it, and we're making Joe's room into Joseph's room. I hope that's all right."

"Of course it is," Mom says. "We wouldn't want it any other way, would we, Albert?"

Dad tickles Joseph under his chin. "Mary, it's just like you said the day this little man came into the world, he's going to be the most loved baby in Nebraska."

"He sure is," Thomas says. "With all that education you got coming, Sis, he'll have the smartest mom too."

Chapter 27

Kurt and Lainey

On the way back home from Alma, Kurt admires his gold wedding band, which sparkles in the warm afternoon sun that shines through the windshield of Lainey's old SUV. He touches the miniature Cape Hatteras Lighthouse dangling from the rear-view mirror, and his revived hardware store memories allow him a cherished look into his past.

That Saturday April morning in 1948, three years after returning from Germany to live with the Edwards, Kurt parks outside the hardware store. Mrs. Edwards needs vegetable seeds for the garden, and this is the only place in Alma to get them.

As he shoves the heavy wooden door open, the brass bell overhead jingles. Mr. Hansen, the store's proprietor, waves. At the counter, Kurt takes a list from his pocket. "Hello, Mr. Hansen, are the vegetable seeds in?"

"Just in yesterday." The slightly balding and white-bearded Hansen points. "Got some new bins around the corner. Holler if you need help."

Trying to read the lettering on the bins, Kurt hurries to the rear of the store. Passing a counter, his knee hits something, and a blond-headed boy sprawls across the floor. Kurt starts toward the crying boy to see if he's hurt, but a woman rounds the counter, high heels clicking, yellow dress flaring. She sets the boy on his feet and touches his forehead. "There, there, sweetheart, it's just a small bump." She kisses the boy and wipes his eyes with a tissue from her purse. His crying eases to sniffles. She stands, brown eyes furious, nostrils flaring.

"Mr. Whoever-you-are, are you blind? I saw you looking at those seeds but thought for sure you'd see my little boy and not knock him across the—"

"Ma'am, I—"

"Don't interrupt. If you can't see a little boy right in front of you, you'll be wondering why you have tomato vines growing in your sink and knives and forks sticking up out of your garden."

"Very sorry, ma'am," Kurt mutters in his German accented English while fingering the strap of his denim overalls.

"Not half as sorry as you will be if you don't pay better attention from now on." She takes the boy by the hand and strides to the counter. "I'll be back Monday, Mr. Hansen." She cuts a sideways glance at Kurt. "When your store isn't full of imbeciles who can't see something as big as my little boy."

Catching a sweet whiff of her perfume, Kurt shuffles to the counter. If he didn't know any better, he's just met the wrath of Mother Nature herself. The woman's high heels click a drumbeat tempo across the wood floor. She jerks the door open, and the brass bell rings with shrill, metallic insistence. The door slams behind her, leaving the bell to ring again.

Kurt turns around. Mr. Hansen covers his mouth and laughs. Kurt goes over to the wood stove, rubbing the back of his neck, and waits until Hansen's laughter subsides to chuckles. "She was right," Kurt says. "I was not paying attention. I feel like an id— What is the word? Id—?"

"Idiot, Kurt, you feel like an idiot."

"Yes, sir, that is it. I hope he is not hurt."

"I wouldn't worry about it. Little boys have been getting bumps on their heads for as long as there've been little boys."

Relieved, Kurt sits. The last thing in the world he wants is to hurt anyone, especially a little boy. He admires how the young mother stood up to him. After all, she was only trying to protect her son. Then again, when he recalls her intense brown eyes and her long sun-streaked ponytail tied with a yellow ribbon, including how it swirled about as she told Mr. Hansen she had no time for "imbeciles," he admires her physical qualities also.

"Who is she, Mr. Hansen?"

"Elaine Matthan. She'll be our new teacher this fall. We're glad to have her. Good teachers are scarce around these parts."

"What is her son's name?"

"Joseph. She lives with her parents, Albert and Mary Johnson. Her father has a farm."

Another question hesitates on Kurt's lips, but not enough to halt his growing curiosity. "Can I ask why she is living with her mother and father?"

"It's a sad story, one of the worst to come out of the war for us here in Alma. Sure you want to hear it?"

Hansen's statement jogs Kurt's memory. The Edwards had talked about the young man and woman who loved to visit the river. Then he remembers the worst part: how the man died in the war only three months after they were married.

"I heard the Edwards talking about it. You are right, it is a very sad thing." Kurt's heart aches for her. He knows all too well the tragedies that unfolded for too many families during World War II. His own parents and three sisters all died in the bombing of his hometown.

Since the little boy's mother is single, he allows himself a small hope. Can she ever care for him? His hope fades. He is the enemy. His accent proves it. The scar on his forehead proves it. The way some of the townspeople treat him in the years after the war prove it. Regardless of his past, the Edwards care about him. Still, they know him, beyond the scar across his forehead and the label of German soldier.

Kurt rubs his forehead. Is there any way Elaine can get to know him like the Edwards know him? He stops rubbing his forehead and taps his chin.

She *did* say she would be back on Monday.

Chapter 28

Forgiveness

Monday morning, Kurt rises with the sun, feeds the chickens clucking and scratching around the yard, and goes to the kitchen for a cup of coffee with Mr. Edwards, who's finishing breakfast. Mrs. Edwards sets a plate of eggs, bacon, and toast on the table. "Any plans for today, Kurt?"

"Do you mind … I mean, is it all right if I pick some daffodils?" Kurt rubs his forehead. The Edwards constantly tell him he's learning English well. Reading it and studying it as a schoolboy in Germany is helping, although contractions are a puzzle even they have trouble explaining.

"Have as many as you like," Mrs. Edwards says. "They grow like weeds around the well house."

"Do you have something I could put them in?"

Mr. Edwards scoops the last bit of jelly onto his toast and hands Kurt the empty Mason jar. "There you go. Give it a quick rinse first."

"Thank you, Mr. Edwards." Between bites of eggs, bacon, toast, and sips of coffee, Kurt studies the jar's grape-flavored streaks. "I forgot the seeds Saturday. I need to go back to town for them."

"You paying John in daffodils?" Mr. Edwards asks, pausing

from his toast to grin. "If you are, make sure to rinse that jar."

In his room, Kurt writes a short note, folds it into a long, narrow shape, and tucks it into his shirt pocket. At the well house, he rinses the jar and cuts enough daffodils with his pocketknife to fit. He needs one more item to complete his plan. Unfortunately, it's only available in town.

On Mondays, unlike Saturdays, Main Street in Alma lacks the busy rush of shoppers acquiring necessary basics such as flour, sugar, coffee, or anything not readily available on a farm. Although the lack of people lightens Kurt's step, he still doesn't look forward to the sewing shop. The one time he went there for a zipper for Mrs. Edwards to mend a pair of his pants, the owner and the customers looked at him as if he had just come off the battlefield with a rifle and a snarl, bloody from killing Americans. Kurt hopes this visit will be different, but he has his doubts. Maybe the citizens of Alma will accept him one day, or if not all of them, most of them. After all, Mr. Hansen and the Edwards are nice to him.

Opening the glass-fronted door of the sewing shop results in its bell jingling exactly like the one at the hardware store. Two women cut their eyes toward Kurt. He closes the door and the bell rings again. The same women whisper to each other while shaking their heads. His cheeks warm, but he's determined to get the last item he needs for the daffodils.

Behind the counter, a tall woman with a pair of reading glasses perched on the end of her narrow nose appraises him. "Can I help you? Or is it possible your reading skills—*English* reading skills—have mistakenly led you to my establishment?"

Kurt fights the urge to wrinkle his nose at the sickly-sweet aroma of the woman's perfume. "Very sorry to bother you, ma'am. I am looking for yellow ribbon."

The woman tilts her head back and peers at him over the glasses. *"This* way." He follows her to the front counter, where she points to several rolls of ribbon hanging on a display. "If this isn't to your liking ..."

"This is fine, ma'am, thank you." Kurt pays for the ribbon and scurries out of the sewing shop, vowing to never return.

Back in the truck, he ties a length of ribbon around the daffodils in their Mason jar vase and inserts the note within the green stems. Thank goodness the hardware store is beside the sewing shop. He won't have to drive anywhere and take a chance on missing Elaine. He looks up and down the sidewalk to make sure no shoppers head his way, gives the flowers one last check, and hurries up the steps to the hardware store.

The brass bell's strident ring makes Kurt duck as if it's a bullet whizzing over his head in the war. Nervousness clings to him like the cockle-burrs sticking to his overalls after a day in one of Mr. Edwards' fields.

A group of elderly men circled around the wood stove whip their heads toward him. Freezing in midstep, he supposes they've never seen anyone carrying a Mason jar filled with ribbon-wrapped daffodils down the aisle of this dusty old hardware store before, let alone an ex-German soldier carrying it. As he continues, their eyes follow him and their heads turn, reminding Kurt of several owls huddled in the rafters of Mr. Edward's largest barn.

At the counter, Kurt places the jar in front of Mr. Hansen. "Please give this to Mrs. Matthan when she comes. It is to apolo—" Kurt pauses at the difficult word. He needs to slow down for those when he's nervous. "It is to a-po-lo-gize for Saturday."

The white-aproned store owner glances at the flowers. "I

would, Kurt, but she's already come and gone."

Kurt's mouth falls open. "Come and gone?"

"About fifteen minutes ago, give or take."

"Where is she—" Kurt rubs his forehead. What a dummkopf he is. "I mean, did she say where she is going?"

"I think she mentioned the post office. Maybe the ladies' sewing shop next—"

Kurt grabs the flowers and runs to the door, hoping he can catch her at the post office. About to grab the doorknob he stops. On the sidewalk, Elaine and Joseph stroll by, hand-in-hand toward the sewing shop. Kurt opens the door until the brass bells rewards him with a single, muffled ding. On the steps of the sewing shop, Elaine wipes a smudge from Joseph's face. She stands, and Kurt ducks back in. The brass bell on the sewing shop door jingles. On the sidewalk yet again, he wipes sweat from his brow. Now he has to go into *that* store again.

The jar drips water onto his hands. His coming and going and dodging and ducking has loosened the ribbon around the daffodils, whose heads droop like weary soldiers on the march. He sets the jar on the hood of his truck to straighten the blooms and re-tie the ribbon. That task done, he starts toward the sewing shop and stops, spilling more water on his hands.

Behind the glass door, Elaine's amusement makes his heart flutter as if his chest is filled with butterflies. Brown eyes crinkle. Shoulders bounce. Her girlish laughter teases the corners of his own mouth into a smile.

She takes Joseph's hand and comes out to join Kurt on the sidewalk. "Well, sir, have you come to town to run over another little boy or three?"

"I, uh … no, ma'am, not at all."

Elaine laughs again: light, airy, and possibly forgiving.

Joseph blinks blue eyes at his mother, then at Kurt. Elaine stops laughing. "I'm sorry I gave you such a hard time Saturday, but you really must watch where you're going. Joseph got quite a bump on his head. Now, what do you have there?"

"What? What do I have—"

"In your hand. Is that a new way of washing work boots, with daffodil water?" Her lips crease with a suppressed grin, and Kurt remembers the flowers, along with everything else he has done to get to this moment.

"These are for— I mean, I want to say I am sorry. I did not mean to hurt your son."

"I realize that, Mr. ...?"

Kurt can hardly believe she isn't angry, or how they are actually having a civil conversation. "My name is Kurt Bauer. I help the Edwards on their farm."

* * *

Elaine can hardly believe it. This is the man she yelled at when she and Mom went to town for the pictures. He's also the man she chased away from the river on the day of the picnic for Joe's birthday. Regardless of being an ex-German soldier, which should've been apparent from his accent, he seems decent enough.

"I realize you didn't mean to hurt Joseph, Mr. Bauer." Take the daffodils or not? Put them on the kitchen table or not? Pour them out on the side of the road or not? She takes the flowers. "My name is Elaine Matthan. Joseph, tell Mr. Bauer goodbye."

Kurt kneels beside him. "I am sorry I made you bump your head, Joseph." Joseph slides behind Elaine's legs and peeks at Kurt, who stands. "He is a beautiful little boy. I was the only boy in my family. I had three sisters."

"I really must go, Mr. Bauer. Thank you for the daffodils."

"Please call me Kurt."

She turns to leave.

"Goodbye, E—E-laine-y."

She stops. "What?"

"I am sorry. My English is not good with some words."

Elaine's grandpa called her Lainey when she was a girl. That might be easier to pronounce, but should she tell Kurt? She really doesn't care to make this ex-German soldier feel as if she wants to get to know him. Still, it's never wrong to treat people decently. "When I was around Joseph's age, my grandpa called my Lainey."

"Lai-ney," Kurt says slowly. He tries again, faster. "Lainey. Yes, that is easier."

"Since that's easier, Kurt, you can call me Lainey."

Chapter 29

Filling the Blanks

Elaine's intimate sharing of her childhood name fills Kurt with warmth. "Thank you, Lainey. It is nice to meet you and Joseph."

"You too, goodbye."

Beside Elaine as she walks away, Joseph looks back and waves. Kurt returns the wave and goes in the hardware store. Despite the persistent jingle of the brass bell overhead, he smiles hugely while waiting for the bell to finish ringing. Then he opens and closes the door six more times, ringing the bell in time to the song *Jingle Bells*.

Ring-ring-ring—ring-ring-ring.

The men gathered around the stove, mouths hanging open and eyes widening, stare as if he he's lost his mind. He stares back, grinning. No, he hasn't lost his mind, anything but. He closes the door with a final ding and passes the still-gawking men. Their heads follow him again, as if they're a group of curious old owls.

At the counter, Mr. Hansen nods. "Well, now, does someone have spring fever, or did cupid's arrow hit the bulls-eye?"

Kurt doesn't answer. Nothing matters except Lainey forgiving him. Her beautiful smile from the ladies' shop door plays in his mind like a movie. He can't wait to see her again.

Mr. Hansen clears his throat. "Didn't you need seeds Saturday?"

"Seeds?"

"Seeds. Garden. Saturday. Why you came in."

"Yes, sir, thank you for reminding me."

Kurt takes a few steps, and Hansen clears his throat again. Kurt stops and Hansen points. "In the back, remember?" Kurt looks around. He's in the middle of the men gathered around the warm stove.

One gray-bearded codger, wearing a sweat-stained felt hat with a pipe hanging from his lips, removes the pipe. "Son, take my advice and go back to Germany. You German boys will never be able to handle our American women."

Kurt shrugs. The old man might have a point.

Nearing the seed display, he stops at the counter where he bumped into Joseph. He places his hand on the smooth wood and closes his eyes. Lainey kneels beside Joseph, her sweet voice tenderly calming him. When she stands and scolds Kurt for bumping into her son, fire fills her beautiful brown eyes.

Hansen laughs. "Right there in front of you, Mr. Lovesick Idiot."

Kurt takes Mrs. Edwards' list from his pocket and scoops seeds from one of the bins into a brown paper bag.

* * *

At the truck, Elaine hands Joseph the daffodils. "Hold these for Momma while I open your stubborn door."

He takes the Mason jar. "He gave us flowers, Momma. Yellow flowers, like your hair."

"You mean like the ribbon in my hair, don't you?" He nods. "I thought so. Let's get you in the truck so we can get home to

Grandma and Grandpa."

He grins at her through the yellow blooms, his blond curls a shade lighter. "Okay, Momma."

Pulling from the curb, she slows for a woman crossing the street to the post office. Joseph's barely visible eyebrows, the same shade as his hair, are knit together. "Momma, that man's got a mark on his head. Did he get hurt?"

"I imagine so, but he's all right now. That mark is called a scar."

Joseph's blue eyes squint. "A scar?"

"Remember when Grandpa showed you the mark on his finger? He cut a piece of rope and wasn't careful. When a bad cut heals, it leaves a mark. That mark is called a scar."

"How did the man cut his head?"

"I have no idea. Having a mark on your head is better than having a cut, don't you think?"

"I 'member Grandpa now. His finger bleeded. Scars is better than cuts."

Elaine tousles her sweet son's hair.

Could Kurt have gotten the scar in the war, and since he mentioned his sisters in past tense, saying he *had* three sisters, could he have lost his entire family?

During the war, Elaine rarely considered how the families of the enemy fared, but the German people had suffered too, in some ways *much* worse. Before the war's end, the radio news described how German towns and cities were bombed and burned out of existence—towns with families, towns with children, towns like any other European country. At least no one in America had experienced such a nightmare, although Pearl Harbor was nightmare enough.

Regardless, the horrors of war had visited its share of grief upon her and Joe's family, as well as other families in and around Alma. Those wounds ran entirely too deep, always reminding her of how she lost Joe.

Glad to be back home out of a college dorm, Elaine parks in front of her parent's house. She considered more education, but when the job offer came after she graduated with a four-year degree, she accepted. She could always go back to school, but she missed Joseph terribly, which helped with the decision. The arrangements with her parents and the Matthans—keeping Joseph while she was away—was a blessing. Still, that didn't lessen how much she hated being away from her precious son.

When she and Joseph top the porch steps, Mom opens the door. "What have you got there, Joseph, daffodils?"

"Yellow flowers, Grandma. A man gave them to Momma."

Mom takes the jar. "That's nice of him." In the kitchen, she sets the jar on the table. "What's this nice man's name?"

"He said his name is—"

"You can tell grandma after lunch." At the sink, Elaine wets a cloth for Joseph's hands.

"Elaine?"

"What, Mom?"

"What's wrong with telling me now?"

Elaine closes her eyes. She'll have to tell Mom everything or be questioned relentlessly until she does. She makes a sandwich for Joseph and sets that and a glass of milk on the table.

Leaning against the sink, Mom crosses her arms. "Well?"

"*Well* yourself, Mrs. Nosy. He's the German POW who came back to live with the Edwards after the war."

"Imagine that. The same one you yelled at in the street that day." Mom sits at the table. "A lot more had to happen between you two for him to go to the trouble of picking you a jar of daffodils."

Elaine sits also. "For all I know there's a snake in that jar and he's out to get a few more Americans." Elaine shoves the jar toward Mom. "Maybe you should make sure it's safe."

Mom returns the jar to the center of the table. "Stop that nonsense and tell me what happened."

"While Joseph and I were in the hardware store Saturday, Kurt came around a corner and accidentally knocked Joseph down. He bumped his head and started crying."

"Kurt? You're on a first name basis already?"

"How so?"

"You just called him Kurt."

"He told me his name when he gave me the flowers. Satisfied?"

"I see how it is. You gave him a tongue lashing when he knocked Joseph down, and he felt so guilty he brought you flowers."

Elaine tilts her head to one side. "Who is she, one of the women at the sewing shop? Or maybe it's one of those old men who hang around the hardware store."

"Who's who?" Mom asks, eyes narrowing.

"Your spies."

"I'm just curious, is that a crime?"

Elaine says nothing. If Mom knows the answers, she has a few questions of her own. "What do you know about him besides he lives with the Edwards?"

"I know more than I wish I knew." Mom takes one of the daffodils from the Mason jar. "Remember the day you yelled at him? Not long after that I saw Betty Edwards in town and asked about him. She said he was only seventeen when a group of German soldiers came to his hometown and forced all the young men to go with them."

Elaine didn't know the German leaders treated their people so badly. Then again, what they did to the Jews was an abomination she could never imagine. "Did all his family die in the war? They must have, or he wouldn't be here now."

"I'm not sure. Betty said he went back after the war but didn't stay long." Mom slides the daffodil back into the Mason jar, hesitates, and pulls a folded piece of paper from within the green stems. She hands it to Elaine. "A love letter already?"

Shaking her head, Elaine takes the paper.

Dear Mrs. Matthan,

I asked Mr. Hansen your name. I hope you do not think I am forward. Please forgive me for being clumsy Saturday. I am sorry about Joseph. I hope he was not hurt. Please accept the flowers. Mrs. Edwards allowed me to pick them. I hope you like them and I hope you and Joseph can forgive me.

Kurt Bauer

Mom pulls the edge of the note down. "Well?"

"You're full of 'wells' today, aren't you?"

"I am, until you fill them with answers."

"He apologized, that's all."

"That was very thoughtful, wasn't it?"

"Yes, Mom, I guess it was." Elaine balls the note up and throws it at Mom. "Maybe he won't run over any more children in the hardware store now."

* * *

On the way home, Kurt can't get the picture of Lainey smiling at him out of his mind. Window open, he slices his hand through the cool air flowing past the truck. A mile passes.

He waves at a man on a tractor plowing a field. Humming an unknown tune, he taps the steering wheel while nodding his head to the rhythm. Within another mile, the memory of Joseph waving makes him smile, but his recollection comes with regret: it's a shame the little boy's father is dead.

He takes a few envelopes from the mailbox, drives up the short path to the Edwards' home, and gets out. To the side of the white frame house, as Mr. Edwards plows the garden spot, the fragrant soil turns over beneath the blades. On the other side of the house, Mrs. Edwards hangs laundry in the crisp spring breeze.

Kurt takes the bag of seeds to the clothesline. "I have all the seeds we need for the garden, Mrs. Edwards."

"Goodness, Kurt, how many times do George and I have to tell you it's okay to call us by our first names?" She picks up the empty basket. "It's about time, don't you think?"

"Yes, ma'am. It just seems … not respectful."

"I think you mean 'disrespectful.' We've known each other quite a few years, can't you try?"

"I will try, Mrs. Edwar— Betty, I mean."

"There now, doesn't that sound better than Mrs. Edwards? Don't forget to call Mr. Edwards—I mean George—by his first name too." Kurt tries not to grin at her name slip. Betty's right. George sounds much better, especially when she says it.

They go inside. At the kitchen table, as he takes the small bags of seeds from the large bag, Betty sits across from him. "When do I get to know what you did with a Mason jar full of my daffodils?"

"Remember when I forgot the seeds Saturday?" She nods. "When I was walking to the bins, I accidentally hit a little boy with my knee."

"Was he hurt?"

"He fell and started crying. His mother came and— Well, she was angry. She told Mr. Hansen she would be back today, when there were no im-be-ciles in the store. Did I say that right?"

Betty waves the question away. Kurt often asks about his pronunciation, and she always tells him he's doing fine.

"This woman called you an imbecile?" she asks. "Did the boy stop crying?"

"He did," Kurt says, nodding. "After she left, Mr. Hansen said I shouldn't worry."

"But you worried anyway."

"I was sorry I hurt her little boy. I took the flowers to apologize."

"Who was this person, Kurt?"

"Her name is Lainey Matthan. Her son's name is Joseph."

"You mean Elaine Matthan, right?"

Kurt rubs his forehead. "Her name is hard for me to say. She said when she was a girl, her grandfather called her Lainey."

"Does that mean the daffodils worked?"

"I hope so. Joseph waved at me after we talked."

"What about Elaine?"

"She was not angry any more. She did say I should watch where I was going. She was right, I did not like seeing her little boy cry because of me."

"Well, it was an accident." Betty pauses. "You want to see her again, don't you?"

Kurt doesn't answer right away. Every so often, either George or Betty mentions how it would be nice if he found a wife. He agrees but never says so. Maybe he rubs his forehead so much because he'd like to get rid of his scar. Then again, he'll probably keep his German accent until he's old and gray.

Betty shares a soft smile. "You're mighty deep in thought, Kurt. You *do* want to see her again."

"I would like to. She is very ... how do you say ... big-willed?"

"Strong-willed is more like it. All of us farm women have to be like that."

"Mr. Hansen said she is going to be the new teacher this fall. She must be very smart."

"Do you know what happened to her husband?"

"Mr. Hansen said he died in the war. I heard you and George talking about him once. Is there anything else?"

Betty pours lemonade and asks if he wants any. He says no, and she sits again. "You may have heard some of this while George and I were talking. I'll tell you what I know in case you missed anything. She and Joe—that was her husband—used to go to that nice spot on the river."

"Where I go fishing, you mean."

"That's it. They practically lived there from the time they met until he left for the war. He managed to come home before he left for Europe, and they got married. He went back to Fort Leavenworth the next day. Three months later, Elaine found out she was expecting. She went straight home to tell her folks and found out Joe had been killed."

A wave of sadness presses on Kurt, like when he returned to Germany and was told his own family had died. "Death is not the way a family should start. I wish someone had stopped Hitler long before he came to power."

"It was a horrible time for Elaine and her family, and Joe's too. I can't—" Betty's mouth hangs open.

"What is wrong, Betty?"

"I was going to say 'I can't imagine,' but you know I can since we lost our own son. I know you can too, since you lost your own family."

She pauses for lemonade. "It took Elaine a good while to get back to the business of living. She stayed home with her parents until the spring after Joseph was born, then went to college. Her and Joe's parents kept Joseph, but she came home as often as she could. Every so often we'd see her and Joseph in town. He's a cute little boy, looks just like his daddy. It's nice she's going to be our new teacher."

"I just remembered something," Kurt says. "I met her before at the river. One afternoon I went there to fish, and a woman was there alone. She was … well, I knew she was going to be a mother soon. She was angry with me like when Joseph was crying. She told me to leave because her family was having a picnic. I left right away."

"You never said anything about that."

"I thought how I might feel if my family were planning something nice and a stranger barged in. Still, I hope I would not have acted like she did."

"You might have if you were—like you say—going to be a mother soon, and your husband had died in the war not long ago."

Kurt regards the woman who's befriended him to the point of allowing him—the former enemy—to share her and her husband's home. "You remind me of my mother, Betty. Before she would argue with someone, she would try to look at their side. She would have liked you."

Betty pats his hand. "I'm sure I would've liked her too, Kurt."

Kurt often marvels at how Betty and George have accepted

him into their home, and he is more grateful to them than he can ever put into words. Regardless, he wants to try, because the opportunity rarely presents itself in a busy farming household.

"Betty, do you and Mr. Edwards—George, I mean—know how thankful I am that you asked me to come back?"

"I remember that day, don't you? You jumped up off the porch step and hugged us both." Betty's eyes crinkle with humor. "George was so funny, turned red as a beet. He wasn't used to a man hugging him, still isn't. To answer your question, I'm sure we know how thankful you are. Realize this though, if you hadn't been who you are, we wouldn't have considered it. We heard about some of the POWs, how they were bitter and hated being here. You were nothing like that. We knew you almost a year before we asked if you wanted to live with us. We had plenty of time to see the goodness in you."

Kurt pauses for a sigh. "I wonder if Lainey will ever let me get to know her like that?"

"As you well know," Betty says, patting his hand again, "anything's possible. Still, you shouldn't get your hopes up. Joe was killed by Germans, and the last person she might want to marry is a German."

Kurt lowers his head. "I understand."

Several quiet seconds pass. Betty's fingertips raise his chin. "Don't get down on yourself, okay? She might like to get to know you. How that might happen, I don't know. There's another thing to think about. Is she—or will she ever be—ready to have another relationship?"

Kurt doesn't have an answer to those questions either.

And he doubts he ever will.

Chapter 30

Story for a Son

In bed, warm from the sun shining on her quilt, Elaine closes her eyes as Joseph's feet patter in the hall. The door creaks open and his feet patter toward her. "Wake up, Momma!" he yells, shaking her shoulder. "It's my birthday!"

"What's going on?" Elaine groans. "Who's bothering me in the middle of the night?"

"It's mornin', Momma. Rise and shine like you tell me all the time."

"Oh, no, it's still night and I'm having a dream" —she grabs him and pulls him into bed— "about a monkey waking me up!"

Squirming in her arms, Joseph squeals laughter and wiggles away, red cheeked. "It's not time for tickles, it's time for my birthday." He holds up his hand and spreads his fingers. "I'm this many—five years old—just like you told me. Can we go to the river now so you can tell me about my daddy?"

Elaine can't help grinning at his cute self. She sits up and stretches. "I'm hungry. We need breakfast first."

"I'm hungry too, Momma. I want eggs and bacon and biscuits and sausage and pancakes and ham. Oh, and oatmeal too."

"Where would you put all that? That's a lot of food for a five-year-old boy."

He raises his pajama top and pokes his navel. "Right in my

belly, Momma."

"Your belly isn't that big, you monkey. Are Grandpa and Grandma up yet?"

"Grandma's making coffee. It smells good, when can I have some?"

"No time soon."

"That's not fair."

"Are you ready for your first present?" She pulls him to her for a hug.

He squirms out of her arms. "I get hugs all the time. A present is supposed to be special."

"You don't think my hugs are special?" Elaine covers her face. "Boo-hoo-hoo."

Joseph pulls at her hands. "Don't cry, Momma, I'm sorry. Your hugs are special. *Very* special."

She hugs him again. "And so are yours. Do you remember how all your grandpas and grandmas are meeting us at the river for a picnic?"

"You said after we go first and come back. Don't forget the quilt you said you and Daddy liked."

"I won't. Go find Grandma. I'll be there in a few minutes, okay?"

"Okay, Momma." Joseph runs away, a streak of blue pajamas and thumping feet fading down the hall.

* * *

At the No Trespassing sign now hanging askew on the fence post, Elaine steers into the rutted road. "Hold on, Joseph. It's been a while since Momma's been here. I'll go slow but we might get bounced."

Joseph places one hand on the seat and one hand on the door. "Go fast, Momma, I like to bounce."

"Uh-huh, like on your bed."

The truck bounces. The suspension squeaks. Despite Elaine's efforts, the right front tire slides into a gulley, jarring both her and Joseph. He whips around to look at her. "That was a *bad* one, Momma. You better slow down."

Elaine stops on the last rise before starting down the final stretch of road. She can hardly believe more than five years have passed since she's been here, when she gave the Matthans the framed wedding picture of her and Joe before Joseph was born.

Visions of her and Joe's wedding night flood her mind: Joe changing his clothes behind the oak. Her unbuttoning her dress so it barely slips from her shoulders. Him singing while they dance. Her singing near the end with him remarking how fine her voice is. Then finally, when they make love on the old quilt, warm beneath the blankets she brought.

He promised to come back to her, but how can that happen now? She covers her face so Joseph can't see her crying. He touches her hand. "Momma, can I wipe your tears?" To have such a sweet son is amazing, so amazing she stops crying and lowers her hands. Joseph wipes her cheeks with a corner of the old quilt.

"Thank you, sweetheart. That's exactly what Momma needed."

"Can you be happy now?"

Nodding, she hugs him tight. What a gift Joe has given her. Joseph pulls away. "All better?"

"I certainly am. Do you know how much I love you?"

He spreads his hands as far as he can in the truck. "I know, Momma, this much!"

"That's exactly how much I love you too. Let's go see mine

and your daddy's special place. Can you carry the quilt by yourself?"

"I can, I'm strong." He raises an arm and pulls back his sleeve. "Grandpa said I'm getting muscles."

"Oh, my! Can I touch it?" He nods, and Elaine pokes his arm. "I think Grandpa's right." She shifts the truck into gear. "Let's go."

At the bottom of the path, before it levels out to the river, Elaine hits the brakes.

Beneath the tree is a picnic table, its new wood white against the backdrop of the rolling, gray water. Between the tree and the river, daffodils stand tall, yellow heads bobbing in the breeze.

She parks and holds the driver's door open as Joseph climbs out. They go to the oak, where she places her hand on the coarse bark. The charred remnants of the fire Joe built to keep them warm on their September wedding are still here, except someone has placed a ring of large quartz rocks around them. "Someone has been taking good care of this place, Joseph. The table and flowers and rocks weren't here before."

"I like it, Momma. I like the flowers too." He faces the river. "The water's talking, like when you tell me goodnight. Wish … wishper? Is that what you said it was?"

"Whisper, sweetheart. I think it's saying hello-o-o-o, Joseph, it's nice to meet you."

The table, the daffodils, the rocks—who would do all this?

"Okay, little man, help me spread this old quilt and I'll show you something your daddy showed me."

When the quilt is ready, she picks him up, rolls to her back, and hugs and tickles him. He squeals with laughter, squirms away, and jumps to his feet, breathing hard. "Momma!" He takes a breath. "Stop tickling and show me!"

"Can I get a hug without tickles first?"

He wraps his arms around her neck. "There. Now show me."

"Did you forget something?"

"Ple-e-e-e-e-ease? Is that better?"

"That's a good boy." She lies on the quilt and pats the empty space beside her. "Lie down and look up and tell me what you see."

He lies down. "I see leaves." Sunlight flickers in his eyes, and he darts a finger upward. "I see lights, Momma, like on the Christmas tree."

"Exactly right, just like on the tree. Your daddy showed me those lights a long time ago. From right here on this very same quilt, we looked up at the light shining down through those leaves. What do you think of that?"

No grin. No smiling blue eyes. "Momma, you never told me what Daddy was like."

"I was waiting for this special day. He was shy when we met, but I tricked him into taking me fishing."

"Fishing here?"

"Right here."

"That's his guitar under your bed, right?"

"He tried to teach me how to play. I wasn't very good."

"Did you falled in love after that?"

Elaine holds in a giggle at *falled*. "We figured out we were in love when we went fishing. We had our first kiss here too."

She sits up to take the three pictures of her and Joe from her jeans pocket. Joseph has seen the framed picture of them getting married on her dresser, but she keeps the original three photos in a copy of *The Call of the Wild* that Joe gave her on their first and only Christmas together. "These are pictures of your daddy and me. This one was taken right here, see?"

Joseph leans close. "He looks like a boy, Momma, like me in the mirror." She gives him the picture. He studies it, eyes squinting, and places a fingertip on the log where she and Joe were sitting. "Where's the tree?"

"That was an old log the water washed up. The water took it away again." She trades that picture for another. "This is when your daddy and I got married."

"This is like the one in your room. I like it 'cause your dress is pretty and Daddy looks like a soldier."

"That's right, he was a soldier." She trades pictures again. "This is the day Daddy left to fight in the war. See the ribbon he's holding? It was one of my hair ribbons."

Joseph looks from the picture to the ribbon in her hair and back to the picture again. "I like yellow." He studies the picture a second longer. "Momma, what's war?"

Elaine expected this question and had planned an answer that his five-year-old intellect could comprehend. "War is when the soldiers from different countries fight each other. Sometimes the good soldiers need help. Your daddy was helping the good soldiers fight the bad soldiers."

"Why isn't Daddy here now?"

Elaine expected this question too. Pausing to gather the answer, she kisses her son's smooth cheek, catches a whiff of strawberry jam from the toast he ate with breakfast, and runs her fingers through his baby-soft hair. "Remember when a wolf killed one of the baby cows this spring?"

"I 'member."

"Remember how we talked about if a living thing gets sick or hurt and can't get better, they go to Heaven?"

"I 'member that too, Momma, but why's *daddy* not here?"

"Just like when the baby cow got hurt, one of the bad soldiers hurt your daddy. Just like the baby cow he couldn't get better, so he went to Heaven. I'll see him again one day, a long time from now. So will you, but only after you live your life and have children and grandchildren of your own."

"But that's too long away, Momma," Joseph says, his tender voice pleading. He traces Joe's face with a fingertip. "Do you think my daddy in Heaven cares if I have another daddy? Then, after a long time, I can be with my daddy in Heaven?"

This is the first time Joseph says anything about not having a daddy. Elaine assumed his two grandfathers were filling that void, but her son's question suggests they're not. Not wanting him to see her cry, she turns from the truth in his tender voice. If only Joe could somehow come back to them both, what a miracle that would be. After all, he promised her he would, and— A huge sob shakes Elaine's shoulders. *Oh, Joe, I miss you so much. So much. So mu—*

"I'm sorry, Momma. I didn't mean to make you sad."

Elaine wipes her eyes. "You didn't make me sad, sweetheart." She hugs Joseph tight, then looks him in the eye. "It's just that I miss your daddy too. Sit down again and I'll tell you something that might help you understand why I haven't found you another daddy."

He plops down cross-legged and waits.

"Like when you don't want me to be sad, your daddy didn't want me to be sad either. He said if he couldn't come back from the war, I could find another man to love."

Joseph's faint eyebrows knot together. "Well doggone, Momma, what're you waitin' for?"

Elaine can't help but laugh. Leave it to her son to lighten her mood. "You got 'doggone' from Grandpa, didn't you?"

"Well, what *are* you waitin' for?"

"I'm waiting because your daddy and I loved each other so much. That means I'm not sure if I can love another man enough to have him be your daddy."

"But, Momma, you can love us all. If I have another daddy, I'll tell him to share. You can love my real daddy in Heaven and another daddy too."

"I …"

"What?"

"I never thought about it like that."

"You always tell me I'm smart." Joseph lies on the quilt and clasps his hands beneath his head. "I'll be quiet. You think about it."

Elaine faces the river. In the five years and six months since Joe died, she never looked at another man twice, much less considered one as a second father for Joseph.

Can his idea, as simple as it is, work? Not without giving some man a second glance it won't. Is it time for that? No. Definitely not.

Then again, if she can find someone as nice as Mr. Edwards, who probably planted the daffodils, put the rocks around the old fire, and put the picnic table here, "definitely not" might turn into definitely maybe.

Chapter 31

Chance Meeting

On the way back to the river, with bags of food in the back of the truck for the picnic, Elaine turns into the path behind Mom and Dad, who just turned in behind the Matthans.

And is amazed.

The ruts are scraped smooth, likely with a blade on a tractor. The potholes are filled too, making the ride to the river as smooth as the main road.

"Where did all the bounces go, Momma?"

"I'm not sure, but I'm glad they're gone. Now we can keep our teeth for lunch."

Joseph touches his teeth. "I'm glad, Momma. I wanna save mine for Grandma's fried chicken."

Grinning, Elaine shakes her head. Her boy is a mess—a wonderful, lovable, joy-to-her-heart mess.

Nearing the oak, the two trucks ahead of Elaine separate, revealing a tractor driven by Kurt Bauer, who waves.

Joseph peers over the dash. "Who's that man on the tractor, Momma? He's not my daddy, is he?"

"That's Mr. Bauer. Do you remember the day he gave us the flowers in town? It's been almost a year."

"I waved when we left."

"I thought you didn't like him? You hid behind my legs and wouldn't talk to him."

"I'm a big boy now. Did he fix the road?"

"It looks like it."

"Did he plant the flowers and bring the picnic table and put those rocks around the old fire too?"

"I don't know, he might."

"You told me to say thank you when somebody's nice. Are you gonna say thank you?"

"We'll see."

Kurt shuts the tractor off. The engine's clatter and black smoke from the exhaust fades. He walks over to her window. "Hello, Lainey. I didn't know you and your family were coming." He points toward a short section of wash-boarded path. "I will leave after I scrape that place." He leans down. "Hello, Joseph. You are getting to be a big boy."

Joseph raises his arm "See my muscle?"

"I see, I see. I should go, Lainey. I hope you and your family have a nice day." Kurt leaves for the tractor.

"Thank you, Kurt. Thank you for fixing the road too. Joseph, tell Mr. Bauer goodbye."

Joseph crawls into her lap and sticks his head out the window. "Did you bring the table and put down the rocks and plant the flowers? Yellow is my favorite color, my Momma's too."

Kurt comes back. "Yellow is my favorite color too. Did you like your smooth ride down here?"

"It's okay, but I like to bounce."

"You did all that and fixed the road too?" Elaine asks.

"This ..." Kurt's nostrils flare; he's either enjoying the breeze or carefully considering his answer. "This place is special to me."

Elaine pauses too. What's he hiding with his hesitation? There's one way to find out. "Why's that?"

"I think it is a place where love can grow."

"Well, everything you did is nice," Elaine admits, although she's not quite sure what he means.

"I'll leave and finish the road another time," he says. "I don't want to stir up any dust." He leaves again.

"Wait, Mr. Bauer!" Joseph yells, leaning out the window again. "Do you like fried chicken?"

"Hush," Elaine says. "He might have some other work to do."

"He's nice, Momma. I want him to eat lunch with us."

Kurt comes back again, and Elaine opens the truck door. "*Do* you like fried chicken? You can consider it a thank you for all the work you did."

"Are you sure?"

"I can introduce you to Joseph's grandparents. They'd appreciate knowing who did all this work."

"Can I help carry something?"

She gives him a bag from the truck and starts to turn for another. Instead, she places her hand on his arm. "Kurt, I need to apologize for something. Even though it was over five years ago, I remember the day I told you to leave from here. I … well, I was upset. Still, that's no excuse for being rude."

"You don't need to apologize, Lainey. Betty told me what happened to your husband." Kurt's blue eyes soften. His arm is warm beneath Elaine's fingertips. Words not quite formed fly through her mind like songbirds scattering beneath the slashing talons of a hawk.

Joseph tugs her dress. "I'm hungry, Momma. Give me a bag

and let's go eat."

Elaine takes her hand from Kurt's arm. "I just wanted to say I'm sorry, and—"

"C'mon, Momma. I don't like cold chicken."

"I better get that boy a bag before he worries me to death."

Elaine introduces Kurt to everyone. Joseph adds how he fixed the road, brought the picnic table, put the rocks around the old fire, and planted the flowers. He looks up at Elaine. "We have to say thank you when someone does something nice, don't we Momma?"

"That's why I invited Kurt to lunch."

"I certainly enjoyed the smooth ride," Mom says.

"Me too," Sarah says.

"It is very nice to meet you all," Kurt says. "The road has needed attention for a while."

"Spring's busy for us farmers," Dad says.

"George has kept us working hard with all the planting," Kurt says, nodding. "We have many new animals being born too."

"*So,*" Will says, his word like a shotgun blast, "you don't like farm work."

Sarah, in the middle of unwrapping food, snaps her head toward Will. "I didn't see you scraping the road, Will Matthan."

Their lips tighten; their eyes narrow. Except for the leaves fluttering in the oak, silence fills the conversation.

Kurt lowers his head, and Elaine does too. Will's unspoken accusation hangs over the picnic table: *So, you don't like farm work. I bet you didn't mind killing Americans either.* He takes Joseph's hand. "Let's go down to the river. You might as well come with us, Al."

Elaine watches them walk away. Maybe Dad will talk to Will. She's never seen or heard him act so unreasonable. It's understandable though. He lost his son like she lost her husband.

She unwraps a warm loaf of Mom's bread. The delicious aroma normally makes her mouth water, but her mouth is as dry as a field of drought-stricken wheat. Will's question still sticks in her mind—not because she doesn't understand it—but because she doesn't understand why she asked Kurt to stay in the first place. After all, the last thing she wants is a relationship with him.

* * *

At the water's edge, Will lets go of Joseph's hand. "Don't get too close and fall in."

"I won't, I'm a big boy." Joseph picks up a stick and swishes it in the water.

Al grins at Joseph. "That boy is a mess." He faces Will. "All right, Will, you didn't ask me to walk down here for the heck of it."

"Was it that obvious?"

"You're usually not one for understatements. That's the biggest understatement I've heard in a long time."

"Can I help it if I'd rather have—" Will lowers his voice so Joseph can't hear. "Can I help it if I'd rather have Joe here than that—"

"Will?"

"What?"

"You're not being fair to that young man."

"What's fair got to do with it?" Wills asks, trying to keep anger out of his voice.

"To be fair," Al says, "we need to know a person first. What do you know about him?"

"Sarah mentioned seeing him in town one time and how he lives with the Edwards. I told her I didn't want to hear it."

Al crosses his arms. "Here I am, thinking you're such a level-headed person. Kurt can't help how the Nazis drug him off to make him fight. Haven't you heard how they did that to boys who weren't even eighteen? They practically kidnapped them from their families."

"How do you know that?"

"Betty Edwards told Mary. Like I said, he can't help what happened to him. If you got dropped in the middle of a battle, you'll do what you need to do to stay alive."

"Maybe, but—"

"Betty also said his mother and father and three sisters died when their town was bombed. That's one reason he came back. Another is how well the Edwards got to know him while he was helping them before the war ended."

"Well," Will says, rubbing the back of his neck, "I guess they know what they're doing."

"He wasn't much more than a boy when they met," Al continues. "Would you believe he actually broke down crying and hugged them when they told him he was welcome to come back and live with them?"

Will pauses. George wouldn't let anyone live in his home unless he thought highly of him. "It goes against my grain, Al, but I'll give him a chance."

"It's the decent thing to do." Al faces the picnic table. "I was surprised Elaine asked him to stay."

Will glances toward the table also. "Why's that?"

"I've wondered if she'll ever meet someone. I'm not saying Kurt is that person, mind you. I'm saying I'd hate for her to go through life alone."

"I told Joe that very thing." Water splatters, and Will turns to see Joseph digging a hole in the mud beside the river. He faces Al again. "All I want is what's best for Elaine and Joseph."

"That's what we all want, Will."

"I know, Al. Thanks for telling me about Kurt. Maybe I won't act like a jackass around him again anytime soon."

* * *

Lunch done, Elaine drinks lemonade. Joseph hops from beside her and runs around the picnic table to Kurt, who's leaning against the oak. "Mr. Bauer, will you come with me to the river? I want to make the water go in a hole I made."

"If your mother doesn't mind. You have to call me Kurt, all right?"

Joseph runs back to Elaine. "Can Kurt go with me to the river, Momma? He said he would if you let him."

"If I let him, huh? You have to look out after him and make him behave, okay?" Joseph runs back to Kurt, who winks at her.

"Thank you, Lainey. I am sure Joseph can take care of me. I saw those big muscles, remember?" Joseph takes his hand and leads him to the river.

"I think Kurt reminds Joseph of Joe," Elaine says to no one in particular. "I showed him some pictures of Joe this morning, and told him all about him. I tried to explain about the war too."

"How did he take all that?" Mom asks.

"He seemed to understand. When we drove up, he asked if Kurt was his daddy. I think he remembered what I told him and didn't ask again."

"Kurt does resemble Joe. His hair, anyway."

"Listen up everyone," Elaine says, facing Sarah, Will, Mom, and Dad. "I don't want Joseph to know Kurt was an enemy soldier. We'll probably see him here and around town once in a while, and that might make him think of Kurt as someone who hurt his daddy. Are we clear on that?"

"Elaine?"

She faces Will, who was quiet during lunch. Maybe Dad helped him rethink his treatment of Kurt. "Yes?"

"I'm sorry for how I acted while ago." Will glances at Dad. "Al told me how Kurt lost his family, and how the Edwards trust him enough to live with them. The least we can do is give him a chance."

"I'm glad you see how we shouldn't judge someone before we know them, Will. Unfortunately, for all of us, I understand how losing Joe might make us do that." Elaine stands. "I think I'll see what mischief Joseph is getting Kurt into."

Nearing the river, she can't help but grin. Shoes off, Joseph has Kurt down on his hands and knees, helping him dig a trench from the river to a rapidly filling hole.

"Look, Momma, we're making a pond. It's like Grandpa's on the farm."

"I see that. I see your muddy feet too."

He dips his toes in the brown pool. "This is how I clean 'em. I wanted to step in the big water, but Kurt said it was dange-rush. What's dange-rush, Momma?"

"It means you could get hurt."

Kurt wipes mud from Joseph's feet. "I'm sorry. I should have told you what that big word means."

"That's okay, Momma's a teacher. She tells me about big words when she reads to me in bed."

"I like to read too." Kurt stands to face Elaine. "What books do you like?"

"I like Stuart," Joseph says. "I like the Christmas book too."

"I never heard of 'Stuart,'" Kurt says.

"*Stuart Little*," Elaine says. "It's about the adventures of a mouse who has human parents."

"Betty gave me *The Call of the Wild*. I have trouble with some of the words."

"I like that myself. It's on the agenda for my older students this year." She points at Joseph's shoes. "Which reminds me … put those on, you muddy monkey. I've got lesson plans to make for Monday."

"But, Momma, you said we might catch a catfish."

"When you get time," Kurt says, "I can meet you and Joseph here. Betty makes delicious fried catfish."

"We'll see. Would you like that, Joseph?"

"I would, Momma. A *lot*."

"Good." Elaine kneels to dip Joseph's muddy shoes in the water. "Let's clean these shoes so you don't track mud in Grandma's house."

Chapter 32

Second Love

At the kitchen sink, about thirty minutes after supper, Elaine dries the last plate. Dad's excited about the corn crop this year. He and Thomas have been working later than normal, evidenced by the muffled roar of two tractors in the field behind the house.

One comes closer and its diesel clatter ends. Boots clomp on the back-porch steps. The screen door squeaks open. "Got another full wagon with that load," Dad says. "Looks like the best crop we've ever had."

Elaine puts the plate in the cabinet. "So you keep saying."

"So I'll keep saying until it's all in from the fields. Where's your mother? I need some help throwing this load in the crib for cornmeal and chicken feed. Joseph can help too while Thomas keeps working."

"They went to town. She said something about buying a new hat with all the money you're making."

"Uh-huh. Like she needs another hat. Besides, the stores are closed by now."

"I'm teasing. She's on the phone and Joseph's in his room."

Dad goes to the refrigerator for lemonade. "Is Kurt taking you and Joseph fishing tomorrow?"

"He hasn't mentioned it."

"I think he's taken you at least three Saturdays a month since we met him at the picnic."

"Joseph enjoys his company."

"And you don't?"

"I sure do. It gives me time away from questions like that."

"That's what you get for teasing me about hats." Dad sips lemonade. "How's Kurt coming with his reading lessons?"

"He's doing well."

"Don't you get tired of using *The Call of the Wild* all the time?"

Elaine crosses her arms. "The last time I checked, *I'm* the one with the teaching diploma."

Dad empties the glass. "Just asking, honey."

The unmistakable sound of Joseph's shoes thud in hall. He runs in, Mom a few steps behind him. "Momma, Momma! Grandma said the fair's coming tomorrow!"

"How do you know that?" Dad asks.

"Because Mrs. Hansen just told me," Mom says. "I think we all should go." She faces Elaine. "Would you like to ask Kurt?"

Elaine kneels by Joseph. "What if grandma and grandpa take you instead? I'd like to have a little time at the river by myself."

"Aw, Momma, I want to see Kurt."

"What if us three go next Saturday?"

"I get to go two times?"

"I take that as a yes."

* * *

The next day, as soon as Mom, Dad, and Joseph leave for the fair, Elaine drives to the river. She enjoys her time here with Joseph and Kurt, but once in a while she prefers to go alone, sitting and reading or lying on the quilt while the sunlight filters down through the leaves like it did when she and Joe visited so long ago. Between breaks from reading, she relives the moments they spent together, from the day they met at the hardware store, to their honeymoon night on the quilt at the river, to when he told her to live her life as happy as possible if he didn't return from the war.

The comment Dad made, about how many times she and Joseph went fishing with Kurt over the last few months, touched a nerve. Still, she's come to care about Kurt, for his gentle nature with Joseph, his gentle nature with her, his patience during reading lessons, the way he watches her with his intense blue eyes—but love? A tipping point is coming. Her varying mood whenever she's around him—one-minute leaning close to place her hand on his arm, the next, discreetly avoiding his touch—proves it. Confused as ever, she needs a breakthrough to clear her confusion. How that might happen, she doesn't know.

Elaine spreads the quilt and goes to pick a rose from a bush that Betty Edwards grew from a cutting and gave Kurt to transplant near the daffodil bed. He said he transplanted it because daffodils don't bloom year-round, and he wants her to have flowers for as much of the year as possible. On the quilt again, she sniffs the gorgeous bloom: sweet, delicate, and with petals of the deepest, darkest crimson she's ever seen. The warmth of the September day, along with the murmur of the river rolling by, relaxes her to the point of drowsiness. She closes her eyes and Joe appears, saying he loves her, saying he'll come back to her no matter what.

* * *

Kurt swallows the last bite of a tomato sandwich. Across from him, Betty sips lemonade. "Since we finished work early, what're your plans for the afternoon?"

George pauses from his sandwich to snort laughter. "That's obvious."

"How so?" Betty asks, facing him.

"I told you both how I met Mrs. Hansen in town yesterday, and how she told Mary about the fair. That means Mary, Albert, and Elaine will take Joseph today, and Kurt's going fishing."

"Now, George, you know Kurt takes Elaine and Joseph to the river to be with them. Fishing is just an excuse."

Kurt stands. "Is anything wrong with that?"

"Didn't say it was," George says, "but you always let them take the fish. I'd like some for us once in a while, if you don't mind."

Kurt pat's George's shoulder. "Then I know what I'm doing today."

At the bottom of the path leading to the river, Kurt slows. Elaine's truck is parked by the oak, and she's lying on the quilt in the shade. He parks, takes his fishing gear to the tree, and sits in the grass beside her. She's sound asleep, a rose and a book on the quilt beside her.

Without a single doubt he loves her. Since the day they met, the memory of her flashing brown eyes keeps him company, while her smile during their fishing visits here—the most beautiful smile he's ever seen—fills his dreams nearly every night.

She's never hinted at love—neither single kiss nor knowing glance—although she sometimes touches his arm when they share a book, or smiles at him when he comments about certain characters. But one such occurrence gives him reason to believe she feels more for him than only someone who spends time with her son.

They had spent a long day at the river. Finding the Edwards getting ready for bed, they enjoyed leftovers for supper and settled down on the sofa to listen to the radio. Joseph, curled at Elaine's side, soon fell asleep. Not long after, Elaine lay her head on Kurt's shoulder and also dozed off. Over and over, Kurt yawned, but he stayed awake to cherish the moment. Elaine's chest rose and fell with sleep. An occasional sigh escaped her lips. Unable to control himself, Kurt turned his head to take in the sweet aroma of her sun-drenched hair, loving the softness of the silky strands against his nose. She blinked, smiled, and snuggled deeper into his arm, causing hope to etch itself into his heart more deeply than he ever thought possible.

On the quilt, sunlight dances on her as if she's covered with flickering fireflies. He wants to ask her to marry him, but his fear that she'll say no and end their relationship trembles on his lips every time he considers it.

Elaine told him about these visits, including how she enjoys the peace and quiet of being here alone. He should leave, but he'll wake her first because the old truck usually backfires when it starts, and it might startle her. He kneels on the quilt and touches her cheek with the rose. She mumbles something. He touches her freckled nose, and her eyes barely open. He smiles and starts to say hello, but she pulls him down and kisses him, running her fingers through his hair.

Stunned, Kurt is amazed. Although his wish is coming true, he's afraid to ask Elaine why she chose this moment to finally kiss him. If he does, she might stop, and that's the last thing he wants. He slips his fingers into the soft strands of hair at the nape of her neck and pulls her to him. What a dream. What a dream.

* * *

To Elaine, Joe's dream lips are his living lips: firm, yet soft and smooth. She holds him close, loving the feel of his warmth against her. "Oh, Joe, I missed you so much."

Her dream shudders and jars her awake. She's not holding Joe, she's holding Kurt, who's sobbing miserably. "Kurt, what—" She pulls away. "How did you get here? Why are you crying?"

"I was trying to wake you and ..." Wiping his eyes, he stands. "You need your time alone." Head down, still wiping his eyes, he leaves for his truck.

Elaine runs after him and blocks his way. "Why are you upset?"

"You kissed me."

"That upset you?"

"No, Lainey, it was—" He raises his head. "It was what you said."

What she said? What had she— "Did I call you Joe?"

"You said you missed him. I don't know why I ever thought ..."

Cheeks wet from crying, he lowers his head again. He looks so miserable, so utterly heartbroken, as if—

Of course, he's in love with her, and to mistake him for Joe, especially during their kiss, hurt him terribly.

"I was dreaming, Kurt. I didn't do anything wrong and neither did you. I was dreaming, that's all."

"I need to go." Kurt steps around her, but she blocks him again.

Anger floods Elaine with heat. If he loves her, he needs to be a man and own up to it. "You're not going anywhere!" she yells. "It's time we settled this right here and right now, do you hear me?"

"If you can't love me, I understand." He takes a step back. "But I can't be Joe."

"Kurt, please." Elaine steps closer. "I know exactly who you are and I care about you. It's … it's not easy, okay?" She takes his hand. "Let's sit. I feel silly standing here like this." She leads him to the picnic table. He sits, head down, hands clasped between his knees.

"Look at me, I'm not going to talk to you like you were some school boy."

Kurt faces her. No hint of his usual soft smile. No hint of interest in his usual crinkling eyes.

"Look, Kurt, I won't apologize for my memories and I won't apologize for loving Joe either. I'll always love him no matter what." He looks away; she shoves his shoulder. "Damn you, look at me! How do you think I feel by having to justify my love for Joe to an ex-German soldier?"

Usually pink, the scar on Kurt's forehead flares red. "You're just like the rest of the people in Alma who hate me. At least the Edwards were willing to get to know me. You still judge me for what I was instead of who I am now. Tell Joseph I'm sorry we can't go fishing anymore." Kurt leaves for the truck.

Elaine stands. Let him go or not? She sits. Love is too much work when the love of her life promised to come back and didn't. Life is better alone.

The truck cranks and roars backward in a semi-circle. The bumper crashes into the oak, the engine stalls, and Kurt smacks the steering wheel. A second passes. The truck sputters to life.

Elaine runs to her truck, slams it into reverse, and backs up. Dirt flies from the tires on Kurt's truck. She shifts into forward and accelerates into the path's entrance, blocking his way. The only way he can leave now is if he tries to drive through oaks and maples.

He gets out and goes to her window. "You hate me, let me leave."

She gets out. "I don't hate you, but you need to understand how much Joe means to me."

Kurt waves his arm toward the oak by the river. "Why do you think I planted the daffodils and made the picnic table and put the rocks around those ashes?"

"What's that got to do with anything?"

"Betty told me how much this place means to you. Don't you know I'd die right this minute if it would bring Joe back to you? I can't, so I did all those things to try to bring him back that way."

"Well, it worked to the point of me dreaming about kissing him. That's why I thought you were him."

Kurt takes a deep breath. "I'm sorry I said you hate me."

"Welcome to Joe's world—he had to deal with my mouth too." Elaine goes to the front of his truck and leans against the fender. "How will you explain this dent to Mr. Edwards?"

Kurt leans beside her and folds his arms. "It's a farm truck. This dent is the same as the other dents."

Grinning at his humor, Elaine bumps his shoulder with hers. "If you plan to joke with me, you need to smile so I know it's a joke."

"I'm not joking. That dent *is* the same as the other dents."

"'It's' and 'I'm,' huh? I see some of my contractions are rubbing off on you."

"Always the English teacher."

"You forgot to smile, we need to work on that. Do you

understand I'll never stop loving Joe, regardless of whether or not I get married again?"

"Does that mean you won't love the next man you marry?" Kurt smiles. "Or do I get to try to make you love me?"

Elaine smacks his arm. "If that smile means you'd marry me if I didn't love you, you have lost your mind."

"I see what you mean about Joe dealing with your mouth."

"You do? Why aren't you smiling?"

"I'm not joking." Kurt turns to face her. "Maybe a little, but we need to be serious. Do we have a chance or not?"

Elaine pauses. Time for a joke of her own. "If I say no, I know the perfect woman for you. Every time I go into the sewing shop, she gives me the evil eye."

"I know that woman," Kurt says. "She gave me the evil eye when I bought the ribbon for those daffodils I gave you. Does she have a daughter? Maybe I can turn her into a German lover and make her mother leave Alma."

"You're still not smiling."

"I'm still not joking."

"Yes, you silly German, we have a chance. Just don't forget, I'll always love Joe."

"How can I forget when you keep saying it?"

Elaine turns to face him. "I'm disappointed."

"In what?"

"That you haven't tried to shut me up with a kiss. It's about time, don't you think?"

Chapter 33

Kurt and Ruth

At home again, Kurt parks Lainey's old SUV in the driveway. As the Cape Hatteras Lighthouse figurine sways from its string on the rear-view mirror, a final memory erupts from his heart.

His Lainey, beautiful in her mother's wedding dress, smiles at him as she walks the church aisle. Beside him, George Edwards and Will Matthan, Kurt's best men, wait. On the other side of the aisle grins Joseph, the ring bearer. Albert, escorting her, flashes a thumbs-up.

What a grand life they shared, one that ended all too soon.

* * *

Done with supper, Kurt settles down in a well-worn easy chair by the fireplace to read. Once more he misses Lainey. As long as he keeps busy, her absence flutters near the edge of his usual upbeat mood like a hummingbird probing the feeder she once kept on the porch. Occasionally though, loneliness arrives with her imagined whispers, unsettles his thoughts with the smell of her favorite perfume, calls his name in the wind that moans around the corners of their old house. Those times usually hit late at night, with the creak of a settling board or the ticking of the clock on the fireplace mantle. Tonight is one of those nights. He enjoys the book, but the pangs of not being around someone who brings life into his heart and home prick him into an uncharacteristic melancholy.

He checks the time, almost ten. What's Ruth up to? He misses her stopping by like she did after Lainey died. She visited fairly often then, saying she didn't want him to become a hermit. For a while she dropped by so often, he was afraid she might catch him in his underwear.

He's grown accustomed to his and Ruth's routine. Like a sweat-stained cap that fits his head perfectly, they've sold their wares together at the Farmer's Market every Saturday for almost a year and a half. Her teasing banter, which he enjoys immensely, pokes a humorous thorn in his side, both before lunch and during.

Since he's older—and blatantly honest with himself—he admits to caring for her, possibly enough to believe he loves her. Not just friendly love either. She's on his mind more often these days, and it's on nights like this when he imagines her sitting at his side on the sofa, keeping him company with her gentle ways and quick wit. In the past few months he's considered proposing, but his feelings confuse him. Many a night, after considering them, he ends the evening with a single thought: *After all, old man, it's hard to know what to do when you aren't sure if it's love or if it's loneliness.*

She might care for him—more than simply friends—but he isn't sure. She never mentions her husband, not even in passing. Lainey said she moved to Alma after his death. Also, as far as Kurt knows, she's never formed any attachments since arriving, which suggests she's not interested in any. Her two children, who, as she said earlier today, only visit when they have time. Sometimes they don't even come for Christmas. Her grandchildren keep in touch on the Internet, sharing pictures and messages through emails. Even though she jokes about cell phones, technology gives her few problems.

Never caring to dog-ear a page of one of his favorites, Kurt places a marker in the book, eases up from the chair, and stretches.

* * *

Joe enjoys the calm of the evening, the warm flicker of fire, the scent of woodsmoke. He also enjoys Kurt's book. *The Call of the Wild* was his and Elaine's favorite. Most of the people he inhabited over the years spoke English, but many didn't. This resulted in his confinement in a mental prison, the bars made of unrecognizable words instead of cold steel.

Kurt shuffles to the fireplace. A wooden chest, its rich, almost-black surface resembling mahogany, rests on the mantle. Joe admires the craftsmanship. A brass plate is tacked near the bottom, but he can't make out the engraving. Kurt rubs the smooth wood, slightly warm from the fire's rising heat, and sighs.

He goes to the kitchen and flips a light switch, pours dog food into one bowl, cat food into another, and opens the back door. "Joe, Samantha, come and get it!" The retriever runs toward Kurt from the direction of his dog house, tail wagging.

Joe mentally frowns. *Oh, great, the dog's named after me.*

Kurt scratches the dog behind the ears. "You seen Samantha?" A meow echoes in the yard. A set of green eyes appears in the dark, growing brighter as the cat silently pads into the circle of light.

Kurt sets the food down. As his pets crunch away, he raises his eyes to the starry sky. The sight brings the sting of sadness to Joe's soul. *I didn't see the constellation Orion when Elaine and me stayed late at the river, but I still remember that night. Many's the time I've wished I could control a person's eyes so I could have a decent cry. Too bad I can't do that now.*

Kurt returns to the kitchen. Washing his supper dishes, he occasionally rubs his neck. Joe senses Kurt's demeanor—slow and little sad—and imagines the old man isn't looking forward to sleeping in a cold and lonely bed.

Dishes done, Kurt locks doors and flips light switches. In the bedroom, he dumps his pockets, drops his keys on the dresser, and Joe gets a better look at the picture of the boy he noticed this morning. The grinning young fisherman, around twelve or thirteen, holds a huge catfish while standing by a much younger version of Kurt, who has blond hair like Joe's. The boy has blond hair too, but it's curly like Joe's instead of straight like Kurt's. *Where are you now, young man? All grown up with a family of your own? What about that fish, did you catch it from the same river Elaine and I visited? In the long list of things I'd like to do one more time, one of them would be to go fishing there with her again.*

Kurt completes his bathroom ritual and dons pajamas. To Joe's relief, he remembers his slippers. Like this morning, he sits on the bedside to study the picture on the nightstand. Silent minutes pass. He kisses a fingertip and touches it to his wife's lips. In bed, he pulls the chilly blankets up around him and attempts to read the book he brought from the living room. He yawns, reads a couple of sentences, and yawns again. A few pages later, his eyes close and open … close and open.

Sleep takes Joe like it takes Kurt: gradual, dreamlike. As the book slowly drops to Kurt's chest, a memory bubbles to the surface of Joe's thoughts, translucent globes of hope, each rising from the river's murky depths.

A lazy summer afternoon, Elaine in his arms.

Her hair soft upon his brow. Her breath sweet upon his cheek. Her kisses warm upon his lips.

The river's flow whispers a gentle serenade. A breeze rustles the oak leaves overhead. Sleep takes him and Elaine into dreams of a life together.

I love you, Elaine.

* * *

Kurt's eyes flutter open, waking Joe. Rain taps on the window. "Uh-oh," Kurt says. "No picnic today, Ruthie."

Darn, Kurt, you and Ruth are a lot more fun together than you are by yourself. Don't let a little rain mess things up. Invite her over so she can perk you and this old house up.

Like yesterday morning, Kurt sits on the edge of the bed to take his wife's picture from the nightstand.

The name on that lampshade is Lainey? I would've been about Kurt's age had I lived. I don't remember any Lainey living around Alma. Lainey. Didn't I hear him and Ruth mention someone named Lainey? If anyone ever called Elaine Lainey, I'd know it. Kurt's wife must be someone he met outside of town.

The pungent fragrance of coffee drifts from the kitchen, and Joe licks his mental lips. Kurt dresses quickly, this time keeping the warm slippers on instead of exchanging them for boots.

He fills a mug, starts to sip, and the phone rings. Cordless in hand, he sits at the table and sips the steaming coffee, scalding his tongue in the process.

Doggone, old man, that hurts. As old as you are, don't you know better than to drink coffee that's too hot?

At the freezer, Kurt pops ice into his mouth. The answering machine beeps. "Kurt, honey," Ruth says, "it looks like our picnic is a washout. I was thinking—" Kurt spits the ice in his palm and pushes the handset button.

"Hey, Ruthie, what're you thinking?"

"Are you screening your calls now, old man?"

"I tried to sneak in a sip of coffee before I answered and scalded my tongue." He pops the ice back into his mouth. "I'm putting ithe on ith wight now."

"Ithe?"

Kurt removes the ice. "Ice—i-c-e—ice."

"Oh. Anyway, since it's raining I was thinking about cooking a pot roast and bringing some over for supper. Can your tongue handle it?"

Kurt's mouth waters.

Get her over here, old man. A good meal and a little fun might do us some good.

"Ruthie, you just magically healed my tongue. Any chance you have a loaf of your bread? I have a bottle of red wine that'll go great with a meal like that."

"It sounds like you want to take advantage of me and my pot roast, you old pervert."

Joe tries to smile, and Kurt does. "Why, Ruthie, hasn't that been your fantasy for years?"

"You wish. Open the wine at four and let it get some fresh air. On the way I'll run by the market and pick up something for my sweet tooth. I'll be there around five. See you later."

The conversation amuses Joe. He's known many older couples over the years, but none compare to these two. Along with the delicious prospect of pot roast with homemade bread and red wine, the evening looks promising.

Kurt trades his slippers for boots, puts on a cap and a jacket, and splashes through the yard to the barn. He places a stick of oak on a chopping block and hefts an ax to split it. Joe guesses it'll be the first of many for the fireplace for tonight, so he shuts the eyes of his consciousness.

* * *

Done stacking the wood by the fireplace, Kurt gathers cleaning supplies from the pantry. He wipes the stove, refrigerator, and counters. Checking the pantry again, he finds an old feather duster and shakes it outside. The wind blows dust back into his face, setting off a sneezing fit. In the living room, swishing the feathers over the end tables and the fireplace mantle, he chuckles softy. He resembles a farmer hanging onto a chicken that has no intention of being Sunday dinner.

Satisfied with his dusting, he returns to the kitchen and fills a bucket with hot water for mopping.

A scratching sound comes from the door. "Darn it," he says, opening the door. "I'm sorry, you two, I forgot to feed you." Joe and Samantha patter in; wet feet muddy the floor. Kurt fills their bowls. Good thing he planned to mop.

His pets finish eating and return to their outdoor houses. Kurt mops the floor and waits in a chair at the table for the yellowed linoleum to dry.

When the wet sheen is almost gone, he stands. "Kurt, old boy, what you need after all that work is more coffee." He empties the decanter into a mug, puts on another pot to brew, and returns to his seat. As far as he's concerned, these cold, rainy days are prime examples of why the good Lord made the coffee bean.

Raising the mug to drain the last drops, he wrinkles his nose at the sour aroma of his underarms and glances at the clock over the stove. Time for a shower before Ruth gets here, if he hurries.

In the bathroom, he throws his clothes in the hamper, turns

the water on as hot as he can stand, and steps into the steaming stall.

* * *

At the touch of hot water, Joe blinks his mental eyes. *I see you're getting spruced up for your date, old man. Go ahead, I've got some thinking to do.*

That medal hanging outside the bathroom, along with what's left of Kurt's accent, tells me he's German. He's also about the right age to have been in the war, but how the heck he got to Nebraska, I don't know. He was married and had a son, but his wife in the picture is dead. As far as Elaine, I doubt I'll figure out what happened to her. Other than that, who knows?

Out of the shower, Kurt dries himself with a coarse towel in need of fabric softener. *Durn, old man, take it easy. That towel feels like sandpaper.*

Kurt massages some kind of lotion into his knees and elbows, then spreads shave cream on his face.

Amused by his wildly pointing eyebrows, Joe studies the old man's reflection in the mirror while he scrapes his gray stubble. *That's quite the routine you have there, Kurt. I'm glad you aren't into plucking your eyebrows, but they sure could use a trim. Huh, his nose is twitching. He's slipping on his robe. I bet he's going for more coffee.*

In the kitchen, as Kurt rinses the dregs from his mug, someone knocks on the door.

The door window, foggy from the cool, rainy day, blocks his view. He wipes the chilly haze with his hand, which reveals Ruth's frown. He opens the door. "You're a bit early, aren't you, Ruthie? Planning on catching me in the nude?"

Ruth's eyes dart from his, to his robe, to his feet, and she bursts out laughing. Every time she catches her breath, a fresh wave of laughter takes hold, even to the point of her grabbing the door frame to steady herself. Kurt crosses his arms to wait.

Ruth's giggles gradually subside. She takes a tissue from her purse. Wiping her eyes, she shakes her head. "Oh yeah, baby, catching you in the nude's been my dream ever since we met."

She takes a crock pot from a table on the porch by the door. "You better get dressed. If I have to look at those legs" — she points at his feet with the toe of her dripping shoe— "or those crooked old things you call toes any longer, I might ravish you right here on the kitchen floor."

Kurt uncrosses his arms. "Now look here, old hen, I—" He stops to make sure his robe is tied. If anything were hanging out, Ruth might have a durn stroke laughing. "I better put some clothes on," he says, glad everything is secure. "I *might* be back in a minute." His feet slap the hardwood floor in the hall.

"That's a good idea!" Ruth yells after him. "You remind me of one of those shirtless hotties on a romance novel!"

Kurt closes the door, which muffles her cackling laughter. He puts on underwear, socks, a shirt, and gets one leg in his pants.

Knock-knock-knock.

On one foot, Kurt grabs the door knob. "What?"

"Hey, Hot Ass, I'm running home to change. Do you need anything from the grocery?"

"Can you pick up some shame from the drugstore? You need a good dose."

"Who needs shame when they've got spice? Remember what I said about a meal being mediocre without spice?"

"Good grief, don't I know it. As far as what I need, you crazy old woman, the dignity my clothes can give me is a start. Drive safe."

Chapter 34

First Date

While Kurt puts his other leg in his pants, Joe shares his shoulder-bouncing chuckles. Laughing like this is better than not laughing at all, but it isn't the same as laughing in his own body. Nothing compares to a knee-slapping roar from way down deep that squeezes tears from his eyes and takes his breath away. Ruth's one of the funniest women he's ever known, and he's known a lot of funny women over the years, even residing in a few. Add Kurt to the comedic mix, he and Ruth are a male and female version of Laurel and Hardy. There's no telling what else might happen this evening.

Fully dressed, Kurt digs around in the cabinet under the bathroom sink until he finds an artifact from Joe's past: a bottle of Old Spice aftershave lotion. Joe winces at the slight alcohol sting, but he still enjoys the out-of-style fragrance his father wore, and which he borrowed from time to time so long ago.

Kurt goes to the living room. He adjusts a picture or two, fluffs the sofa pillows, and snaps his fingers. In the kitchen, after shoving the mop, bucket, and detergent in the pantry, he eyes the coffee maker.

Uh-huh. Ruth interrupted your coffee break while ago, and you're ready to try again.

Kurt fills the mug, sits, and sips a bit more carefully.

221

A car horn beeps. He goes to the window on the door and pulls back the curtains. Ruth shuts off the headlights and emerges from the car, bag in hand. He splashes through the drizzle. "That didn't take long, Ruthie. Did you clean out the market?"

She gives him a bag. "Let's get in out of the rain before we wash off your Old Spice."

"Did I put on too much?"

"It's just easy to recognize."

They bring everything to the table, and Kurt closes the door. "Can I take your wrap, madam?"

Wearing a long overcoat that almost reaches the floor, Ruth turns around. "You certainly can, kind sir."

Kurt slips the coat off her shoulders, revealing a stylish turquoise knee-length dress. Joe shares the old man's eyebrow rise. *I doubt Ruth usually wears anything as nice as this. She seems like a jeans lady to me. That's what she had on at the Farmer's Market.*

"Wow, Ruthie, you clean up mighty fine."

"Thank you for noticing."

"I meant the dress, not you."

"Why you old buzzard, after being married to my best friend for over forty years, don't you know better than to joke about a lady's looks?"

What the heck is wrong with you, old man, making a comment like that to this nice lady?

"If I offended you, Ruth, I apologize. After you carried on like you did when you caught me in my robe, I can't help but tease you."

Ruth pats his arm. "There, there, don't fret. Just remember, comments like that rarely help a man" —with a lightly mascaraed eye, she gives Kurt an exaggerated wink— "get lucky. Now that first one, when you said I 'clean up mighty fine,' that might help a fella get to first base, at least."

Kurt grins so huge his cheeks ache. Ruth holds up her hands as if to fend him off. "Whoa, now, I was just kidding. Can you can pour me a sip or three of wine?"

Kurt fills a glass. "I'll have coffee now and wine with supper. Can't let you drink alone, can I?" He refills his mug and joins her at the table, to clink the mug to her wine glass. "How about a toast? To Ruthie and Lainey, the finest two women in all of Nebraska."

Ruth sips wine. "Where's the hard stuff, making such a speech? Either that or you *are* trying to get lucky. Look, I'll let you in on a secret." Ruth leans close, her lips near Kurt's ear. "I didn't bring any."

"You didn't bring any what?"

Ruth sits back. "Viagra, of course."

"No little blue pill for me, Ruthie. Regardless of what Lainey might have told you, I've never had any … uh … failures in that department. Besides, I'm too worn out for any such foolishness."

"Thus the Viagra. Don't worry, I'm worn out myself." Ruth clinks her wine glass to his coffee mug.

Kurt drinks coffee. "When's supper? That pot roast smells great."

I remember Mom's pot roast smelling like that in our kitchen at home. The aroma of beef makes Joe attempt to lick his phantom lips. *"It made my mouth water like yours, old man.*

Being familiar with the kitchen from all her visits, Ruth gets a fork from a drawer and inserts it into the roast, which almost falls apart. She gets a platter and a carving knife from a cabinet.

"All right then. If you set the table, I'll slice."

Kurt does so and pours himself a glass of wine. Ruth brings over the platter of sliced beef. Potatoes, carrots, mushrooms, and onions steam on the side.

Kurt aims a fork at a slice of beef, and Ruth clears her throat, stopping him. "I have a small request."

"Anything, Ruth, anything at all."

"Do you mind if I say a blessing?"

Kurt's cheeks warm.

If I were you, old man, I'd be embarrassed too. I imagine you have a lot to be thankful for.

Kurt takes Ruth's hand. "Nothing would please me better."

Ruth bows her head. "Dear Father, thank you for the friendship of this man and his wife. They have filled my last years with more happiness than I deserve. Thank You for this meal and all your blessings, amen."

"Amen," Kurt says, patting Ruth's hand. "Thank you for that and thank you for your friendship. More importantly, thank you for your friendship to Lainey. I tried to be her rock when she was sick, but you were her feather-bed of comfort. She thought the world of you."

"As you well know, the feeling was mutual." Ruth clinks her wine glass to Kurt's. "A toast to avoid too many jokes tonight and enjoy an evening of calm and peace. Do you have any wood split for the fireplace?"

"Sure do. I'll get it going right after supper."

As Kurt chews bites of juicy beef, along with tender carrots and sweet onions, Joe's phantom taste buds pop as if he's enjoying the meal himself. Between swallows of food and sips of wine, the conversation includes gardening, his greenhouse, and her baking, making Joe think about his years growing up in Alma, and also about Elaine.

All these years I've wanted to come home and find out what happened to Elaine. Some reunion this is turning out to be. To top it off, I'm stuck in some old German soldier too. If he has anything to do with Elaine, I don't know how. Where the heck can she be?

Chapter 35

Elaine and Ruth

December 17, 1997

Elaine raises the morphine pump control, presses the button, and returns the control to the bed.

She touches the scars beneath her nightgown. Two years of radiation, chemo, and surgery, and all she has to show for it is a chest with one breast.

She presses another button to recline the hospital bed at the foot of her and Kurt's bed—the bed they shared for over forty years. No matter, she enjoyed a happy and fulfilling life. The only thing that could've made it better is if she had spent it with Joe.

Death challenges her, but the challenge of dealing with pain is entirely different. She presses the morphine pump button again and leaves it on the blanket that covers her frail body. The pain can be debilitating, but she's grateful her humor is lurking just below the surface of an occasional grimace. She eyes her thin frame. There's so little left of her, she wouldn't even make a decent scarecrow. If she were hanging in a field, the crows would *caw-caw* with laughter.

In the kitchen, Kurt stirs soup. The spoon tapping the side of the pot sounds like a muted bell around the neck of a cow that's moved in. Despite having no appetite, Elaine will take a few sips to help him feel more positive. Well, as positive a husband can feel with his wife dying from cancer, unable to share his bed because she might soil the damn sheets. Not an occurrence that makes her smile in the least.

Enough of the pity party, what was she about to do? Oh, yes, her book, her *favorite* book. The binding crackles in protest as she opens the faded hardcover. Has Kurt noticed this book never leaves her side these days? Probably not, since he knows Jack London is one of her favorite authors. He wore out his original version learning to read English and bought a recent paperback version to replace it. *The Call of the Wild*, this exact copy from 1943, is not only *her* favorite, it was also Joe's favorite. She never told Kurt that. Anyway, it isn't so much the book as it is the treasures inside.

The spoon still taps. She takes the pictures from the yellowed pages. Although the black and white photographs are somewhat faded, each detail is as clear and vibrant and everlasting as when she first began treasuring them this way after Joe died in December of 1944.

Taken in July, the first is of her and Joe standing by the Republican River on the evening before he left for basic training at Fort Leavenworth. The second, taken the next morning, is of her and Joe at the train station in Holdrege. Her arms are around his neck, his are around her waist, and the yellow hair ribbon she just gave him dangles from his fingers. The third was taken in September, after their wedding at the office of the Justice of the Peace in Holdrege.

1944.

1997.

Fifty-three years.

How completely and utterly amazing that number is, which doesn't matter in the least.

Like sparks bursting upward from their honeymoon fire, the years slip away, rising with flare and flicker, pinpricks of light dancing among the stars, embraced by the black of night to simply—

Disappear.

It could have just happened. Could have.

She presses her fingertips to her lips.

Presses them to Joe's smile.

A single tear traces a warm trail down Elaine's temple, past her ear lobe, down her neck. Another follows, which will leave a wet spot on her pillow. Kurt might see it, but she's beyond worrying about such trivial things.

His footsteps echo in the hall, so she tucks the pictures into the book. *Soon, Joe, I'll see you soon. God willing, we'll get to start all over again.*

Kurt brings a tray to the bedside table. "Got your soup warmed up, Lainey. Got some crackers to go with it."

Elaine leaves her book on Kurt's bed. "Can you help me sit up, sweetheart?"

"Yes, ma'am, I sure can."

Elaine raises the bed. Kurt gently lifts her so she can sit straighter, but a soft moan escapes her clenched teeth. No doubt he can feel her bones through her nightgown. No doubt he would give anything to not cause her pain.

He places a pillow behind her. "I'm sorry, Lainey."

"It's all right, I can handle it." *Maybe with a triple dose of morphine.* He turns for the tray and she pushes the white button again. *Why doesn't this stupid thing work?*

Kurt pulls up a chair, sits, and offers her a spoonful of soup, his hand beneath it to catch drips. She sips the semi-salty liquid, nibbles a cracker, and swallows more soup. "That hit the spot, sweetheart, thank you." Kurt's expression—sad eyes, deep wrinkles across the faded scar on his forehead, no hint of a smile—communicates his concern.

Elaine pats his arm. "I'll have another spoonful in a few minutes, okay?"

"All right, Lainey."

Someone knocks on the kitchen door, and Kurt leaves. Elaine dabs her lips with a napkin. That should be Ruth.

Ruth appears in the bedroom doorway, Kurt behind her. She holds a small foil-wrapped package. "Just in time for lunch, I see. Elaine, how would you like a slice of my bread with your soup? It's still warm, fresh out of the oven."

"I could go for that, Ruth. Sweetheart, do you mind if us ladies have a chat? Don't worry, I'll have more soup."

"Holler if you need anything." Kurt closes the door behind him.

Ruth sits in the chair and scoots closer. "Do you have any idea how much he's going to miss you?"

"As much as I'd miss him if it were the other way around. I can count on you to see him through the rough spots, can't I?"

"That you can, hon." Ruth unwraps the foil package, releasing the fresh-baked aroma of her famous bread.

Elaine licks her lips, trying to work up enough saliva to swallow. "You know what? That soup would taste a lot better with a piece of your bread dipped in it." Ruth dips the bread and holds her hand under it while Elaine takes a bite. "Mmm, mm, that's what I call a meal. Set it there by the bowl."

"Can't you eat more now?"

"For what? So I can fill out my burial dress?"

"I'm sorry if I can't smile. Leave it to you to joke on your death bed." Ruth puts the bread aside. "Your phone call was rather cryptic. You have some errands for me?"

"Three to be exact." Elaine reaches under the covers for four envelopes. "Open yours after I … well, you know. When Joseph comes, give him the one with his name on it."

Ruth takes the envelopes and reads them. Elaine knows the third one, with Kurt's name on it, will make sense, but she waits to see how she'll react to the last one.

As she reads it, her eyes widen. "Okay, Kurt and Joseph and I have envelopes." She puts the four envelopes in her purse, beside her in the floor. "But how in the heck do I give Joe his?"

"That's part of one of my requests. I hope you can give it— and me—to Joe. Not now, of course, but later, after Kurt passes."

Ruth's mouth falls open. "After Kurt passes? Do I have a séance and invite you and your two husbands so you three can figure out who gets who in the afterlife?"

"Don't be silly" Elaine says, narrowing her eyes. "This old hen is still scratching around the yard with a clear mind."

"That remains to be seen," Ruth says, her tone doubtful. "Answer me about the séance and I'll let you know if your cheese has slipped off its cracker."

Elaine points to the dresser. "See those books? Get the one with the blue cover."

Ruth goes to the dresser and touches one of several books between two bookends "This one? *The Ghosts of Longing?*"

"That's it."

Ruth takes the book to Elaine sand sits. Elaine opens the book and closes it. "We've discussed a lot of things over the years, but I doubt we ever discussed this. Is there any chance you believe in ghosts or spirits, or maybe possession?"

"I believe in the soul, if that's what you mean. I've also heard and read some interesting ghost stories that made me wonder about that sort of thing, why?"

"It's going to sound crazy, but when Joe left Alma, he said he would come back to me no matter what. Of course, he—"

"Oh, hush. You know that's impossible."

"Because he died in Europe?" Elaine pats Ruth's hand, "That's what I was about to say, Ms. Interrupter. Regardless, if there's such a thing as ghosts or possession, he might still be out in the world looking for me. Who knows, maybe I'll become a ghost and go looking for him too."

Ruth leans back in the chair and folds her arms. "Old hen, I think you've about scratched any claim to logic out of this discussion."

"Logic?" Elaine waves a bony hand at Ruth. "As far as logic, I know the value of it because I'm a teacher. Regardless, love is a powerful thing, especially the love Joe and I shared in the short time we were together. Believing we'd find each other again has been a comfort over the years."

"I can see that. Still …"

"I told you how it was when Joe died—it's something I never quite got over. Holding on to the hope that he'll come back to me is a large part of what helped me get over the grief. If it weren't for that … if it weren't for Joseph …"

Ruth tilts her head to one side. "If it weren't for Joseph, what?"

Although Elaine isn't sure what her best friend will think of this story, she thinks she'll understand. After all, she understands how much Joe's death affected her. She sits a little higher in the bed.

"I never told anyone this. It was about a week after the news came about Joe. It was a Saturday, and Mom and Dad were in town. They were worried, but I told them to get out of the house and stop hovering over me like a doggone wasp buzzing over a nest. I told them I'd be taking a nap. I think that was the second time I'd ever been dishonest with them. The first was when I married Joe without telling them."

Ruth's eyes narrow. "What did you do if you didn't take a nap?"

"I drove to the river—you know where I mean—and I thought about jumping in."

"You mean killing yourself?" Ruth asks, her tone climbing higher.

"I thought about it. Well, until I thought about being pregnant with Joe's baby. Even if it hadn't been for the baby, I don't think I'd have done it. Anyway, that's what I did, and I'm glad I'm here to tell you about it."

"Me too," Ruth says, adding a slight grin."

"Will you take care of Joe's letter for me?"

"As long as I don't have to die to do it. What's the other request?"

"This one might sound loonier than that one."

Ruth leans back in the chair again. "All right, lay it on me."

Elaine taps the book with a fingertip. "This says it might be possible—might be—for the ghosts of people who have died to exist within close friends or loved ones."

"What the heck are they supposed to be doing in there?" Ruth asks, chuckling at the same time. "Enjoying someone else's sex life?"

Elaine rolls her eyes. "*You* would. I'd be too embarrassed."

"You always were a prude, hon."

"Well, *hon*, this book says the ghost might try to find its way back to the person they loved most in life."

"*Now* I see where this is going. You think Joe's in someone close by, and he's trying to get back to you."

"Despite your tone, which says my cheese has not only slipped off my cracker, but cancer ate it too, my theory is Joe might show up when Kurt's time gets near."

Ruth's eyebrows scrunch into a knot. "What's Kurt got to do with this?"

"I think he and Joe are linked through their mutual love for me. Like the book says, Joe's ghost, or spirit, or whatever we might call it, might come to Kurt. If that happens, when Kurt dies, Joe might be set free so we can be together again."

"Oh, sure, maybe he's inside a unicorn," Ruth says sarcastically. "Shoot, why stop there, maybe he's inside Joe. I know how much you love that dog. If I didn't know any better, I'd say you named him after Joe because you've never been able to let him go. Come to think of it, I *don't* know any better."

Elaine pops Ruth's hand. "Hush your horse hockey and listen. I want you to read that letter to Joe when Kurt is close to death. If Joe is near, I want him to hear it."

"How do I know I'll be there when—you know—*then?* He could pass anywhere at any time."

"I have one more request to help with that."

"I thought there weren't any more?"

"Hey, I'm dying, sue me."

Ruth laughs out loud and Elaine joins in. Maybe Kurt can hear their laughter. If so, he'll smile at knowing she and Ruth can still carry on like this.

Ruth takes a tissue from a nearby box and wipes her eyes. "Okay, what's this request about?"

Elaine knows Ruth will do almost anything she asks, but this might shake her. The signs are there, she's seen them herself. The question is how Ruth will take her suggestion.

"I want you to marry Kurt."

"Well flip me a pancake, Elaine, how many kids should we have? Two? Eight? A doz—"

"Don't you love him?"

"I—" Ruth blinks once, twice, and Elaine gently squeezes her best friend's hand. "It isn't all that hard to see when another woman has feelings for her husband. I imagine part of it is because of the way your ex treated you. You've never had a man treat you decently, or with respect like Kurt does, right?"

"All this time I thought I was hiding it. I had no idea a man could be so nice to a woman until I met you and Kurt. You know I wouldn't come between you two for anything."

Elaine squeezes Ruth's hand again. "Except for Kurt and Joseph, you're my best friend. As far as you and him getting together after I move on, couldn't it happen?"

"With you, Elaine, anything is possible." Ruth leans close to palm Elaine's cheek. "You're the best friend I've ever had, old hen. As much as Kurt is going to miss you, do you know how much I'm going to miss you too?"

As a boy, Joseph's blond-headed, blue-eyed, sweet-as-can-be self always had the perfect answer.

Elaine opens her arms wide.

"I know, this much!"

Chapter 36

Death and Birth

Elaine hugs Ruth goodbye. Minutes later, except for the soft clank of Kurt washing the soup pot and bowl, the house is quiet again.

A spasm of pain shoots through her middle, like a giant hawk's talons slashing her insides. She snatches the morphine control from the bed and jabs the white button.

Please, God, I can't take much more of this.

The pain hits in wave after wave, concentrated in her middle, worsening each time. The location makes no sense; even the doctors said nothing about it. Another wave of agony takes hold, almost like a birth contraction. Jabbing the button again, she holds it until her thumbnail turns white. She tries to call Kurt but another pain takes her breath, doubling her over.

Please, God, why can't I just die and be done with it?

The deep blue of the bedroom curtains fades to the color of fog over the fields, milky white and subdued to the near point of nothingness. The golden daffodils on the wallpaper wither to a sickly yellow. The ceiling and lights pulse in time with her slowing heartbeat. The *tick-tock* of the clock on Kurt's nightstand slows as if it needs winding. On the dresser, Joseph's picture of him holding a catfish, Kurt at his side, shrinks to the size of a postage stamp. The wood grain in the dresser wavers like the haze hanging over a scorching road in summer. The tiny lines twist over and over, until they form a pretzel of polished walnut. Everything fades to white, like the mythical white light described in some of her life-after-death books. The light intensifies, slowly enveloping her, wrapping her in a blinding white sheet of brightness.

She's ready. Ready to see Joe.

Another pain wrenches her, so crushingly intense that she expects her frail body to tear apart.

The light fades into darkness.

The darkness gives way, step by step by step as if waking from a dream. Elaine's surroundings grow bright again, but still too bright to focus. *Am I in heaven? Joe, where are you? I'm—*

"Wow, honey, I can see the baby's head."

What? Whose head? Who are you and what are you talking about and—? Wait a doggone minute, why can't I talk? Am I paralyzed?

The room comes into focus. A white sheet covers her legs, drawn up nearly to her chest. Sweat trickles from her forehead into her ears.

Did I pass out? Am I in the hospital? Another tearing pain. *Oh my God, what's happening to—*

"It's a boy, a healthy baby boy. Ten fingers and ten toes." A shrill cry, like Joseph's when he was born, comes from behind the sheet.

A baby? What? How? I thought I was dying?

A young man, maybe in his late twenties, beaming a huge smile, steps from behind the sheet. "You did great, Rachel, we have a son." He kisses her. "I love you, honey."

Who's Rachel and who are you sand why are you kissing me?

"I love you too, Adam. Is he okay?"

Why did I say that? Who's Adam? Who's Rachel? What the—

A man in blue scrubs and a white mask steps from behind the sheet. "Here you go, Mrs. Lewis, see for yourself." He places a beautiful baby boy wrapped in a blue swaddling blanket on her chest. Or is it Rachel's chest?

I'm so-o-o-o confused.

As the two parents marvel at their new baby, Elaine doesn't blame them one bit. Adam holds the small hand. "Nice to meet you, Son. Your name is Samuel Lewis."

Elaine marvels at the baby too, but she marvels more at her strange life-to-death-to-life transformation. *Those pains make sense now. They were exactly the same as when Joseph was born.*

The doctor returns to Rachel's side. "Sam needs another Apgar score." A nurse takes Sam to a nearby table.

Adam faces the doctor. "Thanks for everything, Dr. Michaels."

"Congratulations on your new son. Is his sister excited about having a little brother?"

"She can't wait to see him," Rachel says. "How long before we can go to our room?"

"We'll have you on your way soon so he can have his first meal." The doctor steps behind the sheet. "I'll add a few stitches while they're checking Sam. Adam goes to visit Sam while the doctor works.

My book must have been right. I'm now a ghost, or whatever it is that truly makes me me, and I'm living within this new mom. This should be an interesting experience, especially since it's been so long since I had Joseph.

The nurse places Sam in Rachel's arms, and Adam escorts them along the hall.

Elaine's excitement at starting a new life of sorts mingles with sadness. Time after time she wishes Joe could have been with her when Joseph was born. Aside from his death, that's one of the most difficult parts of their story. Still, Joe gave her a wonderful son, and she couldn't be any prouder. *Joseph was such a cute little fellow, smart too. I remember—*

Oh, no, Kurt! I can't imagine what he's going through. Ruth should be there soon and comfort him. It'll take time, but she'll help him find happiness again.

Adam holds Sam while the nurse helps Rachel into bed. He touches the tiny toes and fingers, the delicate, translucent nails, and ends by kissing the pink forehead.

Well, Mr. New Daddy, isn't he amazing? That's exactly how I felt the first time I held Joseph.

Rachel pulls the hospital bed sheets, stiff and smelling of starch, around her. "Don't you think Sam's ready for his first meal?"

"If he's anything like his dad he is," Adam says. He takes Sam over, who knows exactly how to nurse.

Rachel looks up at Adam. "Yep, just like his dad."

Adam blushes; the nurse pats his arm. "Don't be embarrassed, Mr. Lewis. Just remember, they're all Sam's for at least six weeks."

Adam's face turns a deeper shade of pink. Rachel bursts out laughing while Sam, Elaine can tell, isn't happy that his meal is interrupted. He begins to cry, but quiets when he finds his mother's nipple again.

The tiny lips nuzzling Rachel's breast cause Elaine's motherly urges—along with a bit of melancholy—to return.

If you're out there, Joe, I'm praying as hard as I can that we find each other again. I'm here and I'm hoping, and I pray you're hoping too.

Chapter 37

A Brother's Special Smell

Adam snaps his fingers. "I need to call Mom and Dad and Hope."

"Did you forget my parents in the waiting room?" Rachel asks.

"Good idea, I'll tell them first."

Adam's sneakers squeak on the newly waxed floor as he rounds the corner to the waiting room. Rachel's parents are relieved Rachel and Sam are doing well and want to know when they can see Sam. Adam tells them right after he phones his parents and Hope.

He takes out his phone and calls them, and they're equally relieved. "Is Sam there, Grandpa?" Hope asks in the background. Adam's dad gives Hope the phone. "Has Sam been born, Daddy? I didn't hear what you told Grandpa."

"He was born a little while ago. He and Mommy are fine."

"What's he look like?"

"He looks like you when you were born. He has the same color eyes and hair too."

"Daddy?"

"Yes, honey?"

"Grandma said new babies smell special. What's special smell like?"

"You'll find out when you see him."

"But when?"

"Tomorrow, okay? Mommy and Sam are tired."

"Can you kiss Sam and Mommy for me? I've been good. I helped Grandma make cookies."

"I'm sure you've been good, honey, you're the best. Can you save me a cookie? I bet they're especially good since you helped Grandma."

"They are, Daddy, chocolate chip! I'll save you some. We can take some to Mommy and Sam too."

"Mommy might like one, but all Sam can have now is milk."

"But cookies are good with milk."

"Sam doesn't have teeth to chew a cookie. They'd upset his tummy too. You know how it feels when your tummy hurts."

"I don't want his tummy to hurt, he might cry."

"He's going to cry, honey. That's how he lets us know when he's hungry, or when his diaper needs changing."

Hope grows quiet. Adam can almost see her blue eyes crinkling while she ponders this information. "I've got to go, okay? I'll be glad to kiss Sam and Mommy for you. I love you, honey, bye-bye."

"I love you, Daddy. I love Mommy and Sam too. Bye!"

The doctor stops by after Rachel's parents leave, telling Adam and Rachel she can go home tomorrow.

* * *

The next day, when Adam opens the door to Rachel's room, Hope patters to the bed. "Mommy, Mommy! We need to show Sam to Grandma and Grandpa Sand go home!" Adam goes to the bed. Hope hasn't even seen her tiny brother cuddled in Rachel's arms, having his breakfast.

"You want to see him, honey?" Rachel says. "Don't forget my hug and kiss."

Adam gives Hope a boost. Her eyes open wide and her lips form an O. She twists around. "Hold me still, Daddy. I want to see what special smells like, like Grandma said." Adam holds her close, and she sniffs Sam's fine wisps of hair. "Mmm, he *does* smell good. Do I ever smell like that, Mommy?"

"You sure do, because you're special too. Isn't he beautiful?"

Adam slides a chair over for Hope. On her knees, she leans over to place her finger in Sam's hand. His fingers close, and her fine, blonde eyebrows arch. "He likes me! He is *very* beautiful, Mommy." She touches one of his cheeks as it works in and out while he nurses. "He sure likes to eat."

Adam clears his throat. He takes a tissue from a box by the bed and dabs his eyes. Rachel looks around Hope. "Are you okay over there?"

"I couldn't be better." He wraps his arms around his family.

Hope squirms. "You're squishing me and Sam, Daddy. Can I hold him now?"

"You can," Rachel says, "but you have to sit and be still."

Hope plops into the chair. "Is this good? Am I being still?"

Adam takes Sam. "Do you mind if I hold him a minute? I haven't seen him since last night."

"Okay, Daddy, my turn next."

Adam slides a chair from the corner, sits beside Hope, and holds the warm blue bundle in the crook of his elbow. "Hey, Sam, I'm your Daddy." He kisses his son's soft brow. "And I love you more than I can say."

* * *

Elaine attempts to smile at the family's interaction, but only for a moment. It's been years since Joseph was that age, and he never had a sibling. Time and time again she wished otherwise, so this little taste of what she missed makes her ache for Joe even more.

Okay, I'm here and I'm doing this, but for how long? It's nice and all, and this family is wonderful, but come on, it's been over fifty years since I've seen Joe and—

What am I thinking? If Joe's been living this way for over fifty years, I can't imagine how he feels.

Elaine's heart breaks all over again. She hoped for the same beginning with Joe as Adam and Rachel are experiencing. Seeing this young couple so in love—so in love with their family—should make her happy and hopeful. Instead, it dredges up the pain of everything she lost when she lost Joe.

Adam stands. "Okay, Hope, are you ready to hold him?"

"Yes, Daddy," she says while nodding, her blonde curls bouncing. "It's my turn now."

He positions Sam within her arms so her elbow supports his head. "We have to hold his head up because he can't yet. You got him?"

"I got him, Daddy. You stay close, okay?" Adam slides his chair closer.

"Hi, Sam, I'm Hope, your big sister. You're the first brother I ever had. I hope we can be best friends. I'll teach you everything I know, okay?" Sam sticks his tongue out and pulls it back in. A bubble forms on his tiny lips, breaking as he yawns. Hope's eyes open wide, and her lips again form an O. "Does all that mean he knows I'm his big sister?"

"I'm sure it does," Rachel says.

Hope is the sweetest thing. I guess I need to get over my self-pity and start enjoying this family. There's no telling how long I'll be here.

Chapter 38

Christmas

At the bathroom sink, while Rachel brushes her hair, Elaine watches, not at all happy.

The kids are tucked in. You're fresh from a shower. Adam's ready for bed earlier than normal. You've been counting the weeks on the calendar too, darn it, so I know exactly what's on your mind.

Rachel glances through the bathroom door at Adam. "Is that a good book, hon?"

In bed with his latest paperback, Adam keeps reading. "It's all right."

Rachel applies lipstick and glances at Adam again. He gives her a sideways look.

How in the world do I handle them having sex? Maybe he'll go back to reading and I won't have to deal with it tonight. And to think, Ruth teased me about this very thing when I told her about ghosts living in people.

The paperback plops to the nightstand. Adam slips up behind Rachel and points at a tube of lotion by the sink. "Need some help with that?"

Elaine eyes him in the mirror. *Lotion my foot. I'm not ready for —*

Rachel hands him the lotion. "That'd be nice." He squirts several cold dabs along her shoulders, and she shivers. "You're supposed to rub it in your palms to warm it first."

"I'll remember that next time," Adam says, winking. He massages the lotion into Rachel's shoulders and upper arms. She closes her eyes.

I—am—not—ready—for— Oh my, it's been a while since Kurt rubbed my shoulders like that. Elaine concentrates on Adam's warming hands rubbing Rachel's bare skin—until something still warm, but soft and moist, caresses Rachel's neck below her ear. *Is he kissing her neck? My goodness, he's better at that than Kurt.*

Adam dots warm kisses down the curve of Rachel's neck to her shoulder. In the middle of sharing her moan, Elaine stops. *Quit that, you silly old woman. You act like you've never had sex before.*

Adam continues kissing Rachel's neck and shoulders. She opens her eyes to see Adam in the mirror. "I saw those checkmarks you've been making on the kitchen calendar."

He pauses the kissing and looks up. "Six-weeks today. Will it be okay?"

"The doctor said it should be fine my last visit."

Adam turns Rachel to face him. "Did I tell you how much I like your doctor?"

"What you *better* do is show me how much you love me, regardless of my flabby belly."

"I love you, honey, flabby belly included." He kisses her lightly, which sends shivers through Rachel. Rachel responds by writhing against him and kissing him deeply.

What the heck happens when they do more than kiss? What happens when he—when she—oh my!

Adam's lips move to Rachel's throat. She runs her fingers through his hair and pulls him to her, and she and Elaine moan with pleasure. More kisses and caresses go well below Rachel's neck. Adam picks her up and carries her to the bed. He throws his pajamas in the floor, pulls her nightgown up, and rubs her legs.

She slides her feet along the cool sheets. "Smooth, aren't they? I shaved them just for you."

"Just for me? Then I'm not the only one keeping up with the weeks on the calendar."

"I keep a small one in my pocketbook. Mine has a big star on today instead of a check mark."

"I'm worthy of a big star?"

"Only if you perform" —Rachel licks her lips— "and I mean well."

"That is *not* going to be a problem." Adam climbs into bed. Rachel raises her bottom. He pulls the nightgown up and lowers himself onto her.

This isn't right! I love Joe and Kurt, not Adam, regardless of how great this feels.

Attempting to close her eyes, Elaine finds herself in a calm, quiet state, almost like daydreaming.

Okay, I'm here but not quite. I'm still with Rachel because I can feel her, sort of like when I couldn't see Mom or Dad but could somehow sense they were at home. This definitely comes in handy.

Let's see now … close my eyes tight, tight as I can, not too tight, even less. Oh, my, Rachel's about to— Okay, okay, just a little tighter, like trying to go to take a nap. There, that's it, just enough to where I should be able to fall asleep. Yeah, right, Elaine. You were enjoying Adam as much as Rachel was, and you know it.

* * *

Elaine shares Rachel's smile—one of many that have made Rachel's cheeks ache—as she takes Sam's cupcake with a single candle to his high chair. Friends and family are gathered around the dining room, chatting and smiling too. Sitting beside Sam, Hope frowns up at Rachel. "Do you think he'll know how to blow it out?"

Adam sets a tray of cupcakes on the table for the guests. "We don't want him to get burned either."

Rachel holds the cupcake out of Sam's reach. "Sam, you pucker your lips and blow. Can you do it?" Rachel does as she describes. Instead of paying attention, Sam reaches for the flame.

Hope pulls his hand down to the tray. "Like this." She puckers and blows. Sam puckers, but his tongue comes out to make a sound similar to when he has a particularly messy diaper. Hope faces Rachel. "I think I better do it, Mommy."

Everyone sings Happy Birthday, and Hope blows out the candle. Rachel takes it from the icing and gives Hope the cupcake. "Give that to Sam while I throw the candle away."

Hope sets the cupcake on the tray. Sam touches the icing, frowns at it on his fingertip, and looks at Hope, a question in his narrowed eyes.

"It's icing, Sam. You eat it."

Sam slaps the cupcake, which lands in Hope's thick curls. She snatches it from her head and stomps to the trash container, throws it in and stomps back to Sam to waggle her finger at him. "That was not nice, Sam-u-el Lewis! Not nice at all!"

Elaine shares another of Rachel's cheek-aching grins at how Hope waggles her finger in time with each section of "Sam-u-el's" name.

Adam waggles his finger at Rachel. "Now, now, Mommy, don't make the situation worse."

"Me? You're grinning like a nut yourself."

"It's not funny." Hope crosses her arms. "Not funny *at all.*"

Adam takes a napkin from the holder and wipes her curls. "At least this yellow icing matches your hair."

"Clean it good. I don't want ants to eat my head."

Elaine attempts a grin. Yesterday afternoon on the deck, Hope and Sam watched a line of ants carrying a piece of a chocolate chip cookie away, crumb by crumb.

What a mess they are. Experiencing them growing up has certainly been a blessing. A year has passed in no time.

Rachel takes a cupcake from the tray and feeds it to Sam. "More?" Sam nods, brown bangs flopping up and down.

As long as I get to enjoy this family, I can deal with this way of living, but I wonder what next year will bring, or how long I'll stay here?

***

Adam opens the front door; cold air chills his cheeks. "Come on, Hope. I want to get to the Christmas tree lot before it closes."

Hope tightens her shoelace and hops off the sofa. "I wish Sam could come."

"He's too young right now. If he doesn't wake from his nap before we set the tree up, it'll be a surprise." At the door, Hope waves to Rachel on the sofa. "Try to keep Sam asleep 'till we get back, okay, Mommy?"

"Help Daddy pick out a nice tree. The one last year looked like a toothpick with spinach wrapped around it."

In the car, Hope climbs into her seat and clicks the belts. "I liked our tree last year."

"It was pretty skimpy," Adam says, backing out of the driveway. "We couldn't hang many balls on it either."

"Do you think Sam will pull them off this year?"

"He should mind better now. You we're a handful when you were a year old yourself."

Hope holds up her fingers. "One plus one is two. That's how old Sam is. Can one more year make Sam be good?"

"You've got a point, honey. It didn't help you much either."

"Was I a terrible two?"

Adam glances at Hope in the rear-view mirror. "Were you a terrible too what?"

"Mommy said Sam is in his 'terrible twos.' Did I have those?"

"All two-year-olds have those."

"Did you?"

"Mommy says I still do, when I don't hear her because I'm watching football."

Hope nods, blonde curls bouncing. "She says you zone out."

"It sounds like you and Mommy are ganging up on me."

"Only when you watch football, Daddy."

At the Christmas tree lot, while Adam holds Hope's hand as they walk through the rows of Spruce and Fir trees, the spicy evergreen scent surrounds them. Adam lets go of her hand. "Go pick us out a nice one."

"All by myself?"

"Why not? You're a big girl now."

Hope runs along the rows of evergreens, sometimes darting back and forth between the rows, her red stocking hat turning this way and that as she considers each candidate. She pauses at tree after tree, frowning at each one, and steps through a small opening in a row. "There it is, I see it!" Adam brushes through the thick evergreen branches, their scent even stronger. She waves and points at a shorter than average tree. "I like this one, Daddy, it's just my size."

The tree *is* shorter, but it's one of the fullest trees on the lot. "I think you're right, honey, it's just like you—short and sweet and perfect."

"I'm not perfect, Daddy, see?" Hope sticks her tongue through the hole where her two top front baby teeth were a few days ago.

Adam laughs. "Sweetheart, you're absolutely perfect. One day you'll be a beautiful young woman with a smile that'll make all the boys come running. When that happens, I'll have to chase them away from my little girl."

"But you said I'd be a beautiful woman—that means like Mommy—so I won't be a little girl then."

Adam kneels beside her. "Don't you know a daddy's little girl is always his little girl no matter how big she gets?"

"I'm glad, Daddy. You can help me find a husband exactly like you one day."

"Uh-huh, one day a long time from now." Adam waves a clerk over. "Let's pay for this tree and see what Mommy and Sam think of it."

"Yay! Mommy said we could get new lights the next time we go shopping."

Chapter 39

Not a Very Merry Christmas II

Adam has the stand ready before leaving for the Christmas tree lot, so a few minutes after returning home, the tree is up and watered. Hands on her hips, Hope nods her approval.

In sock feet, rubbing his eyes, hair sticking out at wild angles, Sam shuffles into the living room. Adam sits on the sofa to see what Sam thinks of the new tree.

"Hi, Sam," Hope says. "Did you have a good nap?"

Sam yawns and looks toward the top of the tree. "Wha-is-sit, Hope?"

"It's a Christmas tree. Can you say Christmas tree?"

Sam sticks a finger in his mouth, looks up again, and pulls the finger from his mouth. "Cwiss-mus twee."

"That's right. What color is it?"

Sam rolls his eyes, and Adam almost laughs. Sam knows his colors but sometimes mixes them up.

"Ellow?"

Hope giggles. "Not yellow, green. Can you say green?"

"Geen."

"You got it, Sam, very good!" She sniffs one of the branches. "Now the house smells like Christmas."

"It's a special smell," Adam says. "Like Sam when he was born."

"That's silly, Daddy."

"Why's that?"

"He doesn't smell like a Christmas tree."

"He sure doesn't, but I'll be glad when he doesn't need pull-ups."

"Yuck, me too." Hope pulls one of the branches toward Sam. "Smell it, Sam." He touches the tip of his nose to the bristly branch. His eyes move side to side as if he doesn't know what to make of this thing poking his nose.

Rachel comes in from the kitchen. "How about taking us to dinner, Daddy? We can pick up the new lights too."

"Tonight?"

"Yes, tonight. Football can wait."

"That's a good idea, Mommy, dinner and lights!" Hope jumps into Adam's lap. "Us girls are better than any old football game."

"What about Sam?" Adam says. "He's not a girl."

"Now, Daddy, stop teasing. You know what I mean."

Sam crawls onto the sofa beside Adam, and Rachel sits beside him. "He knows what you mean, Hope. He's just trying to be a pain." Rachel kisses Sam's head.

* * *

Sweet with the aroma of baby shampoo, Sam's hair tickles Elaine's phantom nose.

In some strange way, kissing Sam reminds me of kissing Joe. Maybe it's because he has blonde hair like Joe's. I've been waiting two years now. Where can he be? Who is he with? What's be doing? Better yet, how can I find him?

Oh, that's stupid. If he's living like me we're spirits, and my books didn't say how two spirits find each other. Do they meet and go to Heaven? They must, because I doubt they get another chance at life.

At the restaurant, Rachel orders a dish Elaine never tried back home in Alma, in farm country. *Grilled salmon, sautéed green beans, and white wine? Why not?*

The delicate pink morsel melts in Rachel's mouth.

Not bad. Kurt was always a meat and potatoes man. We should've tried grilled catfish instead of fried. Huh, I wonder how many meals Joe has tried while living in other people?

Rachel sips wine. Beneath the table, she slides the open toe of her high heels along Adam's leg.

Uh-oh, someone's gonna fool around when the kids are in bed. Elaine pauses. *Oh, well, I suppose some of the people Joe has been with are married. I wonder if he stays around during sex?*

Oh, that's silly, thinking things like—

Wait a minute, if Joe has been doing this for over fifty years, how many people has he lived in? Besides that, what causes people like us to change who we're with? I doubt he stayed in one person all that time. If I could change people on my own, I wouldn't know how, and if I could, I wouldn't know who to change to. Do I stay with each person until they die? If that's how it works, I'll be with Rachel a long time.

On their way home, when Adam steers the car onto the road where their house is located, Hope sings Jingle Bells, and Rachel turns around to sing with her.

A muscle spasm grips Elaine's middle. Her stomach twists into a knot, then loosens and tightens again, exactly like when she died. *Is Rachel sick? Was the food spoiled?*

Sam points toward Hope— "Light, Hope"—and she whirls toward the car window beside her.

"Mommy! Daddy! It's the—"

Outside the car to the right, what can only be a train's horn blasts Rachel's eardrums. She jerks toward the window, the train's brakes squeal, and a glaring white light blinds Elaine. "Adam, go!" Rachel yells.

He hits the accelerator. The car lurches forward until the impact of the train tears through it, ending the family's screams.

An icy wind embraces Elaine. Intensifying, it chills her to the bone, as if she's flying through the cold night air after falling from a great height.

Oh my God, what's happening to—

Chapter 40

Transformation II

—me?

The pain in Rachel's middle—it's gone. I'm warm again too, but why can't I see anything? That sensation was so strange. It was as if I were pulled from Rachel and pushed into—

Another person?

But who?

And how?

Does it matter? I could ask those questions all night and never answer them. All I can do now is wait and—

Oh no, the train hit the Lewis's car and my family is dead. It makes no sense. One minute everyone's fine, the next minute they're gone. God, please take them into Heaven and give them peace and comfort, and I could use some comfort myself. Life is so short. I wish I could have my own body so I could cry. What a terrible thing to happen to my family.

The person Elaine is in rolls over, so whoever it is must be asleep.

I guess I should calm down and see who I'm with. I hope it's a woman instead of a man. I'm not ready for that at all.

Elaine's first sensation of this new body is of a woman, but someone different from Rachel. Rachel felt supple and graceful, as if molten glass had been poured into her very being, magnified many times over when she and Adam made love. Elaine loves that feeling. She reveled in it during her and Joe's honeymoon night at the river, the warmth multiplying with each tender kiss, intensifying with every sensual caress. This new person carries an innate chill within the older body, and although she's feminine, supple hardly describes the slight aches in the muscles and joints. Elaine imagines they might creak, like the barn door at home. The woman snores lightly.

A nap sounds like a good idea. I have a feeling I'm going to need it.

* * *

A loud buzz wakes Elaine. The woman fumbles for a clock and smacks the button. Quiet fills the room. Eyelids blinking, she rolls back to the middle of the bed.

It's about time you woke up and turned off that dreadful noise, whoever you are. Can we get our day going? I'd like to see who I'm with and where I am.

The woman swings her legs off the bed, and a nightstand with a lamp and an oddly familiar shade comes into Elaine's view. The woman slips her feet into slippers. Elaine tries to get a better look at the shade, but the woman hurries toward a bathroom. She dons a thick robe and steps to a sink with a mirror above it.

Ruth! Is it really you? I can't believe it. I've made it back home and I'm with Ruth!

Ruth rubs her neck, wets a washcloth with warm water, and scrubs her face and eyes. "Time to get moving, old girl. That bread won't bake itself."

My goodness, Ruth, has it really been almost two years since we had our last talk before I died? I'd love to see the look on your face if you knew what I've been doing. Huh, especially the sex part.

Regardless, I'm happy to watch you get your day going. It'll help get my mind off the Lewises, God rest their souls.

Wearing blue jeans and a pink flannel shirt, Ruth goes to the kitchen. She sets the oven temperature and pours cereal and milk. As she finishes the last bite, the oven dings. She slides six long loaf pans of risen dough into the oven, sets the timer, and rinses the cereal bowl and spoon.

Elaine attempts a frown. *Well darn, I didn't get to see her make the dough. That's okay. Although she never shared that recipe with me, she shared plenty of bread. What a great friend she was.*

Ruth starts a pot of coffee, retrieves the morning paper, and peeks at the bread. The aroma of the browning loaves drifts from the oven. She pours coffee and sits at the table. Unfolding the paper, she gasps. Elaine reads the article with her and understands why. A family of four living in Kansas was killed when a train struck their car. A few lines down she reads the names of the family—*her* family. Adam and Rachel Lewis, and their children, Hope and Samuel, all died in the crash.

I can't believe they're gone, or how Adam forgot the train crossing. Wait a minute, how can I say that when I didn't think about it either? That crossing should have a signal. They all should have—

Why haven't I thought of this? Since Rachel died, and since I changed who I was with, does that mean for me to change again, Ruth will die?

I feel you rubbing your neck, Ruth. I know I'm causing it but I can't help how I feel. Elaine closes her eyes, blocking her outward awareness. *I can't do this right now. Maybe I can sort it out while Ruth continues with her day.*

* * *

Ruth turns a few pages for the rest of the story, which includes a picture of the parents and their two children. "Such a tragedy," she says, shaking her head. "All gone in an instant."

She finishes the cooling coffee, checks the oven timer, and gathers the rest of her market items. The timer dings. She wraps the loaves in a towel and places them in a Styrofoam cooler. Loyal customers love a warm loaf or a slice fresh out of the oven, especially with homemade blackberry jam or honey from one of the other vendors.

At the Farmers Market, she takes the cooler to her vendor table, slices a loaf for samples, and covers them with a clear plastic lid to keep them warm. As she sits to wait for customers, Elaine's old SUV rolls by. "Well, well, if it isn't the old coot himself. I think I'll walk over and surprise him."

Chapter 41

Meeting for Lunch

S*lam!*
Good grief, Ruth, scare a person half to death slamming your car door like that. I suppose it doesn't matter. I've about used up all my theories about the train hitting my family's car.

I know I prayed for them to go to Heaven, but maybe the children can have another chance at life. There's too much hope in people for death to be the end. After all, without hope, what's left? I need to stay strong in my hope, for Sam and Hope and for Joe too.

Ruth goes to a vendor table and readies her bread for sale. As she waits for customers, she turns toward an old SUV pulling into the Farmer's Market and remarks about surprising Kurt, which thrills Elaine. *I'm so happy to see my sweetheart and find out how he's been doing since I died. Give him a hug for me, Ruth.*

Ruth hurries toward Kurt and slips her hands around his waist and squeezes. "I know who that is," Kurt says. "Are you trying to hijack me and steal my spinach, old gal?"

"No, old man, I'm just stealing a squeeze from your broken-down body is all. You can keep your spinach." Elaine catches a hint of wood smoke and fresh air from Kurt's clothes.

They separate, then joke about being old. *Listen to you two, you're like teenagers teasing each other. I wonder if you're more than friends yet.*

At Ruth's booth, Kurt places his box of spinach on the table alongside her bread. "I hope I get a good price for this last box. That'll be it for a while."

"Don't you need to pick up your order from the hardware store? I'll work on selling my bread and your spinach while you're gone. That'll save you from making the trip later."

"You know what, Ruthie? You're one smart and considerate lady. Now I know why my wife thought so much of you."

"Aw, go on," Ruth says, waving the comment away. "Stop being nice before you throw me off my game. Besides, how long did it take you to figure out I'm smart and considerate? Your wife—and my best friend I might add—knew it the minute I warned her about old roosters like you."

"If you don't know my opinion of you by now, maybe this will help." Kurt kisses her cheek. "Besides, we both know you're full of fertilizer."

"All spice here, old rooster. Wouldn't life without spice be a mediocre meal?"

"Got that right, Ruthie. Mediocre meals—or conversation— never happen around you. I'll be back quick as I can. Then we can head over to the diner and see if you can spice up that stuff Bill calls meatloaf."

What a pair they are. I'm happy for them both, especially Kurt. I'm glad he didn't whither up and blow away after I died. No doubt I have Ruth to thank for that.

Kurt climbs into the SUV.

He's off to that old man cave of a hardware store. I wish I could see that place again. When I think back to how I met Joe there, and Kurt too, I'm amazed.

But what about Joe? Could he be nearby, maybe even with Kurt like my book said? If he were, I sure wouldn't know it.

About twenty minutes later, Kurt returns to joke with Ruth about taking all the money from selling his spinach and running away to France. Ruth tells him Mr. Jenkins bought all the spinach because of some diet his wife has him on. For a few minutes they joke back and forth about being old again. Deciding to end that kind of talk for the day, they climb into Elaine's old SUV for the drive to the diner.

Elaine's miniature lighthouse swings back and forth from the rear-view mirror. *My lighthouse. I loved Cape Hatteras and the Outer Banks. Maybe Kurt and Ruth will get married and honeymoon there. I doubt it since it's such a long drive. Besides, I need to keep reminding myself that I don't know how he feels about her yet.*

At the door to the diner, Kurt and Ruth joke about Elaine corrupting him, and Ruth mentions how much she misses her.

I've missed you too, Ruth, both of you. I never thought I'd die at what I considered to be a fairly young age. None of us is promised a single day, so we'd better make the best of each one while we're alive.

Inside, Bill Jenkins tells Kurt about Ruth's unwillingness to compromise on the price of her homemade bread. Elaine doesn't blame Ruth one bit, because Bill gained many a customer by having Ruth's famous loaves on hand every Saturday to serve to the lunch crowd. He follows up with a joke about spinach, which leaves them laughing. Kurt gives his order, joking about how Bill's meatloaf is a "stool sample," and Ruth gives her order, saying she wants plenty of spinach in her salad because she's not due a physical with her doctor anytime soon. Her joke doesn't get the same laughs as Kurt's joke. Bill leaves, and Kurt tells Ruth her joke was fine except for the timing. Ruth answers by calling him a "knot-head," then asks about something Elaine hasn't noticed: a bandage on Kurt's ear. Kurt tells Ruth his dermatologist sent a sample to check for skin cancer.

Elaine shakes her phantom head. *That old hard head. How many times did I tell him to wear a big hat like mine when he was out in the sun? I'm sure he'll be okay. I don't remember seeing a spot on his ear, so the doctor probably caught it early.*

Kurt and Ruth spend the rest of their meal discussing various subjects, most of them centered around how people live with too many unnecessary complications. Ruth specifically mentions the obsession some have with cell phones, or "dumb-ass phones" as she jokingly calls them. Considering how Ruth has a phone in her purse, and how she emails her grandchildren easily, the irony of her comment isn't lost on Elaine.

Done with lunch, they return to the Farmer's Market. Ruth suggests having a picnic tomorrow at Lainey's Grove, if the weather cooperates.

Is that what they're calling it now? I don't mind, but I've always thought of it as the place where Joe and I fell in love. Regardless of what they call it, I'd like to see it again. I couldn't begin to number the memories Joe and I created there. Maybe Kurt will fall in love with Ruth soon. She already loves him, so it could happen.

Then again, even when I was alive, it was sometimes hard to tell what he was thinking, but I can tell he likes having her around. Still, loneliness isn't something to base a relationship on, but it can be a consideration.

So, old man, when are you going to stop wasting time and see the light?

Chapter 42

Bare Legs and Crooked Toes

The next morning, as Elaine enjoys the coffee Ruth sips, a light tapping on the window over the sink catches her attention. Ruth pulls the curtain aside. Clouds darken the sky, hanging low like a tattered gray curtain with rain drizzling down. Ruth shakes her head. "Well, there goes the darn picnic, old man."

Elaine is disappointed, but when Ruth places a fingertip to her chin, she recognizes her friend's expression. *I've seen that look before. I bet you're thinking about a way to salvage the picnic.*

Ruth takes a cell phone from her purse and dials Kurt's number. The answering machine plays his recording.

Are you still in bed, sweetheart? Except for weekends, when I'd get up early and cook breakfast, you were up with the chickens. Well, we never had chickens, but if we'd had chickens — Oh hush, Elaine, and listen.

Ruth starts to leave a message, but Kurt picks up, telling her how he burned his tongue while drinking hot coffee.

"Ithe," huh? It's a wonder he has any skin left on his tongue, as much as he did that while I was alive.

Ruth reveals her backup plan—making supper and bringing it over—and Kurt is hooked like a catfish. Ruth occasionally brought pot roast over when Elaine was sick. Kurt never admitted it, but she could tell he liked Ruth's pot roast better than hers. It never worried her—she liked it better than her own too. Ruth and Kurt finalize supper plans, with him mentioning a bottle of wine he has that will be perfect with her pot roast.

Why you old dog, are you planning to get my best friend drunk and take advantage of her? Elaine attempts a phantom smile. *Ha, I know better than that. If anyone plans to take advantage of anybody it's Ruth.*

Ruth tells Kurt she'll arrive around five, ends the call, and sets her hands on her hips. "All right, Ruthie, it's time to get rolling."

Imagine that, I finally get to watch Ruth cook her famous pot roast. Maybe I'll learn some of her secrets.

Ruth takes a crock pot from a cabinet and fills it with carrots, potatoes, onions, and mushrooms. Next, she preheats a cast iron skillet, salt and peppers a roast, and sears it until the meat forms a brown crust. Vegetables chopped, she returns them to the crock pot and adds the roast and some beef stock.

That took no time at all, Ruth. You remind me of a miniature tornado swirling around in here. I never thought of using beef stock. Maybe that's why your roast was better than mine.

Ruth takes a break for a bite of lunch, the last of the coffee and, with the dishes in the sink, removes her apron. "Time for a shower, old girl. Then I need to find something to wear."

I agree, a hot shower would feel wonderful. By the way, I'm glad you talk to yourself like that. You always thought it was a habit you needed to break, but I get to know what you're up to next. And you're always up to something.

The shower loosens Ruth's muscles and relaxes Elaine. Toweled dry, Ruth removes the shower cap, dons a robe, and goes to the closet, where she purses her lips while jerking racks aside with a clatter. The dress to the right, beside the door, catches Elaine's eye. *How about that one? I always liked how it looked on you.*

Ruth plucks the hanger and holds the turquoise, knee-length dress to her shoulders. "I don't believe Kurt has ever seen me in this. Elaine always liked it, so maybe the old coot will like it too."

What a mess you are, Ruth. If you and Kurt ever do get together, there won't be a dull moment in that old house.

Ruth hangs the dress on the door frame, trades the robe and slippers for jeans and a sweater, and runs a brush through her hair.

Good idea. Who wants to get fancied up when that roast will take a while to cook. To Elaine's surprise, Ruth dons a coat, unplugs the crock pot, and a few minutes later is driving through downtown Alma, smiling and humming.

I know what you're up to, Ruth. You're planning to surprise Kurt by dropping off the crock pot and going back home to get ready.

Leaving town, Ruth glances in the rear-view mirror. "As mature as that old goat and I are, I like to think we can handle it like adults. Don't you think so, Elaine?"

If you're talking about romance, yes, I think you two can handle it, but what took you so long? Well, maybe you waited out of respect for me, which I understand.

On Kurt's porch, Ruth places the heavy crock pot on a table, where Elaine once kept flowers. She tries to look through the foggy window, but Kurt's nowhere in sight. Ruth knocks hard on the wooden door, and footsteps plod inside. Kurt's gnarled hand wipes the haze on the window away, revealing his blue eyes peering at Ruth. He opens the door, bare legs and feet protruding from beneath a bathrobe.

"You're a bit early, aren't you, Ruthie? Planning on catching me in the nude?"

Ruth's eyes dart from his, to his robe, to his feet, and she explodes with laughter. Every time she catches her breath, a fresh wave of laughter takes hold, even to the point of her grabbing the door frame to steady herself.

My goodness, Ruth, I haven't laughed like this in ages. Careful now, we don't want to wet your jeans.

When Ruth's giggles subside, she takes a tissue from her purse. Kurt crosses his arms. She wipes her eyes, shakes her head, and Elaine waits. This situation is made to order for her always irreverent best friend.

"Oh yeah, baby, catching you in the nude's been my dream ever since we met." She picks up the crock pot. "You better get dressed. If I have to look at those legs" — she points at his feet with the toe of her dripping shoe— "or those crooked old things you call toes any longer, I might ravish you right here on the kitchen floor."

Vintage Ruth. You asked for it, sweetheart, and I'd say you got it.

Mouth hanging open, Kurt uncrosses his arms.

Aw, I almost feel sorry for him. Almost.

"Now look her, old hen, I—" He glances down, as if he feels underdressed. "I better put some clothes on. I *might* be back in a minute." His feet slap the hardwood floor in the hall.

"That's a good idea!" Ruth yells after him. "You remind me of one of those shirtless hotties on a romance novel!" She takes the crockpot to a counter.

I wish you knew I was here to see that, Ruth, that was priceless. If I'd been standing next to you, I'd have smacked you a high-five.

Ruth plugs the crockpot in and goes down the hall to knock

on Kurt's bedroom door. "What?" he asks, his voice gruff.

"Hey, Hot Ass, I'm running home to change. Do you need anything from the grocery?"

"Can you pick up some shame from the drugstore? You need a good dose."

"Who needs shame when they've got spice? Remember what I said about a meal being mediocre without spice?"

"Good grief, don't I know it. As far as what I need, you crazy old woman, the dignity my clothes can give me is a start. Drive safe."

Ruth, I've always loved that saying you have about meals being mediocre without spice. I don't know what I would've done without your special brand of spice in my life over the years. I'm sure that goes double for Kurt. Now, let's get dressed and get back here to see what happens tonight.

Chapter 43

Prayers and Appreciation

At the mirror on the back of her bedroom door, Ruth troubles herself over a stray lock of hair, whether she has on too much makeup, whether the red polish on her nails is dry, whether her lipstick matches, whether she has on too much perfume, whether her high heels are too high, whether her new pair of panty hose has a run or not, whether—

Stop that, you look fine. I wish I could tell you how beautiful you are.

Ruth finally sighs, dons an overcoat, and grabs her purse. At the grocery, she buys a few last-minute items, foregoing anything sweet.

Since it's one of the weaknesses you were always trying to steer clear of, I could have sworn you'd grab a container of butter pecan ice cream. Maybe you're being good because you're going to indulge in that wine.

At Kurt's again, Ruth beeps the car horn. He splashes out, she hands him a bag, and Elaine sniffs the aroma of Old Spice. Ruth tells him they need to get inside before the rain washes it off. He asks if he's overdone it, and she says it's recognizable. Elaine loves the sweet aroma, especially when Joe used a splash of Will's Old Spice from time to time.

Inside, Kurt offers to take Ruth's coat. His face lights up

when he does.

I knew you'd like that dress, sweetheart. Great job, Ruth.

Kurt makes a joke, or rather, *tries* making a joke, saying he means the dress looks nice instead of Ruth. Elaine wants to shake him. *Kurt! Didn't I teach you any better?* Ruth's spice takes over, and she lets Kurt know clearly, but in a teasing manner, that joking about a woman's looks isn't acceptable.

Blushing, Kurt apologizes, reminding Ruth that after their meeting earlier, when she caught him in his bathrobe, their joking has become a habit. Ruth seems to see his point, but Elaine knows she isn't about to concede it. Instead, Ruth jokes about his behavior not helping him get lucky romantically and then asks for a glass of wine.

They sit, Ruth with wine and Kurt with coffee. He clinks his mug to her glass. "How about a toast? To Ruthie and Lainey, the two finest women in Nebraska."

You better be nice to Ruth, darn it. She went to a lot of trouble for you.

Since he made such a sincere comment after his former one about the coat, Ruth accuses him of hiding a stronger beverage, or either he is, yet again, trying to get lucky. Then she admits to not bringing any Viagra, and Kurt claims he never needed any, despite what Elaine might have told her.

My goodness, Ruth, now I feel bad for Kurt. When it comes to wit, I think he might have met his match in you. And no, he never needed any help, as he calls it, "in that department."

Ruth's joking about Viagra clears the air, causing Kurt to laugh and say—and her to agree, clinking her wine glass to his coffee mug—how they're too worn out for any such foolishness.

Kurt sniffs the air.

Uh-huh, you're smelling Ruth's fine meal she made for you.

"When's supper?" he asks. "That pot roast smells great."

Elaine agrees. *As good a cook as Rachel Lewis was, God rest her and her family's souls, no one makes a pot roast like Ruth.*

Ruth slices the roast while Kurt places silverware and plates on the table. He pours wine for himself, and Ruth brings the steaming platter of sliced beef, with potatoes, carrots, mushrooms, and onions on the side, to the table.

Kurt licks his lips.

Yes, Kurt, it looks wonderful. If you marry Ruth, you might need to go on a diet.

When he starts serving himself, Ruth asks to say a blessing. He agrees, bowing his head as Ruth bows hers.

"Dear Father, thank you for the friendship of this man and his wife. They have filled my last years with more happiness than I ever deserved. Thank You for this meal and all your blessings, amen."

I hope you know how much you meant to me, Ruth, and mean to me now. I wish I could tell you one more time. Maybe that old man will say something.

"Amen," Kurt says, patting Ruth's hand. "Thank you for that and thank you for your friendship. More importantly, thank you for your friendship to Lainey. I tried to be her rock when she was sick, but you were her feather-bed of comfort. She thought the world of you."

There's the kind and gentle man I married. Thank you for telling Ruth that, Kurt. Now, instead of all the joking, I think we should have a quiet evening together.

Ruth suggests the same thing, asking for a calm and peaceful evening by the fire, and Kurt says he'll start a fire in the fireplace after supper.

Thank goodness. I can't think of a nicer way to relax after such a delicious meal. Besides, you two need to discuss the relationship you need to start. It's not like you'll live forever, you know, so it's time to get frisky.

Elaine stifles a phantom giggle. *Oh, my, I suppose I did become a prude as I got older, but I sure enjoyed mine and Joe's honeymoon night at the river. Mmm, mm, mm, how I loved me some Joe Matthan, beefcake that he was. Now, if I can just figure out if he's with Kurt like I'm with Ruth.*

Chapter 44

Joe and Kurt, Elaine and Ruth

Kurt swallows his last bite of roast beef. "Ruthie, that was absolutely the best meal I've had in a good long while." He sops gravy with bread and pops the combination into his mouth. "Mmm-mm."

Ruth dabs her lips with a napkin. "Thank you, sir. It makes me quite happy to know I've still got what it takes to please a man ..." She waits while Kurt sips wine. "... at least in the kitchen."

He sputters and coughs. Patting his back, she hands him a napkin. "Is the timing of my punch lines getting better?"

Kurt clears his throat. "Sure, but that one almost killed me." He wipes his lips. "If we're finished, let's get these dishes washed. Then I'll get the fire going."

"I'll handle the dishes while you start the fire." Ruth takes their plates to the sink. "I won't be long."

Kurt brings their glasses. "As long as you don't think I'd take it for granted that you'd wash the dishes by yourself."

"Your sweet wife said you were a good dishwasher. She also said you two took turns between washing and drying, unless you had something more pressing to do." Ruth squirts soap into the sink. "As far as I'm concerned, I'd say building that fire is more pressing."

Kurt winks. "I agree. See you in a bit."

He gathers newspaper and kindling, then matches from the holder on the mantle. The soft clatter of Ruth washing their dishes drifts from the kitchen. They enjoyed a nice supper and stimulating conversation, even after his dumb remark about her dress. What else might the evening bring?

The leather sofa's low-pitched squeak announces Ruth sitting. Is she watching him? Maybe. After all, this evening was her idea.

He prods the last piece of wood into place with a poker. The flames flare, warming his cheeks. "This dry oak is rolling along pretty well. I hope you don't get too warm."

"I've been looking forward to this all afternoon," Ruth says. "This cold, rainy day has me chilled to the bone."

Kurt sits a discreet distance from Ruth. Seconds pass, then more, and he covers his eyes.

"What's wrong?" Ruth asks.

"It's Christmas Eve, darn it, and I didn't get you anything. We even talked about it yesterday."

"It slipped my mind too. That's all right, presents and such are mostly for younger folks." She pats his hand. "Besides, I couldn't ask for a better way to spend Christmas Eve."

"That's nice of you to say, but—"

"I'm not just saying it, I mean it. Regardless of not giving each other gifts, I appreciate the reason for the season. I'm sure you do too."

"That I do."

Ruth faces the fire again, and Kurt watches her. It flickers on her face and in her eyes, highlighting contours and shades of color. In some strange, ghost-like way, she resembles Lainey.

Minutes pass. Ruth faces him again. She brushes her

fingertips along his cheek, a hint of a smile on her lips. She's never touched him like this. He closes his eyes. Does it mean what he hopes it does? Does she think more of him than just a friend, or more than just the husband of her best friend, now passed away?

He opens his eyes. "Ruth, there's something I've wanted to ask you for a while now, so I'm just going to ask it. Before I do, I want you to know I value your friendship, and I don't want to lose it. That means you can be honest when you answer."

"Would you expect otherwise, old rooster?"

"Dumb question, huh?"

"Go ahead, we'll see"

"What's been on my mind is if there's more to us than friendship. Think so?"

"You know me, old man, I like being straightforward. For me it is, and it has been for some time now."

Kurt exhales the breath he's holding. Another question—one he's never considered—pops into his mind. "Can I ask you something else?"

"You know you can."

"If we become close—not just friends—would we betray Lainey's memory?"

Ruth slides closer. "Kurt, if there's one thing I know in my heart, Elaine would most definitely *not* think we're betraying her memory."

* * *

Warm from the fire, full from the meal, and half-asleep, Joe perks up. *Did Ruth say Elaine?* He mentally shakes his head. *I'm not about to jump to any conclusions, but if she said Elaine, she could be talking about my Elaine.*

Kurt sits straighter on the sofa. "How do you know Lainey

would give us her blessing?"

"She told me so," Ruth says. "I've kept it hidden from you, but I wasn't about to get anything past Elaine."

She said Elaine for sure that time. So, Ruth sometimes calls Kurt's wife—the woman who was her best friend—Elaine. If they're talking about my Elaine, how could she have met and married Kurt after I died? Besides that, how could she marry a doggone ex-German soldier too?

Kurt rubs his neck. "What couldn't you get by Elaine?"

"That I love you . . . and have for a long time."

"Lainey knew you loved me and wasn't upset?"

"You silly old man, she knew I was no threat. Believe me, Elaine is the best friend this old gal ever had. I tell you truthfully, if I could die and bring her back to you, I'd do it in a heartbeat. That's how much she meant to me, and how much you mean to me too."

Kurt pauses to rub his chin. "Would you believe I told Lainey the same thing about Joe before we got married? I'd gone to the river to go fishing, and she was there."

Joe's name hits him with the same blinding force as the exploding grenade that killed him.

He said my name! Oh my God, it all makes sense. I've finally made it back to Elaine! She must have met Kurt and married him after I died. If that's true—if all that really happened—

The next realization slams into Joe as if a second grenade explodes with the first, bracketing him with twin concussive blasts.

If Elaine was Kurt's wife, that means she's passed away. Then why have I been living this nightmare life for so long, even longer than I was actually alive?

Joe clenches his mental teeth, stops, and draws back his

spiritual hand as if to slap himself.

You fool, stop feeling sorry for your stupid self, people die all the time. Like the Jewish boy in the concentration camp and the British girl with her leg almost blown off, some die a lot younger than me. I had eighteen years when they had hardly no time at all.

Joe pauses as another idea comes to mind.

And they didn't have a chance at love like I did. I managed to find the love of my life and marry her, and then I was blessed with our perfect honeymoon.

But …

No, dummy, forget any 'buts.' If what Kurt and Ruth say is true, Elaine had as happy a life as she could've had without me, and that's all I ever wanted for her.

Joe attempts a snort. *C'mon, Elaine, I thought I knew you better than that. Couldn't you have married an American instead of a durn German?*

Then again, Kurt said he would have given up his own life to bring me back to her. That's a heck of a statement for an ex-German soldier to make. I've been with him two days, and I haven't seen anything to make me think he's a bad person. In fact, he seems to be a fine person. That medal on the wall beside the bathroom door doesn't have to mean anything bad. He's got that scar on his forehead, so maybe the medal was for being wounded, like American soldiers get the Purple Heart. From what I know so far, I have no reason to do anything but give him the benefit of the doubt. After all, giving someone the benefit of the doubt never cost anyone anything. Maybe he or Ruth will say what happened between Elaine and him to make him say he'd die to bring me back.

"Yes, Kurt," Ruth says. "Elaine told me all about that day at the river. That includes how you told her you'd die if it would bring Joe back. She said she had no doubt you meant it, exactly like I meant what I said about me dying for Elaine. She also told me how the day you told her that was the turning point in your relationship."

Kurt lowers his head. "I don't think she knew how much I cared for her until I said that. It was obvious how much she missed Joe. I hated how Joseph didn't have his father at home with him."

What the— That boy in the picture in Kurt's bedroom is my son, and his name's Joseph? Could I have made it back to Alma to know I'm a dad? It was that night—that one night—our honeymoon night we spent at the river. If Elaine hadn't tricked me into coming home, I wouldn't be a dad. Imagine that.

Kurt rubs his neck. "Is your neck bothering you?" Ruth asks.

Kurt stops rubbing. "I woke up with it off and on since yesterday morning."

"Is it something like an itch, or a tingle? I've been feeling the same thing lately." She snaps her fingers. "I know, the love bug has been gnawing on our old hides and he's just getting through—to you that is."

Kurt slides his arm around Ruth's shoulders. "You mean that about Elaine, that you'd die to bring her back?"

"I know it's easy to say since it can't happen, but I'm as sincere about it as you were about Joe."

Kurt pulls Ruth toward him. "Well, old hen, since we have Lainey's blessing."

She slips her arms around his neck. "It's about time you figured that out, old rooster."

Chapter 45

Sleepover

Ruth kisses Kurt, embarrassing Elaine.

Isn't this strange, my best friend and I kissing my husband at the same time. At least it's not what Rachel and Adam were doing six weeks after she had Sam, or all those other times too.

Ruth ends the kiss and pinches Kurt's cheek. They both grin.

Aw, look at them, acting like two kids on a first date. Now they can spend the rest of their lives together.

They kiss a few more times, pausing between them to mention how they've been thinking about each other lately.

The fire now burns to a flickering glow, allowing a chill to creep into the room. Kurt adds another piece of split oak, stirs the embers, and returns to Ruth's side. "I could use another glass of wine. How about you?"

"I'll have a sip of yours. I like it but I know when to stop. Besides, I still have to drive home."

A hesitant grin quirks the corners of Kurt's mouth.

"Out with it," Ruth says. "Whenever you think something's funny, you never keep it to yourself."

Kurt's grin blooms into toothy smile. "You could always stay."

She's not going to take too well to that suggestion, Kurt, not too well at—

Ruth bursts out laughing.

Kurt crosses his arms, leans back against the sofa, and glares at Ruth.

Uh-huh, I've seen that look before. Although I have no idea what the joke is either, you don't like being left out of it. Come on, Ruth, tell him. It's got to be a good one.

As Ruth's laughter slows, Kurt uncrosses his arms. "You obviously think you're a natural-born comic, old girl. What's got you so stirred up?"

"I did bring Viagra!" Laughing again, Ruth falls back to the sofa.

Oh, please, Ruth, you did not. Stop all that nonsense.

Through Ruth's squinting eyelids, Elaine catches a glimpse of Kurt. He waits patiently, arms again crossed, his head slowly shaking back and forth. This time it takes considerably longer for Ruth to calm down. When she finally does, Kurt, who's rubbing a finger along his tightened lips, cuts his eyes at her. "C'mon, Ruth, you're kidding, right?"

"I knew if I told you that, the look on your face would be worth a million dollars." She shakes his knee. "And it was."

"Good grief, woman, I thought Lainey had my number, but you're insufferable." He bumps her shoulder with his. "But I'll suffer you anyway."

"I'm glad to hear it. How about that glass of wine? All that laughing made me thirsty."

Bring enough for me too. Ha, never mind, I'll share Ruth's. After all, I'm sharing my husband with her.

Kurt returns with the wine. "Here you go, Ruthie, have a sip."

"My, that's good. Ready for some?" He takes a swallow and sets the glass on the end table.

"Ruth, there's something I've always—"

Pop!

Ruth twists her head toward the fire. "Goodness, that scared the fool out of me. Did you hide a firecracker in one of those pieces of oak?"

"It's just moisture in the wood."

The sudden noise scares Elaine also. *That was unexpected. I hope it doesn't happen again. Ever since Joe died, I hate unexpected things.*

"What were you going to say?" Ruth asks.

Kurt goes to the fire, prods the wood with the poker, and comes back. "I was going to say I always wondered what Joe looked like. I'm pretty sure Lainey kept a few pictures of him, but she never offered to let me see any. I was afraid it would seem like I was prying if I asked."

I didn't show you any of those pictures because I remember how much it upset you when I called you Joe that time. If you want to see one now, it's all right with me. If Ruth has one with her, I'd like to see one myself.

"You really want to see what Joe looked like?" Ruth asks.

"I would," Kurt says, nodding. "All these years I've had a picture of him in my mind, and I wonder about it. I guess he looked a lot like Joseph."

"Elaine gave me a picture of her and Joe. It's in my purse."

"Why'd she give you that?"

"Does a woman need a reason to give her best friend a keepsake?" Ruth stands. "Don't answer, you don't have a reason."

Ruth goes to the kitchen for her purse. On the sofa again, she takes her wallet out for the picture. "Thomas took this the day Joe left for basic training." She gives Kurt the picture.

"Have you seen him lately?"

"At the river a few months ago. If there's ever a man who loves to fish, it's Thomas."

"I know, even to the point of never getting married."

Kurt turns on the lamp at his end of the sofa and squints at the old photo. He takes a pair of reading glasses from his pocket. "I should learn to put these on first by now." Glasses perched on his nose, he studies the picture again, turns the lamp off, and returns the picture to Ruth. "Nice."

Ruth looks at the picture before slipping it into her wallet, and Elaine enjoys seeing the old photo. *Look at us, we were so young and so in love. How I miss you, Joe.*

Ruth returns the wallet to her purse. "It's such a shame Joe died in that war. Elaine told me about the day she found out. It was a heartbreaking time, for her and Joe's family too."

Heartbreaking isn't quite the word for it, Ruth, but it's as good a word as I can think of. I had no idea how I'd survive without Joe, but Joseph helped with that. Then Kurt came along, and I remembered what Joe told me about having a happy life if he wasn't able to come back. I wonder how he'd feel about me marrying a man who was a German soldier? But Kurt was much more than a German soldier. In fact, that was the least of who he was, back then and now too. I hope Joe would realize that.

Kurt drops the reading glasses on the end table, leans back on the sofa, and takes a deep breath. Ruth stretches and yawns. "It's been a wonderful evening, but it's time I head home."

Kurt says nothing. Ruth shoves his shoulder. "Don't you have anything to say?"

"Dinner was nice."

"What about us, Kurt? Aren't you happy about us?"

"I appreciate you making me see something I should've

seen a long time ago. I imagine we're about to be the talk of Alma."

"It's not like our friends aren't used to seeing us together."

"True." Kurt pauses. "That means they'd understand."

"Understand what?" Ruth asks, tilting her head to one side.

"They'd understand if you spent the night."

"You aren't smiling like when you asked me before."

"I guess I'm tired. Besides, I owe you a meal."

"What? Burnt toast and runny scrambled eggs?"

"Lainey always said I made a great omelet. I'll make you one if you stay. Hash brown potatoes too."

"You're still not smiling. You just want a dishwasher."

"I'll handle it."

What in the world has gotten into you, sweetheart? One minute you're your regular jokey self, the next you hardly have anything to say. Maybe Ruth will stay to perk you up again.

"What would I sleep in?" Ruth asks.

"I've got extra pajamas." Kurt shrugs. "It's no big deal."

"Where would I sleep?"

"In the spare bedroom. I don't expect you to sleep with me."

"Would you throw me out if I did?" Ruth says, shoving his arm.

Kurt's shoulders bounce with a silent chuckle. "Not unless you have cold feet."

"It's about time you smiled. Okay, you have a guest for the night. If you have flour, I'll make biscuits to go with that omelet."

Kurt stands. "Can you help me put sheets on the spare bed?"

"It's the room with the bathroom across the hall, right?"

"That's it."

In the bathroom, Kurt takes clean sheets from the linen closet. "I have a new toothbrush and toothpaste. I'll leave those and a new bar of soap in the bathroom. Clean wash cloths and towels are in the linen closet."

Kurt's efficiency concerning the linens and other items surprises Elaine. *You must have figured all that out after I left. Good job, sweetheart.*

He helps Ruth smooth the last wrinkle from the quilt and goes to the door. "Holler if you need anything."

"Except for the other things you're putting in the bathroom" —Ruth pulls him down by the shirt and kisses him— "and that, I'm good."

Kurt starts to turn but stops. "What time would you like to get up?"

"Eight's fine. Goodnight, you old rascal, sleep well."

See you in the morning, sweetheart. Maybe a good night's sleep will help whatever's wrong with you.

Chapter 46

Dreams, Nightmares, and Questions

Joe ignores Kurt's bedtime routine.

I sure wish I could've come home to Elaine instead of to some old German soldier. Ain't that a fine howdy-do? Besides finding out I have a son, I'd like to know is if there's anything else for me to learn, or do I just stick around with Kurt until he dies? I guess it won't be that bad. Ruth will be here to keep things interesting.

Still, all through the years I've believed there was more to my existence than this. Like with the last night Elaine and I spent together—the only night we spent together—when I told her no matter what, I'd do everything I could to get back to her, I honestly thought I'd never die. Do I have to give up all the hopes I've kept for over fifty years?

What a dumb question. Joe attempts a sigh. *Instead of worrying about that stuff, I might as well look forward to hash browns and an omelet in the morning. If Kurt gets a good night's sleep, maybe I can have a sweet dream of Elaine on our honeymoon too. It's been a while since I had that particular dream, but after everything I found out tonight, maybe it'll happen again.*

Joe closes his mind's eye. Kurt's body—his slowing heartbeat, the gentle rise and fall of his chest, the relaxing warmth trapped by the blankets around him—signals sleep.

Yeah, hash browns and an omelet sound great ... and Ruth's ... Ruth's biscuits too.

Darkness gradually turns to gray.

Then to white.

Almost blinding white all around him.

Joe picks his way through snow, over trees, and stops.

Across a tree blasted to the ground by artillery, wearing a dark green coat with a swastika on the sleeve, a man lies dead. From a gaping wound in his side, frozen blood is pooled in the snow beneath him. The neck of a wine bottle protrudes from his backpack. A hand, black and bloody, takes the bottle. Another hand, also black and bloody, *pops* the cork. "Here's to you, Joe." The voice is James's voice. "You were a good friend for the few days I knew you. We always had each other's back no matter what."

James tips the bottle and Joe tastes bitter wine, barely any grape to it at all.

James swallows. "At least I killed that damn German that got you. Let me get some help to carry you outta these woods." He takes a single step. Something thuds the back of his helmet and he falls to his knees. Dizzy and disoriented, he can't get up. His vision slowly clears to a contrasting black and white haze, which focuses on a man. The man holds a rifle, and on the end of that rifle, a bayonet shines in the sunlight.

The man spews several words in German. Joe raises his hands—the still bloody, the still black hands. Then more words, thick and southern-accented, come from his and James's mouth.

"Please, I surrender. Please."

More words from the tall, thin man in front of him: a gray

and black scarecrow spitting and snarling in rage. Soot-black hair sticks from beneath a helmet with a strange symbol: a circle of feet that turn over and over and over and over—

Cold steel pierces Joe's chest and withdraws. Hot blood fills his throat and runs down his chin. James falls to the blinding white snow. A final breath leaves him, a cloud of white dissipating in the frigid air of the Ardennes.

Joe wakes.

Kurt rolls side to side in the bed, rubbing his neck and mumbling in German. The rolling slows. The German words fade. He stops rolling and speaking altogether.

Damn, I haven't had that nightmare in years. Even though I blacked out before that German stabbed James, the stress that led to James's dying must have somehow imprinted itself onto my consciousness. Anyway, that's the only thing I've been able to figure out since then. Hell, I even tasted the wine in the dream.

Joe listens to Kurt's breathing, which is completely normal again.

Could my nightmare have affected Kurt? He seems okay now. Still, it's strange how we both were having a nightmare at the same time.

Kurt rolls over to snore softly.

What a hell of a way for James to die. Then me, with my stupid self, all I could think about was how a grenade killed me. I couldn't have been more wrong. James and the boy, the girl and the doctor— no one should have to die like they did.

I was still alive though. I didn't know how or why back then, and to this very second—even after coming back home and finding out what happened to Elaine—I don't know. Could everyone's hope draw them along on a crazy trip like mine, like a huge cosmic black and yellow garden spider drawing a web back and forth between the tomato stakes in Mom's garden, but with the stakes being people's pasts? I doubt it, but I think hope is a powerful thing. Maybe it's powerful enough to do more than people can imagine. I hope so, because I hate to think I'm going through all this for nothing.

Kurt wakes, swings his feet to the floor, and clicks the lamp on. "All that wine," he says, rubbing his forehead.

"All that wine" is right. It feels like your bladder's about to pop. Take care of it so we can get back to sleep. Kurt shuffles to the bathroom, lifts the commode lid, and opens the fly on his pajamas. *Good job, old man. Let's get back to bed so I can have a chance at a decent dream.*

Kurt snaps his fly, takes a few steps across the chilly bathroom floor, and stops outside the door to stretch. His hand touches something cold, something metallic. The German medal glints in the lamplight. Kurt stares, blinks, and rips the medal from the frame's corner. The frame crashes down, scattering shards of glass across the cold hardwood floor with a clatter.

What the hell? What's wrong with you, Kurt?

Kurt flips the overhead light switch and glares at the medal in his hand. Hot blood rushes to his face. Pressure fills his veins. Throat muscles convulse.

C'mon, old man, what's gotten into you? I've never known you to be so upset.

"Why?" Kurt says, still glaring at the medal. "Why couldn't the damned Nazis have left me the hell alone. If one of you were here right now, I'd—" He rushes to the kitchen, flips on the light, and again glares at the medal. "None of you bastards are here, but this" —he slams the medal to the table— "will damn well do."

Calm down, Kurt! Throw that medal in the trash and get back to bed before you scare Ruth half-to-death.

Kurt jerks a jacket on, shoves the medal in a pocket, and forces his feet into a dirty pair of boots by the kitchen door.

Where the hell do you think you're going? C'mon now, calm down!

Kurt snatches the door open; the curtains fly in his face. Rain still falls; puddles fill the yard. The old SUV shimmers in the umbrella of light from the porch. He splashes to the barn and jerks the door open, then tugs the chain on the overhead light and slams the medal to the cut and gouged chopping block.

Kurt! What are you—

Kurt wrenches the ax from the block and raises it high over his head. Shoulder muscles tighten. Hands squeeze tighter. He brings the ax down and strikes the medal a glancing blow. A pause. A heavy inhale and exhale. A rub of his neck that's more of a slap. He raises the ax again and hits the medal hard enough to jar his arms. Kurt's face muscles contort into a hard frown. The medal, bent double, is stuck in the chopping block.

You hit the damn thing, are you satisfied? Maybe you'll forget this foolishness and—

What the— He's getting a screwdriver? He's digging the medal out? Dammit, old man, enough is enough!

Kurt throws the screwdriver to the dirt floor and raises the ax. "One more time, you bastards, just one more time."

Pain flares in his and Joe's chest—a searing pain that radiates down his left arm in a white-hot arc to end at his fingertips.

Dammit, Kurt, you're giving yourself a heart attack!

Kurt drops to his knees. Another jolt of pain hits Joe, the same as the first. Kurt falls forward and rolls onto his back. The light hanging from a rafter sways with a gust of wind.

"Lainey," Kurt moans. "Ruth … where's Ruth?" His eyes close.

Darkness engulfs Joe. Rain rattles the barn's tin roof. Lightning burns through Kurt's eyelids. Thunder follows, booming and echoing like distant artillery rounds exploding in the night.

I can't believe you're going to die out here in this damn barn all by yourself—and me with you. I haven't felt the cold on the back of my neck yet. Maybe Ruth heard you and she'll get an ambulance out here. Come on, Ruth, this old fool needs you.

And I do too!

Chapter 47

Discovery

Ruth's inaction puzzles Elaine. When Kurt stomped down the hall, Ruth rolled over, so she must have heard him. She rolled over again when Kurt slammed the kitchen door, but she stayed in bed.

Ruth! Why aren't you up looking out the window? Come on now, let's—

Ruth throws the covers back and goes to the window. In the open barn doors, light glows. Kurt's shadow moves on the dirt floor.

We need to go see what he's doing out there, Ruth. Please go check on him.

Ruth rubs her neck. "What in the world would get that old man out of a warm bed in the middle of a cold, rainy night? He might not like it, but I'm going to see what he's up to."

Shoes on, she goes to the kitchen and looks through the kitchen door window. The fogged glass hazes everything, so she opens the door. Within the circle of light illuminating the barn's dirt floor lies Kurt.

"Kurt! Oh my God!" Donning her coat, she starts toward the barn, then whirls back inside and calls 911. The dispatcher says an ambulance will be on the way.

Ruth splashes through the cold rain and muddy yard to the

barn and kneels at Kurt's side. "Kurt, can you hear me? Hang on, help is coming!" She unzips his jacket and presses her ear to his chest. To her and Elaine's relief, his heart beats steadily. "Thank God! Why would you come out here like this? It doesn't make any sense!"

I don't understand either, Kurt, this isn't like you at all!

"Please stay with me, Kurt," Ruth begs. "We just found each other. I can't—" Ruth's warm tears run down her cheeks. "I can't lose you now."

Don't die, sweetheart, you can have many happy years with Ruth yet, and me too! I'd love to stay here with both of you until … well, until then, but not now!

* * *

Ruth's voice stirs Kurt. "Ruth?"

"Hush and lie still, help's coming."

"I'm—" He raises his head but it thumps to the ground. "I'm jus' … jus' gon' rest."

The pressure on Kurt's chest eases, so Joe stops expecting him to die any minute. *Do like Ruth says, you hardhead, or I'll figure out a way to make you wish you did.*

A siren wails from the highway.

"They're almost here," Ruth says.

Tires splash in the driveway. Red lights circle the yard. Two doors slam; footsteps splash toward the barn.

"Ruth, I—"

"Don't try to talk, help is here."

"I'm … I'm sorry, Ruth. I'm … I'm—" His face contorts; his eyes widen. Joe feels pain explode in his chest and shoot down his arm.

"No! Kurt, please, no!"

An EMT kneels by Ruth. "Ma'am, do you think he's having

a heart attack?"

"I think he might, please help him!" She backs out of the way. The EMT opens Kurt's jacket and rips his pajama top open.

The familiar ice-cold hand grips the back of Joe's neck, followed by the building pressure that threatens to squeeze him into a molecule-sized ball.

Damn! That's the quickest transition to the second warning I've ever had. If you want to live, Kurt, it's time to fight. Past time. C'mon now, we got this!

The pressure on Joe intensifies. *One more step and we're gone. I had hoped—*

A new sensation hits—a sudden jolt concentrated in Kurt's chest. It hits again, forcing him into unconsciousness.

* * *

Elaine can't believe what she sees. Kurt's body jerks and arches as the electricity of a defibrillator pulses through his chest.

"Let me check his heartbeat." A second EMT places a stethoscope on Kurt's chest. "We have a steady rhythm. Let's get him ready for transport."

"Thank you, Lord," Ruth says. "Will he be all right?"

"Too soon to tell, ma'am. We'll transport him to the Harlan County Hospital. You might want to get some of his things together and come right away."

Ruth kneels by Kurt and holds his hand. "I'll be right on, Kurt, soon as I can." He doesn't open his eyes.

"Okay, ma'am, we need to go," the EMT says. Ruth moves aside. They lift Kurt onto a stretcher and carry him through dwindling rain.

Ruth splashes behind them. Elaine tries to see Kurt while

the men place him in the ambulance. One man stays in back. The other man slams the twin doors shut and climbs in through the driver door. The swirling red lights disappear down the road.

"What am I doing standing here like an idiot?" Ruth splashes to the house. "I need to change and pack a bag for Kurt and get to the hospital—now!"

Take your time, Ruth. We don't need to have an accident on the way.

Ruth dresses, packs Kurt's bathroom items, and hurries from the house to stop by the SUV. The light still glows in the barn. She goes inside to turn it off. An ax and a screwdriver lie on the dirt floor, and on top of the wood block, gouged and bent nearly double, a small, brown metal circle gleams in the light. She picks it up. "What in the world?"

Elaine recognizes the simple medal Kurt was awarded for being wounded in battle, the American equivalent of the Purple Heart. Some minor official gave it to him when he returned to Germany and reported in at his hometown.

I don't know what was going on out here with you and that medal, Kurt, but I hope we find out.

Ruth drops the medal in her purse. "Old man, when you're up to it, we need to have a talk."

That's right, Ruth. If anyone can get make him talk, you can.

Chapter 48

Hospital

A hand touches Kurt's arm. "He should be regaining consciousness any time now."

Joe tries to shake his head, to blink his eyes. *Whoever you are, I'm awake, okay? Wait a minute, where am I and who am I with? Did Kurt die on me? Did—*

"Poor thing, I guess he's worn out."

That's Ruth! Kurt didn't—

"No doubt, Mrs. Richardson. Emotional stress can tire a person as much as physical stress. From what you were saying, Mr. Bauer had a traumatic night."

"I never heard that about stress. I was wondering why he slept until morning."

"The doctor should be in to check on him soon."

Rubber soled shoes squeak across the floor. A door swishes open and thumps closed. Joe assumes it's the nurse leaving the room. Nearby, pages flip hesitantly.

Ruth must be reading a magazine. I don't hear anyone else, so Kurt must be in a private room instead of intensive care. That means he should be all right. Well, at least until Ruth gets to the bottom of this crazy business with that medal. I don't know what got into him with all that—

"Uh-h-h-h."

Well, well, if it isn't sleeping friggin' beauty himself. You hear that, Ruth? Wake up, old man. Let's see how bad off you are.

* * *

Fingertips cool and soft touch Kurt's cheek. "It's Ruth, Kurt, can you hear me?"

Kurt opens his eyes. "Where— Are we in the hospital?"

"Not we, you. They say you might have had a heart attack. Can you hear me?"

"Don't you know the difference between a heart attack and an ear attack?"

"I see they saved your sense of humor. How do you feel?"

Kurt tries to swallow, but it's like choking down a mouthful of cotton balls. "Can I have something to drink? My mouth feels like I'm one of those 2,000-year-old mummies on National Geographic."

"How about ice chips, Mr. Mummy?"

"How about a beer?"

"Did they have beer in ancient Egypt? It doesn't matter, all you're allowed is ice chips." Ruth pushes a button on the bed rail, and Kurt tilts upward. She raises a cup to his lips. "Here you go."

He crunches ice and swallows. "Whoa, that's good." Ruth raises the cup again, but he waves it away. "How long have I been here?"

"Since last night. Do you remember any of it?"

"I was in the barn, right?"

"We'll talk about it later. You need your rest."

"What about this heart attack business? How bad did I mess up?"

"The emergency room doctor said you might have a small amount of damage, but nothing to keep you from recovering.

We're lucky the EMTs came so quickly. They had to shock you to get your heart back to a normal rhythm."

"You sure that's all they did? I feel like a tractor ran over me. Maybe you snuck into my room and ravished me in my sleep." Kurt grabs Ruth's hand and shakes it. "Since my toes got you all hot and bothered."

"We need to get you well before anyone does any ravishing, okay?"

Kurt attempts a weak smile. "I have no problem with that, Ruth, no problem at all."

"More ice?"

"I'm good. Did the doctor say when I can go home? What's his name anyway?"

"*Her* name is Dr. Richardson. Imagine that, the same as my last name."

"And you love it."

"I sure do. Now you'll have to listen to *two* Richardson women—one here and one at home."

"Great. Can I have some more ice, Doctor Ruth?" Ruth tips the cup, the hint of a grin at the corners of her mouth. "Okay, Ruthie, what's so funny?"

"Have you ever heard of Dr. Ruth?"

"Should I?"

"She's pretty famous. She's an expert sex therapist."

"Does she make house calls?"

"I doubt it, you pervert. By the way you're acting, I'm beginning to doubt you had a heart attack too. Anyway, don't worry about that Dr. Ruth. You'll have your hands full with this one."

"Tell me something I don't know."

Ruth pushes the button that lowers his bed. "Lie back and

rest while I finish the article in this magazine. Then we'll be ready when the doctor comes."

"I can sure do that," Kurt says, closing his eyes.

* * *

Instead of concentrating on the article, Elaine concentrates on last night.

You were a lot easier on Kurt than I thought you'd be, Ruth. If he did something like that when I was alive, I'm not sure if I could wait to ask him about it. You're being smart, I suppose, but I hope you mention it sooner than—

Ruth stands and drops the magazine in the chair.

Go get him, Ruth.

* * *

A sigh comes from beside Kurt. "Tired of reading, Ruthie, or did you miss my pretty face?"

"About last night …"

"What happened to later? This isn't later."

Ruth shows him her watch. "It's five minutes' later. That's good enough for me."

"It's too personal to talk about here. Can't you trust me on that?"

"If there's one thing I can do" —Ruth taps his nose— "I can trust you."

"Good. It's not like I could get up and run away."

Ruth purses her lips, which worries Kurt. She leans against the bed rail. "While you're stuck in this bed, there's something else I want to tell you."

"Go ahead, I'm waiting."

"I'm staying with you when you get home. Care to argue about it?"

"Who's arguing? When a man gets home from the hospital,

wouldn't he want his wife to stay with him?"

Ruth tilts her head to one side. "Did you say 'wife?'"

"Why not?" Kurt asks, patting her hand. "That way, if you stay at my house, the neighbors won't gossip."

"You'll do the darnedest things, like having a heart attack to avoid getting down on one knee to ask me to marry you."

"You never said when I can go home. I'll ask then if you can wait, but you might have to help me back up."

"Maybe three days, so they say."

"Can you wait that long?"

"I can wait. Besides, you don't know my answer."

Kurt winks. "I think I know."

"That's all right." Ruth kisses his cheek. "I'll let you think you know me so well. You'll have a lot more to learn once we get married. I bet you won't like some of those things either."

"Vice-versa, I'm sure."

Ruth makes a growling sound in her throat. "That's the understatement of the century, old man."

Someone knocks; a woman with long red hair comes in. She wears a white smock and carries a clipboard. A stethoscope hangs around her neck.

"Hello, Dr. Richardson," Ruth says. "I was just telling Kurt how long his stay might be."

"Good morning, Ruth, and to you, Mr. Bauer. I'm happy to see you're still in the land of the living. However, if you try another stunt like you did last night, Ruth might be attending your funeral. Surely we can agree that's something you'd like to avoid?"

"Yes, ma'am, no doubt about it."

"I didn't think you'd argue with logic. I need to listen to your heart."

She places the stethoscope, cold even through his hospital gown, to his chest, then listens, moves it, and writes a few notes on a clipboard. "I imagine you're quite active, yes?"

"Did my manly physique give me away?"

The doctor glances at Ruth and returns to Kurt. "I was asking because you have a good chance of getting back to normal activity if you follow my directions. You're in excellent shape."

"Thanks, I think so too."

"For a man your age."

"Oh. I guess I better stop with the jokes."

"Forgive him," Ruth says. "It's all I can do to forgive him myself at times."

"As far as my activity," Kurt says, eyeing Ruth, "during the growing season I do quite a bit on my farm. I don't *try* to stay active. It's my lifestyle and I enjoy it."

"Is Ruth part of that lifestyle?" Dr. Richardson asks. "When she and I met last night, I thought she might be a good influence on you."

"She hasn't been but she will be. If I heard her right, she's agreed to marry me. Isn't that right, Ruth?"

"Actually, he just asked. I intend to make him get down on one knee and propose properly when he's able."

"Congratulations to both of you." The doctor faces Kurt. "Some studies suggest married men live longer. Did you know that, Mr. Bauer?"

"What about married women?" Ruth asks.

The doctor taps her pen on the clipboard. "I'm not sure the results of that study have come out yet. They'd be quite mixed, I'm sure."

"I'm surprised they've come out for men," Kurt says. "Now,

is there any way I can get out of this place sooner than three days?"

"That's one of the reasons I stopped by." The doctor studies her clipboard. "Your test results look remarkably good for a man who's had a heart attack. In fact, we aren't sure you had a heart attack at all. Sometimes those symptoms mirror other issues, like stress. I understand you were out in a barn last night, pounding on an old medal with an ax. That sounds like a man under a lot of stress to me. Is that statement accurate?"

"I'd … uh … well, I'd say that's how it was." He glances at Ruth. "I have some strong feelings about that medal—personal feelings I'd rather not go into right now."

"We're clearing it up as soon as we get home," Ruth says. "Unless he wants to stay single."

Dr. Richardson puts the pen in her pocket. "We have some fine counselors here. I can make an appointment if you'd like."

"No, thanks," Kurt says. "When my wife was alive, she and Ruth were best friends. I trust Ruth as much as my wife did."

"I'm relieved to hear that. If you ever have the need, we're here for you."

"If I have the need. Now, you were about to tell me if I can get out of here quicker than three days."

The doctor consults the clipboard again. "From what I see, and from what my colleagues and I agree on, probably tomorrow. However, I'd like to see you again in a week. The EMTs had to use a defibrillator to get your heart back to a normal rhythm. It seems fine now, but I want to keep a check on it for the next month or so." She glances at her watch. "I'll let you make your wedding plans, see you in the morning."

"It's a date." Kurt watches the doctor leave the room. Grinning, he faces Ruth, who slowly shakes her head.

"You, sir, are a scoundrel."

"Why, Ruthie, you're just figuring that out?"

"Of course not. Your wife was my best friend, remember? I probably know more about you than *you* know about you."

"I doubt she knew I had a thing for redheads. What do you think about wearing a red wig on our honeymoon?"

Ruth covers her eyes and peeks over her ringed fingers. "It'd be cheaper than Viagra."

Kurt slaps his leg. "Ha! Doggone, Ruthie, the timing of your punch lines keeps getting better and better."

"Being around you, you old fool, does it have a choice?"

Chapter 49

A Decent Proposal

Ruth parks the old SUV in the driveway, and Kurt unbuckles his seatbelt. "Yep, the old place is just like I remember."

Joe tries to grin at the remark. *C'mon, old man, you've only been away a few days. Try over fifty years and see how you like that.*

Ruth unbuckles her seatbelt. "Listen to you, acting as if you've been gone a month. Do you feel like you were swept up in a tornado?"

"That's a good way to put it." Kurt opens the SUV door. "Let's get inside."

My, you're impatient, sweetheart. You do sound like Dorothy from The Wizard of Oz, wanting to get back home. Maybe Ruth should buy you a pair of ruby-red work boots to remind you not to do anything foolish enough to land you in the hospital again.

At the porch steps, Joe and Samantha run to meet him. "Hey, you two," Kurt says, patting their heads. "Did Ruthie take good care of you while I was gone?"

Ruth twists her lips to one side. "You act as if I'd let them starve."

"They're good company out here on the farm."

"I know, I know." She unlocks the door. "Ready?"

"I can't wait to have a cup of my own coffee. Maybe some of that leftover pot roast from the other night too." Kurt goes inside. "It sure is great to be home." He pats Ruth's shoulder. "And I'm glad you're here with me."

"Please don't ever do anything so foolish again," she says, her tone serious. "I didn't show it at the hospital, but I was scared to death."

Elaine attempts a nod. *I was too, Ruth.*

"I'm sorry," Kurt says. "I promised to talk about it, and I will, but I'd rather enjoy a few days of peace first."

"Don't wait too long. I want it behind us so we can look forward to the future."

"Speaking of the future." Kurt takes her hand and leads her to the kitchen table. "Okay, Ruthie, cop a squat."

"Uh-huh, you saw *Pretty Woman* one time too many in the hospital while I was back here feeding Joe and Samantha."

"Regardless of my being in love with Julia Roberts, I'm about to ask you to marry me, *exactly* as you requested. Can you please sit?" She does, smiling, and Kurt rolls his eyes. "You're enjoying this entirely too much, you know."

"If our roles were reversed, wouldn't you?"

Kurt holds the edge of the table and eases down on one knee. "Ruth, you meant the world to Lainey. She constantly surprised me in life, and she still surprises me now, even after she's gone. So, with her blessing, will you marry me?"

Ruth takes his face in her hands and kisses him soundly. "Does that answer your question?"

"I just got out of the hospital. Are you trying to give me another heart attack?"

"No, but you better be fully recovered in time for our honeymoon."

"Don't worry, remember what the doctor said about my manly physique?"

Joe wants to smirk. *Manly physique my rear— Well, our rear end, old man. I hope you have fun on your honeymoon, because I ain't hangin' around that night to find out. Talk about nightmares.*

"Actually, what the doctor said is you were in good shape for a man *your* age." Ruth pulls his nose. "You didn't think I heard that part, did you? When I met her, she was wearing a Santa hat. Did you realize you were in the hospital on Christmas day? Anyway, she said she would take the hat off when she came to check on you so you'd take her seriously."

"You two won't let me get away with a darn thing, will you?"

"Someone has to keep you rooted in reality, you old farmer you."

"I guess you're right." Kurt groans. "If I don't get up soon, my reality is gonna be aching in the morning. Give me a hand, please."

Ruth takes his elbow. He slowly stands, and she steers him to a chair. "Have a seat while I make coffee and fix you a sandwich."

"You handle the sandwich, I'll handle the coffee. I feel like I need to move around. If I stayed in that hospital much longer, I think my joints would have locked up."

Ruth slices roast beef while Kurt measures coffee. She bumps his hip with hers. "I feel like an old married couple already. When can we make it legal?"

"In a hurry, old girl? Or is that because of what I said about the neighbors gossiping?"

"Phooey, you hardly have any neighbors. Besides, you know I've never given a fig about what others think. I do give a fig what I think, and I think I'd like to tie the knot sometime soon. Don't you feel that way too? No teasing this time."

"What's today? I got all fumbled up while I was in the hospital."

"It's Monday."

"Well durn."

"What are you durning about?"

"Saturday might be as good a day as any. Is that too long a wait for you?"

"Good idea. How about we do it at the river?"

"You talking about the wedding" —Kurt winks— "or the honeymoon?"

Joe attempts to shake his spiritual head. *Oh, you're a real card when that medal isn't on your mind. You shouldn't forget Saturday so doggone easy, I was there, remember? Let's see what happens when Ruth makes you deal with whatever reason you had for acting like an idiot.*

"Mmm, mm, mm," Ruth says, her lips a tight line. "You're always joking about something."

Elaine agrees with Ruth's sentiment. *He wasn't so darn jokey before I died, Ruth. Maybe that's because it rubbed off from being around you for two years.*

* * *

Kurt takes a pad and a pen from the top of the refrigerator and checks the calendar on the door. "Happy Thursday, Ruthie. Two more days before we get hitched."

Folding laundry at the table, she looks his way. "Haven't you checked your list enough?"

"You don't know it yet, but I like to keep things in order." Kurt places the point of the pen beside the first sentence on the pad. "I called Dr. Redhead. She says I'm ready to rock your world Saturday night. Check."

"Not without Viag—"

"All our friends are invited to the wedding. We haven't had any pre-marital sex to make you blush. Check."

"Would you stop doing—"

"Bill's got the food lined up. Check."

"What about alcohol?"

"Good idea. I might need to get you drunk before—"

"Kurt Bauer, behave!"

Kurt scribbles a few words. "Bring plenty of wine. Check."

"Did you ask John at the hardware if the Masonic Lodge minds him bringing their chairs?"

"Sure did, no problem."

"Can you write down something about having nice weather?"

"Good point. We might need a fire if it turns cool. A *big* fire."

"A fire?" Ruth raises a sock as if she's about to throw it at him. "Do you really think a woman wants to stand around a fire in her nice clothes? We'll watch the weather reports and modify our plans to suit. If we need to make any last-minute changes, I'm sure everyone will understand."

"You're right, Ruthie. All our friends are a good bunch of people."

"Yes, they are. I'm glad we have friends like them."

"Now that that's settled, how about a more pressing question." Kurt rubs his stomach. "What's for supper?"

"Old man, it's not too late for me to pull out of this thing if you go acting like I'm the only one around here who can make a menu."

Kurt raises a single bushy eyebrow. "You're kidding, right?"

"Not about supper I'm not. You've got a microwave. Being

a bachelor for two years, I'm sure you know how to defrost."

"You had me worried. For a minute I thought I was losing my bride before she's my bride." He opens the freezer. "Are chicken breasts on the propane grill okay? If you don't mind, Ms. Ruthie, you can make us a tossed salad."

"I didn't picture you for a propane grill. I thought you'd be hardcore charcoal all the way."

"I'm trying to modernize. You have your cell phone, I have my propane grill."

"What you have is no sense whatsoever, old man. That's okay, I love you anyway."

"Good." Kurt slips on his jacket. "I better check the grill. It's been a while since I used it." As he turns the doorknob, a pair of his underwear hits the door beside his head. He faces Ruth. "What?"

"Don't blow yourself up. That would ruin the wedding."

Hey, Kurt, I think Ruth's getting better at joking than you are. Joe pauses. Still, I'm not sure about seeing the river again. I mean, I want to see it, but what if the memories Elaine and me made there upset me? They're strong enough to do almost anything.

My goodness, I can't wait until the wedding. I don't think I've been this excited since Joe and I got married, not to mention our honeymoon there. It's certainly a magical place, so magical that almost anything might happen.

Chapter 50

Betrayal

Kurt leaves to clean the grill. Ruth finishes the laundry and takes a list of wedding guests from her purse to make sure they haven't forgotten anyone. Satisfied, she places it on the refrigerator beneath a miniature magnetic Cape Hatteras Lighthouse. Closing her purse, she stops when she sees Kurt's ax-beaten medal.

"Old man, we need to get this out of the way before Saturday." She snaps the purse shut. "And tonight will be as good a time as any."

I agree, Ruth. That business needs to be over and done with. I'm sure we'll end up in front of the fire after supper, so why not take your purse to the living room? You know, be prepared, like a Boy Scout.

Ruth takes her purse to the living room.

* * *

In the barn, Kurt clenches his fists while glaring at the wooden chopping block. He draws his work boot back as if to kick it, but he doesn't. Joe is sure he's thinking about Saturday night. *You need to forget that mess until you and Ruth sort it out. It can't be important enough for another ambulance ride to the hospital.*

Kurt removes the dusty grill cover, rolls the grill outside, and raises the lid. He can almost smell the last meal he cooked for Lainey—grilled tomato slices with oregano and parmesan cheese—still clinging to the blackened grates.

Whatever you cooked on here the last time sure smells good. Did I get a whiff of cheese? Let's try whatever it was tomorrow night.

Kurt returns to the barn and sits on the chopping block. He rubs his eyes a few times, and warm tears trickle down his cold cheeks.

Believe me, old man, if you're thinking about Elaine, I know how you feel. Look at it this way though, you got to have a lifetime with her when I only had about a year. Go ahead and cry. I can't count the times I wanted to sit and have a good cry myself.

"I acted like a real imbecile Saturday night, Lainey … a lot more than when I met you at the hardware store." Kurt takes a handkerchief from his pocket and wipes his eyes. "That damned war …"

I wonder if that medal reminds you of how you lost your family? I get it if it does, but wear my durn pants like I'm wearing yours and see how it feels. I can't count the times I've wanted to beat the hell out of the guy that killed me, exactly like you beat the hell out of that medal.

Kurt shoves the wet handkerchief in his pocket. "I'll get through it, Lainey. Maybe with your help, and Ruth's, we can get this mess straightened out. I sure hope so."

You and me both, old man, you and me both.

At the kitchen counter, Ruth stops slicing tomatoes. "Were you okay out there? That took a while."

"I sat down and talked things over with Lainey is all. Had me a little cry too."

"I know you miss her. Are you better now?"

"I feel like she's watching over us. Since you said she wanted us to get together, I know she's happy."

I'm more than happy, sweetheart, but I want you to be happy too. After all, that's what Joe wanted for me.

"Oh, she's happy," Ruth says, giving him a hug. "I really do believe that."

Kurt kisses her cheek. "You know what the future Mrs. Ruthie Bauer? You sure know how to make a fella feel loved."

Ruth's warm embrace comforts Joe as much as it comforts Kurt. *You're right, you old fart. I got some nice hugs over the years, but Ruth's hugs are some of the best I ever had. Well, except for Elaine's.*

"All right then," Kurt says, "let's fix us some supper. Your hug has given me an appetite."

Ruth winks. "Just for supper?"

Kurt grins hugely. "There you go again, getting better and better with the timing of your punch lines. Before you know it, I'll have you breaking them up at the diner. Maybe the hardware store too."

Ruth resumes slicing tomatoes. "I might try the Farmer's Market—or the diner—but I'm not getting mixed up with you and your buddies at that musty, old hardware store."

Kurt picks up a piece of tomato. "You don't want to associate with a bunch of old degenerates like us anyway." He pops the tomato in his mouth, and Joe enjoys the tart, sweet slice.

Ruth points the knife at Kurt. "Old degenerate, instead of eating our tomatoes, light that grill. Doesn't it need to be heated before you use it?"

"Yes, ma'am, right away, ma'am." Kurt hurries out the door, leaving Ruth and Elaine shaking their collective heads.

* * *

Kurt adds a stick of wood to the fire. "That chicken was

309

pretty darn good." He joins Ruth on the sofa and pats his stomach. "Whew, I'm stuffed."

"I ate too much myself. You're right, your chicken was delicious."

The fire flickers orange and yellow in the fireplace, radiating warmth into the room. A spark pops now and then; the embers crackle like sleet blown against the window by a gust of icy, plains-driven wind.

Ruth takes her purse from the end table. "It's time to get this over with, old man."

About to put his arm around Ruth's shoulders, Kurt jerks it back. "Get *what* over with?"

She opens her purse, brings out her clenched hand, and drops the damaged medal into his lap. He picks the medal up. "Huh. I guess you found this in the barn."

"Maybe you were too upset about Elaine to see it was missing. Don't you think it's time we sort this mess out?"

He stares at the small brown medal, now almost a V in his hand. "If it can be."

"What do you mean by that?"

"It depends, Ruth."

"Depends on what? No, forget that. We're going to hash this out regardless of what you think it 'depends' on, especially since it landed you in the damn hospital."

"You don't have to curse about it."

"Don't look at me like that, Mr. Bugeyes. I'll say it again if I have to. Damn-damn-damn. I'll say worse if—"

"Ruth, I—"

"Don't 'Ruth' me. I don't want to see you in the hospital again."

None of us does, sweetheart. Please do like Ruth says.

Ruth's right, Kurt. Like I said in the barn, it isn't worth another trip in that ambulance. Let's get it over and done with.

"Okay, okay, calm down," Kurt says. "Yes, it has something to do with this medal. And the war. And what I'm afraid I might have done. It's hard to believe how many coincidences must've happened for me to end up in Alma, not to mention meeting and marrying Lainey." Biting his lower lip, he shakes his head. "Even though it looks like every one of them happened, the thing that *made* them happen wasn't a coincidence, just everything after."

"What in the world are you talking about?" Ruth asks, her voice rising. "Elaine told me how you came to Alma as a prisoner in the war. She also told me how the Edwards offered you a home if you had no reason to stay in Germany after you went back."

"That's a good thing," Kurt says, not looking at her. "I'm talking about a tragic thing. I mean as tragic as it gets."

"You mean how you lost your family? No doubt that played a part in why you came back and applied for citizenship. You weren't the only German man—German boy, really—to do that. I'd have done the same thing."

So that's how he ended up in Alma. I thought this house and barn looked familiar. This is the Edwards' farm, where the river is, and where Elaine and I—

Kurt gives Ruth the medal. "Put that away. I don't want to look at it."

She drops the medal on the end table beside her purse. It twirls in an echoing metallic circle until Kurt reaches over to slap it down.

Ruth shoves his arm away. "Did that make you feel better? If it did, good. Now what—"

"Just … just …" Kurt's hands tremble. "Just hold on, please." He bows his head.

"Kurt, what—"

"Can I see that picture of Elaine and Joe again?" He raises his head. "The one you showed me Saturday night?"

Ruth takes the picture from her wallet and gives it to Kurt.

Sweetheart, why do you want to see that again when you hardly looked at it the last time? Ruth's only trying to help, okay? Please listen to her.

Kurt turns the lamp on, perches the reading glasses on his nose, and studies the picture. He slowly stands and shuffles to the fireplace mantle, then takes a magnifying glass from beside the mahogany chest that Joe saw earlier. Placing his hand gently on the chest, he rubs it. "Lainey, I'm so sorry." He returns to the sofa and studies the picture again.

Joe feels the old man's shoulder muscles tightening and his heart thudding faster. *Is he looking at me? Why would he look at me like that?*

That's why I didn't frame these pictures when we got married, Kurt. I knew they'd upset you. It didn't take forty years of marriage to figure that out.

Kurt returns to the sofa and leaves his glasses and the magnifying glass on the end table beside him. "I wanted to see that again." He fingers moisture from his eyes. "To be sure." He gives Ruth the picture.

"To be sure of what?" Ruth drops the picture on the end table beside her and whirls to face Kurt. "Spit it out already."

"I think—" Kurt clears his throat. "I don't know how to tell you this, Ruth, but God help me, I think—no, I know—I killed Joe."

Like when Joe saw James staring into his eyes from the

mirror he took from his pocket over fifty years ago, the meaning of Kurt's statement batters his consciousness to the edge of passing out. *What the— You think you killed me? Just from looking at a picture?*

No, sweetheart, you've got to be mistaken. That was ages and ages ago. How could you remember what Joe looked like?

Ruth's mouth hangs open. She closes it and looks Kurt dead in the eye. "How could you recognize Joe from a picture taken that long ago?"

"He's familiar. At least his blond hair and profile is. There's another thing I remember about that day that makes me think I killed him."

Kurt lowers his head. "It was …" His chest expands with a huge inhale. "Joe had a yellow ribbon tied around his wrist that day. It's exactly like the one Elaine is giving him in the picture."

He buries his face into Ruth's shoulder. "I wish I could take it back and give Joe and Lainey their lives." His shoulders heave with a sob. "But I can't."

You son-of-a-bitch, you took me away from Elaine and cry about it? I wish that damned fake heart attack had killed you so I could get the hell away from you. You got the best of her and all I got was a memory.

The shock of Kurt's statement drills into Elaine's being, but only for a moment. *Kurt, please, if you did kill Joe—and I'm not sure you did—you must've been protecting yourself. I know you and I know your past. You were—and are—a good man, just as good a man as Joe was. Neither one of you could do anything about that terrible war except try to stay alive so you could come home to your loved ones. Ruth will tell you the same thing, won't you, Ruth?*

* * *

Ruth holds Kurt while he sobs.

Can his story be true? The coincidences for it to have taken place are unimaginable. The only way to find out is to ask him more about that day.

She pulls away. His eyes are red and his nose is running. She gives him a tissue from her purse.

"You need to tell me more than that before I believe you killed Joe. Out of all the men in the war, surely he wasn't the only one to wear a yellow ribbon on his wrist."

Kurt wipes his eyes and nose. He balls the tissue in one hand and squeezes it again and again, as if he's making a fist to punch the wall—or himself. "I can tell you what happened. Don't know what good it'll do."

"Go ahead, but leave out any upsetting parts."

Kurt settles back against the sofa and faces Ruth. "I don't know how I lived through it, but artillery hit our position at dawn. I thought I was the only person alive except my Corporal. He was a cold-hearted bastard, mean as they come."

"You could've left that part out," Ruth says.

"Sorry, but it's real when I think about it. Anyway, we were out of ammunition, and I saw him behind a tree. He liked to wound men and finish them off with a bayonet. I was lying on the ground behind a tree. All I wanted was to stay alive."

Huh, that corporal sounds like the guy in the nightmare I had, when Kurt was having his nightmare too. He hit James in the back of the head and screamed at him and then drove that bayonet into his chest. I hate this. I don't like wishing Kurt was dead. After all, he made Elaine happy.

"All you had was a rifle with no bullets?" Ruth asks.

"I had one grenade left."

"Was Joe there all by himself? That doesn't sound right."

"He was with a Black soldier. We heard about them, but we

thought they were kept apart from the white soldiers. When they—"

"They served in their own artillery units," Ruth says, nodding. "I read about them on the internet once."

"When they—"

"It seems …"

"It seems what, Ruth?"

"I can't remember right now. Go ahead."

"What is it? Is it important?"

"Elaine said Joe wrote her once about some Black artillerymen joining them. He was getting to know one. I think his name started with a J. John maybe, or Jimmie."

James, Ruth, his name was James, dammit.

She waves her comment away. "I need something to jog my memory. What were you saying?"

"They were coming right at me," Kurt says. "We were told we'd be shot on sight if we surrendered. I had no choice but to throw the grenade."

Ruth raises a hand to her mouth, then lowers it. "Did you … well, did both …?"

"The shock wave made the Black soldier drop his rifle, and I …"

"You used the bayonet?"

"He fought me with one of those folding shovels that soldiers carried on their backpacks. I cut his hands and face before he" —Kurt touches the scar on his forehead— "hit me and knocked me out. He was still there when I woke up. Half of my face was in the snow soaked with my own blood. I played dead by holding my breath so it wouldn't cloud and by keeping one eye open, even though it had snow and blood in it. The last thing I saw was him leaving. Then I passed out again. I woke up in an Army medical unit a few days later and was sent here as a prisoner."

"Okay, that's how you ended up in Nebraska and that's how you got that scar," Ruth says, almost cringing at the pain Kurt must've felt from his wound. "But how does that prove the man you killed with the grenade was Joe?"

"He looks exactly like the picture, Ruth, that's how."

"Where was this at?"

"The Ardennes Forest, during the Battle of the Bulge."

Ruth covers her eyes. "Good Lord above. Elaine said the Army eventually told her that's where he died."

Kurt blinks. "I told you it was him." A single tear rolls down his cheek.

Ruth considers shaking him but doesn't. "Kurt, I want you to listen to me. As much as it hurts, as guilty as you think you might be, you aren't. It was war. As hard as it is to hear, that's all it was, war. I know you—Elaine knew you too."

Kurt lowers his head. Ruth lifts his chin, none too gently. "Listen to me, you were no damn Nazi. Those—I can't even call them people—*bastards* took you away from your family and forced you into their war. All you're guilty of is trying to stay alive."

"That's what I've been trying to tell myself since I saw that picture. Deep down I know it's true. There's something else I keep thinking about. Something that tears me apart inside. I need to stop thinking about it, because if I don't ..."

"'If you don't,' what? Since it already put you in the hospital, we know what it'll do. Whatever you're talking about, if you get it off your chest tonight, you won't have to think about it anymore. In fact, I won't let you think about it anymore. Now tell me what's going—"

"It's not that easy."

"Kurt, I—"

"Joseph, Ruth, I'm talking about Joseph."

"Elaine said you were wonderful with Joseph. She said she couldn't ask for a better man to help raise him."

"Except Joe, and I took Joe away from him."

"Look, we both know—and agree—it wasn't your fault. It was the damn war, Kurt Bauer, and I won't hear you say that again."

"I know it's not my fault. Not really. What tears me up inside is remembering how Joseph talked about his daddy not being with him. When he was little, he told me how, after a long time, he would go to Heaven and see his daddy. Once he told me how a bad man's soldiers hurt his daddy, and how he wished they hadn't so he could be at home with him. That's me, Ruth, the bad man's soldier." Kurt wipes his nose. "Dammit, that little boy deserved to have his father with him and that didn't happen because of me."

"Well, *dammit,* old man, didn't we just agree it wasn't your fault? Joe might have gotten killed some other time. You remember the war, you remember how many servicemen and women all over the world died, and from all the other countries too. If Joe hadn't died that day, he might have another day. You absolutely do not know otherwise."

Kurt rubs his forehead, and Ruth pauses to watch his eyes. Is she getting through to him, even just a little? Regardless, she isn't finished, not by a long shot. She turns on the sofa to fully face him. "Listen, Kurt, there's something else you need to understand. As hard as it was for Elaine and Joseph to lose Joe, millions of other women lost their husbands and millions of other children lost their fathers, but—"

Kurt looks away. Ruth grabs his face and turns him back toward her. "Don't you dare turn away from me, Kurt Bauer. I'll call off the wedding, don't think I won't."

Kurt turns on the sofa until their knees touch. "Okay, Ruth. I'll listen, but I don't know what good it'll do."

"You *better* listen, this is important. As hard as it was for Elaine and Joseph to lose Joe, millions of other women lost their husbands and millions of other children lost their fathers, but how many weren't able to find a man like Kurt Bauer to fill that void? I'm betting entirely too many did not."

"I … well, I guess you have a point," Kurt says, the tension in his voice easing. "The only reason I had that medal was because I was wounded. It was like the United States version of the Purple Heart. I figured I'd earned it. What a dumb thought that was, one of the dumbest thoughts I've ever had."

No, sir," Ruth says, using her firmest tone possible. "The dumbest thought you ever had is thinking all you were to Elaine and Joseph is the man who took Joe away from them. You know better than that. You helped her do what Joe wanted her to do, to move on with her life and find love again. She told me that herself. If Elaine and Joe were here right now, if they knew everything we know, they would agree with every single undeniable fact. You need to agree too, and I mean right this minute."

You tell him, Ruth. That's exactly what Joe wanted for me and that's exactly what Kurt did for me. As much as I miss Joe, war killed him, not Kurt. He was just a boy trying to stay alive.

"I hear you, Ruth, I really do." Kurt sniffles and wipes his nose. "But when I finally leave this earth, I hope I get to see Joe. I'd—" Filled with emotion, his voice breaks. He clears his throat and wipes his nose again. "I'd like to ask him to forgive me, you know? Still, that's an awful lot to forgive."

No joke, old man. I get what Ruth's saying, but—

"I think he would forgive you," Ruth says. "Maybe he already has. His dying was a tragedy—certainly it was—but you coming here to Alma was a miracle. And understand this, you meeting Elaine was a miracle too."

In the middle of wiping his nose once more, Kurt lowers the knotted tissue still in his hand. "How's that? My belief in miracles is about used up."

"Well," Ruth says, rubbing his shoulder, "you need to keep believing in them regardless, because this *is* one. Elaine told me how you two met in that old hardware store. Did you know that's where she met Joe? He was trying to earn money for college by giving guitar lessons. She showed up the first day."

Kurt's eyebrows rise, which wrinkles his forehead and scar. "Really? I didn't know that."

"You know it now," Ruth says, glad she can finally smile. "She had to nearly beg him to take her fishing on their first date at the river. According to her, it was *on* after that."

The wrinkles on Kurt's forehead relax. "Imagine that. That old store must be full of memories."

"And miracles. The place at the river is full of miracles too."

"More miracles? How can there be more mira—?"

"Just hush and listen, old rooster, before this old hen pecks you. Yes, the place at the river is filled with miracles, like the miracle of you and Elaine falling in love there. I don't know if she ever told you this, but she and Joe were married in secret. She tricked him into coming home by telling him his mother was sick. When she picked him up at the train station in Holdrege, she told him she wanted to get married, and they did."

Kurt tilts his head to one side. "You're kidding. *My* Lainey lied to Joe about his mother?"

"She felt terrible about it, but nothing would've stopped her from marrying Joe. Honestly, the way she told it, she was a nervous wreck after Joe got his draft notice. She said her nerves calmed down after they got married."

"What's that got to do with the river? They went there on their first date and spent a lot of time there. What makes that a miracle?"

Ruth takes the picture from the end table. "That's where they spent their one night together after they were married. Do I have to tell you what that means?"

"I'm not sure what you—" Kurt's mouth falls open. "Good Lord, you mean that's where Joseph was conceived?"

"Don't you think that qualifies as a miracle? It was their first time together—their *only* time together. A woman is only likely to conceive within a few days of ovulation, so …"

Kurt waves the comment away. "Okay, Dr. Ruth, I get it."

"I thought you would. Another reason Joseph is a miracle is because Elaine said she might not have lived to meet you if it hadn't been for him."

"What?" Wrinkles furrow Kurt's scar again. "Are you saying she might've killed herself?"

"She said she thought about it. I imagine her looking forward to Joseph being born helped her cope with losing Joe. So, yes, Joseph certainly was a miracle."

"I guess Lainey told you how I accidentally bumped into Joseph at the hardware store. If that hadn't happened, it's a fair chance we might not have gotten to know each other."

"Absolutely true," Ruth says, glad that Kurt's forgotten his guilt. "All Joseph did was bump his noggin, but Elaine told me how she laid into you for hurting him."

"That she did. I never met a woman with so much spirit. She was very protective when it came to Joseph."

"Of course she was. He was her miracle."

Joseph certainly was my miracle, like with the miracle of me meeting Kurt in the same store where I met Joe. My life is over now. So much has passed. Joe and Kurt and I did the best we could, but I still wish I could have another life to spend with Joe.

"You got that right," Kurt says to Ruth. "If anything on this earth is a miracle, Joseph sure is. I love him like he's my own son."

You old German bastard, he isn't your son, he's mine. Kurt grins, which, despite Joe's remaining anger, gradually becomes his grin. *Well, you do know he's my son, just like you know Elaine loved me first. At least that's something I got on you.*

Huh, you already said you know she loved me by saying you would have died to bring me back if you could. I'm still not too keen on living out your days with you—with you killing me and all— but what choice do I—

A cold chill drags the hint of a memory from Joe, followed by numerous scenes he experienced in the war, scenes that sometimes plague him.

A wife or a mother, a daughter or a sister, a father or a brother. For every man I killed, those relatives lost a loved one. If I were accused like I'm accusing Kurt, I could only say I was trying to stay alive like he was. After all, giving someone the benefit of the doubt doesn't cost anyone anything. If I don't give Kurt the benefit of the doubt, especially after getting to know him and what he did for Elaine and Joseph, I'd be a hypocrite all day long.

Gratitude fills Elaine with love for her best friend. *My goodness, Ruth, you were a treasure in my life and you're a treasure now. Thank you so much for helping Kurt see he shouldn't feel guilty for what happened.*

Elaine pauses at a sudden thought. *But what about Joe and I? Since I'm living like this, he must be living the same way. There has to be a reason for it, and I'd like to know what it is.*

Uh-huh, I was never patient when I was alive, especially when it came to making love to Joe on our honeymoon. But now, when it comes to the chance of us getting together again, there's only one thing I can do, and that's to hope.

Chapter 51

Wedding Plans

Kurt opens his eyes.

Sunlight filters through the curtains, yellow and bright and cheerful. The aroma of coffee makes his mouth water. Ruth must be up already.

He stretches and rolls over, to smile at Elaine's picture.

"What a night, huh, Lainey? Not that I didn't already know why you thought so much of Ruth, but I got a good dose of what she's capable of when it comes to knowing people."

Me too, old man. Ruth may be a mess in the humor department — and keeping you straight — but she sure has a head for perspective. The last thing I thought I'd do is look at the perspective of someone who killed me, but she sure helped me do it.

Fully clothed, hair brushed, face washed, Kurt points at himself in the bathroom mirror. "Hey, you old coot, you need to call Joseph and tell him about the wedding. And I mean now."

He follows the delicious aroma of coffee to the kitchen. Ruth closes the refrigerator, carton of eggs in hand. "I almost threw these away because of the cholesterol. Then I remembered your heart trouble was just a pain-in-my-behind trouble."

He pecks her cheek. "The only heart trouble I have is you."

He takes the phone from its cradle. "I'll let Joseph know we're tying the knot. He probably won't make the wedding, but—"

"But he'd like to know, right?"

"Seems you didn't interrupt me so much before I proposed."

"Will you tell him about your hospital visit?"

"I don't see the need, do you?"

Ruth points at the chair at the table. "Sit down and call. Tell him I said hello while you're at it."

Kurt dials. "Matthan residence," Joseph says.

"Mighty proper there, boy. Why don't you come back to Alma and take your old step-dad fishing?"

"Hey, Kurt, I wish I could."

"I know, I know. Life, kids, and loving your wife is more important."

"I learned that from you, remember?"

"Sure do. Look, I've got some news for you."

"Good news, right?"

Kurt grins at Ruth. "Ruth proposed and I can't think of a good reason to say no."

"It's about time you two got together. Mom loved Ruth like a sister. She'd be happy for both of you."

"I'm glad to hear you say that. I've got something else on my mind while I'm at it. I don't know if you ever thought about it, but I plan on leaving you this place. Of course, it'll be yours to do whatever you want with it. Maybe one of the kids or grandkids would be interested in it. Heck, it might even make a nice retirement spot. You know, get away from all the rat race of the city."

"That's not a bad idea. Mom and Dad's farmer's blood sometimes makes me want to get away from all the hubbub. I'll tell Joe about it. He enjoys his new job in crop sciences, so he might want to get some hands-on experience one day."

Well knock me over with a buzzard feather. I get to hear my son on the phone and find out I've got a grandson named Joe. Sounds like more of Ruth's miracles. I wouldn't have missed this call for the world.

* * *

Ruth places the last breakfast dish in the cabinet. Kurt rinses his coffee mug and leaves it in the sink. "Don't wash that. I'll need it later."

"It's a wonder you don't overdose on coffee. I had one cup out of the entire pot."

He leans against the counter. "Do you realize we haven't talked about what we're wearing for the wedding tomorrow?"

"It's a good thing we aren't nudists," Ruth says, poking his side. "No one would have an appetite for the food."

"Ha! Ain't that the truth." Kurt snaps his fingers. "Hey, I've got a suggestion."

"What? That I wear a red wig for the ceremony as well as the honeymoon? You either love me for my own hair color or not."

"What if you wear Elaine's wedding dress? It was handed down from her mother. I bet you would look great in it."

"I don't know," Ruth says doubtfully. "A lady might not want to share her wedding dress with the woman who's marrying her widower. Something from my closet will do."

"Something from your closet?" Kurt asks, his tone skeptical. "Don't you know what Lainey would say about that?"

"I can guess, but still ..."

Guess, my foot, Ruth. First, I'd say it's your wedding day. Then I'd say if you don't wear it, I'll make your neck feel like it's going to itch off on your honeymoon night. At least try it on, please?

"Can't you at least try it on?" Kurt asks. "Please?"

"You get it out," Ruth says. "Elaine wouldn't mind, but I wouldn't feel right about going through her things."

"I'll meet you in the spare bedroom." As Kurt leaves, the memory of Elaine's wedding dress tugs at her with a thread of sadness.

I remember hoping my own daughter would wear my dress one day. It wasn't meant to be I suppose. I hope what I'm going through means I'll never have to say that about Joe and I finding each other. I have to believe it can happen.

Kurt returns. In front of the mirror on the back of the door, Ruth holds the dress to her shoulders. Her eyes fill. Kurt rubs her back. "Tears, Ruthie?"

"Elaine said she wanted to be my maid of honor if I ever found someone. That never happened, as you well know. Those thoughts were special to us. More than special."

"You were as close as any two women I've ever known. Never had a cross word that I know of. Lainey always told me you were the sister she never had."

"I felt the same, Kurt, I truly did."

"I'll make more coffee while you see how the dress fits." He kisses Ruth's cheek. "I think it's going to be fine."

Ruth holds the dress up again. "This is beautiful, Elaine. It makes me feel like you're right here with me."

I am, Ruth, I just wish you knew it. Elaine mentally smiles. *But that would ruin the heck out of the honeymoon. Please do me the favor of bringing your own nighty. Oh, phooey, what am I thinking. There's no way I'll be hanging around that night.*

Ruth dons the dress and finds Kurt by the dribbling coffeemaker. She turns around a couple of times. "Well?"

"Whoa, Ruthie, you're looking good. When all those old coots coming to the wedding see you, they'll try to take you away from me."

"I can't think of a one of them who would want me more than you, old man."

"I don't know," Kurt says, pouring coffee. "You look as fancy as the last milk cow I had. Poor old thing keeled over after the neighbor's bull jumped the fence and came over for a visit."

Ruth gives Kurt a sly grin. "Is that a hint of what you have in store for me Saturday night?"

"Yeah, right. We'll probably be worn out from the wedding and fall asleep on the sofa in front of the fireplace or TV."

"Regardless, I appreciate you saying I look nice. The dress fits perfectly."

"It sure does. I'll never look as nice as you do."

"You'll look dashing, I'm sure." Ruth and Elaine eye the stitches in Kurt's ear. "Weren't you supposed to get those stitches out this week?"

Kurt touches his ear. "I've been kind of busy with a few things. You know, like maybe having a heart attack and spending a few nights in the hospital, on Christmas day of all days. Then there's planning a wedding and sorting out my past so I don't end up in the hospital again. Just run of the mill stuff farmers like me do every day."

Ruth crosses her arms. "Poor thing. Maybe the dermatologist can work you in today."

"I'll give her a call while you change."

"Good idea. I'll be right back."

* * *

When Kurt dials the dermatologist's office, he gets a busy

signal. As he dials again, Joe shares his frown. *It's hard to believe I've only been with you six days. Except for the clipped ends of the stitches, you look okay to me.*

This time a recording plays, and Kurt grunts at it. "Huh, here we go, customer no-service." He presses the appropriate numbers. "Appointments," a voice says.

"Good morning, appointments, this is Kurt Bauer. I might have missed my appointment to have my stitches taken out. Would you have an opening for today?"

"Hold, please."

"Such a cheery disposition," Kurt mumbles. A recorded message concerning the importance of using sunscreen plays in the background, and Joe agrees with it.

You should've listened to a message like that a long time ago, you old hard-head. Then we wouldn't have to worry about this ear mess.

"You didn't miss your appointment, Mr. Bauer. It's for one this afternoon."

"Glad to hear it."

"Do you have any other questions?"

"I don't think— Yeah, yes I do. Will my test results be in today?"

"How long has it been?"

"I was there last Friday, a week ago today."

"You can ask the doctor. Anything else?"

"Guess not, see you at one."

Kurt cradles the phone. "It's about time something convenient happened around here."

Darn, old man, ain't that the truth. I'd roll your eyes for you if I could.

"I heard that," Ruth says, coming from the hall. "What's convenient?"

"I thought I missed my appointment but I didn't." Kurt taps his wristwatch. "It's this afternoon at one."

"Good," Ruth says, nodding. "I can pick up a few things while you're getting un-stitched."

"Is that what they're calling it now?"

"I was attempting to come up with a Kurt-colloquialism."

"I might use that on the receptionist. They sound like they need perking up down there."

"You behave. They're under enough stress as it is by putting up with people like you every day."

Kurt scratches his head. "You might have a point."

I agree with that too, old man. Ruth, are you sure you know what you're doing, marrying this guy? Yeah, I guess you do, and yeah, I'm just joking. I guess he's okay, for a hard-head.

* * *

Kurt chuckles when the dermatologist removes the last stitch. The scissors *clank* into the tray. "This procedure isn't something most patients find amusing, Mr. Bauer. Am I missing something?"

"Something Ruth said, Dr. Peterson. She called this my un-stitching."

The doctor removes latex gloves. "I don't think I've heard you mention anyone named Ruth."

"She's my fiancée. We're getting married tomorrow."

"Congratulations. Is she someone I know?"

"I've seen you at the Farmers Market. Ruth makes the best bread in Alma."

"I know Ruth. My husband gets a loaf every other weekend or so. He and the children manage to eat it all before I can get any. I assume the market will be closing with winter setting in. We've only been here since the spring."

"This past Saturday was the last day. She sometimes does special orders."

"I'm not about to bother a newlywed, Mr. Bauer." A grin teases the corners of the doctor's mouth as she hands him a checkout form. "Please drop this off at the desk. Good luck tomorrow."

Kurt eases off of the examining table. "I was wondering about my test results."

"The lab's backed up, but the area I removed didn't have any usual signs of malignancy. I'll call when I hear anything."

At the front desk, the receptionist studies the form. "I see we don't get the honor of a return visit, Mr. Bauer. I take it the un-stitching went well?"

"Nope, no return visit. I hope not anymore, if you know what I mean. Are you gonna use that word now? The one I used earlier when I signed in? Un-stitched?"

"I don't see why not. Yes, I know exactly what you mean. I hope to not see you again either."

Kurt goes out into the warmer than average December afternoon. Parked in her car beneath a red maple, where the remaining leaves flutter in the breeze, Ruth waits. Kurt settles beside her, snaps the seat belt, and points at his ear. "Good as new. Not that it'll help me look any better tomorrow."

"Phooey on that. I told you I'm not worried about how you look." Ruth touches his ear. "What did the doctor say about the test results?"

"She said the lab is backed up but my ear is fine. The results should be in early next week."

"It never takes that long for any of mine."

"That's because you're special, Ruthie. Can we go home now?"

"After we run by the courthouse for the marriage license. Don't tell me you forgot?"

Kurt rubs his nose. "I was testing you."

"Uh-huh, sure you were." Ruth buckles her seat belt. "Oh, remind me to call my kids when we get back. With so much going on, I forgot to tell them I'm getting married. They likely couldn't make it anyway, but I'd still like to tell them."

"It's those busy lives, living like rats on a wheel until we learn to appreciate the finer things in life, like growing old."

Ruth starts the car. "It beats the heck out of the alternative."

The irony of Ruth's statement strikes Joe as odd. *How about my kind of alternative? I don't even know if I'm getting old or not. Kurt seems to be in good shape, so I guess I'll be here a while longer.*

Elaine's no happier about Kurt's late test than Ruth is. *That durn lab needs to get on the ball. Until those results come back and I know there's nothing to be concerned about, I'm going to worry.*

Chapter 52

Secret Vows

At the kitchen window, Elaine shares Ruth's disappointing view. Saturday morning has dawned chilly and gray. Rain threatens from low clouds, dreary and ominous.

Kurt and Joe enter the kitchen. Kurt slips his hands around Ruth's waist. "I wouldn't worry about it too much, old girl. What does the weather forecast say?"

"I haven't turned on the television. I'm trying to predict the weather like you farmers claim you can do, by looking at the sky."

"That's not how we do it. We read the Farmer's Almanac."

"Is there a copy around here?"

"I'm just pulling your leg. I got up in time to see the early weather forecast. It's supposed to start like this but clear off by noon."

Ruth leaves Kurt's arms to turn on a small television on a counter in a corner of the kitchen. She and Elaine are just in time for the local weather forecast, which confirms what Kurt said. Ruth clicks the TV off. "Old man, you're right about a lot of things, and I'm glad, but not as glad as you are."

Now, Ruth, Elaine scolds, *you know as well as I do how a lot of that is your influence. That's okay, he's happy and so are you.*

Kurt places his palm to his chest. "Are you saying that I, me, this guy right here, has an ego?"

"Just a tad," Ruth says. "A healthy one, that is."

Kurt winks. "As should we all."

"I suppose you're right. You need to be wrong sometimes though, before you get a big head."

Joe shares the old man's grin. *I'm right here in this guy, Ruth, and I can tell you this—I think it's too late to worry about him having a big head.*

"Regardless of the threat to the size of my head," Kurt says, "it looks like this wedding is a go."

"We have the license," Ruth says. "The minister's ready except for asking us about the vows. Have you given them any thought?"

"Who's had time to think? I imagine he'll help us out with whatever questions he might have when he gets here."

Doggone, Kurt, I wish I could ask him a question or two myself. I'd like to get a professional opinion on whatever it is I'm going through.

"There's one more thing we need to do before he gets here." Kurt pours coffee and sits at the table.

Ruth sits beside him. "Did I forget something?"

Kurt reaches into his pants pocket and takes it out to reveal a diamond ring and a wedding band. Elaine immediately recognizes the rings Kurt placed on her own finger so long ago. *Just perfect! What a wonderful idea, sweetheart.*

"If you aren't one for surprises," Ruth says. "Those are Elaine's, aren't they?"

"I had them sized to one of your rings. I think Lainey would be pleased."

Blinking back tears, Ruth looks up at Kurt. "I don't know how I'm going to get through the wedding without crying my eyes out. I just wish I had thought about a ring for you."

"I'll use the one from when Lainey and I were married. I think it'll be fitting to have our rings together again, on the fingers of the two people she loved so well."

Kurt's unexpected sentiment surprises Joe. *Old man, I'll hand it to you, and to you too, Ruth. It's obvious both of you were a large part of Elaine's life that gave her years of happiness. I wish I could tell you both how grateful I am.*

Elaine wants to cry—wishes she was able to cry—then warm tears stream down Ruth's cheeks. "I don't know how to thank you. You are the dearest man."

He is, isn't he, Ruth? That's why you're marrying him like I did.

"Ruth, you being you and agreeing to marry me is all the thanks I need."

I think Ruth's the one who deserves the thanks, you old German. Hold on there, are those tears I feel running down your wrinkled cheeks? Okay, I'll admit what you did was nice—real nice—but we're gonna have to stock up on tissues if this keeps up.

* * *

Kurt sips coffee while Ruth swallows scrambled eggs. Someone knocks on the front door, and she stands. "I bet that's the minister."

Kurt clunks his coffee mug to the table. "At least he's on time."

"You behave, old rooster, or this hen's sleeping in the guest room tonight."

Following her to the door, Kurt pops her bottom. "Tell that hogwash to someone who'll believe it. You know you can't wait to get hold of my manly physique." He pops her bottom again, this time adding a firm squeeze.

Ruth swats his hand away and opens the door. "Good

morning, Minister Mattaniah."

"Morning, Ruth, morning, Kurt. Are you ready for your big day?"

Kurt waves him inside. "Isn't that why you're here?"

"I'll do my best, Kurt, if you will."

"He'll do the best he can," Ruth says.

Sitting on the sofa, Kurt pats his shirt pocket. "Yep, got my little blue pill right here."

Ruth sits beside him. "See what I have to deal with, Minister?"

The minister takes the chair by the fireplace. "Proverbs 17:22. A merry heart doeth good like a medicine."

"Cool beans," Kurt says. "I can save my little blue pill for when my bride's a grouch."

Ruth shakes her head. "Lord help him. He knoweth not what he does."

Eyes crinkling, the minister takes a pad and pen from his pocket. "Do we forgo the wedding and jump right to the honeymoon?"

"Please don't encourage him," Ruth says. "He's bad enough as it is."

Kurt faces the minister. "You know, I've often wondered about your name."

"Why's that?"

"I never heard of Mattaniah. What's its origin?"

"It comes from Israel, where my parents are from. It means the hope of God."

"That's interesting," Ruth says.

Elaine and Joe simultaneously attempt a nod.

It is interesting, Ruth, but Joe never mentioned any meaning to his last name. It's similar to Matthan though. That's quite a coincidence.

Mattaniah and Matthan. What a strange coincidence. Since they mean the same thing, my name and the minister's must be derivatives of the original name.

"The hope of God," Kurt says. "Let's hope that's a good sign for today. What do you think, Minister?"

"I take good signs when and where I can get them. Have either of you given any thought to your vows?"

Kurt shakes Ruth's knee. "Anything with obey, right, Ruthie?"

"I agree." Ruth shoves his hand off her knee. "As long as you're the one doing the obeying."

"All right then." The minister clicks the pen and jots something on the pad. "There'll be no obeying in this marriage whatsoever." He clicks the pen again and returns it and the pad his pocket. "I have a suggestion. Sometimes I like to question the prospective bride and groom separately, because it seems easier for them to open up. If that works out, I take the best of each person's ideas and combine them into vows."

Kurt raises an eyebrow. "That can be a surprise, can't it?"

"I agree." Ruth says, eyeing Kurt.

"It's something I've been working on lately," the minister says. "After we talk, I'll let you know whether or not I think I can put together an exceptional service out of the ideas you've given me."

"I'm willing," Ruth says.

"Me too," Kurt says. "I like a good surprise now and then."

Chapter 53

One More Kiss

Beneath the oak at the river, Ruth waggles a finger at Bill Jenkins and John Hansen. "I know Kurt's a bad influence, so no untoward remarks during the ceremony, got it?"

Sitting with their wives while waiting for the wedding to begin, the men look at each other and grin, and Kurt laughs. "You sure got our number, Ruthie, but don't count on them behaving any better than you'd count on me behaving." He waves at Thomas, who's sitting nearby.

Thomas returns the wave. "How 'bout we forget all this weddin' business and go fishin', Kurt?"

Ruth grabs Kurt's hand and leads him to the oak. "Don't you even think about it, Kurt Bauer."

"And miss rocking your world tonight, Ruthie? Not a chance." Kurt looks at the blue sky. "The weather sure turned out nice. Maybe Joe and Elaine had something to do with it."

Ruth looks up into the blue sky also, then faces Kurt. "We may be the married couple to be, but I like to think the married couple of long ago is right here with us. Let's take a moment to enjoy that thought on this beautiful day."

Through the old oak's bare branches, the sun shines shadows that resemble butterflies on everyone. A soft breeze hints warmth, despite winter's grip. The aroma of leaf mold and the watery flavor of the river whispers by.

The gathering crowd speaks with hushed tones. An occasional laugh likely reveals a story about one of Kurt and Ruth's humorous interactions at the Farmer's Market, or at the diner.

The grass, green and lush in the summer, is brown and frost-bitten. Footsteps crunch among the chairs when another friend arrives.

That's a good idea about enjoying this gorgeous day, Ruth. I don't even mind if it's winter because all I see is the night Elaine and me spent here on our honeymoon.

Ruth, you're such a dear friend to think Joe and I are here with you. Still, I see this place as Joe and I saw it on our honeymoon. How I miss him.

Minister Mattaniah leaves the crowd to join Kurt and Ruth. "Are we ready?"

Joe and Elaine share their nods. The minister takes a paper from a worn and scuffed Bible.

"We're gathered here today to join Kurt and Ruth in marriage. They have entrusted me with their vows, and to speak about what has influenced their mutual love and respect. Also, I will speak about their love and respect for two very important people—Kurt's deceased wife and Ruth's best friend, Elaine, and Elaine's first husband, Joe Matthan."

"The theme for this ceremony is hope, for without hope, where would we be as loving and caring people? Our hopes, of course, can be dashed to pieces, as Kurt's were when he returned to Germany and discovered how his family had been killed in World War II. Elaine's hopes suffered the same fate when she discovered how her beloved husband, Joe, had lost his life in that same terrible war. Even though these tragedies occurred, hope lived on. Kurt returned to Alma, to be welcomed into the family of George and Betty Edwards, while Elaine gave birth to Joe's son, Joseph."

"I would be remiss if I didn't mention Joe and Elaine's relationship. Ruth has told me how they secretly married and spent only one night together before Joe returned to his base. I don't know about anyone else, but I consider Joseph a miracle. Not only is he a miracle because he came to be from one night of a committed and loving marriage, he's also a miracle because, if not for him, Kurt might not have met Elaine. However, that's a subject for another time."

The minister shares a slight smile with the crowd. "I imagine Kurt will enjoy explaining that story, humorous as it is, to those who would like to know more."

"Ruth also mentioned Joe's wish for Elaine, to move on from the tragedy of his death if it occurred. His fondest desire was for her to have a happy and fulfilling life, and, if possible, to find love again. Ladies and gentlemen, that is love—unselfish, pure, and giving love."

"Ruth also tells me how Elaine had the same wish for Kurt, telling her so from her death bed. Again, the perfect combination of unselfish, pure, and giving love. This is how Ruth came to love Kurt, with Elaine's blessing."

"As we go through our lives, we learn what is important, and we each should hope that, as we live, we can learn the importance of forgiveness. Forgiveness is the key that opens the door to miracles. Of this we should have no doubt. Elaine and the good people of Alma forgave Kurt for fighting against this country in war. Yes, it took time, but they soon learned that only the most infinitesimal portion of Kurt was a soldier, because the largest part of him was, and is, a good and decent man."

The minister's statement weakens Joe's remaining resentment toward Kurt. Although he understands how Kurt was only defending himself in the war, he knows he hasn't completely forgiven him, and it's been grinding at his conscience ever since Kurt admitted to killing him.

Well, Kurt, I understand about the war and how it was. I'm glad you were there to love Elaine and Joseph, and to help them have the happy life I wanted for them. I'd be a fool to hold a grudge and not see that. I forgive you, old man. Just stay alive long enough for me to enjoy some more of Ruth's great cooking, and maybe to see my son and grandson.

Minister Mattaniah pauses. A warm breeze flips the remaining leaves on the ancient oak with a whispering rustle. He bows his head. "Let us pray. Father, please bless this marriage. Allow love and hope to flourish within it, and please be with Kurt and Ruth all the days of their lives. Amen."

Amen to that, Elaine agrees. *May those days be many.*

"And now the vows. Do you, Kurt, take Ruth, to have and to hold from this day forward, for richer or poorer, in sickness and in health, till death do you part?"

Kurt can't take his eyes off of Ruth. "I do."

"Do you, Ruth, take Kurt, to have and to hold from this day forward, for richer or poorer, in sickness and in health, till death do you part?"

"I do." Ruth winks at Kurt, which he returns.

"The rings please."

Kurt gives Ruth his large, golden band, keeping her ring at the ready.

"Kurt," the minister says, "repeat after me." Kurt places the ring on the tip of Ruth's finger. "With this ring," the minster continues, "I thee wed, and with it, I bestow upon thee all the treasures of my heart. And for all our lives to come, I promise to share with you forgiveness, hope, and love."

Kurt repeats the vows and slides the ring onto Ruth's finger.

The minister faces Ruth, makes the same request, and she works Kurt's ring over his gnarled knuckle.

"I now pronounce you husband and wife. Kurt, you may kiss your bride."

As their lips join, a warmth envelopes Joe and Elaine—a warmth they haven't experienced in ages. The kiss is more than real; it spans time itself as honeymoon memories course through them, until Kurt and Ruth's kiss lingers long past a customary wedding kiss.

"Hey, Kurt!" Bill Jenkins yells. "Is that what eating all that spinach does for you?"

"Break it up you two," John Hansen adds. "You've got all night."

Kurt and Ruth separate. Kurt grins like a twenty-year-old looking forward to his honeymoon. Flushed, Ruth fans herself with her bouquet. "Oh, my, Kurt, where did that come from?"

"Me, Ruthie? I thought it was you."

"I don't care who it was. We just need to make sure we find it again later."

"I'm not sure about that." Kurt raises a bushy eyebrow. "But I'll do the best I can."

Chapter 54

Phone Call

Ruth's eyelids flutter open. Beside her in bed, Kurt kisses her cheek. "Hello there, old girl."

"I see it's morning. Have you been watching me sleep?"

"I—"

"Never mind." She rubs her temples and winces. "My head feels a bit thick. Too much wine, I suppose."

"Do you remember dancing with Bill Jenkins?"

Ruth lowers her hands and whips her head toward Kurt. "Say what?"

"You two were doing the twist." Ruth covers her head with a pillow, which Kurt tugs. "C'mon now, you did a fine job. Bill couldn't even keep up." A muffled voice comes from under the pillow. "What's that, Ruthie?"

She lifts one side of the pillow. "I said to please fix some coffee. *Strong* coffee, okay?"

"I think I just heard the pot starting up."

Ruth pulls the pillow back down. Kurt winks at Elaine's picture, slides his feet into slippers, and pulls some of the covers off Ruth. "C'mon, Ruthie, rise and shine, a new day is starting." Ruth moans and waves him away. He ambles down the hall, grinning and chuckling while following the welcome aroma of freshly brewed coffee.

Smells mighty fine, old man. You definitely know what you're doing when it comes to a pot of coffee.

Ruth lifts the pillow to the unmistakable sound of eggs being cracked. "Hey, Mr. Gourmet Chef!"

Kurt steps to the door, spatula in hand. "Yes, ma'am?"

"I'll have my eggs over-easy. Can you handle that?"

"Your wish is my wish, Ruthie. Bacon's in the pan. Would you like sausage with those eggs too?"

"The smell of your coffee has made me hungry. I'll be good, just bacon."

"My, my, did we work up an appetite with all our strenuous overnight activity?"

"Sleeping is not a strenuous activity, you old buzzard."

"Sounds like dancing with Bill Jenkins isn't the *only* thing you don't remember." Kurt leaves for the kitchen, and Ruth sighs.

"Elaine, what have you gotten me in to?"

Exactly what you wanted to get into. Now get on up, you lazybones, you've got a whole new life to live. Besides, I'm hungry, and that bacon smells good.

Ruth dons her robe. The *slip-slap slip-slap* of her slippers announces her presence to Kurt, who hands her a plate of perfectly cooked eggs with bacon.

"There she is, ready to start the day."

"This looks good, old man, but" —Ruth sits and sips from her waiting coffee cup— "now I'm ready to start the day. As far as Bill and John, when you casually mentioned to them and their wives how we should continue the festivities here, I thought for sure they'd decline."

Kurt joins her. "I figured they'd know I was joking, but I couldn't go back on the invitation once I'd made it. Maybe that'll teach me a lesson."

"You seem to have a hard time learning your lessons, especially about women. You never know when one might fool you."

Kurt raises his mug. "Ain't that the truth.

Mmm, great coffee as always, you old German.

Ruth swallows egg. "I'm glad the ladies made their husbands leave before it got too late. I was tired, I'm sure you were too."

It's been a long time since I carried on like that, Ruth. We were doing okay until we—you—had that third glass of wine.

Kurt picks up a piece of bacon. "Right now I'm hungry. Let's eat before our so-called gourmet breakfast gets cold."

Joe enjoys the salty crunch of bacon and the creamy consistency of perfectly cooked scrambled eggs, both washed down with a warm swallow of coffee. *Good stuff, Kurt. I'm glad I forgave you for blowing me up. I might choke on your cooking if I was as mad as I was when I found out.*

Kurt crunches more bacon.

I still wish I could've talked to that Minister Mattaniah guy about forgiveness being the key to miracles. If I could, I'd ask him about my crazy way of living, and how I only move on when a person dies. Still, if a miracle is in the works for me, that means Kurt has to die. That should be a while yet, since both his heart doctor and the dermatologist say he's in good shape.

Ruth goes to the refrigerator for a jar of strawberry jam, which makes Elaine's phantom mouth water. *Good idea, Ruth. I love the jam I made from Kurt's strawberries.* Eyeing Kurt's ear, Ruth jabs the knife into the jar harder than usual. *Why did you do that? Oh, that's right. I don't like his test taking so long either. Oh, phooey, I'm still a worrier, even when there's nothing to worry about. I suppose it's an age thing.*

But age has nothing to do with when we die, like with Sam and Hope and Adam and Rachel, God rest their souls. I just hope Kurt and Ruth can have some good years together before ... well, before anything happens.

* * *

Kurt pours another mug of coffee. Ruth takes their dishes to the sink, and the phone rings. "Who in the world could that be?"

"Probably someone wanting a special order of your bread," Kurt says, standing. "I'll get it. Hello?"

"Mr. Bauer?"

"You've got him."

"Mr. Bauer, this is Dr. Peterson, at the dermatology office."

"The dermatology office? You're there on a Sunday morning?"

A fork clatters to the floor. Ruth picks it up. She and Elaine watch Kurt.

"I sometimes stop by to check a few things," the doctor says. "I hope the wedding went well yesterday."

"I appreciate the thought, but I doubt you called me on a Sunday morning to tell me that."

"Yes, well, not just that. Your lab results came in over the weekend. Can you and your wife come in tomorrow morning?"

"Can you hold on a second?"

"Yes."

Joe doesn't like the tension in the doctor's voice. *I agree with Kurt, why call on a Sunday?*

Kurt palms the phone, and Ruth's chin trembles. "Why is she calling, Kurt? Couldn't it wait?"

"My lab work is in. She wants to talk to us tomorrow morning."

Ruth turns away, eyes filling with tears as real to Elaine as if they were her own. *Oh, God, now? Not now! They just ... they just ...*

Kurt scratches an intense itch on his neck and returns the phone to his ear. "What time?"

"Eight, if that's all right."

"We'll be there." Kurt cradles the phone. He takes Ruth by her shoulders and turns her facing him. "Take it easy, Ruth, we don't know anything for sure. Maybe she talks to all her patients in person when a lab test comes in."

"I'm not sure." Ruth rubs her neck. "What I am sure of is I don't like it, not one bit."

Neither do I, Elaine agrees, *neither do I.*

Joe understands exactly how Ruth feels. *Damn. Just, plain, damn.*

Chapter 55

Goodbyes

Half-asleep, Ruth slides her hand to the other side of the bed. The sheets are cold. The sheets are lonely. She listens for the sound of Kurt's breathing below her, where he now lies in the same hospital bed Elaine used almost four years ago. Ruth checks the time, 6:44, and listens again. Kurt breathes slow and steady, the rhythm of sleep.

She rises to don slippers and a robe, the usual routine. Oxygen tube okay? She adjusts it slightly and kisses his scratchy cheek. "If you're up to it, sweetheart, I might have to give you a shave today." No hesitant flutter of eyelids. No smile. No joking about his bedpan.

She shuffles to and from the bathroom and settles into the chair she placed beside him a week ago. "Old man, what I wouldn't give to have you well and in our bed so I could wake you with my cold feet."

She pulls the blanket up to his thin shoulders and leans back in the chair.

The last two years are both a curse and a blessing. When they visited his dermatologist, the lab test results were as frightful as they imagined.

The biopsy discovered malignant melanoma.

Having every confidence beforehand that the skin sample

was a minor benign growth, the doctor was almost as upset as Ruth. She apologized over and over, but Kurt, true gentleman that he is, attempted to ease her guilt from when she told him his ear was fine. "Dr. Peterson," he said, placing a gentle hand on her shoulder, "please stop apologizing. Now that we know what we're dealing with, let's deal with it the best we can." He offered his hand. "If you do your part, I'll do mine, deal?"

With tears in her eyes, the young woman in her first year of practice, according to her diploma on the wall, took his hand and shook it gently. "You have a deal, Mr. Bauer."

All those involved—friends and family plus Minister Mattaniah and medical personnel—supported Kurt as much as anyone could, and he amazed everyone with his resilience in facing his predicament.

Ruth gently rubs his scratchy cheek with her knuckles. "You certainly gave it your all, didn't you? That included keeping our funny bones tickled."

Kurt's lips purse slightly.

"I'd love a smile, sweetheart, but I better let you rest while I remember our trip. Thank the good Lord for helping you through all your treatments so we could go." Ruth shakes her head. "Listen to me prattling on about things you already know. I suppose it's a sign of how I miss talking to you without the strain of cancer eating at us. Now, let's see how much of that day I can remember."

During Kurt's longest remission—a six-month stretch—he and Ruth visit the Outer Banks, making the same trip he and Elaine made. On the way back, when they stop at a farm stand in the little town of Grandy, North Carolina, another coincidence concerning Kurt's past—and Joe's—occurs.

Ruth strolls around the stand, picking out fresh vegetables, and a memory teases her mind. It isn't until she stops to study a bulletin board that the memory—Elaine and Joe's memory—becomes crystal clear. She whirls around, sees Kurt examining a display of tomatoes, and waves him over. "Kurt!"

He joins her, tomato in hand. "They have some nice-looking stuff here. Let's get some tomatoes for the trip home."

"Never mind that, look here." Ruth gestures toward a bulletin board. "This is a World War II memorial to the men from Grandy." She points at a picture. "I think that man is Joe's friend, James. Remember how I couldn't remember his name?"

James? That's right, his full name was James Daniel, like it's written underneath that picture. It's been a long time, but I still recognize him. Yep, he said he was from Grandy. It's good to see you, buddy, even if it's only in a picture.

Oh my, that's James all right. Joe wrote about meeting him. Then years later, when Ruth and I became friends, I told her all about him. It's nice how the store owner still remembers the men who fought in the war.

"That *is* him," Kurt says, touching the picture's edge, curled and yellow. "If it wasn't for him, who knows where I would've ended up."

"You're absolutely right," Ruth says. "When I think of all the coincidences that took place for your life to have turned out like it did, I'm amazed."

Joe agrees with Ruth's assessment. *I'm amazed myself, especially when I think about how that day affected Elaine, Kurt, and me. The main thing, Ruth, is Elaine had a really fine life, one you and Kurt were a large part of. I sure wish I could thank you both in person.*

Ruth wraps her hands around Kurt's arm and leans her head against his shoulder. "Joe and James, two remarkable men. Thank you both for your sacrifice."

Kurt points at a yellowed newspaper clipping entitled *Massacre at Wereth*. "Lord have Mercy, they even have a clipping about that. Thank God I wasn't involved."

"What's it about? I never heard of the place."

"Because, like the clipping says, those men were massacred."

"You—" Ruth's mouth falls open. "You mean they surrendered and were still killed?"

"I heard about it from some of the soldiers before that last fight I was in. I'm glad this article's here. Not many people know what happened to those men, and they need to be honored properly."

I remember James telling me about those missing men. Now I know what happened to them, much as I hate to hear it.

Kurt gives Ruth the tomato. "Hold that for a second." Tomato in hand, she steps aside. Kurt straightens himself as much as possible, squares his shoulders, and salutes the picture. Hot tears fill his eyes as he lowers his hand to his side.

Done with her memories, Ruth leans from the chair for a tissue from a box on the dresser and wipes her eyes. "What a day that was, sweetheart. I'll never forget it as long as I live." She gently shakes Kurt's shoulder. "Rise and shine, old man. We've got another day to spend together." She runs her fingertips through Kurt's remaining hair.

Joe attempts a sigh at the comforting touch of Ruth's fingertips. *Ah, Ruth, what a fine lady you are. Your touch reminds me of how Elaine did the same thing on our dates at the river. You're a comfort to me, but I'm not sure about Kurt. I can't sense him waking at all.*

Ruth shakes Kurt's shoulder again. "Come on now, time to wake up." She touches his hands, ice-cold and pale, the veins a ghostly blue. She wraps a blood pressure cuff around the shrunken bicep and pushes the button. The machine beeps: fifty over thirty-five. The Hospice pamphlet on the kitchen table—she'll throw it in the trash. No, she'll burn the damn thing.

She removes the cuff and caresses Kurt's forehead, pink except for splotches of white. "I wish Joseph and Elizabeth could be here. We didn't think it'd be this soon, did we, old man?" She wipes her eyes again.

Joe attempts another sigh, this one of resignation. *I envy you, Kurt. I'm about ready to move on myself, and I don't mean to another person either. If I've run out of hope for Elaine and me, how long do I have to go on like this?*

Elaine shares Ruth's grieving, crying hot tears as if they were her own. *You go on if you're ready, sweetheart. I know how it is to suffer in this bed. I'm not sure if what happened to me will happen to you, but maybe you'll move on to where you're meant to be, since you had a long and happy life.*

But—

I had a long and happy life too, so why didn't I move on when I died? Is there still hope for Joe and I? If there is, I can't imagine how that would happen. Maybe there's a miracle left for us yet.

Kurt's breathing slows. Slows more. Even more. His lungs empty with ragged, rattling effort, waiting … waiting … before slowly rising again.

Ruth straightens in the chair. "Elaine, it's time I did what you asked me to do. If you can hear me—and I do think it's possible—maybe Joe can hear me too. From everything you told me, you loved each other as much in one year as you and Kurt did in in all the years you spent together, so I think it's possible he can hear me too."

Joe concentrates on Ruth's every word, on every sound that Kurt's ears can manage to take in. A rustling noise comes from Ruth's direction, what sounds like sheets of paper being unfolded.

"Here goes, Elaine and Joe. I hope you can hear me."

Dear Kurt,

We spent over forty happy years together, and I'm grateful to you for more than you know. I could count on you like I knew the sun would rise and set and like I knew the stars would come out at night. You helped me raise a wonderful son, teaching him so many things he might not have known otherwise.

Yes, you indulged me when I was quiet and wanted to spend time at the river by myself, never questioning me one single time. I have to laugh as I write this. Maybe that's because I'd no longer be so quiet when I came home.

So thank you, Kurt, for everything. Most of all, thank you for understanding me so well.

Love always, your Lainey.

The chair creaks. Joe hears Ruth's footsteps shuffle across the wood floor toward the bathroom.

I had no idea Elaine would go to the river alone. Maybe she went there to feel close to me. To think of her sitting there all alone, probably upset at times, maybe crying, it's—

An overwhelming wave of sadness and anger engulfs Joe. *We only had a year! And all these years I've held on to some idiotic hope of finding my way back to her. Why live like that without it being possible, or without some kind of goal? What the hell was the point?*

Ruth's footsteps shuffle toward Joe. The chair creaks again.

She places a cloth, wet and cool, on Kurt's forehead. More paper rustles. Joe concentrates again, waiting for Ruth's words.

Now my letter to Joe, Ruth. I have no idea if you can hear what I wrote you, Joe, but I pray you can. I'm here, so maybe you are. It has to be possible. There's no other explanation for my being here.

Dear Joe,

I don't know where to start, but I wish I could start over with you again, back at the river after we were married. As I write this, I remember that night as if it had just happened.

You and that place were my heaven, and I hope you know that.

Our son looks and acts so much like you. He's serious, of course, like you were before I loosened you up, but he's blessed with a wife who can make him laugh, and that laughter, as silly as it may sound, keeps their marriage fresh. You would have been a wonderful father, and I wish with all my heart you could have known him, if at least for only a brief moment in time.

When the news came of how you were killed, it almost killed me too, but our parents helped me through it while Joseph kept me centered. Thank you so much for him. As a baby, and a sweet little boy, he was my miracle. As a man, he is my pride.

And, Joe, if you know about Kurt, I want you to know I was able to do as you had hoped because of him. Yes, I had a happy and fulfilling life, and if not for Kurt, and you, I'm not sure that would have happened.

I've asked Ruth to do something for me, and I know I can count on her. It's not simple, so it will take some doing. You might even see her there, or you might not. What's important is it's something I really want.

One more thing. I still have one of my favorite yellow hair ribbons tucked away. It's the one I wore when we went to the river the night after we were married. I take it with me when I go there. I sit on the old quilt and hold the ribbon to my face and daydream of you reaching up to pull it so my hair would fall around my shoulders. I've enclosed it in this letter, and I've asked Ruth to take it from the envelope. If it's possible, I want you to see it one last time.

Hey, I can hope, can't I?

Now I must go. I am so sorry in so many ways about so many things, but I'm never sorry I met you.

With all my love, Elaine.

P.S.

Remember the morning we woke after our honeymoon, when you called me darlin'? That was the only time you ever called me that, and I miss it so. Maybe one day, with all the hope I've carried in my heart for all these years, I'll hear you call me that again.

Love, E.

Elaine focuses every ounce of energy she possesses, hoping somehow to reach Joe. *I'm here, Joe! I hear you laughing. I feel our bodies close together. I feel your lips on mine. I hear you saying you love me. I hear you saying you'll come back to me. Joe, please, please, please, come back to me!*

So many emotions bewilder Joe—sadness, regret—but the happiness of how Elaine had loved him so much, and always did, overwhelms him. Still, the words she had written fill him with desperation—desperation for Kurt to open his eyes for one last time.

"I read most of your books, Elaine," Ruth says, "those life-after-death ones. If there's one thing I believe I've learned, it's that concerning death, hope, and love, anything is possible. Here goes."

Ruth holds out her hand; the yellow ribbon dangles from her fingers. Elaine begs and hopes with all she is that Joe can sense her presence.

Like an old memory attempting to surface, the skin beneath Ruth's ear tingles. "Elaine?" She looks around. "Is that you?"

Joe wills Kurt to open his eyes, concentrating furiously. They barely move.

Dammit, he's so far gone, I don't know how— Wait a minute, being so close to death, could he hear me and could I help him open his eyes?

I know you're tired, Kurt, tired and ready to move on. If you can hear me, if you can sense me, do me this one last favor and open your eyes. I want to move on too, move on and stop this insane way of living and dying over and over and over again.

Ruth and Elaine focus on Kurt. His cheek muscle twitches ... his eyes barely open ... and he smiles. "Oh, my goodness," Ruth says, collapsing into the chair.

Elaine isn't sure, but she believes she recognizes the smile that brought her so much happiness. *Is that you, Joe? Are you really here? I wish I knew for sure but—*

Elaine stops mid-thought. If Joe's really with Kurt, she's about to—

No, not that—I can't lose you all over again!

Kurt's eyes blink once, twice, slowly close, and his smile fades.

"One last miracle." Ruth folds the letter and returns it to the envelope. "I sure wish Minister Mattaniah had been here to see this."

Thanks, old man. Seeing Elaine's ribbon was … I don't have the words. Maybe this moment, along with all the others, is why we got together, and I can move on to where the good Lord wants me to be. After all, our lives are over in this world, and that means I get to see her in the next world.

Ruth wipes her eyes with another tissue from the nearly empty box. "Unbelievable." She kisses Kurt's cheek—

And cold grips the back of Joe's neck.

No! Please don't make me go on like this. Let me go—let me go so I can be with Elaine!

The cold intensifies, sending the sensation of icicle shards piercing his upper spine, and a sudden realization slams into Joe's being.

Ruth's been talking about Elaine like she's— Oh, God, please don't let her be here with Ruth. That means I have to leave her after I just found her!

Ruth lies her head on Kurt's chest and holds him. He takes three deep breaths, each slower than the last, until his chest fails to rise again.

And that terrible, crushing pressure engulfs Joe.

No, God, not again—how long do I have to live like this?

Kurt's heart continues to beat. Ruth and Elaine listen.

The *thump-thump* slows …

gradually fades …

into silence.

The bolt of light rips Joe from Kurt and thrusts him away from the old man's already-cooling body. It flings him into darkness, ending his hope of ever seeing Elaine again. Ruth's crying echoes back and forth, bounces off the walls of the black void surrounding him.

And then, not at all.

No, please, I forgave Kurt! Wasn't that why I was here? Why make me keep living like this?

I can't do this anymo—

Chapter 56

Promises Kept

Inside the airliner, a red light blinks on the far wall, toward the cockpit. "Ladies and gentlemen, this is the captain speaking."

"I'm glad," Ruth says. "We'd be in trouble if he were somebody else."

"As we start our descent …"

Joseph clicks his seat belt. "I want to thank you again for inviting me, Ruth. Did I ever tell you I always wanted to visit the cemetery where Dad's buried?"

"Not explicitly, but I figured it out when you accepted my offer so quickly. Your mother would be glad you made it. That's why she left enough money for both of us."

"I thought Kurt left the money. That's what you said after the funeral."

"If I did, I'm sorry. Some days I didn't know which way was up after he died."

"That's understandable."

Ruth clicks her seatbelt. "Come to think of it, I didn't tell you about the letter your mother wrote me about this trip. You know about the one she left you, and the one I put in Kurt's suit pocket before the funeral. She left one for me and one for your dad. She included the money in my envelope. Anyway, the last time we spoke, she asked me not to open mine until after she died."

"You didn't tell Kurt about it, or about this trip?"

"You read the letter to your dad. She wrote to keep the reason for this trip to myself because it might upset Kurt."

"I can see that. We all like to think we'll be buried beside our spouse one day."

The airliner shudders from turbulence. Ruth waits for it to stop before she continues. "Do you have any idea how much your mother loved your father?"

"That letter made it clear. Most of the time she was an open book, but other times ..."

"You mean the time's she got quiet, right?"

"Exactly."

"That's because your dad, even though she loved Kurt, was her dream. I wasn't too surprised at my envelope because she hinted at it the last time we talked. Since she and Joe couldn't be together in life, her last wish was to be together in death. As you can see by how we're winging our way over the Atlantic, I'm determined to honor her wish."

"Mom loved you like a sister. She knew she could count on you." Joseph faces the window, then turns back. "Did Mom ever say why Dad's body wasn't brought home? She never mentioned it to me, and I didn't want to pry."

"She did. Instead of getting in touch with her about your father's body, the Army contacted the Matthans. Apparently, it seems, there was some sort of mix-up. Your mother didn't ask the Matthans about it until the year after the war was over. She said they all met—her mother and father too—and had a long conversation. It took a while, but they eventually agreed to let your father's last resting place be in Belgium."

"Oh." Joseph's flat tone suggests he doesn't agree. He faces the window again. "Well, I guess they thought that was the right thing to do."

"Joseph?"

"Yes?"

"You might not agree, but I think it was for the best too. If you turn around, I'll tell you why." Joseph faces her, and she shares a soft smile. "You're wondering why that is, right?"

"If you have some sort of insight, I'd like to know."

"Consider this trip. Consider what your father meant to your mother. Then consider what it might have done to her to have him buried where she could visit him every day."

"You mean she might have mourned herself to death?"

"Not since she had you. Otherwise, who knows? She wouldn't have been the first woman to do that, or the last."

Elaine understands her son's perspective, but she agrees with Ruth. *She's right, Joseph. Even though the Matthans never said so, I think they considered what it would've done to me to go through the pain of bringing Joe home. The day I found out he died, it was ... well, I wouldn't want to go through that again. So yes, I think we made the right decision.*

"I didn't think about it like that," Joseph says.

"I'm sure you know this," Ruth says, "but when a subject is personal, we sometimes judge it before we think. Another example is when you found out Kurt was a German soldier. Did it make you think any less of him, or any differently?"

"Not at all, but I— No, no *buts* about it, Kurt was a good man. Even when he was a soldier he had to have been a good man. Or a good *young* man." Joseph pauses. "Enough of that, how have you been?"

"I'm doing okay out in the country. You saw Samantha and

Joe, they're getting on in years too. I didn't want to drag them into town and make them live cooped up in a house.

"I meant how have *you* been doing? You know, after your heart attack. I was surprised your doctor let you make this trip."

"Don't you worry about this old girl, there's a lot of life left in her yet. Besides, who'll make the best bread in Alma if something happens to me? Not my doctor I bet."

Ruth looks past Joseph, out the window at the puzzle-piece tracts of land looming closer. She didn't tell her doctor about this trip, so what her doctor doesn't know won't hurt her. Still, the beautiful Dr. Richardson—who gave Kurt such a hard time in the hospital concerning his heart—will, no doubt, give Ruth the same hard time if she ever finds out.

* * *

Checked in and unpacked, Ruth sits on the hotel bed to phone the Ardennes American Cemetery. The representative confirms the arrangements. Ruth cradles the phone, which rings.

"It's Joseph, Ruth. Have you unpacked? Is your room nice?"

"I've got everything tucked away."

"I've been looking over the restaurant menu for breakfast. Kurt would've loved to sample some of this food."

"I'm sure he would. He'd still say anything he grew at home was better."

"He'd probably be right." Ruth yawns. "I'll see you in the morning. Goodnight."

* * *

Ruth snaps her eyes open and rolls over to smack the alarm clock that isn't there. Recognizing the yellow hotel curtains illuminated by the sun, she rolls over to the nightstand and

361

smacks the annoying buzz into silence.

"If this is what jet lag is all about, they can keep it. Thank goodness I'll only have to deal with it one more time."

She returns to the oversized pillow. "Today's the day, Elaine. I don't know what to expect, but I've had more ups and downs in the last couple of years than I ever thought possible, so who knows."

She struggles up from the bed and takes two pills from a bottle on the nightstand, then washes them down with water from a crinkly plastic container. "Lord, I appreciate getting here. Now I can do what I came here to do. After that, whatever happens, happens. Well, if you don't mind, I'd like to get home first. I'd hate to put the burden of having Joseph fly my old bones all the way back to Nebraska for the funeral."

She sips more water, steadies herself with a hand on the nightstand, and rises from the bed. "This old girl is about used up, Elaine, but I'm bound to do what you asked."

I don't know how to thank you, Ruth. You've been as much of a friend to me after I died as before. When it's your time, maybe I can thank you with a big hug. Elaine pauses. *But for me to do that, my time will have to come also. It's too bad I don't know when that might be, or if I'll live this way for as long as Joe has. Eventually, I guess, I'll find some peace in my predicament.*

* * *

After breakfast and a taxi ride, Ruth, with Joseph beside her, knocks on the door to the visitor's building at the Ardennes American Cemetery. A dark-haired man wearing an equally dark suit opens the door. "You must be Mrs. Bauer." He faces Joseph. "And you must be Mr. Matthan, Private Matthan's son. Please come in, I'm James Anderson." Mr. Anderson closes the door behind them. "It's nice to meet you both."

"Mr. Anderson," Ruth says, "I don't mean to be rude, but I'd like to know why you called this morning and asked us to meet you here before the service."

"Yes, ma'am, I'm sure. Please take a seat over by the table."

"Does the lockbox on the table have anything to do with this?" Ruth asks as she sits. Joseph places the mahogany chest holding Elaine's ashes on the table by the lockbox.

"It does." Mr. Anderson turns the lockbox facing him. "After you called to request the service, we checked our records and discovered we still have some of Private First Class Matthan's personal possessions. I didn't mention it on the phone this morning because I was afraid it might upset you or Mr. Matthan." He unlocks the box and opens the lid. "I'll be back in a few minutes. Mr. Matthan, since you're next of kin, these things are yours to do with as you see fit."

Joseph takes out the items. First comes Joe's dog tags followed by three photographs, their edges yellow and curled with age. A yellow ribbon, creased and stained, is last.

Elaine expects none of this, especially the yellow ribbon stained with Joe's blood. Grief washes over her, nearly as painful as when she got the telegram about Joe.

"Oh, my goodness," Ruth says, rubbing a strange but familiar tingle on her neck. "Elaine told me about these things, but I forgot all about them." She studies the photos. Joseph does the same with the dog tags. The photographs are faded, Elaine sees, except the one Thomas took at the train station in Holdrege, the same day she gave Joe the yellow ribbon now coiled on the table.

Ruth takes the ribbon and holds it beside the picture. Once again, as Elaine has done since Kurt died, she gratefully shares her best friend's tears.

A slight, metallic ghost of a whisper comes from the table as Joseph slides the dog tags to the center. Ruth takes a tissue from her purse and wipes her eyes.

"It's kind of an emotional thing, isn't it, Ruth?"

She gives him the picture. "The picture … the ribbon … it's … it's everything, really. The others are faded, but that one is almost as clear as the one I have at home. It was taken right before your father boarded the train at Holdrege, when he left home for basic training."

Joseph takes the offered ribbon from Ruth. "Are you telling me this is *that* ribbon?"

"It certainly is. When your mother gave it to Joe that day, she made him promise to keep it tied around his wrist for good luck. She told me he tied her hair with it on their first date too."

Joseph turns the ribbon over in his hands. "I think I remember something about their first date being at the river."

"And most of the ones after that day. They dearly loved that place. You've been there, you know how nice it is."

"We went there a lot when I was growing up, but I don't remember the first time. Mom said it was when she took me there to tell me about Dad. It's a special place, all right. Kurt kept it up so nice all those years. The daffodils he planted have spread everywhere. When they're in full bloom, they wave in the breeze like an ocean of yellow."

"The rose bush he planted is gorgeous in the summer," Ruth says. "There's nothing sweeter than those original blooms. Those newfangled hybrids hardly have any smell at all."

She returns the photograph to the table. "I have a suggestion. I'll have copies made of these pictures for you from some I have at home just like them. Anyway, unless you really want these things, I'd like to place them with your mother."

"I'd like the dog tags," Joseph says, picking them up. "You don't mind, do you?"

"Not at all. Your father and mother would like that."

Of course, I would, Ruth. Thank you for having the ribbon and pictures placed with Joe and me. I think that's very fitting.

* * *

On a wide expanse of frostbitten grass, hundreds of white stone crosses surround Ruth and Joseph and the Army chaplain who led them to Joe's grave. The cross, with its deeply carved name, stands out among the rest.

Joseph S. Matthan
PFC, 106th Infantry Div., Nebraska
Dec. 17, 1944

The dark soil has been opened to accept the small chest, wrapped in plastic, that Joseph holds. A young Army soldier in full dress uniform waits nearby. His breath plumes in the cold. Joseph kneels, places the chest in the earth, and stands.

Ruth takes an envelope from her purse. Elaine recognizes it as holding the letter she wrote Joe, which is the one Ruth read before Kurt died. Ruth placed the bloodstained ribbon and the pictures in the envelope before she left the visitor's center.

She holds out her hand toward Joseph. "Will you help me down, please?"

As he takes her arm, the soldier steps forward. "Ma'am, can I help?"

Ruth looks into clear blue eyes—eyes that seem strangely familiar to Elaine. *I know I wrote Joe how he might be here, but that's a hope that has to be beyond coincidence.*

"Yes, young man," Ruth says, taking his arm. "Thank you."

The freshly turned soil reminds Elaine of when she and Joe took their first walk after Sunday dinner, when she met his parents. The same aroma rode the breeze from several plowed fields that wonderful day.

Ruth unwraps the plastic, opens the chest, and places the envelope inside. She gently closes the chest, touches the polished stone cross, and rests her fingertips on the smooth, mahogany surface, the final resting place of her best friend.

Her kind and gentle gestures touch Elaine's heart. *As dear as you are to me, Ruth, I do wish we had remembered to bring a daffodil to place in my chest. No matter. I still believe in hope and miracles, so maybe it'll be taken care of.*

Ruth rubs the chest. "This is goodbye, Elaine. Now I have to leave you here, thousands of miles away. I want you to know I'll always carry you in my heart, exactly like I know you carried Joe in yours. I love you, Elaine. Until we meet again."

As tears stream down her cheeks, Elaine shares the emotional release. *I love you too, Ruth. Thank you for everything. And thank you for making Kurt's last years so special.*

* * *

Joseph takes Ruth by the elbow and eases her up. Stepping away, she wipes her eyes with a tissue from her purse. She must want to give him a chance to say something, or to say goodbye.

Joseph's chin trembles.

The polished stone cross reflects the sunlight. The cross that holds his father's name. The father he never knew. The father he wishes he knew.

He doesn't want to cry in front of Ruth or the men but ...

Fighting tears, he drops to the ground to place one hand on the cross and one hand on the wooden chest, both warmed by the rising sun. He bows his head. To deny the sadness welling inside him is no longer an option. He releases it in huge, shoulder-shaking sobs. Like when he had cried while holding his son for the first time—the son who bears his father's name—hot tears trickle down his cheeks, except this time they stain the dark earth where his father's and mother's remains now rest.

Ruth comes over. She rubs his shoulder and cries with him. Elaine joins them, sharing their pain.

Joseph's sobs gradually subside. Ruth offers him a tissue and shuffles away, shoes swishing in the grass. He hasn't noticed until now, but the faint smell of the brown grass brings back childhood days of fishing at the river with Kurt in early spring, before the grass turned green again.

Joseph sucks in a huge, soul-cleansing breath and traces the deeply engraved letters in the shining stone cross with his fingertips. It doesn't seem to be a fitting memorial to the man he's heard so much about, the man whose name he shares, the man his mother had obviously loved so much.

"Dad, I sure wish I had known you. From everything I've heard, you would've been someone to admire, someone to look up to in a million different ways. I want to thank you for being the type of person who, even at your young age, had your wife's happiness in mind. Somehow, some way, I hope you can be together again. Thank you, Dad, and you, Mom, for being my parents. I'll never forget you." He stands to rub the warming stone of the cross one more time. "I'll make sure my kids and grand-kids never forget you either."

Someone sniffles. Joseph faces the young soldier. "Sir, are you all right?"

The young man wipes his blue eyes. If Joseph doesn't know

any better, by how Ruth described Dad's eyes from Mom's recollections, they could be a perfect match.

"Yes, sir, I—" The soldier clears his throat, rubs his neck, and lowers his hand to his side. "I'm—" He swallows. "I'm sorry for your loss. All these men—including your father—gave so much for you and me and for everyone back home too. It's impossible to say how much I appreciate his and your sacrifices."

Ruth gives him a tissue. "We appreciate your service also, young man."

"Sir," Joseph says to the chaplain, "please say a prayer for my parents."

* * *

Returning to the taxi, Ruth grips Joseph's arm tightly. The day has left her as drained as the day Kurt died. She hates to ask, but her curiosity can't stand it.

"Do you mind telling me what you and that young soldier were talking about after the ceremony?"

"That's right, you were busy with the chaplain." Joseph pats her hand. "What time is he picking you up for your date?"

"Phooey, tell me or not, I don't care."

"Why, Ruth, what happened to your jokie side?"

"I'm only teasing, but I'd like to know."

"I was asking how long he'd been stationed here and where he might go next. He said he's heading to Afghanistan soon."

Ruth blinks up at him. "Afghanistan?"

Because of what happened to the World Trade Center. You know, 9/11."

Ruth says nothing.

At the taxi, she turns for one last look at the multitude of crosses, each representing the life of a person unable to fulfill his or her hopes and dreams.

She shakes her head. Why, with all its sadness—and all the sadness it still brings to the families of those young men and women who give the ultimate sacrifice—does war continue? More importantly, what does humanity lack in its heart and soul that allows such evil to start these wars, like Adolf Hitler started *this* war?

The taxi leaves for the panorama of the peaceful Belgian countryside.

Ruth glances at Joseph, agreeing with his wish that Joe and Elaine can somehow—however that might be—find each other again.

How that might happen, who knows. They might hope to find themselves at the river again, lying on a faded patchwork quilt beneath the old oak.

Talking … laughing … dreaming. Maybe even fighting a huge catfish.

Then again, why not have the chance to meet as young people once more, to enjoy the wonder of the first glowing realization that they were about to fall in love?

Ruth smiles.

That's what I'd hope for, Elaine. How about you?

Chapter 57

Hope

September 6, 2014
Alma Elementary School, Alma, Nebraska

What will he say when it's his turn? It's just his name, but Mrs. Hansen asked everyone to tell their whole name—even their middle name—and he hardly ever tells anyone that. His new English teacher is nice enough, but why say all that? His hands sweat. Why is he so nervous? Maybe it has something to do with starting sixth-grade and moving to a new town.

Mrs. Hansen's eyes settle on him. An ice-cubed size lump forms in his throat. Is he last? Out of everyone here, is he really last?

"I believe you're last," Mrs. Hansen says. "Please stand and tell us your name. Then we can get our day going."

He stands and faces the class. They all stare familiar stares.

"Um … my name's—"

The door opens. A girl about his age, bangs hanging in her eyes, comes inside. She wears a green and yellow backpack, faded jeans, and a frown. "I'm sorry I'm late, Mrs. Hansen. My mom's car wouldn't start and I had to catch a ride with a neighbor."

"That's all right, we're just finishing up our introductions. Go ahead, young man. Then this young lady can tell us who she is."

The boy can't tear his eyes away from the girl. "My name is Joseph—Joseph Samuel Matthan. I like to be called Joe, like my great-grandpa."

The girl closes the door.

"I'm sure she's happy to meet you," Mrs. Hansen says. "If you face the rest of the class instead of her, they might like to meet you too."

Cheeks warming, he faces the staring eyes again. Should he say the same thing? That's dumb. Add a bit more? Maybe.

"My name is Joseph Samuel Matthan. Um … my family just moved here to the old Edwards place. I hope you'll call me Joe." *You dummy, you already said that.*

The teacher goes to Joe and nudges him toward his desk. "We'll make sure to call you Joe, okay? Take a seat so we can finish."

The girl goes to the front of the room.

"Before you start," the teacher says, "I'm asking everyone to tell us their middle names. I think it's an interesting addition to who we are."

"My name is Elaine Hope Johnson. My family just moved here from Holdrege. We're going to live on the Johnson farm with my great-uncle." She looks Joe in the eye, the hint of a grin teasing her lips. "I think I'll like Alma."

Mrs. Hansen sits at her desk. "Some students have asked to be called by their middle names. Do you have a preference?"

"I like Elaine."

"Elaine it is. Please take a seat in front of Joe." Elaine drops the backpack beside the desk, sits, then raises her hand.

"Yes?"

"What you said about names reminds me of something. Can I ask Joe a question?"

"Since we're getting to know each other, go ahead."

Elaine faces Joe. Freckles lightly dot her nose. Brown eyes with hints of green around the center pull him in. "I never heard of your last name," she says. "My dad told me names can have a special meaning. Does Matthan?"

"It does, sort of. My grandpa told me it has something to do with hope."

Elaine smiles, and something tugs in Joe's chest, something a poet might describe as a heart-string being plucked, like when he plays Great-grandad's guitar. The clear, harmonic chord resonates in his ears, also like the guitar, but similar to a song he might've heard in a dream.

The sound fades. Elaine's brown eyes crinkle with ... another question? Some of the kids are giggling because it sounded like he said his name has something to do with her, or rather, her middle name of Hope. He laughs too, and so does Elaine.

"Okay, class," Mrs. Hansen says, "let's get started with our reading."

Elaine, still smiling, turns around and takes a textbook from her backpack.

"Please turn to page forty-four," Mrs. Hansen says.

Joe opens his book, and page forty-four appears. He always likes it when that happens. It's like magic, like his hopes have come true. All around him, pages flips.

He looks from the book to the back of Elaine's head. Her brown hair, streaked with sun, shines in the overhead lights.

Each silky strand stands out, almost like spider webs misted with dew.

But something else catches his attention, something that causes his fingers to reach for Elaine's sun-streaked ponytail. Surprised—and a bit shocked—he forces his hand down to the desk, resisting the unexplainable urge to pull the yellow ribbon from her hair.

Afterward

As an author, I enjoy mixing fact with fiction. This book, along with many of my others, is no exception. Saying that, it amazes me when facts surface to weave fiction together much better than I ever could without them. For those interested, a quick internet search will reveal the facts I shared with this book.

The first fact revealed in this book is the actual massacre at Wereth, Belgium, during the Battle of the Bulge. Having never heard of it, I was shocked to learn how members of an SS Panzer Division tortured and killed eleven African-Americans serving in the 333rd Field Artillery Battalion after they had surrendered.

Although segregation existed in World War II, the second fact is how some African Americans from the 578th Field Artillery Unit took up arms and fought with the 424th Infantry Regiment from the 106th Infantry Division, who were white. This is how I joined Joe and James together on their patrol in the third chapter. For those who've noticed how I placed James with the 333rd, which isn't the 578th, please forgive the inaccuracy, for I dearly wanted to include the Wereth story.

For the third and final fact that helped me weave this novel together, imagine German prisoners of war brought to America and then used as farm labor in the Midwest. Yes, it really happened, which further added fact to my fiction with Kurt Bauer's story.

In actuality, some German POWs did stay in America and marry after the war, which made me understand Kurt's story even more poignantly.

In closing, like Ruth's observation near the end of chapter fifty-six, let us all remember how, no matter who we are, we are human, and it should be our fondest hope for humanity to end all war.

J. Willis Sanders
2/20/2022

Book Club Questions

1. What did you like best about this book?

2. What did you like least about this book?

3. What other books did this one remind you of?

4. Which characters did you like best?

5. Which characters did you like least?

6. If this book were a movie, who would you choose to play the characters?

7. What other books by this author have you read? How did they compare to this book?

8. What feelings did this book evoke in you?

9. If you got the chance to ask the author of this book one question, what would it be?

10. Which character in the book would you most like to meet?

11. What do you think of the book's title? How does it relate to the book's contents? What other title might you choose?

12. What do you think the author's purpose was in writing this book? What ideas was he or she trying to get across?

13. How original and unique was this book?

14. Did this book seem realistic?

15. How well do you think the author built the world in the book?

16. Did the characters seem believable to you? Did they remind you of anyone?

17. What did you already know about this book's subject before you read this book?

18. What new things did you learn?

19. What questions do you still have?

20. Were you happy with the ending?

Please enjoy the first chapter of *The Yearning of Hope*, coming later in 2022.

The yawn began as a slight tickle in the back of Sam's throat. He grabbed the cushioned bar at the front of his car seat and waited. The tickle grew until he squeezed his eyes shut in a head-shaking, mouth-wide-open yawn that stretched his lungs before he released the huge breath in a single, sighing rush. His yawn done, he rubbed his eyes with his fists, blinked several times, and frowned at Hope. His sister's excitement concerning this thing she called Christmas was keeping him awake. She paused her chattering, and though the warm air from the car's heater and the gentle motion of the curving road attempted to put him to sleep, he faced the window beside him.

In the evening sky, a huge, bright ball hung over the treetops lining the road. Sam knew the word and it wasn't ball. Hope told him the word one night as they stood on the front porch in their pajamas, watching it. He touched the glass with a fingertip, and part of the word popped into his head. If he said that part, maybe he could remember the rest. "M-m-m-o-o-o ..." He paused. There was another sound, one where his tongue had to do something differently than with the first two sounds. He touched his tongue to the roof of his mouth behind his teeth. "N-n-n." He grinned. The word was moon.

His breath fogged the glass as he licked his lips, still sticky from the candy cane his mother had given him when they left the place Hope had called a "mall." He gave the haze a quick swipe, chilling his fingertips.

In the back seat beside him, Hope leaned forward. "Daddy, since Sam is two this year, you can hold him up to put the angel on the tree." She faced Sam. "What do you think, Sam?"

Sam clapped his hands. "Daddy! Cwismus twee!"

She continued talking, but so quickly he couldn't understand most of her words. Her hands fluttered about like when she ran around the living room, trying to catch a paper airplane she had showed him how to make this morning.

Sam shot his hand to his neck, where an intense itch below his ear made him frown. He rubbed it, fingertips still cool and damp from the window.

Hope turned to look at him. "What's wrong, Sam, got an itch?"

"Itch, Hope," Sam said, nodding.

She smiled. "Then scratch it." Sam did, but the scrape of his nails barely eased the irritating tingle below his ear.

The car slowed and turned, shifting Sam in his seat. He grabbed the cushioned bar again. The headlights shined through trees and along another road, this one without yellow lines down the middle. The car straightened, so Sam relaxed his grip on the cushioned bar.

"Mommy," Hope said, leaning forward again, "lets sing Jingle Bells. Jingle bells, jingle bells …!"

"Jingle all the way," Sam's mommy sang, looking over her shoulder. "Oh, what fun …"

Sam clapped his hands again. "Fun!"

"It is to ride …"

A light shone in the window behind Hope, highlighting her thick, blonde curls like the head of the angel she had showed Sam at the mall.

He pointed. "Light, Hope," and a loud, blaring sound burst through the car, shaking his body and hurting his ears. Hope whirled around and screamed.

"Adam! Go!" Sam's mommy yelled.

As the car lunged forward, the light grew brighter and the sound grew louder until a crashing, tearing sound that Sam had never heard before ripped through the car.

Darkness surrounded him. He floated in the air like when Daddy tossed him up and caught him.

But no one caught him. No one hugged him. No one said *I love you, Sam.*

Cold air enclosed him, chilling his ears. The feeling was like this past Halloween, when he ran through his front yard with his bag of candy and fell in the dewy grass. He had cried while Hope helped him up and brushed him off. "It's okay, Sam, look" —she held his bag up for him to see— "you're a hero, you saved your candy!" Not a piece had spilled, and he grinned, though he had no idea what a "hero" was at all.

A sudden warmth embraced him. The weightless feeling disappeared, but the darkness remained. He tried to open his eyes but couldn't. A shrill, metallic noise jangled nearby.

Phone?

Mommy?

Daddy?

Hope?

About the Author

J. Willis Sanders lives in southern Virginia, with his wife and several stringed musical instruments.

With several novels published and more on the way, he enjoys crafting intriguing characters with equally intriguing conflicts to overcome. He also loves the natural world and, more often than not, his stories include those settings. Most also utilize intense love relationships and layered themes.

Although he loves history, he has written several contemporary novels as well, and some include interesting paranormal twists, both with and without religious themes.

He also loves the Outer Banks of North Carolina, and he has written three novels within different time frames based on the area, what he calls his Outer Banks of North Carolina Series.

Other hobbies include reading (of course), vegetable gardening, playing music with friends, and songwriting, some of which are in a few of his novels.

Another genre he enjoys is thriller novels, so he has launched a series with a main female character named Reid Stone.

To follow the author's work, please visit any of the following:

https://jwillissanders.wixsite.com/writer

https://www.facebook.com/J-Willis-Sanders-874367072622901

https://www.amazon.com/J-Willis-Sanders/e/B092RZG6MC?ref_=dbs_p_ebk_r00_abau_000000

Readers: to help those considering a purchase, please consider leaving a review on Amazon.com, Goodreads.com, or wherever you purchased this book.
Thank you.

www.ingramcontent.com/pod-product-compliance
Lightning Source LLC
Chambersburg PA
CBHW011157190726
48286CB00009B/2811